CONQUEST OF ARMAGEDDON

THE BLACK TEMPLARS are one of the most determined Chapters of Space Marines – refusing to take a step backwards, no matter what the consequences. When one of their units goes missing in the ork infested jungles of Armageddon, an elite squad is sent to investigate. Their mission is further complicated by the presence of a key Imperial officer who has crash-landed behind enemy lines. Hunted by both the savage orks and the corrupted Chaos Space Marines, the Black Templars must call upon every ounce of their faith and firepower if they are to survive and rescue their lost battle-brothers.

A WARHAMMER 40,000 NOVEL

CONQUEST OF ARMAGEDDON

Jonathan Green

For Jake, one day.

A BLACK LIBRARY PUBLICATION

First published in Great Britain in 2005 by
BL Publishing,
Games Workshop Ltd.,
Willow Road, Nottingham,
NG7 2WS, UK.

10 9 8 7 6 5 4 3 2 1

Cover illustration by Klaus Scherwinski

A CIP record for this book is available from the British Library.

ISBN 13: 978 1 84416 196 6
ISBN 10: 1 84416 196 X

Distributed in the US by Simon & Schuster
1230 Avenue of the Americas, New York, NY 10020, US.

Printed and bound in Great Britain by
Bookmarque, Surrey, UK.

See the Black Library on the Internet at
www.blacklibrary.com

Find out more about Games Workshop
and the world of Warhammer 40,000 at
www.games-workshop.com

IT IS THE 41st millennium. For more than a hundred centuries the Emperor has sat immobile on the Golden Throne of Earth. He is the master of mankind by the will of the gods, and master of a million worlds by the might of his inexhaustible armies. He is a rotting carcass writhing invisibly with power from the Dark Age of Technology. He is the Carrion Lord of the Imperium for whom a thousand souls are sacrificed every day, so that he may never truly die.

YET EVEN IN his deathless state, the Emperor continues his eternal vigilance. Mighty battlefleets cross the daemon-infested miasma of the warp, the only route between distant stars, their way lit by the Astronomican, the psychic manifestation of the Emperor's will. Vast armies give battle in his name on uncounted worlds. Greatest amongst his soldiers are the Adeptus Astartes, the Space Marines, bio-engineered super-warriors. Their comrades in arms are legion: the Imperial Guard and countless planetary defence forces, the ever-vigilant Inquisition and the tech-priests of the Adeptus Mechanicus to name only a few. But for all their multitudes, they are barely enough to hold off the ever-present threat from aliens, heretics, mutants – and worse.

TO BE A man in such times is to be one amongst untold billions. It is to live in the cruellest and most bloody regime imaginable. These are the tales of those times. Forget the power of technology and science, for so much has been forgotten, never to be re-learned. Forget the promise of progress and understanding, for in the grim dark future there is only war. There is no peace amongst the stars, only an eternity of carnage and slaughter, and the laughter of thirsting gods.

Priority level: Magenta Alpha
Transmitted: Battle-cruiser *Valiant*, Task Force Sparta
To: Adeptus Astartes battle-barge *Divine Fury*, Armageddon High Orbit
Date: 3893999.M41
Transmitter: Astropath Prime Macort
Receiver: Astropath-terminus T'Lok
Author: Lord Inquisitor Hieronymous Klojage
Thought for the Day: The wage of negligence is utter destruction.

Greetings Lord Marshal Brant,

I have recently received a communiqué from Lord General Antre Dashparov of the Tartarus Hive Command that has raised questions in my mind as to the role of your Chapter-Crusade within the arena of war that is the defence of the planet Armageddon. The lord general suggests that the Black Templars of the Solemnus Crusade have not been as forthcoming with their aid as might have at first been hoped.

I would appreciate the opportunity to discuss the claims the lord general has laid at your door, in person. Hence, expect my rendezvous with your fleet within the next forty-eight hours, Imperial standard, when I hope we shall be able to resolve this matter to our mutual satisfaction.

As a servant of His Imperial Majesty's Inquisition I shall expect to be greeted with all due pomp and ceremony.

Klojage

Lord Inquisitor Klojage, Ordo Xenos,
His Imperial Majesty's Inquisition

[Message ends]

Priority level: Magenta Alpha
Transmitted: Adeptus Astartes battle-barge *Divine Fury*, Solemnus Crusade, Armageddon subsector
To: Battle-cruiser *Valiant*, Task Force Sparta, geo-stationary orbit above Hive Tartarus
Date: 3897999.M41
Transmitter: Astropath Prime Salaman
Receiver: Astropath-terminus Reis
Author: Marshal Brant of the Black Templars Crusade Fleet *Solemnus*
Thought for the Day: Your honour is your life. Let none dispute it.

My lord inquisitor,

Your epistle is timely in its arrival, for I too have recently received a communication from Lord General Dashparov, and was shamed by the words he had written there. I was incredulous to read the claims he made within it.

Firstly, it amazed me that he would so inadvisably dare to make such claims and question the motives, and actions, of a Chapter of the celebrated Adeptus Astartes. The Emperor's finest owe no allegiance to any, beyond their ancient Chapters and home worlds, other than the Emperor of Mankind himself. Dashparov is fortunate that so many of our vaunted, noble brethren have brought the fight to the blasphemous aliens besieging Armageddon.

Secondly, I would have hoped that Lord General Dashparov might have forwarded to you the file I attached regarding Fighting Company Adlar's actions in the ash wastes east of Tartarus Hive. As he has failed to do so, I too would appreciate the opportunity to defend my Chapter and the actions of the fighting companies under my command, although I would remind you that it is not the practice of the Adeptus Astartes to explain their actions to anyone. The devout battle-brothers of the Black Templars are behoven to no man other than High Marshal Helbrecht himself and the most beneficent Master of Mankind. For, after all, we are all accountable in the eyes of Him Enthroned on Earth.

We will of course be ready for your arrival and await it with anticipation.

The Emperor is beneficent,

Brant

[Message ends]

PART I
NO PITY

ONE
ORBIS CHAOTICA

Five hundred years ago...

HROTHQAR FUROR, RAVAGER of Worlds, Champion of Khorne, threw back his head and bellowed his fury to the burning sky. The howl reverberated across the clearing over the heads of the warriors of his seething warband.

The planet had been theirs for the taking. A new prize for the daemon primarch he had served in the name of Khorne – the awesome daemon-entity the Imperial dogs had so disrespectfully called the Fallen One. A new daemon world.

And now it had all gone to hell, only it was not the hell that Furor had imagined or that his dark lord had longed for. And now even the unconquerable primarch was gone, his daemon blood slaking the inestimable thirsts of the Warrior God of Chaos.

How could it have gone so wrong? How could they have failed?

It HAD ALL begun with the *Devourer of Stars*.

The Daemon Prince Angron, primarch of the World Eaters Legion, had erupted from the warp-realspace maelstrom of the Eye of Terror in a blitzkrieg of slaughter and bloodshed. With his daemonic entourage and chosen Berzerker warriors at his side, and accompanied by a mighty horde of foul mutants, blasphemous daemonhosts and traitorous renegades, Angron had been ready to sate his hunger for blood and his thirst for revenge on the crumbling dominion of the False Emperor of Mankind.

It had been as if the ancient, drifting wreck – in fact several wrecks that had become bound together within the warp – had been sent by He Who Hungers to carry his servants to war; an infernal chariot of the Dark Gods. The Khornate host had taken advantage of the great hulk, using it to move under cover into the Armageddon system.

The gargantuan vessel, now named the *Devourer of Stars*, emerged from the warp in a screaming blaze of sick white light at the furthest reaches of the Armageddon system. Appearing there in the coldest reaches of space beyond the ringed gas giant Iandai, its presence was immediately detected by the system's perimeter monitoring stations.

As the unnatural agglomeration had drifted through the outer regions of the system, blotting out the light of distant stars like an unholy shadow on the face of the universe, in a panic defence craft had been scrambled from the naval facility of St Jowen's Dock. Those same ships made contact with the derelict as it passed the strange, uninhabitable world of Pelucidar, five days after it had first appeared within the Armageddon system. And those same ships, along with the thousands of damned souls trapped aboard them, were obliterated as – pathetic in their defiance – they attempted to halt the approach of the primarch's new flagship.

But the Imperial attack had, incredibly, dealt the *Devourer* a dolorous blow. The propulsion drive of an ancient vessel that made up part of the hulk's gargantuan bulk had been blasted free. As this city-sized section tore free from the rest of the hulk, the resulting plasma eruption had incinerated thousands of Lord Angron's troops, before the propulsion unit was caught in Pelucidar's gravity well and dragged down towards the planet's surface.

The loss of the drive section slowed the progress of the derelict so dramatically that the *Devourer of Stars* did not reach Armageddon until after another month of drifting relentlessly through the planetary system.

The attack on the *Devourer of Stars* had bought the forces of Armageddon valuable time in which to prepare for what everyone on the planet's surface now knew was the inevitable invasion to come. Nevertheless, when that hour came, despite the sacrifices made by the Imperial Navy in the space-borne battles they had fought against the vast hulk, the *Devourer of Stars* overcame Armageddon's orbital defences all too quickly.

As Angron's unholy vessel entered orbit above the planet and the primarch's forces prepared to make planetfall, treachery and sedition showed its blasphemous face in hive-cities across the planet. Nearly half the Planetary Defence Force had turned on their ignorant brethren, now revealed to be followers of the true masters of mankind, their numbers swollen by hordes of cultists who had kept the worship of their secret masters alive in clandestine cells, right under the noses of the Imperial faithful.

Inevitably, and just as the devotees of the Dark Gods had intended, anarchy and mayhem had swept through the hives of Armageddon. In the wake of such planet-wide sedition, Angron's forces were able to make planetfall practically uncontested.

Within a matter of days, all-out war engulfed the hives of Armageddon Prime. The death toll spiralled astronomically. Creatures that should never have existed beyond the realm of Chaos that was warp space – the red-skinned, behorned, daemonic manifestations of violence, slaughter and bloodshed – rampaged through the factory and hab districts of the massive mountain-cities. In their hellish wake, mutants and renegades massacred the civilian population. Monstrous hell-titans – more daemon than Mechanicus creation, being an amalgam of war-machine and warp-spawned entity – stalked the ash wastes battling those feeble-minded princeps and their land battleships that remained loyal to the corpse enshrined within the Golden Throne of Earth.

Angron's unified forces steadily drove the Imperial forces back towards the equatorial jungles and the landmass of Armageddon Secundus. In their wake death, madness and the warp held dominion. The daemon primarch's followers constructed crude, but effective, abattoirs. The blood of Angron's victims was offered up to glorious Khorne in depraved rituals enacted by his loyal devotees, a thousand at a time. Hundreds of thousands, perhaps millions, perished.

Great was the bloodshed carried out in veneration of the god of blood and death, and many were the blood rites carried out to his greater glory by Angron's World Eaters. So great was the slaughter that in the days that followed, it was said that the very rivers had been corrupted and choked with the carcasses of the slain.

But there had been more to the massacre than just the veneration of the Lord of Skulls. The sheer scale of the slaughter committed in the Blood God's name lent power to Angron and his daemon horde, enabling more and more of the offal-drenched creatures to manifest within the physical realm.

As Angron's invasion was taking place, warp storms of terrifying strength and ferocity blew up around the Armageddon system. In the initial phase of the battle for Armageddon, the presence of the warp storms gave potency to Angron and his daemonic horde, enabling the warp-creatures to maintain their physical corporality all the more easily. However, such power always comes at a price, and the surging energy of warp storms is always unpredictable. Angron was playing a game with time, racing to complete his conquest.

But the nature of Chaos is fickle, and before he could finally bring Armageddon to its knees, the warp storms, unable to maintain such ferocity and magnitude indefinitely, began to abate. As they blew themselves out, so Angron's power diminished.

And so it was that the primarch's advance mired amidst the stinking swamps and sweltering jungles of Armageddon's equatorial belt. The daemon primarch, a being of such power that he had been on the verge of conquering one of the most strategically vital worlds in the Segmentum Solar, found himself on the verge of losing all the advances he had made, so tied to the fluctuating power of the warp was he.

Unless he could somehow establish a permanent link to the immaterium, without the unnatural vigour of the warp to empower him and sustain his equally unnatural army, all his efforts would be for naught.

FUROR RECALLED THE past with bitter hatred, tasting the gall of defeat like ash in his mouth. He spat the foul taste away with a snarl, the gobbet of acidic phlegm hissing as it spattered against the knotted skin of a twisted vine-tree. A deep growl rumbling in the depths of his barrel-caged chest, the Chaos Berzerker pushed on towards the foetid heart of the jungle, trailing branches snapping off as his implacable mass barged past. The spikes and cruel ornamentations of his armour scraped gouges through the bark of the enclosing, creeper-wound trunks.

The green gloom closed in around the advancing World Eaters as they left the scorched earth of the burning jungle belt behind them. The vermilion flames licked the petrochemical-polluted skies before disappearing behind the veil of the impenetrable canopy shrouding the rainforest. And they *were* advancing, Furor's anger-maddened mind kept telling him. Warriors of the World Eaters Legion – the chosen sons of Angron – did not retreat. They were advancing towards whatever battles awaited them in the blood-drenched name of Khorne in another arena of the Long War.

It was then that he saw the first of the warp-channelling stones – a roughly sculpted rock ten metres tall, carved with the snarling features of some ravening daemon-beast – and Furor was minded of what Angron had ordered following the dissipation of the inconstant warp storms.

THE PRIMARCH HAD immediately decreed the construction of a monstrous monolith, an esoteric creation of stone and warp essence, that would feed his armies with the energy they needed to sustain their existence in the physical universe.

The building of Angron's monolith had taken many weeks and thousands died in its construction. First there were the bodies spent by the brutal, backbreaking labour. Then there were the thousands more – cultists, mutants and prisoners alike – butchered to consecrate the megalithic structure to the Lord of Skulls, that Khorne might grant them a boon, and Angron's hordes might complete that which the daemon primarch had undertaken in his murderous name. The power of Chaos was certainly growing in that auspicious place now, as acres of jungle withered, blackened and died, or flourished once more with new, unnatural life, drawn to the blasphemous, arcane construction.

At the same time, other smaller, yet similar, structures were erected throughout the jungle – sometimes singly, sometimes as stone circles, as decreed by warp-seer cultists of the Blood God in light of the blood rites they had enacted and the reading of augury-spilled intestines. But all had been constructed with the sole purpose of channelling the energies of the shifting Sea of Souls and containing them on Armageddon, so that Angron might complete his conquest of the benighted hive-world.

The monolith raised in Angron's name already pulsated with dark power, as infernal energies flooded from it in waves to re-energise the primarch's hellish hordes.

During the weeks taken up with the megalithic structure's construction, Angron's armies were forced to engage with the Imperial forces harrying at their heels. The Imperial dogs! They didn't know when they had suffered enough losses, and Furor, along with his fellow Berzerkers, had taken great pleasure in granting them what they so obviously desired, by spilling their blood, decapitating them, dismembering them and gutting them for the blood-hungry Lord of Skulls.

And yet still the forces of the daemon primarch were held at an impasse, trapped within the rotting jungles that divided the landmasses of Armageddon Prime and Armageddon Secundus.

Furor riled at the memory, genetically enhanced muscles bunching at the thought, as if his very flesh rebelled at the concept that Berzerkers of the Blood God could be beaten in open battle.

But the chosen of Khorne did not fail, just as Furor's company was not retreating through the twisted, primordial jungles of Armageddon. They were simply taking the battle for Armageddon to another theatre of war.

This hellhole of a planet would run red with rivers of blood before the Berzerker warriors of the World Eaters Legion relented in their god-given task.

FUROR STOOD AT the centre of the stone circle, in the bottom of the wide crater, the host of his warband arrayed before him. He sensed the fury and bloodlust rising off them like the steam sweated from the sweltering ern trees. And he, in turn, stood before them in all his tarnished glory.

In spite of all that had happened, Furor was still awesome to behold. He looked like a brutal leader amongst a legion of savage slaughterers as he stood atop the blood-drenched altar stone in his ruddy brass and crimson ceramite.

His ancient power armour was crusted with gore and wet with more recently spilled life fluids. It was finished with blasphemous icons and eye-stinging detailing to the glorification of the Legion's dark patron. Its plates were bolter-cratered and scarred by battle but Furor wore his scars proudly, like a conquering rather than a vanquished warrior.

Furor's armour bore the skull rune of Khorne everywhere – often combining the symbol of the World Eaters Legion – from the ceramite kneepads of his armoured greaves to the embossed roundels of his knuckles. It was even fashioned into the faceplate of his helmet, formed from chiselled bone, tarnished brazen metal and chipped ceramite.

In the mighty paw of his gauntleted hand he gripped the haft of a massive chain-axe. It was a brutal close combat weapon, presenting a furiously spinning belt of serrated and hooked metal teeth to the enemy, but Furor's was more savage and cruel than most.

Furor's ancient weapon had bound within its core a Khornate daemonic spirit that was a manifestation of the hunger of bloodlust. Furor had claimed the weapon as his own upon prising it from the stiffening fingers of his one-time commander, having slain him in a death-duel. The daemon-weapon's name, which Furor had learnt during a blood-soaked ceremony of re-consecration, was Qar'Ataleth. Furor had given it a new name, pronounceable by those who could not form the blasphemous syllables of the dark tongue. He simply called it Deathbringer.

As well as his chain-axe, Furor bore a bolter of archaic design, decorated with spikes. At his waist, sheathed in a scabbard of rusted iron and brass, was a gutting knife the size of a short sword. Such knives were carried by many of Angron's sons, for they were part of the equipment used to enact the Berzerkers' many blood rites and depraved cannibalistic rituals, in depraved imitation of the sacred rites the World Eaters had once performed in the Emperor's name.

Furor's hulking frame was bedecked with only a very few of the skulls he had taken in the name of Khorne. There was just one fractured skull for each of the campaigns that the warband of Kossolax the Foresworn had waged against the crumbling Imperium of Man. Eight skulls, eight blood-soaked crusades – the number deemed sacred to the Blood God himself – hung from various parts of his armour. The actual number he had taken for the Skull Throne of Khorne was a thousand times as many.

He removed his helm, revealing the face of a killer, its multi-scarred features twisted into a feral snarl of anger. Furor's head was totally bald and his nose had been debrided down to the bony cartilage beneath. At some point in the past his lips had been removed – by the Chaos Champion himself, truth be told, in adoration of the Skull Lord – so that his face looked more like a death's-head skull than a man.

He set the helmet down on the altar-stone and then unsheathed his gutting-knife. A heavy blade, fully half a metre long, its cutting edge was set with a double row of cruelly piercing fleshhound teeth.

A basso guttural growl rose from the depths of Furor's toughened ribcage as he pressed the tip of the gutting knife into the pale, scar-knotted flesh of his right temple. A bead of dark crimson welled from the spot where the blade punctured the World Eater's skin.

His face set in an ugly grimace, Furor slowly, yet purposefully, drew the blade across his brow, opening up the knotted red scars that already criss-crossed his face. Reaching the top of his nasal ridge, he changed the angle of the cut sharply, crossing the bridge of the nub of his nose and cutting open his left cheek, down to the corner of his lipless mouth. Only then did he remove the blade from his face. Its tip now glistened darkly.

Placing the blade at his left temple, Furor repeated the procedure, forming a mirror image of what he had done before.

He ground his sharpened fangs until his gums bled. The hot coppery taste in his mouth was like a wonderful sacrament to his tortured soul.

Reaching the right-hand corner of his mouth, he stopped in his act of self-mutilation. A cut across the top of each cheek under his darkly smouldering eyes completed the blood rite. Furor's face had run wet with blood, but his wounds were already clotting and healing themselves again – as they had done countless times before – but the skull rune of Khorne was clearly visible, superimposed on his snarling features. His soul, grown black and engorged on the life-blood of countless victims, had been re-consecrated to the Blood God.

Fury like molten quicksilver raced through his brain, ancient bio-neural implants – the knowledge of their making lost along with the world of the daemon primarch's birth – firing hate-pulses into his already raging medulla oblongata.

The champion of Khorne felt an insatiable blood-greed run like liquid fire in his veins, waves of palpable bloodlust washing over and through him.

Furor scanned the crater with growing frustration, which was rapidly giving way to furious anger: a burning blood-rage.

There was no enemy here. A swathe of burning jungle divided the World Eaters from their hated enemies, who had forced them into rout. Furor's anger blazed with an intensity greater than the fires consuming the horizon. Bloodlust, like a red-raw gut-gnawing hunger, was consuming him. All he desired to do now was take more skulls for Khorne.

There might not be any enemy here against whom Furor could slake his thirst for bloodshed but there were warriors whose blood would taste as sweet to the Dark God who demanded that it be spilled in his name.

Furor replaced his horned helm, seeing the world again through its red-tinged visor.

His day was not yet done. And while the hate-fuelled blood of Khorne still pulsed in his veins, he would remain true to the tenets of the World Eaters Legion, ideologies of courage, honour, martial pride and revenge against those that had wronged their order. And as long as he still stood, he would fight, and whilst he could still fight he would claim skulls for Khorne and appease the Blood God with the blood he insatiably desired, as he had for so many millennia.

Furor raised Deathbringer to the burning skies. The angry growls and curses of the World Eaters diminished to become no more than a guttural snarling.

'Sons of the primarch!' he bellowed. 'We came to this damned world in search of war, to bring slaughter and carnage. We murdered, we slaughtered, we brought havoc in our wake, and blood flowed.'

The gathered World Eaters bellowed at his words, basking again in their own martial pride. The assembled cultists chanted their own prayers of praise and adoration to the warrior god of Chaos.

'But now we are denied war,' Furor went on, 'by this world and by the enemy. And yet our master demands blood, requires that our souls be slaked in blood.'

The animalistic roars rose in volume, filling the jungle clearing with their feral voice.

The Berzerker champion thumbed the activation rune on the pommel of his daemon-possessed chain-axe. With a promethium cough, Deathbringer screamed into life.

Furor could be heard over it all: 'Blood will have blood! Khorne requires of you your bodies, your warrior might, your murdering souls. He requires the very life-blood pumping through your bodies. We shall see the sun set in blood, before this day is done!

'Blood for the Blood God! Skulls for the Skull Throne of Khorne!'

The sound of the throng was now that of wild dogs baying for blood, rabid hounds that will not be tamed until they have been unleashed and allowed to fulfil their savage need for slaughter.

Neural transmitters sparked and flashed again and Furor's mind was flooded with waking dreams of death and murder.

Deathbringer still held high in his hand, Furor turned and strode towards the nearest of his companions, Annuz Skrell. In three great strides he was on the bellowing Berzerker. The daemonic axe descended, striking the crimson-armoured warrior's gorget. The teeth bit and Deathbringer screamed even louder.

Reacting on animal instinct, Skrell raised his bolt-gun, aiming it directly at Furor's face. Furor swung up his own bolter and batted Skrell's away as the other depressed the trigger. The explosive round spanged off the auto-reactive shoulder plate of his desecrated armour.

All the time he maintained the downward pressure on his axe as Deathbringer's daemon-soul howled for blood.

Bolters were holstered and the two warriors then brought only axes to bear. Deathbringer shrieked and screamed as it clashed with Skrell's growling chain-axe.

At first the two met each other blow for blow, the teeth of their weapons grating as they clashed and scraped across the ceramite plates of their armour.

Yet Hrothqar Furor had not been marked as the Ravager of Worlds, Champion of Khorne, without cause. He moved quickly, seemingly unencumbered by the massive suit of armour he wore, and started to get blows in under his opponent's guard.

Furor was dimly aware of the clamour of battle rising around him.

Then the fatal blow came. Gripping Deathbringer in both hands, Furor smashed the head of Skrell's weapon aside. Before the battle-weary warrior had time to recover, Furor brought the whirling blade of his own weapon round in a great swing and smashed Deathbringer down against the other warrior's neck. Striking with experienced precision, he hit the exact same spot where his first blow had landed.

Ceramite parted and blood sprayed into the air as Skrell's jugular was severed, the whirling teeth of the daemon-axe tearing messily through the artery.

Skrell faltered as his bio-engineered physique struggled to deal with a wound that would have killed a mortal man outright. The Berzerker stumbled backwards, instinctively putting an armoured hand to the wound, even though there was nothing he could do to seal it. He would have to rely solely on the arcane geno-magicks that had been unleashed inside his body untold centuries before. He fell to his knees.

Before his enhanced body even had time to try to effect a repair, Furor was on top of him, the muzzle of his bolter pressed into the spouting wound in his grox-thick neck.

'You die well, brother,' Furor growled, his voice echoing through the auto-senses of Skrell's helmet. 'The Lord of Skulls will savour your blood, redolent with the vigour and rage of your soul.'

Furor twisted the barrel of his bolter up under the edge of Skrell's horned helm and fired twice. The explosive rounds obliterated his head inside his helmet. A third round exploded the helmet itself.

Annuz Skrell's headless body slumped to the ground, black-red fluid soaking into the mulch.

His chest heaving from the exertion of the contest, the adrenaline flashing through his veins like an electrical storm, Furor looked up from the corpse steaming on the jungle crater floor at his feet.

All around him brother fought brother, hulking terminator-armoured World Eaters gunning down raging Berzerkers. And the opposite was also true, as the remnants of the Foresworn turned on each other like slavering flesh hounds in a feeding frenzy. Flesh-scarred cultists died in droves. Khorne would have his sacrament.

Furor watched it all impassively through his scarlet-tinted visor, as though somehow emotionally detached.

Blood was misting in the air of the clearing around him. The sacrament was accompanied by the battle-cries and curse-oaths of the World Eaters: prayers and supplications to the carnage-seeking, macabre Lord of Skulls.

They would consume this world yet.

Khorne. Khorne. Khorne.

He heard his own voice calling inside his head. It was a mantra to the god of death.

'Khorne. Khorne. Khorne.'

Knotted vocal chords gave the chant voice.

'Khorne! Khorne! Khorne!' he roared, his booming bellows redolent with hatred, anger and a blood-thirst that would not be quenched.

'KHORNE! KHORNE! KHORNE!' The standing stones echoed with the roars of the damned as the red-armoured warriors around him took up the chant.

'Blood for the Blood God! Skulls for the Skull Throne of Khorne!' Furor roared, his armoured feet already pounding the loamy ground beneath his ceramite boots, the daemon-possessed chainsword screeching in his hand as he charged into the throng of his men.

It seemed to the Ravager of Worlds that the blood misting in the air of the clearing was now congealing in the air above the clearing. And there was some-thing else as well: an otherworldliness, manifesting itself at the centre of the crater, feeling like the uncomfortable pressure that precedes a thunder-storm, only a hundred times more intense.

The battling warriors had become more like savage beasts than men. As Furor hacked into the limbs and bodies of his warband, he felt his skin turning to gooseflesh inside his armoured suit, tingling at the building esoteric energies.

The crimson clouds swirled above and around him in a pumping red vortex of building warp-energy. The raw power of the immaterium was taking on substance around them, within the circle of Khorne-consecrated sacrificial stones.

A hungry wind tugged at the Chaos Marines with clawing fingers, its howling sounding like the braying cries of a starving predator. It was as if the very fabric

of the air had been given life and some semblance of
sentience, and was writhing in warp-spawned agony at
the birthing pangs of something not of this reality.
Something born of rage, hatred and vengeance. Something that was as nightmares made pulsating flesh,
being born into the waking world. Something
abysmally dark and with an animal hunger that would
not – could not – be sated.

Minds and souls focused now on nothing but the
act of killing, felt the touch of their ravenous god.
Bloodlust washed across the space between the
stones like a sickness, renewing the dark desires of
their cankered souls, swollen fit to burst with the
blood they had spilled for their thirsting deity. And,
in response, the warriors renewed their battle against
their frenzied brethren.

An unbearable blood-wrath filled Furor. The Ravager of Worlds had become rage made flesh. To
think that they were trapped here, amidst these god-
less jungles, denied the genocide they so desired
against the populace of this oppressed planet. He
wanted nothing more than to take more and more
skulls for his master, until he made for him a new
throne from the bones of those he had slaughtered.

Another of the Foresworn fell to Furor's relentless,
scything blows; ten thousand years of fighting the
Long War making him seemingly unconquerable,
proving exactly why it was that he had been elevated
him to the position of champion.

And the Blood God answered his unspoken prayers.

The hurricane-strength winds quickened to still
greater velocities, sucking the vortex manifested in the
air above them down to the clearing floor.

The sky turned massacre black.

Snaking tentacles writhed inside the tornado of eldritch energies, reaching out from the swirling maelstrom. And there were other things too, moving within the esoteric currents: spirit-entities of malevolent intent, keen of eye and sharp of tooth.

The Berzerkers paused amidst the relentless bloodshed, panting, their breath steaming visibly in the bloody air. An unnatural moment of calm descended over the circle of warp monoliths that stretched out towards a future of untold possibilities and potential.

And there, at its raging heart, amidst flashes of sick white lightning, striking with the rapidity of an electrical storm of untold ferocity, the veil between realities was riven.

As the warp portal irised open, Hrothqar Furor caught a glimpse of another world, shimmering as though through a heat-haze, like a mirage. A world green and lush and full of life – life ready for the taking – where the remnants of his warband might continue their ceaseless battle for the Blood God.

Then Furor knew that his mighty lord Khorne had heard the unvoiced prayers – in his bellows of slaughter, in the roars of sadistic cruelty, in the rabid battle-cries of his brethren – unspoken and yet written in words of blood. The Blood God had heard his champion and answered his murderous prayers.

Their day was not done yet. This world might yet be theirs.

TWO
THE DEVASTATION
OF SOLEMNUS

Twelve years ago…

FROM THE BRIDGE of the mighty battle-barge *Divine Fury*, Marshal Brant of the Black Templars Chapter and the other assembled crusaders looked down on the cloud-wreathed world of Solemnus and at the orbital laser strikes igniting the atmosphere above the largest continent on the planet below. From the *Divine Fury*'s position in high orbit, the coruscating explosions looked like blossoming crimson flowers amidst the dense white cloud cover, incongruously beautiful considering the abominable sacrilege to which they were a testament.

Through the armacrys glass of the oriel window the Space Marines could see the ugly, angular shapes of the alien vessels – no more than rusting conglomerations assembled from chunks of metal debris. They were circling the wrecks of orbital defence platforms like piranhas around a fresh kill.

Several of the larger predatory craft hung in geosynchronous orbit over the broiling cloud beneath them. Beams of rippling energy blasted from the gaping maws of their blunt, archeosaur-headed prows, piercing the cumulonimbus with their intense laser barrage and boiling the water-laden air around them.

Watching the ork assault, Brother-Apothecary Colber felt hatred burn in his heart. But behind the all-enclosing mask of his gleaming white helmet, his expression remained surprisingly impassive – thanks to the nerve-shredding wound dealt him by a manta-gaunt on the ocean-world of Eswulus twenty-seven years before, three years before he had been elevated from the rank of neophyte-medic to the status of full Apothecary initiate.

But righteous fury still blazed inside Colber. From the moment he saw the shark-ships dealing out death to the chapter world below, he made a personal vow that he would not rest until every last one of the vile aliens had been expunged from existence, whether by his hand or others.

'Sigismund's sword!' Brant roared, his cry of anger and heartfelt anguish reverberating from the cathedral nave of the battle-barge.

Every one of the marshal's senior officers and attendants aboard the bridge with him uttered their own disbelieving oaths at the sight that appalled them through the viewing port in front of them.

How had the orks been able to home in on the one place on the planet worth attacking so quickly and so accurately? The greenskins were renowned for their lack of forethought. What power had allowed them to locate the site of the ancient chapter keep with such deadly speed?

Ultimately the alien armada would have found the keep, their own crude communications system picking up comm traffic from the ancient bastion, but the *Divine Fury* had been tracking the ships ever since the Lugnasad Crusade had dropped out of the warp at the edge of the Solemnus system. They had been only a matter of hours behind the invading xenos fleet.

What dread ability did the aliens possess? Had they looted some devastatingly powerful doomsday weapon from another vessel… perhaps one of the drifting derelicts they were prone to colonise as they drifted through space, dropping in and out of the warp at the whim of who knew what powers, carried unguided on the currents of the Sea of Souls?

'Helm, lock in an intercept course. Full power to the plasma engines!' Brant commanded.

Space Marines, blank-faced servitors and servants of the Machine God, hurried to do his bidding.

'Lock every Omnissiah-given weapon onto those abominations and hit them with everything we have!'

The *Divine Fury*'s weapons arrays charged and then, in a supernova fusillade, unleashed the fury of a thousand volcanic eruptions at the ork armada.

As the battle-barge's weapons charged again, the other ships of the Templar fleet discharged their own weapons batteries and moved in for the kill, ploughing through the chill void to engage with the xenos vessels.

The sleeker, faster-moving Gladius-class frigates *Loyalty's Reward* and *In Memoriam* closed on the first of the ork vessels – designated terror ships by the Imperial Navy – pounding them with heavy ordnance as well as devastating barrages of laser fire.

The capital ships of the crusade fleet – the *Hammer of War*, forgeship *Goliath* and the *Divine Fury* herself, fired again. Laser lances pulsed with vaporising light. Gun decks shook with seismic vibrations as weapons crews loaded and fired their artillery pieces, before clearing the breach and re-loading, ready to fire again. Outraged by the sacrilege, the orks were perpetrating against their chapter world, the ships of the Lugnasad Crusade bombarded the rabble of ork ships with everything they had, closing in on the alien constructs in a spearhead formation.

The rusty skin of the nearest of the ork vessels fractured and then detonated from within, its ugly bulk disappearing within an expanding ball of roiling nuclear flame. The first kill went to the Emperor's finest. But only the Lord of Terra Himself knew at this stage how many had already been lost on the planet below.

The chapter keep of Solemnus usually housed up to as many as one hundred battle-ready brethren and neophytes, enjoying a time of solitude and monastic prayer between conflicts. A vital part of the role of those left behind was to protect the planet from invasion and to search out new recruits for the most zealous of the Astartes Chapters.

Ever since Lord Sigismund had assembled the first and largest of the war fleets of the Chapter and begun the greatest crusade the Adeptus Astartes had ever undertaken, the Space Marines of the Black Templars Chapter had scorned the idea of maintaining a single home world. The Black Templars zealously guarded their chapter keep worlds, for they were vital to the continuation of the Chapter itself, founded ten millennia back. Lord Sigismund, once of the Imperial Fists, but known to the Black Templars as first high marshal of their order, had established the Chapter of holy warriors, following the accursed days of the Horus Heresy. Those dark days had seen the Imperium of Man torn apart and brought to the edge of oblivion. To save all mankind, the Emperor had sacrificed himself aboard the Warmaster's battle-barge in order that he might cast down his favoured son Horus.

Such chapter worlds also acted as staging posts for war fleets of what was essentially a fleet-based Chapter. And on every world conquered or reclaimed for the Imperium by the Black Templars of the Adeptus Astartes there stood a chapter keep. Mighty, majestic strongholds eons-old, of untold might they were great bastions that stood as unyielding as the zealous faith of the Templars themselves. Never had there been a more loyal and holy body of warriors in the ten thousand-year history of the Imperium of Man.

And now the marshal's war fleet had returned from its pilgrimage to the Apollo subsector only to find Solemnus and its ages-old monastery-fortress at the mercy of the filthy alien orks. And the ships under Brant's command – the grand battle-barges, strike cruisers and their escorts – were bringing down divine retribution upon the enemy for what they had dared to do.

Standing on the bridge of his fleet flagship, Marshal Brant of the Lugnasad Crusade felt an all-consuming hatred for the xenos greenskins possess his huge bio-engineered frame.

'By all that is holy,' Brant swore, 'not one of these blasphemous alien scum shall escape my wrath and the wrath of the Emperor for the wrong they have done our glorious Chapter this day!' He slammed his gauntleted fist down on top of the command-pulpit at which he stood, cracking the carved granite lintel.

'I swear it in the Emperor's name, in the name of our patriarch Rogal Dorn and in the most venerated name of Lord Sigismund! Every one of them will die and burn in the fiery hell of our vengeance!'

THE DROP POD rocketed through the atmosphere of the planet, buffeted by hurricane-force high altitude winds. Strapped with their locking-harnesses, there was nothing that Apothecary Colber and his retinue could do, other than pray to the Master of Mankind, their gene-father Rogal Dorn and their saintly founder, that they would make planetfall safely. And pray they did, chanting meditative mantras, filling the interior of the screaming drop pod with sanctifying reverberations as it plummeted towards the surface of desecrated Solemnus.

Solemnus was a μ-class world, as grim and dour as its name suggested. It was believed to have been first settled by mankind during the millennia-distant Dark Age of Technology, an almost mythical time pre-dating the Age of Strife. It was a world troubled by storms, the climate of its major landmasses temperate and enduring more or less continual rainfall for ten months of its thirteen-month year. The people of Solemnus who lived beyond the towering walls of the Templars' massive sanctuary were hardy, humourless folk. They made their feudal livings rearing sheep and livestock of all kinds, by mining and quarrying, and through timber production from the swathes of deciduous and coniferous forests that covered vast areas of the damp uplands.

Those same people maintained their own method of government via a system of petty kingdoms and vassal lords. But it was the castellan of the chapter keep who was the true overlord, and effectively governor, of the planet, who represented Solemnus to the greater Imperium. The tithes it paid to the Imperium were the warriors it provided for the Adeptus Astartes. That and the unwavering faith of its populace, numbering several million according to the last census performed by the Ministorum, with the hallowed brotherhood's consent.

A thousand years before, the Black Templars had come to Solemnus to quash the insidious genestealer cult that had held almost the entire planet in its filthy talons. The people only remembered those terrible bloody events now in their legends, but the Black Templars never forgot any injustice done against the people of His Glorious Majesty's galaxy-spanning Imperium. The eradication of the alien cult was inscribed upon the walls of the magnificent Hall of Heroes inside the chapter keep, along with the record of the other battles that had been fought by the Templars that now called Solemnus their ancestral home.

As his thoughts focused on the threatened world beneath them, Colber found himself wondering what fate it was that had befallen the current castellan, Lord Hagan.

Retro-jets firing at the last possible moment, the drop pod impacted before the shattered keep with a ground-quaking thud.

The heat-seared panels of the pod fell open with a resounding clang and Apothecary Colber burst from its plasteel interior. Seeing the smoke-wreathed silhouette of the keep, Colber nearly faltered in his charge.

The Templar stronghold had stood for two hundred generations. Now it was nothing but a burnt-out, vitrified shell, black and broken, like the carcass of some prehistoric behemoth, stark against the icy peaks of the Lammas Mountains a hundred kilometres distant.

The keep had been the largest man-made structure on the backwater world of Solemnus. Now it was just a ruin of its former glory and a cruel reminder of the newly found devastating power of the ork asteroid-fortress. Despite having stood for a thousand years and resisted sieges by the piratical eldar and Chaos renegades in its long history, in one day the greenskin rabble had breached the ancient fortification's walls.

In front of the keep a wide crater had been formed in the surface of the very bedrock of the planet. Something exerting colossal pressures had come to ground at this spot: the ork rok.

As he took in the scene of devastation, the furious hatred Colber had felt when he had first set eyes on the terror ships of the ramshackle ork armada now returned ten-fold.

'Suffer not the alien to live!' Colber cried, raising his reductor, and pointing it towards the shattered shell of the fortress before them.

Doubling their pace, the Apothecary's honour guard charged up the slope towards the broken outer fortifications. The hillside had been pared down to the bedrock, the blackened vitrified scars testifying to scything energy beams having chewed at the exposed granite.

Colber's armour was in stark comparison to that of the battle-brothers who accompanied him. Where their ancient suits of enclosing power armour were almost totally black, with only a few contrasting white or red details, his Apothecary's uniform was almost totally white. He moved like a spectral vision of a Space Marine between his black-armoured brethren.

Drop pods continued to make planetfall on the bleak hillside in a thick black rain. Enraged Templars, their souls full of the fires of battle, bursting forth to take the battle to the orks. The alien fleet had been broken by the superior might of the crusade ships and were being driven from the Solemnus system in the shadow of their blasphemous hulk.

Those orks left behind on the ground seemed oblivious to their predicament, or they simply did not care that they had been abandoned and that the full dreadful might of the Black Templars would soon come upon them in a hail of furious vengeance. Whatever terrible fate had befallen the keep and its guardians, not a single ork would live to glory in their brutish destruction.

A solid gatehouse had once stood before the keep, as big as one of the castles of the feudal lords who once held sway over the populace on a day-to-day basis for their own Templar overlords. There was little left of it now.

Charging through the smashed gatehouse, a drift of ember-blown smoke cleared momentarily and Colber saw lumpen, green-fleshed creatures plundering the corpses of those who had defended the gatehouse. The beasts were pulling weapons as well as pieces of armour from the bodies of the fortress's own human custodians.

Colber felt his stomach knot in anger and grief as he saw that the largest of the xenos scum was trying to pull the bolter from the deathly grip of what remained of one of the keep's superhuman guardians. The Templar had been crushed under several tonnes of rubble, a huge corbel sculpted with the equal-armed cross of the Chapter having crushed his head completely.

And then the battle cry of the Black Templars was spilling from Colber's lips – 'No pity! No remorse! No fear!' – his deep basso voice making the exclamation sound more like a bullish roar.

An Apothecary was a Space Marine trained to undertake the routine medical and surgical duties of the Chapter, particularly on the front line of battle. But first and foremost an Apothecary was a Space Marine, trained to be one of the Emperor's finest warriors. Although those chosen to serve in the Apothecarion of the Chapter were expert medics, they were also expert killers, having been trained to kill the enemies of the Imperium in a myriad ways.

Bolt pistol in hand, Colber threw himself at the greenskins. Pulling the trigger, he felt the reassurance of the weapon kick in his left hand as it hurled round after explosive round into the alien marauders. Green flesh exploded in sprays of foul ichor. Two of the hideous, tusked creatures fell, one with half its head missing, the other with daylight visible through the cavity blown through its chest.

There was a blur as something hulking, and clad in pieces of scavenged armour and animal hides, lunged for the Apothecary. But Colber's reactions were faster. He lashed out with his right fist and the gleaming spike of the reductor attached to his armoured wrist. The reductor was a medicae tool designed to extract the precious progenoid glands that every battle-brother carried inside their bodies, but it made an equally effective weapon. There was a viscous pop followed by a brief, high-speed whirring and then Colber pulled the reductor free. Most of the ork brute's brain seemed to come out with it through the hole of its ruined eye socket.

Colber's fellows fell on the remainder of the ork mob scavenging within the ruins of the shattered gatehouse. In a matter of minutes, with deft strokes of swords and carefully aimed bursts of gunfire, the aliens' carcasses had joined those of the keep's defenders.

More orks were lolloping out of the main keep to repel the Black Templar attackers, armed with crude automatic weapons and hand-axes.

But amidst the raging cauldron of battle, Colber himself paused. There was crucial work for him to do here. Crouching down beside the black-armoured body of the fallen Marine, with a silent prayer to the Emperor, he set about his labour. Far more important even than tending to the wounded on the battlefield, an Apothecary's most vital duty was the guardianship of the future and the continuance of the Chapter.

Those who served the Apothecarion were the keepers of the Chapter's holy biological legacy, the guardians of the Chapter's precious gene-seed. The source of the gene-seed was the Space Marines themselves, each one having been implanted with the mysterious replicating progenoid organs as part of their induction into the Chapter. These miraculous Emperor-created implants absorbed genetic information from a Marine's body. When a battle-brother died, his progenoids could be removed and used to produce further zygote implants for future initiates of the Chapter.

Without the progenoid glands, no further implants could be cultivated, and no new Marines created. And if no neophytes could be engineered then, in time, the Chapter itself would die, as so many had in the past. The Sons of Gorgax and the Silver Stars were now no more than dusty memories, the only evidence of their existence being a record within the Index Astartes. So it was that the life of the Chapter was totally dependant upon the medicae work of the Apothecaries.

With the anointed seals of the dead Templar's gorget and chestplate released, Apothecary Colber was able to remove those pieces of litany-inscribed power armour. Placing the point of the reductor against the Marine's neck, Colber punctured his skin. The point sank into the dead warrior's body with ease, Colber following its course as a sub-dermal mag-res scan on a tiny medicae-augury screen built into the wrist unit.

Then there the swollen slug-like gland appeared on the monitor. Colber activated the arcane device with a thought-impulse and the reductor set to work removing the implant. The progenoid extracted, with practiced speed and ease, Colber did the same with the second of the gene-seeds buried deep inside the Marine's chest, behind the fused bone shell of the ribcage. Cutting tools built into the reductor automatically came into play before the second implant could be taken out successfully.

He could not help but feel a pang of grief as he extracted the glands from the dying Templar. To lose his gene-seed truly meant the end for a warrior, and no matter how many battles he saw, how many dying men he ministered to, Colber still felt the same way. And he was glad, for as soon as he stopped feeling this way then he would be dead himself, a soulless, emotionless creature.

And what good was that to the Chapter, when its warriors needed to feel the torments of anger, grief and moral righteousness to prosecute their crusades against the myriad enemies of the Emperor? What would a Space Marine of the Black Templar Chapter be without passion, without overwhelming love and respect for the Emperor and the sacrifice He had made for the sake of all mankind, and the ability to hate?

The two gene-seeds recovered, Colber transferred them to his narthecium unit, where they would be preserved within a self-regulating, cold-stasis compartment.

'Your death will not have been in vain,' Colber addressed the nameless corpse, as if to offer some comfort to the deceased Templar. 'May the Emperor's warrior-angels guide your soul to His side to fight for His glory for all eternity.'

The whole procedure was over in a less than a minute. His duty done, Apothecary Colber rose to his feet. Having made the sign of the helix across his chest, he followed an advancing squad of initiates and their neophyte charges as they crossed the splintered remains of the stronghold's massive drawbridge into the heart of the chapter keep itself.

IT SOON BECAME apparent to the avenging Black Templars just how devastating the greenskins' attack had been. Under some colossal bombardment the chapter keep's shield dome had failed.

The ancient bastion had suffered both an orbital laser assault and heavy shelling by devastating ordnance that had flattened Earthshaker and Hydra battery emplacements, and levelled whole areas of the fortress-monastery that had withstood every siege ever thrown at the holy citadel in its thousand-year history.

The formidable firepower levelled at the keep had obviously eventually overloaded its ancient void shield generators. When the generators went critical, the very bedrock of the planet had melted and the arsenals of siege guns in the base of the walls had cooked off. The combined explosions brought down a half-kilometre stretch of the west curtain wall.

With that, the keep had been blown open and the orks had stormed in, destroying all before them like a devouring locust swarm.

Colber stopped at the threshold to the chapel. It too was now open to the sky. He had always halted here every time he visited the resting place of Marshal Emrik, the noble crusader who had first brought the Black Templars Chapter to the backwater world of Solemnus. He had done so in the past to allow the air of sanctity of the shrine to wash him clean of war and fill his heart anew with devotion to the Emperor and the Crusade. But now he stopped, his heart and mind gripped in a seizure of shock.

Little remained of the hero's tomb that had not been defiled in some way by the aliens' attack. Emrik's image had once adorned the huge stained glass window at the end of the Hall of Heroes. He had been the keep's founder as well as its first castellan. The window had shown him smiting the grotesque, bloated 'father' of the heretical alien cult that had once held Solemnus in its flesh-corrupting, taloned grasp. Now it was destroyed, just so many shards of broken glass. Little more remained of the Hall of Heroes itself. Its roof gone, the once great, columned vault was exposed to the roiling black clouds of fire burning elsewhere in the building. A smoky pall hung over the keep like a burial shroud pulled over a corpse.

For close to eight hundred years Emrik's tomb had stood unmolested, a monument to the great faith and achievements of this pious son of Sigismund. Raised before an altar carved to resemble the holy cross of the Templars – bearing the ever-present memento mori skull of the Imperium at its centre – it had been a reminder that all loyal subjects of the Imperium of Mankind should be prepared to lay down their lives in service to the Golden Throne, just as the Emperor had made the ultimate sacrifice for humanity.

For eight centuries, four life-sized statues of Templar Marines had guarded Marshal Emrik's rest. At the northern corners the stone-carved crusaders had been genuflecting, their heads bowed towards the chapel altar, their hands resting on the hilts of their swords in silent vigil. The two at the southern end had been standing, holding their bolters across their chestplates in the ceremonial manner.

Only one of the unsleeping sentinels now remained, itself only partially intact. The standing figure was headless; the other three had been totally obliterated by the profane aliens. Even Emrik's black marble sarcophagus had been fractured in two.

One of the banners the ork armies rallied around lay twisted and broken amidst the wreckage. He had seen such alien iconography before. Chaplain Ugo had once said that the grim ork-head images the greenskins carried into battle were supposed to represent the aliens' own brutal gods. But this banner-top was different. The usual green, tusked, angular face had been very deliberately crossed with a red-painted lightning flash. To Brant it looked like a jagged scar. He had seen the bullhead, crooked crescent moon and crossed axe symbols that were markers for various greenskin tribes before, but he had never seen anything like this.

Colber passed through the tomb in slow reverence and appalled shock, with deliberate, measured strides, his heart casting up prayers to the Emperor, that he might preserve the immortal eternal rest of the Liberator of Solemnus and look with a merciful eye upon the souls of all those who had died, fighting to their last breath to stop the ork hordes taking his stronghold.

ON HIS PROGRESS through the shattered keep, Colber had come across the bodies of twelve of his brethren, as well as the broken corpses of the stronghold's serfs and servitors, too numerous to count. Although he had arrived too late to save them, at least he had found them in time to collect the precious gene-seed their lifeless bodies harboured.

Rage withered to an aching sorrow as he came upon one fallen warrior after another. That the alien attack could have cut down so many of his noble brethren was unconscionable! He found not a single one alive until he reached the Crusaders' Chapel.

By now, Marshal Brant's Marines had regained control of the keep and were steadily eliminating the last, stubborn pockets of ork resistance. But those orks that they had found inside the Crusaders' Chapel were already dead.

The ugly alien bodies formed a huge mound of cooling carcasses that dominated the blackened shell of the sanctuary. It had been one of the most ornately decorated devotional chambers in the entire fortress-monastery. The dome of its vaulted roof was hung with the battle-banners of notable campaigns and famous warriors of the Solemnus Keep, remembrances and trophies of past glories.

But the orks had desecrated this last sanctuary, just as they had defiled the rest of the chapter keep. And one zealous warrior had taken his revenge on the alien abominations in memory of his fallen battle-brethren. The lone Templar lay now, atop the mound of alien dead, his armour ruptured, his blood covering the corpses of all those greenskins that had fallen in the face of his holy wrath.

It had not taken an Apothecary to realise that the Templar's wounds would be the end of him. The Space Marine had been cut in half by a rusting cybernetic claw which was attached to a hulking ork's arm. The same ork's head was held in the warrior's unbreakable mortis-locked grasp, the Templar having torn it from the greenskin's body.

Colber turned to Brother-Initiate Kerbas. 'Fetch Marshal Brant,' he said.

Brant stormed into the chapel, with Techmarine Garan, of the marshal's own household, and the doughty Chaplain Ugo following not far behind. Brant looked every part the marshal of the crusade, imposing in his ornately tooled armour and ceremonial robe of office. He was a force to be reckoned with indeed, as one would expect of an Astartes brother who had served his Chapter for almost three centuries.

Colber could see the steely look in the marshal's eyes, as Brant cast his gaze over what awaited him in the Crusaders' Chapel. There was recognition in his gaze too.

'Brother Jarold,' he said grimly.

He knew every neophyte and initiate in his crusade, as well as those who had been seconded to a stay in the chapter keep for a time, having fought side-by-side with all of them.

'Is he conscious?' the marshal asked.

'No,' said Colber, having already carried out his examination.

Brant fixed the corpse-pile with brilliant blue eyes, as cold and hard as diamonds. 'But he's alive?'

Colber met Brant's anxious stare, his expression stony. 'My lord marshal, he is dying,' the Apothecary said with grim finality.

'He is a hero!' Brant suddenly declared. 'He deserves a hero's burial!'

'Or something more,' the crimson-armoured Garan said, his voice an augmetic mimic of a human voice.

All the Space Marines present turned their gaze from the dying Jarold for the first time and onto the Techmarine.

'As you know, my lord, Ancient Brother Dedric died a second death on this day, but his battle-suit can be repaired. My artificers can make it whole again. And Brother Jarold with it.'

WITH A HISS of compressed gas, the stasis containers eased shut. A chilling mist heavy with the smell of cryogenic chemicals drifted through the bio-vault, but the Apothecary barely even noticed it. It gave him some comfort to know that the gene-seed, so highly prized by the Chapter, was safely stored now within the Apothecarion bio-vaults of the *Divine Fury*.

He lingered for a moment, offering up a prayer to the immortal Emperor for the souls of those whose genetic material had been returned to the Chapter after they had given their lives in His service. Colber's hand traced the relief pattern of the Apothecarion helix and the Templar cross on a stasis container's frosted surface.

Yes, it was all stored away safely again now and, Emperor willing, in time it would be used to create new brothers for the Chapter to fill the void left by the appalling massacre on Solemnus.

But not Brother Jarold's biological legacy. Fate, it seemed, or the Emperor, had another destiny laid out for the fallen hero of Solemnus. Brother Jarold would serve the crusade still, and help Marshal Brant's renamed Solemnus Crusade avenge their departed brethren against the hordes that followed the scarred ork.

THREE
LAST STAND

The present day…

THE EQUATORIAL JUNGLES rang with the clamour of battle, strange echoes returning from the scale-bark trees.

Brother-Apothecary Colber of Fighting Company Gerhard raised his bolt pistol, meeting the savage greenskin's charge head on. The gun kicked in his gauntleted hand and the ork was thrown violently backwards, as if yanked by a heavy chain, the front of its thick skull shattered and its tiny brain liquidised by the explosive round.

But where one fell, another three of the foul alien scum were ready to take its place and prove themselves worthy in the eyes of their brutish gods. Truly could the old adage 'might is right' apply to the greenskin hordes, no matter what branch of the xenos genus they came from, whether they were those of the ork clans or what the Magos Biologis referred to as feral orks.

In a moment of mental detachment, as his body fought on against the relentless horde, it seemed to Colber that all of ork-kind were feral, certainly when compared to the civilised nature of humankind. It was even more true when they were compared to the noble majesty of the Adeptus Astartes.

The Apothecary suddenly found himself in a bubble of calm in the very midst of the fighting, as if caught within the eye of a storm. It felt unnatural, sense-numbing, as if he was merely a distant observer to the maelstrom of battle-madness raging all around him. But he made the most of the opportunity and took stock of the battle.

The dense foliage of the jungle was oppressive around them. The fighting company was being forced to make its last stand in a clearing amidst the interminable cloud-forests of the equatorial jungle belt. It was as if the trees, packed in with claustrophobic closeness, were trying to claim every part of the terrain.

At some time in the past this clearing must have been formed when an ancient giant of a tree had rotted through and fallen, bringing down several others with it. This glade was then suddenly exposed to the polluted sky, streaked with ochre petrochemical clouds and the unforgiving glare of Armageddon's sun. Even now, however, the towering, creeper-hung trees and their encroaching canopy threatened to block out the sky and enshroud everything beneath a pall of darkness.

Fleshy-trunked cycads had already taken advantage of the disappearance of the sunlight-stealing canopy and were growing in profusion over the floor of the glade, forcing the Marines to fight the orks through densely packed undergrowth.

Colber had effectively become separated from his fellows by the fighting. He began to move back across the glade to regroup with the other warriors of the fighting company. He stopped as the fallen body of a Templar appeared through the clusters of fern fronds in front of him. It was Brother Kaslon. He had lost an arm to an ork cleaver and even his enhanced physiology was struggling to stem the bleeding from the savage wound.

'Do not worry, brother,' Colber said, bending down to tend the stricken Marine. 'I have something in my narthecium that will halt any further blood loss.'

'There… there isn't time,' Kaslon gasped, his system struggling to allay the effects of shock brought on by the trauma he had suffered.

'But without my ministrations you will die here, brother,' Colber stated bluntly, his tone calming.

'Then let me die here, Brother-Apothecary,' Kaslon managed. 'But take my gene-seed. Return it to the Chapter. That way I can never truly die.'

Colber bowed his head. It suddenly felt very heavy. He despaired when he had to leave a Space Marine's corpse unharvested, for it meant that more of the Chapter's precious, irreplaceable gene-seed was lost.

The brave brother was right. So as Brother Kaslon lost consciousness, the Apothecary removed that which made him a Space Marine and stowed the precious organs inside his narthecium.

* * *

ONCE THE SOLEMNUS Crusade had reached the Armageddon system, and finally orbit over the beleaguered planet, Fighting Company Gerhard and the marshal's own household had carried out boarding actions against the multitude of roks cluttering the space lanes above the war-torn world. The Templars of Fighting Company Adlar had executed a mission into the arid, polluted deserts of Armageddon Secundus, south and east of Tartarus Hive and Clain's Stronghold, following up reports of orks carrying the banner of the scarred ork in that region. They had also been inspired by a vision sent by the Emperor Himself to the devout warrior Brother Ansgar, who had been anointed Emperor's Champion in recognition of that fact.

The Emperor's Champion had claimed to have fought in hand-to-hand combat against the warlord of the Blood Scar tribe, the alien abomination Morkrull Grimskar. Grimskar was an alien general outclassed in terms of cruelty and power only by the guiding force behind the whole of the alien invasion of Armageddon, the Great Beast Ghazghkull Mag Uruk Thraka himself.

And although the Emperor's Champion had not slain Grimskar, the two combatants having been separated during their clash by the death-throes of the monstrous war machine in which they confronted one another, Ansgar had dealt the warboss a mortal injury. Besides, the Scarred Ork himself was dead anyway, for nothing could have survived the nuclear firestorm that engulfed the volcanic caldera in which the gargant factory had been constructed. Ansgar had only just escaped with his life himself, thanks to the beneficence of the Emperor and the primarch.

With the demise of their warlord, the Blood Scar tribe fell into disarray. The various mobs that made up the tribe, that had only been held together by the dreadful force of personality of a leader as mighty and as physically terrifying as Morkrull Grimskar, devolved into mutual animosity and in-fighting. It seemed that the tribe was quite successfully tearing itself apart, finishing the job that the Black Templars had started.

However, it also soon became apparent that units of the Blood Scar tribe were still active on Armageddon. Some of the more powerful individuals from among Grimskar's original horde had declared themselves the new warlords of the Blood Scar tribe and were battling each other, as well as Imperial forces, to prove their supremacy.

And Grimskar's own flagship, the massive derelict hulk *Krom Kruach*, was still active in the space ways above Armageddon. As yet, the *Divine Fury* had been unable to penetrate the cordon of ork vessels surrounding it. The orks had also taken hold of the wrecks of Armageddon's orbital platforms and space stations that they had overcome in the first days of the Third War. It seemed that the Blood Scar tribe would not fall so easily as the humans had at first thought. It was not simply a case of cutting off the head and leaving the body to die.

And even once the orks who had followed the banner of the Scarred Ork had been wiped from the face of Armageddon, and all evidence of them obliterated from the system, there were still the massed hordes of other greenskin tribes, gathered together under the overall command of the master alien tactician and overlord, Ghazghkull Thraka.

The holy warriors of the Solemnus Crusade would not rest until every one of the aliens had accounted for the sacrilege perpetrated by them against Armageddon, the Black Templars and the Imperium of Mankind. For the Templars' crusade for Armageddon was to be their last such undertaking. The reduced size of the Solemnus fleet, their depleted numbers and gene-stocks, could not survive a conflict of the magnitude of the campaign to save the strategically vital, armament-forging world. It was one of the most all-consuming wars fought on Imperial soil in the last five hundred years of the forty-first millennium.

And then reports had reached Marshal Brant and the Marines of the Solemnus Crusade that orks under the banner of the Blood Scar tribe had been seen within the southern equatorial jungles. What Blood Scar orks were doing in that region – known to be feral ork territory, ever since Ghazghkull's first, unsuccessful assault on the planet fifty years before – was anybody's guess. Especially as they were several thousand kilometres from where their presence had last been recorded on the planet's surface.

During Fighting Company Adlar's harrying mission against elements of Grimskar's war host out in the polluted ash wastes, it had become apparent that the orks of the Blood Scar tribe had a genetic inclination to build huge war machines – weapons of mass destruction constructed in the image of their brutish gods. This followed the pattern begun by their use of a rok asteroid-fortress in the attack on Solemnus and their outfitting of the derelict hulk that was the flagship of Grimskar's armies. What the slimy, humid depths of the foetid jungles had to offer them no Marine could begin to imagine.

But Marshal Brant had dared not miss an opportunity to rid Armageddon of their kind forever. Whilst he continued to lead the sword brethren of his own household in a mission to bring about the total destruction of the *Krom Kruach*, Brant had commanded Castellan Gerhard and his company to follow up the rumours amidst the sweltering rainforests that divided the two major landmasses of Armageddon Prime and Secundus.

ALTHOUGH THE FIGHTING company still numbered twenty-three men after the losses it had suffered fighting aboard the ork rok *Gork's Toof*, each one of them more than a match for a savage greenskin, there seemed to be no end to the horde assaulting them now. The jungles obviously provided perfect propagating conditions for the ork spores.

They came at the Marines out of the all-enclosing green, dressed in scraps of leather and animal hides, daubed with crude war paint, waving ungainly handcannons and heavy-bladed cleavers. Some of the feral beasts even carried stickbombs and other heavier weapons; even out here in the jungle they were obviously scavengers.

The way the aliens kept coming at them, despite the terrible losses they were suffering to the Templars' superior skill at arms, made Colber think that it was almost as if they were being herded into the clearing by something the Marines hadn't encountered yet.

And although not one of the valiant Templars was prepared to admit it, these alien savages were slowly but relentlessly, inevitably, wearing them down. For to make such an admission would be tantamount to admitting defeat, in which case Fighting Company Gerhard might as well give up now and abandon their whole crusade. A Black Templar of the Solemnus Crusade would never do that, not after what Morkrull Grimskar and his sacrilegious tribe had done to their chapter world. For every ten of the orks that fell, so did another of Castellan Gerhard's men.

Deep down, Colber knew that – barring an Emperor-sent miracle – this would be Fighting Company Gerhard's last stand. And although he inwardly chastised himself for the implied lack of faith, Colber was a pragmatist at heart; a miracle seemed unlikely. Cerbera Base, the nearest Imperial station, was at least one hundred kilometres away by Techmarine Torrek's reckoning.

And although short-range comms were still operational, for some reason they had been unable to signal the Solemnus fleet in orbit one hundred kilometres above them.

It seemed incredible that the feral orks could be in possession of something so complex, and no doubt requiring huge amounts of power, that they were able to jam the Space Marines' signalling devices.

HIS AUTO-SENSES detecting swift movement above him, Brother Baruch turned his heavy bolter on a pair of bounding orks that were leaping through the canopy of the treeline. The heavy weapons-fire tore great holes through the broad-bladed leaves of the forest vegetation, filling the air with a sticky sap-mist. Through the emerald haze, Colber saw several rounds rip through the shoulder of one of the leaping aliens, tearing a thickly-muscled arm from its body and rupturing the creature's stomach. The greenskin's flight came to an abrupt end as it plummeted from a vine, crashing to the ground amidst the thick foliage covering the jungle floor.

A shell also passed cleanly through the thigh of the second ork, but before Baruch's heavy bolter could do it any more damage the alien had landed in front of the Apothecary, a necklace of teeth rattling around its thick neck. Colber's white armour stood out more than any of the other warriors, their two-toned suits providing at least some semblance of camouflage amidst the obscuring vegetation.

Colber felt as well as heard the clang of the ork's machete-like hand weapon hit the shoulder plate of his armour. With an oath to the God-Emperor, Colber faltered under the blow. The alien was almost as tall as him and was possibly even as heavy as him in his armoured state.

But then it was the ork's turn to falter, the momentum of its attack causing it to put weight on its own injured leg, and in the next moment Colber had recovered. He jabbed forcefully with his right fist, the tip of the reductor popping the ork's right eye and embedding itself in the alien's brain. Colber followed the manoeuvre with a burst of bolt pistol rounds to the ork's midriff. The creature spasmed for a moment, setting its ugly tusked mouth in a snarling grimace, and then the light of life faded from its beady eyes and the ork crumpled to the ground at the Apothecary's feet.

There was the buzz of chatter over the comm, Templars declaiming oath-prayers in the face of the enemy, cursing the aliens with the divine wrath of the triumvirate of the God-Emperor, the primarch and Lord Sigismund. Others were trying to reorganise themselves. Some were trying to call up Castellan Gerhard. Brother Daric's strident tones were claiming that he had seen the commander fall.

All, it seemed, were engaged with the enemy face-to-face. This was the favoured way of fighting for the Astartes warriors of the Black Templar order. It seemed unthinkable that such primitive life forms could put up any realistic resistance to the proud warriors of the Adeptus Astartes, let alone prevail in battle against them. The thought was unconscionable.

In the twelve years since the Scarred Ork's attack on Solemnus, the Templars of Marshal Brant's crusading force had encountered the greenskins again on several occasions and had always ultimately won through. But here on Armageddon, a world subsumed by war, nothing seemed certain any more.

Who knew why the aliens had chosen to attack there and then and with such force that dark day twelve years before? The ways of the alien were as unfathomable to the human mind as it was impossible to stare across the endless gulfs of the Sea of Souls and not go insane at the sight. The ways of the xenos mind were closed even to the all-seeing divine insight of the Emperor himself. And now was it really possible that the foul greenskins had brought low Castellan Gerhard himself, who had led his fighting company since the scourging of N'twus Sune by the piratical eldar twenty years earlier?

And then, in a blizzard of static wash, Gerhard was back online, bellowing for order in the name of the primarch, whose sanctified blood flowed in all their veins, initiate and neophyte alike, and confirming that rumours of his death had been much exaggerated.

Apothecary Colber looked behind him. Standing atop a moss-limned section of tree trunk and towering over those of his fighting company still standing was their commander, Lord Gerhard. The castellan's black and white power armour was slick with alien blood and the slime of pulverised bio-fungal flesh, the prominent Templar cross on his chestplate gouged by the traces of solid munitions fire.

Despite the weapons-fire skimming past him through the air and the occasional shell spanging off his ancient ceramite armour, Castellan Gerhard understood that this would be his company's last stand against the greenskin menace and that it was more important that he rally his troops now in their final defiant defence than fight a battle of subtle manoeuvres. The time for subtlety was past. They were doomed, all of them, but they could still make their sacrifice count.

'Warriors of Solemnus!' his voice rang out over the comm. 'We have nothing to fear from these greenskinned abominations. How can our efforts come to nought when we are the Emperor's finest, his most devout servants? The warriors of the Adeptus Astartes are fear incarnate! Did our noble forefather, Primarch Dorn, not say that one hundred of the Astartes are worth a thousand of any other fighting force loyal to the Imperium?'

The castellan broke off abruptly, took practiced aim with his plasma pistol and sent a screaming ball of roiling blue liquid fire hurtling into a mob of galloping orks. The aliens died with the flesh melting from their bones.

'We have nothing to be remorseful for. We should not count the cost of the sacrifice we make,' Gerhard went on, taking up his speech again, 'for the foul greenskins will find that our deaths come at a high price – one paid in ork corpses. And besides, what nobler way is there to die than in service of Him Enthroned on Earth?'

As the castellan spoke, yet more of the savage orks poured into the clearing. Was there no end to them? Their constant presence on a world of the Emperor's realm was a continual affront to His Imperial Majesty in the eyes of the aggrieved Black Templars.

'And we shall show them no pity as we reap our terrible revenge, just as our brothers who will come after us and avenge the loss of our lives on the heads of the alien host. For the Emperor, for the primarch, for Lord Sigismund and for Solemnus!' Gerhard roared.

'No pity! No remorse! No fear!' The men of the castellan's company took up the battle-cry of the Black Templars Chapter, the same the galaxy over, no matter where the crusading fleets of the Black Templars continued the longest holy war in the ten-thousand year history of the glorious Imperium.

An explosive crash, like the fury of a thunderstorm breaking directly overhead, shook the clearing. It was the sound of a missile launcher firing – several missile launchers in fact.

And then a new swathe of weapons-fire tore across the glade in crackling green lightning arcs and the greasy black fossil fuel contrails of rockets that made even the emboldened Gerhard take cover behind the barrier of the massive log.

Crashing and clumping their way into the clearing between the trees, splintering saplings beneath their iron-shod feet, were yet more orks. But these were dramatically different to those feral creatures the Black Templars had fought so far. They were certainly not what Colber would have expected to see fighting alongside a feral ork tribe.

There were fewer of them, but every one of the new arrivals had been extensively 'modified' by the addition of crude bionic components. Such a practice was common amongst the ork hordes, but the orks now entering the clearing were more rusting metal augmetics than green flesh. They were what the Magos Biologis classed as cyborks.

Where had they come from, Apothecary Colber wondered? But their arrival gave him an inkling as to how the orks had been jamming their long-range comms. The more technologically proficient cyborks would be more likely to have the ability to interfere with the Templars' communications. Colber found himself asking the same question again: what were such highly mechanised orks doing in the untamed depths of the equatorial jungles?

Colber knew clearly that he would soon be fighting at the Emperor's side against the enemies of mankind for all eternity. Not many warriors who had given their whole lives to His service had the privilege of knowing the precise hour of their death that they might fully prepare their souls for it. It was time for him to shed the vestiges of his mortality and be reborn as a warrior angel of the Master of Mankind.

But until the moment when that pre-ordained cleaver took his head from his shoulders, or that explosive round detonated inside his chest, or that particular accursed las-discharge fried the flesh from his augmented skeleton, he would fight to the end to fulfil his duty to protect the precious narthecium that contained the gene-seed of his dead brothers.

Even if he did not survive to fight another day, there was still a chance that the progenoid glands he had harvested from his fallen brethren would, to be reclaimed by the Solemnus Crusade. Perhaps another of his Apothecary brothers would even recover the zygotes from his own carcass when they made the pilgrimage to the site where Fighting Company Gerhard had made their last stand.

With the castellan's personal signifier hanging limply above them, motionless in the humid air, Brother-Apothecary Colber, Castellan Gerhard, Standard-bearer Pelka and the handful of Black Templars that remained of the company that had forged their way to this point in the unforgiving green twilight world prepared to do just that, together.

This was to be their last stand, and the alien greenskins that beset them would pay dearly for it.

PART II
NO REMORSE

FOUR
VALKYRIE DOWN

THE VALKYRIE ASSAULT carrier skimmed over the vast
expanse of jungle, the jet-wash of its engines sending waves rippling away over the lurid emerald sea
of the forest canopy. The forest floor was hidden
from view beneath the all-encompassing cover provided by the densely spreading branches and leaves
of the jungle trees. The endless canopy sealed the
world beneath in the permanent twilight of its
turquoise depths.

The swathes of jungle spread out for a hundred
kilometres in every direction, as far as the eye could
see. There was no end to the lush green vista as the
thick rainforests stretched out towards the horizon.
The only features to break the interminable green
were the occasional dark hole in the forest canopy or
outcropping of vegetation-swathed rock.

The gunmetal grey craft skimmed over the forested peaks and followed the line of the deep-cut valley paths. The Valkyrie's pilot kept her low, wanting to avoid modar detection by the enemy or any of the numerous Imperial factions at large within the southern equatorial jungles.

The Valkyrie's passenger knew for a fact that at this time, as well as the regular patrols of the Armageddon ork hunter regiments operating out of Cerbera Base, supported by elements of disparate off-world Guard forces, it was rumoured that there were as many as five different Astartes Chapters pursuing their own missions into the Green, as the ork hunters termed it. They included the Marines Malevolent, the Angels of Vigilance and the lauded Sons of Guilliman. Such rumours remained uncon-firmed for now, but it seemed likely to Tremayne that there was no smoke without fire. Chances were that there had to be some sort of Chapter presence in the jungles when there were in excess of twenty Chapters fighting for Armageddon in its most des-perate hour of need.

Staring out of the view-port in the side of the aircraft to his left, Lieutenant Nimrod Tremayne of the Armageddon Command Guard watched the jungle fly past as a verdant blur. The lush vibrancy of it was in dramatic contrast to the filthy firmament above it. The sky was a soiled brown, streaked with wisps of chemical cloud, an ever-present reminder, even here, of the reason why Armageddon was such a strategically vital world and such a precious possession to the Imperium. It was a vital node at the centre of the sector's navigational channels and its thousands of weapons shops supplied arms to Guard regiments many light years away.

But Lieutenant Tremayne's troubled mind was not concerned with the scenic vista laid out before him beyond the glass. His anxious thoughts might as well have been a world away. They were fixed firmly on the mission that awaited completion within the haunted depths of the jungle.

The Valkyrie was flying roughly south-east on a bearing of one-three-six, Tremayne judged from the position of the morning sun. He glanced at his wrist-chronometer. It was still only 07.04 hours Imperial standard. They had departed from the wind-swept and sandblasted landing field on the Anthrand Plain at 06.15 hours. They had been flying for less than an hour and in that time had probably covered over four hundred kilometres.

Tremayne jutted out his chin, stretching the tense muscles in his neck, rubbing at sore skin where his tight starched collar rubbed. His jaw ached. He realised he had been clenching his teeth tightly together while concentrating on the mission ahead.

Strapped into the aisle seat, one seat away from him, was Kurn, the leather harness barely managing to restrain his hulking frame. Kurn was Tremayne's personal bodyguard. He was built like an abhuman ogryn. In fact, Tremayne could well believe that there was an abhuman strain in Kurn's genetic heritage at some point in the long distant past.

The two of them – lieutenant and bodyguard – had an unusual bond. Kurn, Tremayne knew, would be faithful to him unto death. And Tremayne would keep Kurn around as long as he was still useful to him.

Kurn was as loyal as a cyber-mastiff and came with a vicious streak to match. He had been a trooper in the Armageddon Command Guard before Tremayne seconded him to act as his personal protector. Before being conscripted into the Guard, Kurn had been a hive-ganger in the lawless under-stack regions of Hive Volcanus.

The first time Tremayne had encountered Kurn had been in the opening days of Ghazghkull Mag Uruk Thraka's invasion of the world Tremayne had sworn an oath to protect on his admission to the upper echelons of the ACG. Ork mobs had stormed the walls of Hive Volcanus and Tremayne had been thrown into the bloody frontline action to repel the invaders at the command of his superiors.

Incredibly, Tremayne had found himself in the position of saving the trooper from certain death, a lucky las-shot taking out the monstrous creature that would otherwise have ripped Kurn's head from his shoulders. Following the desperate street fighting, Kurn had sworn a blood-oath to Tremayne, as was the way of the fiercely loyal hive kill-gangs. He had slashed his forearm, doing the same to the only semi-conscious lieutenant – Tremayne being on the verge of blacking out from blood loss, thanks to a knife wound he had received in the battle. Kurn had then carried Tremayne to the nearest medicae outpost and in turn saved the lieutenant.

Kurn was now utterly loyal to Tremayne who, in Kurn's gang-raised mind, came above even his own home world in terms of where his loyalties lay. Kurn would do anything Tremayne asked of him, go wherever he willed and lay down his life to save that of his master, if need be. Tremayne had subsequently manipulated the simple-minded trooper mercilessly, playing on the sworn debt of his blood-oath.

The scarring disfigurement that was the physical signature of their bond – which a man of Tremayne's mid-hive breeding considered to be a practice more appropriate to the savage culture of orks than that of men made in the Emperor's image – was a constant irritation to a lieutenant with his eye on the career ladder and a desire to dine with the gentry of the upper hives social strata of Armageddon. But all things considered, it seemed a small price to pay for Kurn's eternal devotion.

As well as Tremayne and his bodyguard, the Valkyrie's pilot and navigator, the rest of the mission team was made up of a squad of four Imperial storm troopers. They were dressed in black-grey camo fatigues and carried their trademark hellguns, the power source for each weapon harnessed to the back of the man that carried it.

The lieutenant took in each of the elite soldiers accompanying him on this mission. The team had been handpicked by his superiors in the Command Guard. They were men of the utmost discretion. Tremayne did not recognise any of them. The stony-faced storm troopers all looked alike, especially now that many of them had their faceless, black plastek visors down, in operational readiness. The only one who had introduced himself to Tremayne, with a clipped recital of name, rank and serial number, was the squad's sergeant, one Sergeant Keifer. Indeed, the only thing that made the sergeant look any different from the rest of the elite schola-trained troopers, other than his rank badge, was the fact that he was armed with a short-pattern hellpistol and a carefully oiled chainsword.

Tremayne looked down at his own uniform, comparing it to the dark fatigues of the storm troopers. Dressed as he was, he looked better suited to the ops room or the parade ground than a mission into the unforgiving jungles of his mother world.

But then the mission itself should prove relatively straightforward, he told himself. The storm troopers were only there as a precaution, sent by Tremayne's superiors. It was a simple insertion-extraction mission. They should not even need to enter the jungle itself. They would set down within the boundary of the compound, recover their objective and then leave again immediately.

He should be back at Cerbera Base in time for luncheon and medals.

The storm troopers sat on the opposite side of the gangway to Tremayne and his bodyguard. The elite Imperial soldiers were all focused on the mission ahead as well, carrying out their own subtly nervous habitualised actions, some checking the targeting scopes of their hellguns, others testing their weapon's connection to its power pack energy source. One of the men, sitting across the gangway from Tremayne and a row behind, kept putting his hellgun to his shoulder, from his chest, and back again, in one fluid motion, as if testing his aim and the speed of his reactions.

Sergeant Keifer sat facing the cockpit and the pilot's position towards the nose of the craft, watching the landscape rippling towards him, his helm-visor raised.

From where he was sitting, the unsettled lieutenant could also just see out through the windshield of the Valkyrie. The pilot sat to the right, his navigator in the co-pilot's position to the left. They were both wearing the innocuous, grey flight coveralls of ACG flyers.

The Valkyrie continued to speed towards its classified target destination, soaring just above the treetops. They must be only a matter of some thirty kilometres from the target now.

For the umpteenth time Tremayne adjusted the collar of his uniform jacket.

The snap-shot sniper behind Tremayne kept putting his gunstock to his shoulder and then lowering it again. The red-dot laser-spot of the hellgun's targeter kept flicking up onto the bulkhead in front of Tremayne.

Up, two, three. Then it was gone. Then it would snap up again – for two seconds, its tiny sparkling ruby target spot wavering on the cold steel of the craft's inner hull as the Valkyrie jinked and soared over the jungle, never perfectly still for a moment in its flight – and then down.

Up, two, three, down, two three.

Up, two, three, down, two three.

Up–

But this time the target-spot did not reappear on the bulkhead in front of Tremayne.

At first he felt nervous relief that the incessant target practice had ceased. Then that unknowable sense beyond the usual five came into play and Tremayne's unease increased. He felt the skin at the nape of his neck prickle with gooseflesh and the tiny hairs there stand on end. Slowly, but with great purpose, Tremayne turned his head and looked back over Kurn's muscular shoulder.

There sat the storm trooper, his expression indiscernible, hidden behind the emotionless black glass of his visor, the muzzle of his hell-gun pointing into the lieutenant's face. The sparkling laser made the lieutenant blink.

In that moment, Tremayne knew that he was a dead man.

And it was at that moment that fate – or perhaps it was some higher power, maybe even the Emperor Himself – intervened and a flock of white-winged ibises rose from the jungle canopy in a cacophonous panic as their treetop roost was disturbed by the broiling downwash of the Valkyrie's engines.

At that moment, the pilot's heart lurched in his chest. He knew, of course, that when travelling at approximately five hundred kilometres an hour, if so much as one of the two-metre spanned ibises passed through the turbine of an engine or hit the cockpit's windshield head-on, the results could be catastrophic and would almost certainly spell an end to the mission.

In that split second, to avoid just such an airborne disaster, the pilot abruptly jinked the craft to starboard. Responding to the pilot's sudden course correction, the Valkyrie lurched violently.

At that moment the storm trooper's finger tightened on the trigger, even as he was thrown sideways in his seat. A pulse of intense laser energy zinged past Tremayne's ear; he felt a burst of sudden heat at its passing. The viewing port next to the lieutenant's seat exploded, sending glass spinning into the cabin.

Tremayne turned away instinctively. Diamond-sharp shards lacerated his cheek and sliced open the sparse flesh of his forehead.

A painful hurricane howling assailed his eardrums as the splintered glass of the viewing port was suddenly sucked out of the assault carrier in a rush of high-speed air.

Tremayne cried out in shock and pain, feeling the hungry vacuum created by the depressurising cabin sucking at him bodily, pulling at his clothes and tugging the peaked cap of office from his head.

And then he was slamming his fist against the release-stud of his harness. As long as he remained in his seat he was an easy target. If he moved, there was a slim chance that he would not be a dead man, at least not yet. If he moved it also gave others the chance to react on his behalf.

Even as Tremayne was scrambling out of his seat Kurn was rising, turning as he did so, to face the sniper. But the assassin was on his feet too, the stock of his weapon still to his shoulder. He must have released his harness before making his failed assassination attempt.

There were shouts of surprise, angry barked instructions and a colourful oath to the Emperor from the usually reserved squad.

There was another splintering of glass, followed by a wet crunch and a cry of concussed pain.

Even though he could only just see the assassin out of the corner of his eye as he did all he could to move from his original position, Tremayne somehow sensed that the storm trooper was lining up another shot.

The hellgun spat again, a mere two seconds after the first shot.

Tremayne still lived. Sergeant Keifer did not.

The sergeant's body toppled backwards onto the grilled companionway of the cabin with a loud clang, watery blood, bone fragments and cerebral matter covering the bulkhead behind the dead man. Keifer's pistol clattered to the mesh floor next to his corpse. He had had the gun aimed and ready without a moment's hesitation.

A split second later, the killer adjusted his aim fractionally and dropped a second storm trooper – a high-intensity las-beam popping a targeter-shielded eye and scorching a hole through the man's head, cauterising the grey matter of his brain before the elite soldier could level his weapon.

These men were meant to be the best Command could field, Tremayne's mind reeled. And one man had killed or apparently incapacitated three of them in as many seconds.

The assassin had made his assessment of the situation. He had decided that the more immediate and deadly threat had been Keifer's ready-to-fire hell pistol, and rightly so. He could drop the sergeant, and the other storm trooper, and still be able to bring down the lieutenant with his very next shot. But that didn't take account of Kurn.

As the assassin took aim once more, Tremayne stared down the barrel of his high-powered lasgun in deathly grey terror, looking like a dead man already then Kurn burst into action.

The bodyguard moved surprisingly quickly and with deceptive agility for a man of his size – akin in height and mass to one of the abhuman degenerates that populated the deepest and most polluted fractured dome caverns of the Volcanus underhives. He barrelled into the treacherous storm trooper as he snapped off another searing las-blast. Kurn put his head down and charged like an enraged grox, bringing the man down and knocking the air from him. Kurn's muscled arms wrapped around the assassin's legs and he slammed the storm trooper onto the grilled mesh floor of the hold.

Tremayne would have thought that Kurn's retaliatory assault would have left the man winded – if not with several broken ribs and a punctured lung – gasping for breath and unable to move, existing in his own private world of pain. But not this man.

The horizon pitched violently again and Tremayne found himself thrown backwards into the hard steel of the seat arms. He gasped as he felt the unyielding metal push into the small of his back.

Wincing from the pain, and not knowing when this nightmare might end, he clutched at his back and felt a wet warmth there. He did not need to look at his hand to see the blood now soaking through the fabric of his jacket.

Tremayne forced open his watering eyes, a moan of pain escaping from between gritted teeth. From his position the cabin appeared to be at a cantilevered angle. He couldn't see the sniper, or Kurn.

It was only then that Tremayne realised that the Valkyrie was jinking erratically. Tremayne pulled himself up, another stab of pain making him cry out again. He failed to hear his own voice over the jet-scream of pressurised air being sucked from the interior of the flyer.

He could see the last of the storm troopers now, still strapped in the metal chair where he had been sitting next to the assassin. His head lolled unconsciously on his chest. The visor of his helmet was a broken mess, cruel obsidian shards forced into the man's blood-streaming face. The assassin's gun butt had smashed into the front of his helmet with enough force to shatter the visor, break his nose and force the sharp splinters of plastek into the man's face. Tremayne could not tell whether the man was dead or merely agonisingly unconscious.

He could see Kurn and the assassin now, struggling on the floor of the gangway.

The assassin occupied, Tremayne dared to look to the pilot's position. Beyond the iron-runged steps Tremayne could see little through the cockpit, the pilot's brains having splattered across the inside of the windshield. The assassin's second shot had found a target after all.

And then the prong-branched canopy of the forest was suddenly reaching up to drag the Valkyrie out of the sky.

Tremayne felt the horrendous G-forces ease, but this had the unpleasant side effect of making him aware of the injury in his side all over again. The stunned co-pilot was struggling to regain control of the craft. Tremayne could hear the assault craft protest, the whine of its engines increasing in pitch and drowning the cabin in the tortured sound of screaming air.

There was a groan of pain from the assassin as Kurn struggled to his feet, hauling the man up bodily by the webbing of his anonymous black fatigues. Tremayne braced himself against the steel-backed row of seats in front of him. He popped the catch on the holster holding his own laspistol. This ended here.

The Valkyrie was still bucking and swaying, but Kurn somehow managed to stand upright. The assassin hung from his arms, the man's head mere centimetres from the girdered roof of the cabin.

The pain suddenly forgotten, it seemed to Tremayne that there was a feeling of pomp and poetic justice to this moment. The traitorous storm trooper had made an attempt on Tremayne's life and on the success of a vital covert mission – which in turn could have had a terrible impact on the course of the war for Armageddon itself – but he had failed. Now he would have to pay the ultimate price.

'For crimes against the Emperor,' Tremayne decreed, the moment possessing him, 'I sentence you to d–'

Grabbing hold of Kurn's locked arms tightly to gain a better purchase, straining every muscle in his body, the assassin kicked out with his left leg. A heavy booted foot caught the fingers of the hand in which Tremayne carried his laspistol. Hot red pain made him release his grip. The pistol sailed away through the cabin, hit the facing bulkhead and clattered to the floor beneath the seats.

With a groan of effort, Kurn lifted the assassin higher, obviously intending to crack his head open against the steel girders above him. Suddenly the assassin's right arm was behind his back. A split second later it whipped round again, a jagged-tipped, gleaming fifteen centimetres of steel in his hand. The assassin stabbed the knife blade into the bunched muscle of Kurn's bicep.

The ox of a man let out a wordless cry and dropped the assassin. The man landed in a crouch, leaving his knife in Kurn's arm.

Tremayne ducked down behind the metal seats and began scrabbling for his lost laspistol, feeling a knot of pain-induced nausea clench his stomach. He could not see it. He could not feel it with his desperately sweeping hands, his fingers outstretched. At least for the time being, the gun was as good as lost.

The flyer lurched again.

Tremayne half-stumbled, half-fell out from behind the seats onto his knees in the gangway, fitful red marker lights set into the mesh floor demarcating the route to the rear exit ramp of the plane.

Vulnerable, on his hands and knees, Tremayne looked up at the storm trooper who had his weapon trained on him once more.

In barely more than a minute, as measured on Tremayne's wrist-chronometer, the assassin had wiped out an elite squad of specialist trained soldiers, killed the Valkyrie's pilot, almost killed Tremayne and effectively brought an end to the lieutenant's clandestine mission.

Tremayne wondered who had sent the assassin to kill him – not that such considerations mattered at that precise moment. Was it something personal or were Tremayne and the assassin merely pawns in a game of regicide played by anonymous forces?

Then Kurn was on the assassin again, coming from nowhere, trapping the struggling man in a choking headlock. The bucking of the plane and their own violent struggles brought Kurn and the assassin rolling to the rear of the cabin.

Considering Kurn's size and strength, the assassin was making a good account of himself. They were both fighting unarmed and that meant little to Kurn. A two-fisted uppercut from him was the equivalent of being hit with a sledgehammer.

But where Kurn had the advantage in terms of weight, sheer brute strength and savagery, the assassin was swifter and more agile, even after receiving a beating from the ex-ganger.

Nonetheless, the outcome of the brawl was a forgone conclusion to Tremayne.

And then the unthinkable happened.

It all happened so quickly that Tremayne didn't quite know *what* had happened. One moment Kurn had been lining up for another punch to the assassin's stomach, then the assassin had lashed out unexpectedly with a booted foot, delivering a savage kick to Kurn's ankle. The bodyguard crashed down at the edge of the sealed exit ramp. And now it was the assassin standing over the prone bodyguard. If Kurn was not careful, he was about to fail in his duty to Tremayne and the God-Emperor.

For one frozen moment that seemed to stretch out into eternity, Tremayne stared in horror at the hellgun now aimed at Kurn's head, his own pulse pounding in his ears. The assassin had reassessed the threat factor. Kurn was now the greatest threat to his directive. With the bodyguard summarily executed, he would be able to take his time over his real target. Then time rushed back in to fill the temporal vacuum and it was Tremayne's turn to spring into action.

He had no gun and he was injured. He would have to try a fresh gambit.

With stumbling steps Tremayne staggered towards the rear of the Valkyrie, towards the assassin.

Tremayne hooked an arm around a bulkhead girder and prepared to hang on for dear life. He was sure the Valkyrie carried a complement of grav-chutes but there wasn't time to look for one and struggle into it now. He had to act without hesitation.

Tremayne slammed his open palm down on the hatch-release's activation stud. A red hazard beacon began cycling on the bulkhead above his head and a droning claxon sounded with a similar regular pulse. There was a shuddering clang and Tremayne's world was thrown into disarray. The assassin was hurled bodily through the air.

A rushing wind roared through the cabin with increasing force. Kurn and the assassin both rolled towards the back of the cabin and the widening space where the exit ramp was deploying. Tree tops flashed past them only metres below.

The wind had become a howling gale, slicing through the cabin with its terrible clawing talons, trying to drag all who remained there, alive or dead, out of the back of the assault carrier.

Sergeant Keifer's body tumbled past Tremayne, bounced over Kurn, who was clinging to a flapping net of webbing, and hit the assassin.

The storm trooper scrabbled for purchase, but found none. His hellgun forgotten, desperate fingers clawed at the tug-release of a black harness fastened across his chest.

And then the assassin was gone, lost in the jet-wash of the Valkyrie, sucked out of the back of the hurtling craft.

Tremayne was safe again, but only temporarily.

There was a shuddering clang as the lowered ramp hit something skimming past barely beneath the undercarriage of the assault carrier.

The Valkyrie convulsed, throwing Tremayne against the roof of the cabin and then painfully back against the bulkhead. He struggled to maintain his grip on the girder. It was too much for the co-pilot.

Screaming like a banshee, the aircraft nosedived into the forest canopy and went down.

FIVE
EMPEROR'S CHAMPION

GRIEF. GUILT. ANGER. Hatred.

A rushing maelstrom of emotions – the physical pain of emotional trauma – like a whirlpool sucking him down into its oblivion-black depths.

His mind was torn from his body, hurled through the frozen shroud of the void – the passage of time having no relevance here anymore – to the sweltering world below, to…

…the green-dark depths of the jungle.

The castellan was standing atop the fallen tree trunk at the centre of the cycad-carpeted glade, resplendent in his Templar power armour, the aliens' weapons discharging in the sticky air around him. And Brother Ansgar knew him: he was Castellan Gerhard, the inspiration behind Fighting Company Gerhard, which made up one third of the Solemnus Crusade's fighting force.

Few of the warriors of Fighting Company Gerhard remained. Where once there might have been as many as sixty Templars fighting for the castellan, Ansgar could now only see seven.

As well as the castellan himself, there was the company's standard-bearer, Brother Pelka. The black cross insignia of the Black Templars, surmounted by Castellan Gerhard's personal heraldry, was hidden among the folds of cloth as the gun-shot and scorched banner hung limply from the banner-pole in the stifling air of the glade.

There was also a brother of the Apothecarion, his white armour dazzling in the streaks of misty, copper-stained sunlight piercing the depths of the clearing between the towering trees that created a cathedral-like dome with their canopy.

Four other battle-brothers made up the rest of the company. All of them bore the equal-armed black cross of the Templars on a field of white upon their armour, as well as carefully inscribed passages of holy scripture and the flapping parchment ribbons of purity seals.

Before Ansgar even caught the castellan's words he realised that the grizzled warrior was rallying his troops to the battle-banner of his fighting company that they might make their last stand against the orks, united by their faith in the Emperor.

And then, above the shrieking screams of lasfire and the chugging roar of bolter rounds whipping through the humid atmosphere, Ansgar heard the castellan's voice as if his helmet comm had suddenly been switched to the same channel being used by the fighting company.

'The warriors of the Adeptus Astartes are fear incarnate!' the castellan bellowed, his words clear as an alarm bell sounding on the bridge of the *Divine Fury* warning of an imminent impact. 'Did our noble forefather, Primarch Dorn, not say that one hundred of the Astartes are worth a thousand of any other fighting force loyal to the Imperium?'

As the castellan was addressing his men, a mob of crazed, tattooed orks charged his position. Calmly he fired the plasma pistol held in his left hand. A blazing ball of molten energy screamed from the muzzle of the weapon. The castellan's aim was true. The plasma burst hit the mob at their centre, splashing the bounding greenskins with liquid fire that immediately began to eat away at their flesh and melt their toughened bones.

'We have nothing to be remorseful for,' the castellan went on. 'We should not count the cost of the sacrifice we make, for the foul greenskins will find that our deaths come at a high price: one paid in ork corpses. And besides, what nobler way is there to die than in service of Him Enthroned on Earth?'

There seemed no end to the number of orks pouring into the clearing. It was only a matter of time – and precious little of it – before the Black Templars' position was overwhelmed.

Castellan Gerhard's voice carried as loud as the clamour of battle itself now: 'And we shall show them no pity as we reap our terrible revenge, just as our brothers who will come after us and avenge the loss of our lives on the heads of the alien host. For the Emperor, for the primarch, for Lord Sigismund and for Solemnus!'

Ansgar heard the men of the castellan's company take up the battle cry of the Black Templars Chapter as he ran towards the tree trunk.

'No pity! No remorse! No fear!'

Ansgar felt as much as heard the battery of missile launchers firing, a subsonic wave that shook his body inside his power armour. He saw the castellan ahead of him leap down from his rallying point atop the sundered jungle tree, taking cover from the explosive hail of missile fire now assailing the Templars' position. Flashes of what seemed like green lightning flashed across the glade and the air was filled with the smoky residue of the rockets' fossil fuel emissions.

Reaching the castellan's position, Ansgar turned. Where before the Space Marines' assailants had been orks of the feral variety, armed with nothing more complicated than hacking cleavers and crude solid slug-firing guns – which had caused enough devastation among the isolated fighting company – they were now confronted by another breed of ork altogether.

Smashing their way through the treeline, emerging from the smothering green twilight beyond, was a mob of orks of another degree of savage killing power altogether. Every one of the monsters was a hulking colossus of an ork, extensively modified with rusting bionics that leaked greasy fluid, and sparking electronic components of alien design.

Ansgar had encountered such cybernetic creatures before, on feral Fossalus and then on the moon of Conlaoch. There had been some amongst the unruly masses of the Blood Scar tribe. But he would not have expected to meet them in the foetid depths of

Armageddon's equatorial jungle belt, and certainly not fighting alongside a feral ork tribe. As far as ork-kind went, they were far too 'sophisticated'.

The mechanical augmetics made the cyborks seem even larger and more threatening. It certainly made them even more efficient killers.

The cyborks pounded towards what remained of Fighting Company Gerhard, dousing the Marines with a withering hail of weapons fire. Cycad stems exploded under the barrage. The bitter smell of boiling sap and burning plant fibre scorched the senses.

And then blood was misting in the air too; the blood of the Black Templars as well as that of the aliens.

A Templar was hurled back against the trunk, the force of the impact rocking the tree in its soggy hollow and splintering its rotten bark. The direct hit the Marine had suffered from a missile and its subsequent detonation cracked the chestplate of his armour open and a thin trail of smoke now rose from the smouldering crater in his flesh.

Then the cyborks were on them, clubbing them with their oversized mechanical claws. Crude but effective chain-blades of the aliens' own devising clashed with blade and bolter of the Space Marines.

Ansgar had fought such creatures before – he had battled with the warboss of the Blood Scar Tribe, Morkrull Grimskar himself, for the Emperor's sake – but never had he felt so outnumbered.

What was this treacherous emotion he was experiencing now, despair? The fear that he and his compatriots might not conquer here this day, that they might fall, unnoticed, to the greenskin menace, their pleas for aid unheard by the crusade fleet orbiting this contested world above them?

Ansgar riled against himself and his desperate feelings as a snarling, iron-jawed ork lunged at him. He was a champion of the Emperor, he thought, as he struck the cybork's armoured exoskeleton with the blue-crackling blade of his sword. What did it matter if he died here, this day, so long as he died in the service of the Emperor, bringing down as many of the vile xenos scum as possible?

The power sword bit deep into the ork's body, tearing through both mechanical and living tissue. Dirty brown hydraulic oil bubbled from the creature's side. The beast howled and Ansgar felt a sudden cold stab of pain and a feeling like he had been winded. Warning runes flashed across his visor display, changing from amber to red. He tugged at his sword, trying to free it from the cybork's hulking body, aware that the ork's stinking metal-toothed maw was mere centimetres from his faceplate, its foul breath condensing on the visor-shield.

And then Ansgar was being lifted bodily into the air on the end of the rusting hook of a bionic claw. He was dimly aware of the battle going on around him: the Apothecary emptying the clip of his bolt pistol into a greenskin's augmetic eye, shattering the red lens of its blocky implant; Castellan Gerhard bringing the scripture-inscribed blade of his axe down, half-severing an entirely bionic arm in a welter of white sparks, leaving sundered cables and crackling wires visible like torn mechanical tendons and ragged ripped muscle.

Then the blade was free. The ancient sword gripped tightly in both his gauntleted hands, Ansgar raised the weapon above his head.

'No pity! No remorse! No fear!' The battle-oath of the Templars came readily to his lips. The holy relic he held in his hands hummed as he brought the blade slicing down through the air towards the ork's metal-plated skull.

There was a moment of sharp, cold pain. Then it felt to Ansgar as if he were flying through the air, but at the same time he was seeing his own body skewered to the thick trunk by the cybork's claw from an ever-changing vantage point, his foe's other shearing claw at his neck. Only it wasn't his body anymore that he was seeing.

In the split second left before consciousness left him forever, Ansgar realised that he had been decapitated…

THE RAMP OF the Crusader-pattern Land Raider dropped open, lowered by whining hydraulics, and the gloom of the interior of the tank was suddenly bathed in the dirty sepia light of the contested marshlands.

Kill-team Wolfram was ready. With a shout of 'For Solemnus!' the Templars burst from the back of the Land Raider, weapons held ready for battle, led by their inspiring Chaplain – his crozius arcanum held high – and Emperor's Champion Ansgar – the Black Sword of the Solemnus Crusade pointing the way towards the enemy.

Ten battle-brothers came after Wolfram and Ansgar and comprised the rest of the kill-team. Brother

Jarold was the last out of the rear of the Land Raider which seemed barely capable of containing his immense bulk. The dreadnought had to duck to pass through the exit hatch of the tank and even then the spiked iron halo that crested his machine body grated against the roof of the armoured vehicle.

With Brother Jarold stomping through the swamp behind them, calling down the divine vengeance of the Emperor upon the heads of the savage greenskins, the newly-formed Squad Wolfram moved at engaging speed towards the borders of the jungle and the feral orks' refuge, splashing through the stinking stagnant surface water of the marshes.

The Space Marines all heard the whining roar, the rapidly increasing volume telling them that an object was closing at high velocity.

A heavy munitions shell hit the swamp in front of the Templars with concussive force. It threw up a wall of filthy water four metres high, drenching the Space Marines, showering them with sods of black mud and peaty clumps of reeds. But the Templars did not falter, and pressed on towards the dark, amorphous backdrop of the treeline. It was there that the brooding darkness of the jungle met the mist-shrouded expanse of the swamplands that formed a buffer zone between the Green, as the indigenous ork hunter regiments called it, and the crawling waterway of the Minos River.

Through the mists – the indistinct outlines overlaid with orange wire-frame models by the arcane auto-senses built into the laurel-wreathed helm of the Armour of Faith – Ansgar saw huge snorting behemoths advancing to meet the Imperial tank lines and striding war walkers. The beasts' rumbling bellows and guttural lowing was muffled by the mist, which gave it an even more unsettling, unearthly quality.

Warning runes started to flash at the periphery of his visor. One of the wire-frame models was blinking red, the suit's cogitator trying to reconfigure as something large began to move at speed towards the Space Marines.

It was too close, too large and, incredibly, too fast for them to take evasive action, weighed down as they were by their armour in the boggy marsh.

And then it was on top of them, all tusks, horns and splayed crushing hooves...

RED LIGHTNING CRACKLED across the underside of the darkly massing, monsoon clouds away to the west. West – that was the direction in which their objective lay.

'It looks like a rad-storm is blowing up ahead of us, at the heart of the jungle,' Ansgar said, incredulous. His words sounded distant and somehow dislocated. 'Like that meteorological beast we narrowly avoided in the toxic wastes out beyond the defensive guns of Clain's Stronghold.'

But how could there be such a thing, out here, over the equatorial rainforests, Ansgar wondered? The radiation storms of Armageddon were the unholy offspring of millennia of unchecked industrial pollution on a planet-wide scale and several ecology-devastating wars. Ansgar had understood that for the most part, rad-storms were restricted to the polluted wastes of Armageddon Prime and Secundus.

'That is no radiation storm,' Chaplain Wolfram said darkly. 'Can you not feel it? That sensation of sickness in the air?'

Ansgar *could* feel it. He had endured such feelings before but it had not been in the presence of the crusade's ork enemies.

He had felt it at the Gate of Duranon on the relic-world of Kazalus. He had felt it at the defence of the Shrine of the Immortal Emperor on Macaris Tertius. And he had felt it on board the *Red Slaughter*, as Marshal Brant's Black Templars had pursued their own boarding action against the Carnage-class cruiser.

It was the revulsion felt when confronted by the repulsive insidious presence of Chaos…

IMAGES BLURRED, STRETCHED and warped, reshaping themselves before solidifying again.

A battlefield of churned mud and mulched rotting vegetable matter amidst the all-enclosing forest, devoid of the hoots and trills of jungle animals and birds, strewn with the bodies of black Templars, a sealed box bearing the helix seal of the Apothecarion half buried in the mud.

Trunks grey and withered and yet still clinging to unnatural life, twisted into even more bizarre shapes than they ever had before, an alien outlandishness that was a total anathema to strong, vigorous life itself, as though actual physical corruption had taken hold of the jungle.

A precipitous path hugging an almost sheer-sided cliff face, a raging torrent of filthy ochre water cutting its way through the jungle a hundred metres below.

A storm of untold, unnatural power, like some hungry, feral beast, tearing hurricane-force winds, shredding leaves and even branches from the trees, a deluge of fat greasy raindrops, like a viscous rain of blood, as though the heavens themselves had been cruelly wounded.

The images came one after another, in a barrage of half-forgotten memories, half-remembered moments, sometimes overlapping or blurring into one another, an assault of chaotic visions that made him reel, strobing flashes of light like feverish dreams. Delusional hallucinations. Things that his battle-brethren, but not he himself, had experienced and things which were yet to come to pass–

Horned, leering faces. Ugly statuary encrusted with gore. Jagged-tipped menhirs raking the tumultuous sky like talons. The savage dog-barks of men foaming at the mouth like slavering, rabid hounds.

A vision of the end of the world. A vision of hell itself.

And then the madness of the vision consumed him.

He could hear the beating of his two hearts thrumming in his ears, getting louder and louder and louder until–

They stopped.

BROTHER ANSGAR STOPPED at the gothic-arched portal to the battle-chapel of the *Divine Fury*. He had been in this position before, only hours before Fighting Company Adlar's mission to relieve the Hellsbreach titan pens.

The same feelings of trepidation, tempered with determination and a steadfast resolve, were there too.

The gloom of the vaulted space beyond was redolent with the heady scent of smouldering incense, burning in censers hung on chains from the spans of the roof.

With reverent pride, Ansgar crossed the worn stones of the chapel threshold, consciously trying to slow his breathing and slow his racing hearts, so brimming over was he with zealous excitement and the desire to bring the Emperor's wrath down upon the heads of his Chapter's enemies.

He strode with purposeful steps past shadow-clad statue niches, beautifully carved marble pillars and golden-flamed candelabra that gave the mists of incense smoke an ethereal quality. How many champions of the Emperor had trodden this path over the age-worn flagstones towards the high altar of the battle-chapel before going to war in His name, he wondered?

And as with the last time he had made this walk, the chapel's two statuesque attendants stood waiting. The only difference on this occasion, however, was that their plate armour and monk-like robes showed signs of more recent battle-scars, not yet repaired and made whole. But then, the Solemnus Crusade was in the midst of prosecuting its own campaign here on Armageddon too.

The altar behind them was empty except for a smoking brazier formed from gold and the cranium of a human skull. The banner of the Templar Resurgent stood behind the altar, wreathed in the amber fumes of the censer. The standard was a relic from the time when Marshal Emrik had brought the *Divine Fury* and its attendant fleet to the remote world of Solemnus for the first time, over a thousand years before. It now travelled with the fleet.

The last time Ansgar had been here the altar had symbolically, as well as physically, borne the sanctified wargear of the Emperor's Champion – the Black Sword and the laurel-wreathed helm that represented the blessed Armour of Faith.

That same helm now adorned his head and he wore that self-same armour. The Black Sword was held reverently in both hands before him, for he had been marked out by his Emperor-sent visions and anointed as His champion.

'Brother Ansgar,' Chaplain Ugo said, turning from his ministrations before the altar, 'you come before us again on the eve of battle.'

Chaplain Wolfram turned too, the ruby eyes of his skull-faced helm reflecting back the light of a thousand flickering candle flames from their glittering facets.

'Has the Emperor unwound the knotted skeins of fate for you to see clearly again?' the second priest-marine asked.

'Aye, brother-chaplain,' Ansgar replied.

'And what has He shown you in His glorious beneficence?'

'He has shown me the cruel fate suffered by the brethren of Castellan Gerhard's company amidst the heathen jungles of Armageddon,' Ansgar stated, trying to keep his voice calm even though the passion of the zealot charged his blood. 'He has shown me that we shall soon return to Armageddon to follow them into the alien-infested jungles to recover that which was lost to them – their most precious gene-seed. And he has shown me that this time I shall be going to Armageddon to meet my end in His service.'

There was a long, protracted silence. For several moments no one spoke. Wolfram took a deep breath. Smoke drifted in golden dust-shot swirls through the still air of the chapel.

It was Chaplain Wolfram whose voice eventually brought an end to the portentous hush. 'If that is what has been revealed unto you, then we must ensure that you go to meet your end with your soul shriven. And let us re-consecrate your sword and armour to the Emperor's service, that you might serve Him as His champion to the very end.'

Resting the tip of his sword on the stone step before the altar with his hands on the hilt, Emperor's Champion Ansgar dropped to one knee before the woven image of Marshal Emrik's battle-banner. The two Chaplains placed their gauntleted hands on the metal-wrought leaves of his helm and began to intone the Prayer of Holy Absolution, the prayer of all those who go to die in the service of the Emperor.

For Brother Ansgar had been chosen by the Emperor to be the Crusade's Champion, and he would remain as such – by the will of the Emperor – for as long as the Black Templars waged holy war against the ork hordes on Armageddon, or until he fell in battle against their loathed and detested green-skin foe.

SIX
CRUSADE

BRANT'S CELL WAS as plain and spartan as that of any Templar-brother aboard the battle-barge *Divine Fury*. The only notable difference was the addition of a cogitator unit in the far corner of the room and a pict-screen, which had been set within the re-made lead bars of a stained glass window. The window had been recovered from the ruins of the chapter keep on Solemnus and had originally cast its rainbow-hued light upon the floor of the sanctuary of Marshal Emrik's death-shrine.

Marshal Brant's private prayer chambers were also clad with the stone of fallen Solemnus – there being nothing left of the Black Templars' presence on that world now – like every monastic cell on board the *Divine Fury*. The stones – some bare and featureless, other bearing fragments of plaster murals and yet others blackened and melted by the ork attack on the chapter world – were a constant reminder of the crusaders' dead brethren. They resonated with the psychic residue left in the aftermath of the deaths of the Templars and their servants, killed in the assault on Solemnus.

Brant sat behind a desk of carved – and once fractured but now repaired – stone. When Wolfram and Ansgar had entered, the marshal had been perusing a piece of torn parchment with a transcribed message upon it. The desk, like the fresco-plastered walls of the marshal's private quarters, had been recovered from the ruins of the chapter keep on Solemnus, before the last of its fractured walls was finally torn down, and the Black Templars had quit the planet for good.

Stormy Solemnus would no longer be a recruiting world of the Black Templars Chapter, or indeed any Chapter thanks to the warning beacon left in orbit by the departing Space Marines. Now it was left as a memorial to those brethren who had lost their lives to the Blood Scar tribe's assault on the planet, making it no more, and no less, than another relic of the Black Templars Chapter.

Behind the desk, a fragment of one of the frescos that had once adorned the vaulted roof of the Hall of Heroes covered the entirety of the back wall of the marshal's austere monastic chamber.

This portion of the fresco depicted a scene from the liberation of the planet. A squad of Tactical Marines was driving back the grotesque, six-limbed shock troops of the genestealer cult. The holy warriors' chainswords and bolters were raised high beneath the black-crossed banner of their most pious Emperor-devoted order.

'And then the vision devolved into images of madness…' Brother Ansgar broke off from his recollection, as if unsettled by what he was about to reveal.

'Go on,' Marshal Brant said.

'Yes, go on,' Chaplain Wolfram interjected, offering the younger Marine his calm encouragement.

'And then I experienced the moment of my own death,' Ansgar finished.

Brant said nothing. He remained with his gauntleted fingers steepled to his lips, elbows resting on the stone top of his desk, staring at the ork skull that sat on its mounting plaque in front of him.

The skull was large and malformed – as were all those of ork-kind – with an over-large jutting lower jaw full of thrusting teeth. The tip of one of the largest of the skull's tusks had been cracked off and the top of the skull bore a wide rent in the thick bone where a smiting blow from an ork cleaver wielded by Marshal Brant himself had felled the great beast on Conlaoch.

It was whilst fighting the orks on the colonised moon that the Solemnus Crusade had come so close to catching up with and defeating the Blood Scar tribe before Morkrull Grimskar and the *Krom Kruach* had ever joined Ghazghkull Thraka's assault on Armageddon.

'And you say this vision came to you just as when the Emperor chose you to be the inspiration of our crusade on Armageddon?' the marshal queried.

'Indeed, my lord,' Ansgar confirmed, 'as I was holding my holy vigil before the shrine in my cell, in a moment of prayerful entreaty. It was then that the stones of Solemnus spoke to me with the voices of our departed brethren and the Emperor lifted the fog of uncertainty from the future for a brief glimpse.

'As I said, I saw the valiant last stand of Castellan Gerhard's fighting company as if I was there in the thick of battle myself. Then I pictured the remnants of my own fighting company as had once been led by Lord Adlar – may the Emperor rest his soul – to recover their priceless gene-seed. And last of all, the dark visions of Chaos and ultimately my own death.'

'Foretellings of Chaos,' Brant mused, his voice a low growl. With that he looked up from the sundered skull at last and fixed Ansgar with the red-coal gaze of his replacement augmetic eye and the sapphire-hard needling glare of his one remaining organic eye.

The crusade's lord and ultimate commander knew all about the savage madness of Chaos and its devotees. He had lost his left eye during a boarding action against the *Divine Fury* by Khornate Chaos warriors six years before. The crimson-lensed optical implant and the knotted pink scar that twisted the skin of his scalp and pinched his cheek served as a perpetual reminder of the Black Templars' successful boarding action against the renegade vessel the *Red Slaughter*.

It had begun as an attack by the frenzied, flesh-bonded warriors of the Blood God. The subhuman Chaos creatures had taken the Solemnus fleet by surprise after the holy armada was lashed by the treacherous currents of Warp Storm Gewitter-Wolke.

The *Red Slaughter* rammed the *Divine Fury*, breaching the hull of the battle-barge with the cleaving blade of its prow. The blood-hungry hordes that it carried in its festering belly poured from airlock portals and even torpedo tubes, rampaging through the chambers and sacristies of the crusade's flagship.

It had ended with the Black Templars carrying out their own boarding action against the unholy Chaos vessel. Led by Marshal Brant himself and the Sword Brethren terminators of the marshal's own household, the crusaders had sabotaged the *Red Slaughter*'s engines and made their escape. The *Divine Fury* had then dragged the disabled vessel with it as the battle-barge thundered towards the nearest star. As soon as the collision-locked ships felt the pull of the star's distorting gravimetric forces, the *Divine Fury* fired up its plasma drive and powered free of the deathly embrace of the traitor vessel.

The Chaos craft had slowly spun towards the six thousand-degree surface of the sun, haemorrhaging its internal atmosphere from sundered boarding umbilicals, which burnt off in a superheated flame thirty kilometres long.

Eventually the *Red Slaughter* had crashed into the broiling corona of the sun, burning up in the unimaginable, planet-melting heat of the star, its shields failing in a matter of seconds under the incomprehensible temperatures and gravimetric pressures.

'Well, Brother Ansgar, I can confirm that the fleet lost contact with Fighting Company Gerhard three days ago. You are certain you had not already heard this news?'

'I am, my lord.'

Chaplain Wolfram took a step forward from his place at Ansgar's shoulder. 'It is not our place to question the will of the Emperor or deny the veracity of those messages He sends to the chosen conduits of His holy power, marshal,' the skull-masked priest warned. 'Nay, it is our duty to respect the Emperor's will, act upon it and fulfil His purpose with the fire of zeal in our hearts and His word hot on our tongues.'

Marshal Brant was a wise leader, having served his Chapter for two hundred and forty years, sixty-three of those as commander of the liberation force that now bore the title of the Solemnus Crusade. He was certainly wise enough to listen when a Chaplain of his most devout order offered him counsel. Besides, Wolfram was a true veteran of the crusade as well, being eighty-seven years older than Brant, and having served the crusade as an ordained initiate even longer than the marshal himself.

'So, Chaplain, you are advising me to listen to Brother Ansgar and commit a secondary force from our already depleted crusade to go where our brothers have already gone before and in all likelihood fallen foul of the enemy. And all because of a dream.'

'I am not advising you of anything, my lord,' Chaplain Wolfram said stoically. 'It is merely what the Master of Mankind wills. And are we to deny the plan determined by the Emperor Himself?'

'But, Brother Ansgar, you say that your vision ends in death – in *your* death.'

Ansgar paused momentarily. 'It does, my lord marshal.'

'Then perhaps the Emperor, in His beneficence, has shown you what might happen if this course of action is pursued – sending warriors to their deaths where others have given their lives in vain already. Perhaps He has revealed to you a way to escape such a fate, that our crusade might fight on in His name to the very end against the enemies of His Glorious Imperium.'

'If it is the Emperor's will that I die for this holy cause, then so be it. That shall be my fate. And I, for one, shall accept it gladly.'

Chaplain Wolfram took another step forward and laid his magnificent crozius arcanum on the marshal's desk.

The crozius was a Chaplain's ceremonial badge of office, the instrument of his faith as well as a potent weapon in its own right, with which he might bring down the holy wrath of the Emperor upon the heads of His enemies. Every one was different, unique.

Wolfram's rod of office took the form of a Black Templar cross attached to a sturdy haft. The flaring blades of the cross had been honed to incredible sharpness, turning it into a deadly double-headed axe. The haft of the crozius also contained the weapon's power source and a disruptor-field generator, so that it might smite Wolfram's enemies more effectively than most axes.

'A thousand theologians of the Ecclesiarchy could spend as many days debating the interpretation of the Emperor's Champion's revelation,' the Chaplain said, using Ansgar's formal anointed title intentionally to add weight to his argument. 'It is not us through whom His Most Glorious Imperial Majesty has chosen to speak, lord marshal. It is not our interpretation that is of importance in this matter. It is not required.

'It is Brother Ansgar to whom the Emperor has spoken just as He did before the drop to liberate the Hellsbreach titan pens. It is Ansgar who is best qualified to interpret his vision, in terms of how he saw it. How he experienced it, even in terms of how he lived it. That is our interpretation and it is all the analysis we need.'

Brant lent back in his chair, his gaze moving from Wolfram to Ansgar and back again. Once again he said nothing.

Marshal Brant did not like to speak in haste. It was one of the qualities that made him such a wise commander, and indeed one of the qualities that had raised him to the position of marshal of an entire war fleet of the Black Templars Chapter.

Brant then fixed his gaze on Wolfram alone and spoke directly to him. 'But I am still not certain of the surety of a course of action that would mean deploying warriors where those who went before them have already died. We cannot afford to waste the resources of our crusade before we can fulfil the vow we made to deliver the Emperor's divine retribution upon the orks of the Blood Scar tribe, and indeed all their vile, green-skinned kin.

'Following our attacks on the ork fleet and the events surrounding Fighting Company Adlar's foray into the ash wastes beyond Tartarus Hive, our number is down to only half what it was before we joined High Marshal Helbrecht and the other elements of our great Chapter – not to mention those battle-brothers of other Astartes Chapters – in fighting the Armageddon campaign. It is less than a third of what it was when we set ourselves upon our mission of revenge against the orks that followed the banner of the Scarred Ork.'

'This discussion is purely academic,' Wolfram declared. 'The fact that Brother Ansgar has seen all the things he has described to us means that they will come to pass whatever we decide to do. Our own subconscious actions will lead us to our inevitable fate, no matter what the outcome of this debate is. The future has been set. Fate itself will bring these things to pass, whether we would will it or no. There is nothing we can do to change this. We can only make sure that we prepare as best we can and make the most of this advantage the Emperor has deemed to give us in His great millennia-spanning wisdom.'

'And you say that your visions spoke of Chaos coming to Armageddon?' Brant said.

'Indeed, my lord,' Ansgar replied.

'It has been here before,' Wolfram added. 'Five hundred years ago, the forces of the Daemon Primarch Angron Worldeater – curse his name! – attempted to claim Armageddon as theirs and remake it as a daemon-world in honour of the Warrior God of the Fell Powers. It is not beyond the realms of possibility that Chaos might yet return to harry the forces of the Emperor's Imperium here before our war against the alien is done.'

'Hmm,' Marshal Brant sighed. 'And so our enemies beset us on all sides. It will take a great sacrifice to prevail in this forum. We may well yet all be called to make the greatest sacrifice a warrior of the Emperor can willingly make.'

Chaplain Wolfram took his magnificent crozius arcanum in his hands again, thumbing the activation rune set into its haft. A scintillating blue energy field immediately hummed into existence around the cross-axe head crackling across the four blades of the Templar icon.

'No life given in His service was ever given in vain,' the Chaplain declared solemnly.

Brant's fingers drummed on the stone top of his desk as he tried to weigh up everything that he had heard and everything that he knew still had to be done. Only then would he decide about the course of action the warriors of his fleet would pursue.

'What you say is true,' he said. 'No life was ever given in vain that was given fighting to hold back the encroaching xenos threat. No battle-brother that died in His service ever made a futile sacrifice. And we have sworn not to rest until we have eradicated every last trace of the greenskin from Armageddon.'

A forceful rhetoric had infected the marshal's words. For a moment it was as if he were addressing the entirety of the Solemnus Crusade on the eve of battle, his own passionate zeal bordering on fanaticism firing his words. He slammed his gauntleted fist down on the desk in front of him with an audible crack and a visible clouding of marble dust formed around his hand.

'However, we must temper our zeal by remembering that this is just one theatre of war across a world subsumed by war,' Brant said, submitting his old advisor and the crusade's champion to the flickering, seemingly divinatory, red stare of his artificial eye. 'We cannot commit our entire force to this one mission.'

'My lord, if I might be so bold?' Ansgar petitioned.

Brant indicated for him to continue with a slight nod of the head.

'I believe these visions are more than just a simple catalogue of events past and those yet to come to pass. I believe the Emperor is showing us the way to fulfil our crusade-oath and to bring our last crusade to fruition.'

'It is possible that that is the case,' Brant agreed, 'but as the venerable Chaplain has already explained, the future is already set and we must simply play out our parts, trusting in the course the Emperor has determined for us.'

Brant picked up the scrap of parchment that had been lying on the desk and began toying with it in his huge hands.

'When you experienced the moment of your vision when you were with Chaplain Wolfram leading your battle-brothers to take the fight to the enemy, you were part of a kill-team, were you not?'

'That is correct, my lord, I was.'

'Then that is how it shall be now.' Brant put the transcribed parchment down on the desk in front of him. 'This is our last crusade and the warriors of my own household are still driving our crusade to the very heart of the enemy. The blasphemous monster the *Krom Kruach* still plies the space-lanes of this system, and until the obscene hulk is obliterated from existence altogether, I shall continue to pursue it from the bridge of this flagship or in person aboard the profane monstrosity, if that is the way the Emperor wishes me to bring an end to the Blood Scar tribe.'

Brant sat back in his great chair and inhaled deeply. 'Besides, even now I am awaiting the arrival of Inquisitor Klojage's party. There are those, who we fight with, who are allegedly our allies, who would seek to make our own sacred mission difficult to pursue. It would seem that I must explain our actions to an agent of the Inquisition.' There was an angry inflection to Brant's words now.

Wolfram and Ansgar looked at the crusade's commander in amazement.

'But, marshal, we owe the agents of the Holy Inquisition no fealty,' Wolfram railed vehemently. 'Aliens, heretics and Chaos-worshippers – the enemy without, the enemy beyond and the enemy within – yes, that is the scope of their investigation. But it is not their place to question the actions of a brotherhood of His Imperial Majesty's most holy Adeptus Astartes! Our motives are not their concern.'

'I am fully aware of our position in this matter,' Brant cautioned, 'as I have already communicated to Inquisitor Klojage. But we are in the midst of a war the like of which this world and the Imperium itself has not seen in over eight centuries, since the terrible days of the dread Gothic War. It would not do to create divisions where there need be none and encourage infighting amongst the servants of the Emperor. There is enough of that already, I am sure. Let us leave that habit to the unruly alien hordes.

'We have nothing to hide. The only thing we have to be penitent for is not persecuting our campaign against the xenos scum more efficiently, more thoroughly and with greater success. We cannot allow dissension to muddy the waters when there is still a world to be won.'

Wolfram continued to fume without making further comment.

'Besides, we do not want to encourage a full-blown Inquisitorial pogrom, as happened with the shadowy Relictors Chapter.'

Brant pushed back his chair and rose to his feet. He was taller than both Wolfram and Ansgar, and his sheer presence seemed to increase his stature still further.

'So let it be done, as the Emperor desires. But let it also be done subtly and swiftly. Chaplain Wolfram, Brother Ansgar,' the marshal said, addressing each in turn, with an accompanying nod of the head, 'you shall lead a kill-team strike force into the depths of the southern jungles. You shall search out the flesh and blood of the brave battle-brothers of Fighting Company Gerhard – the lost gene-seed. I then charge you to hunt down whatever threat is lurking in those putrid forests and fulfil the mission the Emperor has set before you. Let His will be done.'

FIGHTING COMPANY ADLAR had been severely depleted by their mission into the ash wastes and the battle to destroy the gargant factory that they found lurking there. Twenty-two brave warriors had lost their lives during the course of the mission, including Castellan Adlar himself. The loss was a terrible one for the Solemnus Crusade to bear indeed.

But ultimately – with the support of a titan of the Legio Magna and the remnants of a regiment of Armageddon Steel Legionaries – they had prevailed and dealt their greenskin foes a dolorous blow.

Forty-two battle-brothers had survived the endeavour. Nine of them now stood before Chaplain Wolfram and Emperor's Champion Ansgar within the smoky hallowed sanctuary of the battle chapel aboard the *Divine Fury*.

First there was Apothecary Bliant, of Castellan Adlar's own command squad. His white armour bore the symbols of both the Black Templars Chapter and the crimson helix of the Apothecarion. He was equipped in the traditional manner of Space Marine Apothecaries, with a reductor gene-seed extractor, and a bolt pistol. He would be a vital part of the team and his particular skills would be needed if the kill-team managed to recover the lost narthecium of Fighting Company Gerhard.

Second was Wolfram's sworn personal protector, Bodyguard Koldo. In the twelve years of their holy campaign, various battle-brothers of the Solemnus Crusade had earned titles that would be unknown amongst other Astartes Chapters. The rank of Bodyguard was just such a one.

Beside him stood the rest of what remained of the Chaplain's command squad from the Hellsbreach planetfall mission that had become a race against time to stop the devious machinations of the Blood Scar orks: Brother-Initiates Hebron and Gildas.

Veteran Sergeant Agravain had agreed that veteran brother Kemen could join Ansgar and Wolfram on their mission. Kemen was renowned for his strength and battle-hardened tactical wisdom by the men of the fighting company. He stood now, his helmet held in the crook of his left arm, his head entirely shaven, and almost a whole head taller than any of the other brothers gathered there at that time. In his right hand he held his lascannon as if it were no heavier than a bolt pistol. His heavy weapons expertise would serve the kill-team well on the mission that lay ahead.

Then there were Huarwar and Larce, the only ones to make it out of Squad Dynadin's assault on the gates of the gargant factory-caldera alive. Larce carried his trademark flamer whilst Huarwar trusted his fate to a Godwyn-pattern boltgun.

The last two warriors who made up the kill-team were Brothers Bladulf and Clust, late of Tactical Squad Lir, although they were almost all that remained of that noble unit of men, following the battle of the gargant factory. Clust's heavy bolter would doubtless serve them well, as would Bladulf's chainsword. His mastery of the close quarters was well documented.

There were no neophytes on this mission. There was too much at stake. It was not going to be the kind of mission where it would be easy to guide and tutor a youthful novice of the fleet, and besides, there were precious few neophytes remaining to the Solemnus Crusade.

The robed Chaplain Ugo stepped forward, his hood pulled up over his skull-helm, fuming censer in hand.

'You are ready?' he asked of his fellow confessor and the Emperor's Champion.

Marshal Brant having sanctioned Ansgar and Wolfram to lead a select force into the jungled heart of the principal landmass of Armageddon and recover the lost gene-seed of their brother Marines, Ansgar and his Chaplain mentor had lost no time in choosing their team from the Templars on board the *Divine Fury* at that crucial hour.

'We are ready,' Ansgar replied.

'We await your blessing, Brother-Chaplain,' Wolfram said, gripping his crozius arcanum tightly to him, 'so that we might go into battle with our souls shriven in the eyes of the Emperor, if we are to face the end of our mortal lives.'

'Then I shall begin. In nomine Imperator,' Chaplain Ugo intoned.

The gathered Marines all heard the wheezing clanking sound coming from the threshold of the chapel and turned to face the incense-wreathed portal of the flagship's sanctuary.

The two-tonne dreadnought's steps rang from the flagstoned floor of the chapel and echoed from the fog-obscured vault of its roof. The smoke from Ugo's censer swirled around the colossal form of the war walker body-carriage in a coiling dance of vortices as Brother Jarold strode up to join the line of penitent Templars.

He was at least twice the height of Veteran Brother Kemen, the tallest of the remaining crusaders present. The dreadnought body was constructed from armoured adamantium. The sarcophagus that bore the vestiges of Brother Jarold's organic form bore the Templar cross of his Chapter, a momento mori skull at its centre, which seemed even more appropriate considering the fate he had suffered to end up like this.

Truly was it said that dreadnoughts were death incarnate. One huge arm of Brother Jarold's armoured body was a robotic power fist. The other was a massive assault cannon, a replacement.

Brother Jarold had lost his original assault cannon to an ork bomber during the Templars' first mission to the surface of war-torn Armageddon. In the battle at the caldera he had had to rely on a sentinel lascannon that had been spliced to his ancient, venerable armour by a Guardsman engineer of no little ability. However, back on board the fleet's forgeship *Goliath*, the Techmarines of the Solemnus Crusade had removed the botched lascannon assembly and replaced it with another assault cannon – a relic as old as Jarold's dreadnought body – much to the veteran brother's relief.

The dreadnought's hull was surmounted by a spiked iron halo, a mark of the incredible bravery Jarold had shown in battle and which had earned him the right to have his mortal remains entombed within the ancient machine. Rising above the halo was a banner-pole which bore the tattered remains of a banner. Embroidered into its fabric was the fiery, semi-circular outline of a planet set against the void of space. Above the burning world, on a scrolled background, could be read the name of the planet 'Solemnus' in proud gothic lettering.

What was it that had woken the dreadnought from his stasis-slumber in his specially modified chamber deep within the bowels of the *Divine Fury*, Brother Ansgar found himself wondering.

'Brother Jarold,' Chaplain Ugo said with a slight inclination of his cowled head, 'can we be of service?'

The dreadnought's basso augmented voice rang from the machine, reminiscent of slamming blast doors or distant detonating explosive charges. 'I am here to pledge myself to this rescue mission.'

For a moment no one spoke.

'I mean no disrespect, Brother Jarold,' Ansgar said, also bowing his helmeted head before the dreadnought, 'but great though your prowess in battle and your holy fervour are, it is not usual for a dreadnought warrior to accompany a kill-team squad.'

The upper body of the dreadnought rotated on the swivel-joint of its waist so that the front of Jarold's sarcophagus was facing Ansgar. The Emperor's Champion felt as though the eyes of the Space Marine buried within the metal body were staring directly at him.

'Is it not the habit of the holy Astartes to respect the wishes and wisdom of their venerable elders?' Brother Jarold rumbled.

'It is, of course, noble brother,' Ansgar said carefully.

'Then listen to the wisdom of an elder, Brother Ansgar,' Jarold's voice boomed from the vox-casters built into the hull of his massive body. 'It is my wish that I join you on this mission.'

'I did not mean to offend you, venerable brother,' Ansgar said, bowing at the waist this time before the hulking dreadnought.

'I realise that one of my… stature, would not normally accompany a select strike force, such as I see gathered here before me,' Jarold went on, 'but, by Sigismund's sword, I believe that this is an exceptional case. I understand that Brother-Apothecary Colber was part of Castellan Gerhard's company when they were lost.'

'That is correct,' Ansgar confirmed.

'Then he is the reason for my presence here. It was Brother Colber who found me as I lay dying atop a mound of ork bodies within the Crusaders' Chapel of the chapter keep. It was he who saved my life and he was also involved in sealing me inside this dreadnought body. If the Emperor wills it also, I would do all in my power to save my Apothecary-brother from the clutches of those foul greenskin creatures that are blasphemous in His sight.'

'Then we will, of course, respect the wishes of an elder,' Wolfram said, even though he had served his Chapter for a century longer than Jarold before the tragic fate that had befallen him at the Siege of Solemnus had seen him interred inside his dreadnought's burial casket.

So with the newly-formed Squad Wolfram awaiting his blessing that they might go to war in the name of the Emperor, Primarch Dorn and Lord Sigismund with their souls shriven, Chaplain Ugo began his dedication anew.

'In nomine Imperator...'

SEVEN
HUNTERS

'HOME SWEET HOME,' Trooper Geist said, stretching himself out on the dusty ground under the intense glare of the sun. 'Don't you just love the smell of burning orks in the morning?'

'Frikk off, Joker,' Ferze grumbled.

Geist grinned at the most morose member of the team, his teeth a slash of white enamel in the grime still coating his face, his smiling eyes hidden behind the lenses of his anti-glare goggles.

The sun beat down on Cerbera Base and the small skinner platoon gathered haphazardly outside a gun post dugout. The stubble-scalped Geist appeared to be luxuriating in the sunlight. He wouldn't be able to stay out in the full heat of Armageddon's sun as it quickly and inexorably climbed higher into the smoke-stained equatorial sky towards its zenith at noon, else he would burn badly and easily dehydrate as well.

Arno Kole, Sergeant Borysko's right-hand man, surveyed the jumble of bunkers, artillery emplacements and trench workings that made up the camp. Almost all visitors to the ork hunter regiment's jungle outpost were surprised by what they found lurking amidst the enveloping green of the never-ending forests, expecting some mighty armoured bastion, all adamantium-reinforced rockcrete walls, ringed by high curtain ramparts and topped with Hydra emplacement towers.

What greeted them when they arrived at the Imperial station instead was at first glance an apparently ramshackle, yet vast, Imperial camp. Instead of curtain walls there were concentric rings of razor wire enclosing further minefield defences. Wooden watchtowers kept a sentinel lookout over the entirety of the base, with heavy artillery emplacements sunk into the ground ready to respond to any enemy assault. Trench works criss-crossed the long low hill on which Cerbera Base stood – giving the loyal Imperials an unobstructed view of the wilderness beyond for several kilometres in every direction – and bunker roofs peeked out from beneath artificially raised mounds.

Indeed, anyone attempting to enter Cerbera Base had to negotiate a veritable maze of defensive works – trenches, minefields and razor wire – all overlooked by heavy stubber positions, lascannon gun crews and secreted sniper posts.

For a kilometre in every direction around the camp the ever-present jungle – the Green, as the ork hunters called it – had been uprooted, burned and cleared. The uneven, scorched and shredded ground between the base and the encroaching jungle was riddled with crater-holes: evidence of the numerous battles that had been fought over this patch of land alone.

At the centre of the camp, set just below the crest of the hill, was the heavily armoured entrance to the command bunker. It was beyond those steel doors that Sergeant Borysko had been summoned as soon as his team had arrived back at the base only an hour before. A profusion of comm masts sprouted from the top of the hill in their own wire forest, the means by which Cerbera Command communicated with their units out in the field and received messages from Armageddon High Command elsewhere on the planet and even in orbit above it.

Down the hill from Kole and the others, a heaped bonfire of ork bodies cast its acrid brown smoke straight up into the breezeless air.

There had been another ill-advised attempted ork infiltration the night before. The greenskins had paid dearly for their daring. It was camp policy that any ork bodies were burned. The ork hunters of Cerbera Base knew better than most of the Imperial ground forces fighting on Armageddon that a dead ork could be as lethal as a live one if not dealt with properly. For whenever a greenskin was killed, its alien physiology caused spores to be released into the air. Spores which, if they landed somewhere favourable for growth, would mean that in time more of the foul xenos monsters could sprout and grow to maturity beneath the ground. And this was all thanks to the death of just one of their fore-bears.

Kole looked at each of the men of the platoon as they lazed in the sun, unpacked and repacked their kit bags, went through the contents of their webbing pouches, checked over their weapons and wolfed down stale ration bars, or gulped cups of cold, stewed caffeine. He listened to them bickering, sharing uncouth jokes, whistling tunelessly, and thanking the Emperor for another day that they had survived out in the punishing jungles. Whatever it took for them to come down after a tour. Whatever it took.

Trooper Goya 'Hawkeye' Gunderson's first priority on returning to camp had been to clean the mud and leaf-mulch off his precious longlas. He was still cleaning it now, rubbing it vigorously with a piece of oil-rag, although to Kole's grizzled eye the gun looked clean enough.

'Lucky' Tannhauser had already found a discarded promethium canister that he had upended to create a playing surface. From somewhere within his mud-smeared fatigues he had extracted a battered pack of cards and was shuffling them deftly as he tried to persuade Masursky to join him in a hand of Macharius's Gambit.

T'bar Klim was making adjustments to his vox-set, the backpack arrangement that he usually carried on his back resting on the ground in front of him. For a vox-trooper, Klim was the most reticent of the group. It was always the quiet ones you had to watch, Kole thought.

Then there was Coburg, called Ox by the other skin-ners for obvious reasons. He was as big and strong as an ork, but not even Raus had such a death wish that he would give Coburg the name ork for a moniker, even if it did suit him.

But it wasn't only his size and strength that made them liken Coburg to an ork, and made them feel uncomfortable whenever he was around. Even now he was preoccupied with attaching another ork tooth to the leathery cord tied around his bulging neck. The fang had been taken from one he had killed on the last day of the team's most recent patrol.

'You some kind of secret ork-lover, Ox?' a smaller man – in fact the smallest in the group – called from where he was sitting on his kit bag, his back to a wooden revetment.

'What did you say, Weasel?' the larger man growled.

'I said, do you think you're some kind of skin, threading teeth like that,' the ratty Trooper Raus repeated, persisting in his foolish goading of the short-tempered, and violent, Coburg.

'Cut it out, Raus,' Kole chimed in.

'Come over here and say that and I'll give you a Catachan kiss,' was Coburg's response to the weasel of an ork hunter.

Raus scratched at the bristly beard infesting his chin. 'Yeah, sure you will, ork-fondler.'

'Right, you,' Ox said, rising to his feet, meaty fists bunching.

'Grab him,' Kole said, addressing Vanderkamp and Ertz, jerking a thumb at Coburg. The two troopers jumped to their feet, each of them grabbing one of the big man's arms.

The men were happy to take orders from Kole. Even though he wasn't their commanding officer, he was still Borysko's second-in-command, and the sergeant wasn't there at the moment.

The ork hunters respected Kole. More than that, most of them actually liked him. They respected Borysko too, and would happily follow him into the green hell beyond the perimeter of the camp. But liking had nothing to do with it.

There was a persistent rumour among the men that Kole could have risen through the ranks further and faster than the grizzled Borysko, but that something had always held him back. Kole did his best to quash the rumours, such as they were, especially the one that Kole's own unwillingness to accept promotion was all that had held him back in all his years with the regiment.

'Okay, Ox, easy,' Vanderkamp hissed in Coburg's ear, Ertz hanging off the brute's other arm.

'See, what did I say?' Raus kept on.

'I'll kill him!' the big bruiser roared. 'Throne! I swear I'll kill him!'

'Coburg, enough,' Kole said, his tone suddenly as cold and hard as ice. 'And, Raus, if you say another word Sergeant Borysko will have you clearing the land mines with that ugly face of yours before we see an end to this wretched war.'

Vanderkamp and Ertz slowly released their grip on the larger man.

'I'm okay, Vanders,' Coburg said, shaking himself free of the two troopers. 'I'm okay.' He glared at Raus as the scout scampered over to where Yeydl and Kasarta were watching the bonfire at the edge of the group.

What passed for calm amongst the ork hunters of Cerbera Base descended over the waiting team.

'How long do you reckon the sarge is going to be, Kole?' Nal Bukaj asked. Kole turned to look at the Kid.

They all called him the Kid. He was the youngest of Borysko's Boys by far, but he was no newbie-juve. Nal swore that he was eighteen but if he was a day over sixteen Kole was Old Man Yarrick's grandpappy. The boy wasn't even shaving properly yet.

But no matter how old the Kid really was it didn't change the fact that he was a superb scout and dropped orks with his lasgun like he had been born to it. He was as much a part of the team as any of them.

Nal Bukaj made up the rest of the scout squad within the team, along with Raus and under Tannhauser's immediate authority out in the field. The Kid had joined the team ten months ago. Borysko had always been reticent about where the boy had come from.

'Don't know, Kid,' Kole said with a sigh.

'Why do you think he was dragged off like that?' the sunbathing Geist asked.

None of them had seen the sergeant since he had led them back into the camp at around 08.00 that morning.

'Probably getting a nukking from Vine for allowing a child to join his platoon and follow him around like a wide-eyed puppy,' Ferze said derogatively.

No one rose to this comment, especially not the Kid.

Kole had to admit that Nal Bukaj was one of the nicest people he had ever met. He had a very pleasant nature and seemed to genuinely care about the team. Hell, Kole thought, how had the wretch ended up out here as an ork hunter, a skinner? Borysko was stubbornly cagey about Bukaj's origins and wouldn't be drawn on the subject, not even by his trusted second-in-command after polishing off the best part of a purloined bottle of amasec.

'More likely Borysko's being given the nod to drag our worthless hides back out into the Green,' Vanderkamp said.

'I hope Sicknote's going to be okay,' the Kid said, as much to himself as anybody else.

'That conniving bastard?' Ferze muttered. 'Probably did it on purpose.'

Umbo Jecks – or Sicknote, as he was more commonly known to the other skinners – had been unlucky enough to fall foul of a concealed ork punji pit trap the day before. Borysko had said he'd been lucky not to lose his foot, or even his whole leg. On the platoon's arrival at Cerbera he had been stretchered off to a makeshift medicae bunker almost as quickly as the sergeant had been ushered away. It wasn't the first time Jecks had suffered some 'lucky' injury that had got him out of a patrol. The accidents that befell him were always enough to get him out of a tour of duty or two, but they were never bad enough to kill him.

'I don't know why they don't give him a desk job,' Masursky mused, half-smiling.

'Probably because they know he's a jinx and he'll only somehow manage to muck things up for them here, rather than one of our missions,' Ferze put in.

It was then that Kole became aware of Priest pacing in agitation. Priest was what the Ecclesiarchy referred to as 'Emperor-touched', a holy fool, and what the rest of the ork hunters called a religious madman.

Such characters were not uncommon among the myriad Guard regiments. The unimaginable horrors they had witnessed on the battlefields had proved too much for their tortured psyches and had broken their minds. Those same horrors had not broken their spirits, however, and emotionally they had taken solace in the one thing they still managed to cling on to – their spirit. As a result their faith became all consuming, the one constant in a universe of terrible, traumatic change, immovable as an Earthshaker cannon, as unshakable as the Palidus Mountains.

None among Borysko's platoon knew if Priest was his true name or a nickname he had been given in some other life. Whatever life he might have had before war descended on Armageddon, no one knew, for he did not speak of it – ever.

The traumas Priest had suffered had taken their toll on him physically as well as mentally. He was lean and thin with a face like a knife. Cheekbones poked through skin where the flesh beneath had wasted away. He was utterly bald as well, and not through choice, as was the case with Geist.

Along with Gunderson he was the other sniper of the team – the best. And here he was now, pacing up and down, wringing his hands frantically.

'Where's the Guardian?' the sniper was mumbling.

'What's that, Priest?' Tannhauser asked, looking up from his card dealing.

'Where's the Guardian?' the agitated man kept repeating over and over. Priest was never one for great extremes of emotion. He now appeared about as distressed as Kole had ever seen him.

'Okay,' Kole sighed wearily, 'who's got his long-las?'

'Whaddaya mean, Kole?' Geist smiled back.

'I mean, Joker, have you got Priest's gun?'

'And why would I have his precious Guardian?' Geist continued to beam.

'Oh, for frikk's sake, Geist,' Kole snapped back, 'it's been a long tour, I'm dog-tired, boot-sore and hungry and need a good night's sleep – at least as good as anyone can get here at Cerbera – and I don't need your idiot games. Look, don't get Priest all wound up. You know what he's like. He's already wound tighter than a Catachan lashworm.'

'Precisely. That's why he does it,' Ferze interrupted.

'Mind your own business, Ferze,' Kole said before directing his attentions back at Geist. 'I'll ask you just one more time, Geist. Where's the poor guy's gun?'

'Yeah, don't wind him up, you nukk-head,' Gunderson added. Of all the boys, Goya Gunderson probably understood his fellow sniper better than anyone. Or at least he was the most patient with him.

'Who said I was winding him up?' Geist said. 'And what happened to innocent 'til proven guilty?' The pained expression on his face and the indignant tone of his voice did little to convince the others of his innocence.

'Geist, you'll be on a charge from Borysko if you keep this up. I'll see to it personally.'

'I haven't got it. Coburg's keeping it warm for him under his fat arse.'

'You idiot, Geist,' Kole spat contemptuously. 'I would have thought that anyone in this team would know better than that, that you would have had more respect for your fellow skinners. After all, it's their better nature you're going to be relying on when it's your arse on the line out there in the Green.'

Coburg lifted himself and felt under the crate he'd been sitting on. But Tannhauser got there first. He pulled out something the length and shape of a las-rifle, wrapped in an oilskin.

'There ya go, brother,' Tannhauser laughed, throwing the longlas to the frantic Priest.

'The God-Emperor shall bring His judgement down upon you. The Lord of Mankind knows what is inside your soul,' the sniper stated bluntly, his tone already calmer, now that he had the Guardian back in his hands.

'Hey, don't have a go at me!' Tannhauser retorted.

'By your deeds shall He know you,' Priest muttered, kissing the holy icon that hung from the same chain as his dog tags. The symbol was the carved image of the almost skeletal Emperor locked within the Golden Throne of Terra. It had been whittled with no great skill from a piece of bone. Then Priest turned away from the others to be alone with his precious Guardian and his Emperor once again.

Indeed, thought Kole. Out of the mouths of madmen came the raw truth of the matter. By their deeds would the Emperor know them all, when it came to the time of judgement.

What deeds did He have in mind for them? And would they be found wanting when the time came?

And how much longer was Borysko going to be?

IT WAS UNCOMFORTABLY warm within the command hub, even this far into the hill and out of the direct heat of the sun. At the centre of the large open space – which had been carved from the inside of the hill itself, like the other rooms, and reinforced with metal plates in places – was a large table emblazoned with the double-headed, blade-winged Imperial eagle. A huge map hung on one wall, covered with red and blue annotations and code-symbols. A group of officers were busying themselves with the map, scribbling on the well-used note blocks and data-slates held in their hands. It was here that Sergeant Pavle Borysko waited in the humidity and sweaty heat.

He was standing in front of a doorway that led out of the map room into the true nerve centre of Cerbera Base, as he had done for the best part of an hour, when he hadn't been pacing the perimeter of the table or perusing the constantly updated map of the jungle belt. An irregular stream of map officers passed through the doorway, into and out of the room beyond, always carrying a torn strip of parchment with them on the return journey. Borysko was rapidly losing what little patience he had had to begin with.

At last, after what seemed like an eternity, an adjutant emerged from the darkened doorway and walked up to the broad-shouldered Borysko. 'The marshal will see you now,' the man said in clipped syllables.

'About time too,' Borysko growled under his breath, as the other turned sharply on a jackbooted heel, but not so quietly that the adjutant couldn't hear him.

The ork hunter sergeant followed the officer, passing through the doorway himself and stepping into a chamber lit by the ambient light of the myriad servitor-manned comms panels and pict screens. A computation of lexmechanics chewed through the information coming into the command hub, making sense of the endless streams of data and transcribing it back into a form that the human operatives could easily understand. Screeds of parchment covered the floor, the fruit of their scribing labours. A coven of whistling and beeping tech-priests moved between the various monitor stations and comms panels, making adjustments here, anointing them with holy unguents there, and all the time intoning the prayers of Optimum Operational Performance.

None of this was new to Borysko, of course. He had been here before. Just as he had met the broad man wired into the metal throne by the stumps of his truncated legs on the other side of the nerve centre. The marshal's greying hair had been cropped close to his skull, unlike his thick moustache.

Marshal Vine had seen his fair share of action fighting the orks of the equatorial jungle before the injuries he had sustained had ensured his confinement within the command centre. Other than his missing legs, the most noticeable of these injuries were the scars of two puncture marks in the side of his throat.

'Ah, sorry to keep you, Borysko,' the marshal said, feigning an apology. His voice was a cracked wheeze. He did not sound at all healthy.

Like hell you are, Borysko thought to himself, but said nothing: a reply was not required. 'What was it you wanted to see me about?'

'Ah, let's not beat about the bush, Borysko. You're going out again, you and your platoon.'

'Now?' Borysko queried. 'I'm a man down and the others have been out on two patrol tours now without a break. I thought we'd be getting a rotation at the camp, sir.'

'Not for you and your boys, Borysko, not this time. They wanted the best and I told them I had the perfect man for the job. So don't let me down.'

'Give us twenty-four hours, then we'll be ready.'

'Ah, in case you hadn't noticed, sergeant, there's a war on. I can't give you twenty-four hours. You go now or there'll be no point going at all.'

'Then there's no point going, obviously,' Borysko muttered under his breath.

'That's enough of your ratshit, sergeant!' Vine coughed, his hoarse voice turning shrill. 'Ah, you always were the most disrespectful bastard of the lot. I only tolerate your insolence because you're one of the best I've got,' the marshal said, his voice dropping to little more than a strained whisper. 'You and your bunch of disobedient men are going on this mission whether you like it or not. And you'd better start showing me some respect or you'll be the ones in the frontline the next time the bloody greenskins attempt to assault Cerbera.'

Vine's tirade of vitriol gave way to a wheezing, coughing fit.

Borysko stiffened. 'So what is this mission that you've handpicked my platoon for, sir.'

'Ah, so you're interested now, are you?' Vine resumed, his coughing paroxysms subsiding.

Borysko took a deep breath before answering. 'Yes, sir.'

'Ah, right then. It's a straightforward rescue mission,' the marshal explained. 'Two hours ago, at approximately 07.11 hours, an ACG Valkyrie went down in the jungle south-west of here. On board was some big shot lieutenant of the ACG. Your orders are to find him and bring him back to Cerbera.'

'With all due respect, if the craft went down in this ork-infested jungle, whoever was on board is already dead, or as good as,' Borysko said. 'Either the crash killed them or the Green will have got them by now, you know that.'

'That's why I can't give you twenty-four hours.'

'It's probably too late already. Two hours will have been enough to see an end to this ACG desk jockey.'

'Ah, I know that and you know that, but top brass are adamant. They want their man back or confirmation of his death. When I say that these orders come from the top, I don't mean Armageddon High Command.'

'What do you mean?'

'Ah, they come from higher than that is what I mean. I could be court-marshalled for even telling you this,' Vine exaggerated, 'but I like you, Borysko, although God-Emperor knows why. I trust you to do this job properly, without any cock-ups. This comes direct from General Kurov's inner sanctum.'

'So we leave straight away?'

'Ah, as good as.'

'Shall I consider myself dismissed then, sir?' the ork hunter asked bluntly.

'Ah, not so fast, Borysko,' Vine said, his voice dropping in pitch again to barely more than a whisper. 'There's one more thing you need to know.'

'ALL RIGHT, LADIES?'

Kole and some of the other ork hunters looked up. It was Sicknote. His foot was bandaged and someone had found him a pair of crutches. They didn't match. And there was a faraway look in his dilated eyes.

'Are you high, Sicknote?' Tannhauser asked. 'And, if so, where can I score some?'

'It's the 'phine they give you, I swear it.'

'You *are* high. How much did they give you?'

'Couple of shots,' Sicknote slurred.

'Couple of shots?' Vanderkamp coughed. 'That's enough to have a man sleeping like a hiver.'

'Not him,' Gunderson said. 'Take more than that to knock out Sicknote. He's built up such a tolerance to the stuff he's practically immune, he's had so much of it on so many occasions.'

'Hey, lads,' Tannhauser suddenly piped up. 'Look busy, the sarge is coming.'

'You couldn't make yourself look busy if you were taking on the whole of Ghazghkull's army single-handed,' Sergeant Borysko snarled.

'What news, sarge?' Kole asked boldly.

'We're moving out.'

'What?' whined Geist, pushing himself up into a sitting position. 'But we're only just back in.'

And then suddenly Borysko had his hand to Joker's throat and Geist was getting the full force of the sergeant's stale lho breath in his face. 'I don't like it any more than you do, you nukk-head. But orders are orders, as Vine was so happy to tell me. Borysko's Boys have got another job to do and so we're going to do it.'

'What is the job?' Kole dared ask, braving Borysko's wrath.

'Some ACG lieutenant – who doesn't know his arse from his elbow, I expect – seems to have got himself into a spot of bother out in the Green. It's our job to rescue his sorry backside from whatever frikkin' mess he's got himself into and bring him back.'

'He won't last a second out there,' Ferze complained. 'This is a waste of time. He's probably dead already.'

'That was my assessment of the situation as well, trooper,' Borysko agreed. 'But which of you would pass up the opportunity to go kick some ork arse?' the sergeant said with a forced smile. 'We'll find what's left of his stinking carcass, scoop it up into Geist's pack and then come back with the evidence. We'll probably be back by this time tomorrow.'

There was no point arguing about it now: the sergeant had made their position perfectly clear. As one man, Borysko's Boys began to ready themselves for another stint on patrol in the rot-stinking forests.

'Sorry I won't be coming with you, fellas,' Sicknote laughed, 'only the medicae says I've got to rest up and keep it dry, or the swamp-rot will set in.'

'Won't it just, Sicknote, won't it just,' Vanderkamp sneered. 'Of all the people out in this shit-hole of a jungle it had to be you, didn't it, Sicknote.'

Sicknote grinned back.

'That's right, Vanders. I have got a reputation to live up to, after all.'

'Anybody'd think you did it on purpose,' Ferze harped on.

The smile on the wounded trooper's face slackened.

'Step into a punji pit on purpose?' he whined. 'What, do you think I'm stupid as well as unlucky?'

'Unlucky?' Ferze spat. '"Lucky" Tannhauser wishes he had your sort of misfortune. Should have been looking where you were going, or perhaps you were.'

'Jecks, your turn will come,' the sergeant snarled.

THE PLATOON WAS ready, with ration packs restocked and weapons fitted out with fresh ammo clips, within half an hour.

As his team began to pick their way through the trench workings, past hidden sniper positions and avoiding the myriad traps set up to snare the unwary, Sergeant Pavle Borysko gazed out towards the thick dark treeline a kilometre away, beyond the main gate of Cerbera camp, from under the brim of his peaked cap, a snarling grimace twisting his features. He hawked a gob of phlegm onto the churned ground, considering what he and his team were going to have to do, what he hadn't told them yet. The very thought of it left an unpleasant taste in his mouth. He couldn't fathom the minds of the pen pushers who made such decisions. It was just too much.

'Sorry, sarge?' Kole said, hearing his commanding officer mumble something sourly under his breath.

'I said, I hate frikkin' aliens!'

EIGHT
THE ANVIL OF WAR

THE MINOS RIVER *traces its path for hundreds of kilometres from the heart of the sweltering rainforests of Armageddon's equatorial belt, which effectively divides the two landmasses of Armageddon Prime and Secundus, to its eventual conclusion, where its waters join with the turbulent currents of the Tempest Ocean. The brackish marshlands that border the Minos River cover an area of land almost as large as the desolate Plain of Anthrand that lies another thousand kilometres to the west. Some half a million hectares are home to an incalculable number of different species of biting insects, including stained-glass winged dragonflies as long as a man's arm, giant centipedes with jaws like steel ork-traps and winding bodies over a metre long and many rare species of dust-winged lepidoptera.*

For an area called the Plague Marshes, with all that title's inherent implications of death and disease, it is abundant in all forms of life, indigenous to the planet and otherwise. The stinking, stagnant black waters of the marshy pools and motionless mired lakes teem with fish, molluscs and leathery-skinned slime eels, as well as a mutant species of albino crab which has a shell as hard as ceramite. There is even mammal life here, with grazing kopi and the hunting clawmoset filling their own particular niche in the predatory hierarchy of the food chain. White ibises and golvers wade amidst the brackish ponds searching for tasty morsels such as dragonfly larvae and mudjacks, while the awe-inspiring talonhawk soars on the thermals that rise from the cooking mists and bogs of the exposed swamplands, waiting to snatch a swift-winged buzzet or even a kopi calf. Only the depthless oceans of the Boiling Sea and the Tempest Ocean have a greater biodiversity and profusion of fauna than the jungles and mangrove swamps of equatorial Armageddon.

And then there are the orks. There are always the orks. Magi of the Genetor Biologis estimate there to be as many as twelve ork tribes claiming territory in and around the Minos swamps alone, merging and breaking up as the aliens' inherent drive towards battle and their natural animosity continue to play a part in their existence, no matter how inspiring a unifying force the Great Beast might be to the other ork clans that have come to make war on Armageddon.

The feral orks have had their own unique influence on their environment and on the ecosystem of this habitat, and it has been a detrimental one at that. With their arrival on Armageddon five decades ago, and with their continued presence in the jungles ever since, the feral orks have effectively become the alpha predator. Without doubt some are killed by the inherently dangerous native flora

and fauna, such as the pernicious death-cup and the strangler vine, but the deadly environment of the jungles – with
its unbearable humidity the perfect breeding ground for
dozens of deadly diseases – seems not to have troubled
their alien metabolisms at all. In fact, the greenskins, and
all the various degenerate offshoot subspecies that came
with them to Armageddon, seem to be uniquely adapted to
this environment or, at least, uniquely adaptable.

It might surprise some to learn that creatures from an
ork 'kulture' that has effectively developed in isolation
from an ork waaagh can use – and indeed do use, in great
proliferation – technology, but more particularly weaponry,
that they could have had no means of creating themselves.
It would appear that this is part of an inbuilt genetic pre-
disposition.

Once a feral ork tribe has reached a critical size, led by
a particularly cunning and strong ork, they will learn to
fight against the indigenous natural predators already living in the jungles and surrounding swamps and ultimately
overcome them, steadily expanding their territory. However, these orks will also learn to scavenge weapons and
other pieces of equipment that they find, left behind by
their foul xenos brethren or make use of, and even cus-
tomise, any Imperial technology they can get their claws
on. Much of what they scavenge is too technologically
advanced for them to make use of, but it does not take
them long to realise the effect and power of any weapons
they find, although many of the tribe will die during the
course of such investigations and experimentation.

And it would also appear that the orks did not come to
Armageddon alone. When a feral ork culture develops on
a planet after the initial greenskin invasion has collapsed
or moved on, other spores left behind by the main assault's

forces can grow to produce life-forms other than the orks themselves. The most common and numerous of these varied life-forms is the squig, which orks appear to use for all manner of purposes, from helping them hunt down prey to supplementing their ravenous appetites. Then there are the smaller cousins of the orks themselves that Imperial forces term as gretchin.

It is believed that several greenskin sub-species, originally brought to our planet during Ghazghkull Thraka's first invasion fifty years ago, have stabilised and colonised areas of the marshes. The humid, foetid swamps also provide perfect conditions in which the ork-genus fungi can propagate. After any skirmishes against the greenskins, ork hunters will always carry out a 'scorched earth' policy on the area, burning anything and everything within a predetermined range, to prevent the ork spores from germinating and, in time, producing more of the rampaging greenskins. But no matter how thorough the ork hunter regiments are, some spores are always dispersed more widely by the wind and come to rest in remote areas where they can grow to ork-bearing size.

There are not only orks, gretchin and squigs at large within the jungles of Armageddon. The orks have also, somehow, brought squiggoths to Armageddon. These monstrous alien beasts of burden are the largest of the squig breed and make perfect mounts and transports in the swamps, better suited to the environment than any tank, and more manoeuvrable in the treacherous pools and bogs into which a vehicle can sink. Squiggoths vary hugely in size from that of an immature grox to something on a par with an ancient archeosaur. Indeed the most gargantuan of the breed are referred to as orkeosauruses.

How these massive creatures came to be in these expansive swamps and the bordering jungles is not clear, but there can be no doubting the fact that such monstrous animals are at large within the lush green heart of our world – for Imperial observers have seen them. Many squiggoths have been tamed by the feral greenskins to be used as beasts of burden and as war mounts for the heavy weapons the orks have managed to scavenge from the jungles and the surrounding hinterlands.

Despite the inevitable incursions of man and ork alike, regions of the equatorial jungles, mesa-top rainforests and the half a million hectare marshlands that border the Minos River remain some of the only unspoilt wildernesses of a planet whose ecosystem, and even weather systems, have been devastated by countless centuries of unchecked industrial pollution on a planet-wide scale.

But on a world such as Armageddon, a world whose name has become synonymous with war, even such an inhospitable and uninhabitable place is a contested theatre of war, where life itself fights a constant savage battle of survival.

– Extracted from 'The Flora and Fauna of Contested Armageddon' Volume VII
By Genetor-Magos Second Class Ursulon Quallm

A PUTRID MIST rose from the torpid swamps. Here and there breaks appeared in the clouds of fog, allowing the sun to penetrate the shrouding vapours and lure insect life from the foetid black pools amidst the feather-reeds and bulrushes. Tangles of persistent knotted widow writhed hungrily across the muddy flats and rampant spagweed moss smothered the hummocks of crimson spine-ant nests.

Shiny black carrion beetles lazily buzzed into the air whilst blue taper-bodied bullet flies zipped between scum-covered stands of stagnant brown water channels. Iridescent opal bugs skittered across the surface of the still pools, water tension keeping them from drowning. Beneath them, terribly mandibled, water-dwelling fang-spiders and flamewing nymphs waited with predatory patience, ready to snap one of the water-skating insects from the world above.

Rightly was this place called the Plague Marshes of Armageddon. It was as inhospitable and hostile an environment as any verdant deathworld, such as notorious Catachan or primeval Derwynia.

The marshlands existed under an almost permanent shroud of low cloud and the air itself over the boggy delta reaches stank of rot, redolent with disease and death-causing spores.

And everywhere the subsonic reports of firing cannons shuddered the rippling pools, the air thick with the *zip-zip* of heavy lasfire.

It was the last place that anyone would expect to find armoured units of the Imperial armies fighting the ork menace on Armageddon, but fighting them they were. Heavy armour painted in the proud, uncamouflaged colours of the Rüstung Armoured Fourth – a mottling of urban grey over-painted with bold red chevrons – powered through the mud-flats, caterpillar tracks tangled with uprooted reed clumps churning the black muck. Ryza-pattern Leman Russ battle tanks hammered forwards, obscured by a perpetual spray of slime and foul water. Earthshaker artillery guns coughed their devastating munitions in arcing parabolas towards the feral ork army from the open decks of Basilisk flatbeds. A monstrous Demolisher rumbled forwards at the head of the armoured line, its dozer shovel-blade pushing liquid slurry, and any of the enemy foolish enough to get too close, ahead of it. Oily black exhaust fumes spluttered from the speeding tanks, adding their thick smoky residue to the general miasma shrouding the marshlands.

The Rüstung Fourth were supported by three squadrons of Armageddon Steel Legion Sentinels, the war walkers blazing away at the opposition ranged before them with searing blasts from their hull-mounted lascannons. There was also a Steel Legion Chimera accompanying their offworld allies, equally out of place in this environment in its ash wastes incursion camouflage scheme. The Legionaries had obviously been redeployed at very short notice, possibly so that should the Rüstung Fourth be successful in their operation, the native Armageddon High Command could at least take some of the credit for the victory.

And in the vanguard of the armoured force, alongside the Rüstung command-tank the *Pride of Kazagrad*, was a monstrous hulk of a tank, a black and white adamantium armoured mobile fortress of the Adeptus Astartes. The Crusader-pattern Land Raider raked the greenskins ranged against the Imperials with sustained hurricane bolter fire as well as assault cannon and multi-melta bursts. Through the cloying swamp mists and the exhaust-fumed fog of battle the given name of the Land Raider could just be seen beneath the splatters of peaty mud. Etched into the scrollwork of a cross-bearing shield was the name *Avenger*. It was a name honoured throughout the Solemnus fleet thanks to the achievements of the Crusader's commander Camlann.

Camouflage and subtlety really were not necessary in this battle. There was nothing to be gained from understated deployment and the element of surprise here. What would win this battle was dogged determination and sheer force of numbers.

Opposing the combined Imperial armoured force of the Rüstung Armoured Fourth, the Steel Legion units and the Astartes Crusader were the fluid ranks of the feral ork army. The size of the greenskin force had surprised the Rüstung Armoured's commanders, as it had the ACG tacticians travelling with them. They had not expected such an organised and cohesive resistance to their efforts to purge the swamps of orks in an effort to keep the Minos River safe for traffic into and out of Cerbera Base. It was testament to the huge size of the feral force banded together from several merged tribes that they had gained the wit to organise themselves so effectively under one warboss. And that warboss had to be an awesome individual indeed, for the alien had to be the strongest and most cunning of all the tribal leaders whose clans had banded together here to repel the Imperial purge.

But this was just one battle, with the Imperials fighting just one ork force, and there had to be a hundred such battles taking place elsewhere across the face of the planet at that time. It was a terrible thing to consider.

The vanguard of the feral force was made up of several mobs of fur-clad orks carrying solid shot firearms and heavy-headed cleaver weapons. There were other units advancing behind them that were even armed with crude rocket launchers. The presence of such armaments among the tribes was a sign of just how much junk Ghazghkull Thraka's waaagh had brought to the planet. It was evidence that the orks and their blasphemous invasion were everywhere, even within the untamed regions of the planet.

As well as the animal hides they wore, the orks had augmented their grotesque appearance with skulls – both human and ork – and other looted trophies. Necklaces of rattling tusks hung on knotted strings of dried sinew around their necks, and the bare skin of their arms and faces was adorned with daubs of war paint. As well as their principal weapons the orks were all laden down with reserve firearms, hunting knives and the like.

Flanking the first wave of orks were several larger brutes riding on the backs of bizarre creatures that were a wild amalgam of bristling, bad-tempered boar and maniacal mechanical augmentation. Their mounts might once have been simple forest pigs but after the orks had got their hands on them, they had become ferocious cybernetic beasts, their tiny brains and savage appetites driven into a frenzy by the introduction of crude adrenal stimulants into their bloodstreams. These same cyboars and their boarboy riders were charging ahead of the infantry frontline, hooves splashing through the muddy channels and stagnant pools, eager to engage with the enemy at the earliest opportunity. They were apparently oblivious to the fact that they were simply putting themselves into harm's way all the more quickly.

The Imperials might have the strength, durability and resistance of their armoured units on their side but the orks, despite their feral, primitive nature, were not without the means to counter the advancing tanks and sentinels. Trudging through the fenlands behind the ork lines were the massed tribes' heavy support.

Gargantuan tusked quadrupeds trudged through the marshes behind the greenskin mobs. With every step, their huge hooves sank a good metre into the soggy ground of the insubstantial swamp, the prints they left behind quickly filling with foamy bog-water. These monsters had vile snub-nosed heads that sprouted brutal horns. Long ivory tusks curved from their gaping misshapen jaws.

The elephantine squiggoths were terrible to behold indeed, the largest of the beasts – known as orkeosauruses – dwarfing even the mighty Land Raider *Avenger*. But what made them all the more terrible, and an even greater threat to the Imperial armour, were the huge howdahs they carried on their broad backs. Constructed from thick pieces of pillaged adamantium, ceramite and steel-plate, lashed together with huge chains, these riveted creations had been daubed with the same basic symbols, reminiscent of the patterns produced by the orks with war paint on their own leathery green hides. Mounted on top of these haphazard platforms were all manner of heavier looted weapons, from chugging cannons to primitive laser devices and temperamental flamethrowers, manned by ork weapons crews.

Goaded by their ork drivers, the squiggoths stomped into battle, the ground trembling beneath their massive feet, sending small wavelets washing across the surface of the marshes. Swamp snakes and spiny-backed newts slithered away from the crushing footfalls of the great beasts, and clouds of sting-flies rose into the air before them, the angry insects' needle-like proboscises unable to pierce the scaly hides of the monstrous squiggoths. And all the while the fearsome, unstable artillery mounted on top of the walking war wagons hurled their volatile payloads at the Imperial armour.

WITH A CRUNCH and squelch the Land Raider ploughed into the charging fur-clad feral greenskins. There was a series of guttural alien cries – which sounded more like dogs barking than any recognisable form of speech – that were abruptly cut off as the orks were either crushed beneath the churning tracks of the tank or buried in the stinking, sodden loam as they disappeared under the hull of the huge war machine.

The top hatch of the Land Raider popped open with a groan of heavy hinges, and a bald-headed Marine appeared atop the *Avenger*.

Commander Camlann looked down from the turret of his tank, surveying the surrounding swamp. Like so many of his brethren within the crusade, Camlann's body had been repaired and augmented with bionic additions by the Techmarines and Apothecaries working within the vaults of the forge-ship *Goliath*. The most notable of these augmentations was an ocular implant, ringed with knotted pink scar tissue, that stood in place of his right eye. However, the red-lensed augmetic had been put in at Camlann's request and had replaced a perfectly healthy organic specimen, rather than an injured one.

But through the implant Camlann saw what the cogitator core of his tank saw – projected trajectories, damage assessments, weapon locks, potential targets located, velocities of other armoured vehicles within the scope of its sensor arrays, reactor temperature levels. Through Old Baleful, as the commander called it, he saw what the *Avenger* registered.

And at that moment he saw a great many things as the battle between the armoured Imperial units and the massed feral ork tribes unfolded.

To Camlann's left an enemy shell hit a stalking sentinel as its lascannon pulsed with blue-white energy bursts. The cabin and the sentinel's pilot were vaporised in a blinding flash of incandescent flame. The scorched and smoking backward-jointed legs of the machine took another five unsteady paces before keeling over into the mud and slime.

Elsewhere, a Rüstung Basilisk was overrun by greenskins, where the alien horrors had managed to sneak through the line of speeding armour, their advance no doubt obscured by the constant sprays of liquidised marsh-mud. The orks piled onto the open deck of the gun carriage, slaughtering the crew with bayonets, knives and their bare hands.

Urged on by their battle-crazed riders, cyboars charged at the armoured units head on, legs pistoning, breaking their blade-tusks, iron skulls and distorted bodies against the hulls of the huge vehicles, but leaving their own impression in the ceramite and adamantium plates nonetheless. The orks riding the cyboars were catapulted from their saddles, some landing on top of the gun carriages and transports from where they proceeded to run riot with their guns and axes.

An ork mob, armed with noisy solid shot hand-cannons, scattered in face of the armoured assault and scurried between the tracked vehicles, where a pair of Hellhounds hosed the feral beasts with burning promethium from their Inferno cannons.

The over-enthusiastic advancing greenskin infantry was slowly but surely being decimated by the combined barrage of Armageddon-pattern sentinel lascannons and sustained heavy bolter fire. The *zip* of lasfire and the chugging roar of the tank hull-mounted bolters were accompanied by the crump of battle cannons and even heavier, more destructive weaponry. The bombard detonations were followed by the squeal of recoil as the armoured vehicles rocked in their advance, quaking as their massive cannons fired.

And then the vanguard of tanks engaged with the howdah-bearing, cannon-carrying ork beasts of burden. The first line of squiggoths were smaller than those that came after them, carrying only one big gun each, rather than a whole weapons platform overloaded with orks and burgeoning with gun emplacements. But they were monstrous creatures nonetheless.

Where the front line of tanks stretched out across the stinking vaporous marsh to the right of the Land Raider Crusader, they began to disappear from sight between the hulking bodies of the lumbering quadrupeds. The guttural hooting and barking of the orks were underscored by the deep lowing of the beasts. Every now and then there came the rumble of flatulence or a snort of bestial bovine anger.

Through the scanning devices of the *Avenger*, relayed via his ocular implant, Brother-Commander Camlann saw another urban camo-painted sentinel stumble and topple backwards, kicked over by the clawing hoof of a squiggoth sporting a ring of bony spines around its neck and with an ungainly missile-throwing weapon bolted to its scratch-built, scrap metal howdah.

A foot as large as a flat-bed half-track smashed down on top of the walker, forcing it down into the clinging mud of the swamp as its frame and cabin crumpled under several tonnes of pressure.

'Emperor's oath!' Camlann cursed as a smoking, shark-faced missile screamed past him, only a metre from the *Avenger*.

Runes flickered and scrolled over the blood-tinged lens of his augmetic, reporting damage sustained by the ancient leviathan, as the Land Raider came under sustained fire from pillbox constructions hanging over the side of a passing squiggoth. At the same time the *Avenger's* logic-engine was calculating distances and angles of fire with which to return fire and eliminate this latest threat to the Templar tank's continued survival.

'Gunnery-Brother Verner!' Camlann called down into the belly of the Land Raider. 'We seem to have a problem. Deal with it.'

'Aye, commander,' the gunnery brother replied.

The side-mounted hurricane bolter sponsons on the starboard side of the tank swivelled upwards and opened fire. Bolter rounds tore great holes in the rusting, patched panels of the howdah in showers of sparks kicked up from the metal by the shell impacts. The orks returned fire, but their gunners found it difficult to keep on target, as the nausea-inducing roll of the great beast's lumbering gait caused their own gunnery position to sway dramatically from side to side, in and out.

The *Avenger* continued to power forward through the marsh, scraping against the tough hide of a descending hind leg of the massive squig beast, as the two leviathans passed each other.

It galled Commander Camlann to let such a prize get away. If he and his crew had been on any other mission, Camlann would have turned his Land Raider round to pursue the gargantuan and bring it down, giving the helpless watching orks a taste of His Most Glorious Imperial Majesty's divine wrath with assault cannon and multi-melta. But that was not the prime reason for the *Avenger*'s presence at this battle in the Plague Marshes. The tank and its battle-brothers had another vital role to fulfil. And once they had executed their duty, Commander Camlann would be able to run to ground as many of the squiggoths as he pleased, with the blessing of the marshal of the fleet and the Emperor Himself.

Armour fired. Mortars and cannon boomed. The report of the shell launches, gun blasts and subsequent detonations echoed across the swampscape. The giant squig beasts bellowed and snorted, their multiple stomachs rumbling like geysers ready to spout. Orks howled and yelled, screaming as they died beneath the tracks of the advancing armour. Men shouted and uttered oaths to the God-Emperor of Mankind. Engine-stacks roared and spluttered as they tried to overcome the cloying slime and muddy waters of the insidious swamps. The smothering mists and choking emissions of the vehicles lent an ethereal quality to the sound.

Everywhere there was the acrid smell of fyceline, promethium fumes, cordite, overwhelming animal gut-gas and the ever-present sickly sweet stench of vegetable rot.

And then, with the tanks and gun-wagons amongst them, what little ordered formation the feral ork tribe had managed to maintain for so long was gone. Ork mobs ran amok between the wheeling vehicles, taking pot shots at any Imperial officer who dared show his head to get a more complete assessment of how the battle was progressing. There was no possible way that they could be acting on any coherent orders in such a situation. They were simply doing what came naturally to them and what they did best, for the orks live for war.

Some of the bolder, or more stupid, greenskins ran up to the tanks in the face of withering sponson fire, in an attempt to shoot their crude hand-cannons in through the narrow slits of viewing ports.

Hearing a bellowing roar, Camlann looked over his right shoulder. One of the larger squiggoth beasts – how many had the feral orks brought to this battle – ten, twelve? – was running down a struggling Hellhound, the machine's tracked wheels having become clogged with some pernicious, tangling vine and thick mats of sickle-reeds. The Hellhound wheeled as its driver tried to free the vehicle. At the same time, the scorched nozzles of its Inferno cannons were turned on the thundering beast as it splashed through the black pools and mossy quagmire.

And then the Hellhound was free, its traction units spraying muck and shredded plant fibre ten metres into the claggy air. The squiggoth came alongside the flamer-thrower tank as it accelerated away, but managed to keep pace as the Hellhound's engines ran up to speed. Two gouts of fire jetted from the Inferno cannons, engulfing the over-sized head of the beast in roiling orange flame and greasy black smoke.

The squiggoth's bellows rose in pitch and changed to a horrible shrill shriek of agony. But the beast did not falter in its charge.

Squiggoths were by disposition bad-tempered creatures, but now this blunt-tusked specimen was consumed by white-hot rage. Nothing mattered other than to hurt the growling metal machine as much as it had been hurt. There was no room in its tiny mind for any other consideration. It would pursue this course of action to the end or until its own demise, whichever came sooner.

The huge lumbering beast did not slow but turned its heavy tusked head away from the Hellhound and then swung it back on the great muscled joint of its neck, smashing it into the side of the tank. The Hellhound was rocked by the colossal impact, the tracks on its starboard side lifting free of the fens altogether, shrieking as they freewheeled in the tractionless air.

The turret of the Inferno cannon swivelled and was then trained back on the squiggoth. The monster swung the massive pendulum of its head again. Tusks like adamantium-tipped warheads punctured the armour plating towards the rear of the Hellhound.

Black fluid, wet with an oily sheen, sprayed from ruptured promethium tanks as the turret-mounted flame-thrower fired.

Fire and fuel mixed, and the inevitable combustion followed.

A sheet of incandescent flame blasted from the side of the tank. Two seconds later the reserve promethium tanks erupted, which in turn cooked off the munitions of the tank's arsenal, the intense heat detonating the bolter rounds inside its loaded heavy bolter.

The Hellhound was torn apart by a searing ball of flame and tarry black smoke that boiled away the surface-water of the swamp in a roiling cloud of steam, hurling pieces of twisted metal, fused engine parts and strips of splintered track across the marsh. Several segments of track clattered off the hull of the *Avenger*. Runes flickered and scrolled over the blood-tinged lens of Camlann's augmetic.

As the smoke and steam cleared, blown away by the shockwave of the blast, lying amidst chunks of burning shrapnel, Camlann saw the squiggoth keel over into the swamp, throwing up another wave of rippling black water. Its head was a blackened and crisped mess, its tiny brain cooked inside its skull by the fiery blast. The orks clinging to the gun-howdah on its back whooped and screamed as the jerry-rigged platform fell apart around them, the kannon the beast had carried crushing several of the greenskins beneath its heavy barrel.

There was the dread grinding of gears, a choking shudder shook that rattled the ancient Crusader. And then the unimaginable happened. The engines died.

'Leith, report!' Camlann barked into his comm.

'This stinking sludge has flooded the pre-combustion chamber,' Leith's report came back. 'The primary engine's stalled. We're not going anywhere.'

'Brother Verner,' Camlann cut in, 'keep that assault cannon primed and loaded. I don't want the *Avenger* to become a sitting target out here.'

'Understood, commander. By the Omnissiah's grace I shall ensure that mighty *Avenger* remains vigilant and ready to repel attackers,' the gunnery officer responded.

'This is it!' Camlann shouted to the *Avenger*'s passengers. 'This is as far as we go. Everybody out! And may the Emperor go with you,' he added.

THE RAMP OF the Land Raider dropped open, lowered by whining hydraulics, and the LCD-shot gloom of the interior of the tank was suddenly bathed in the dirty sepia light of the contested marshlands.

Kill-team Wolfram was ready. With a shout of 'For Solemnus!' the Templars burst from the back of the Land Raider, weapons held ready for battle, led by their inspiring Chaplain – his crozius arcanum held high – and Emperor's Champion Ansgar – the Black Sword of the Solemnus Crusade pointing the way towards the enemy.

Ten battle-brothers came after Wolfram and Ansgar and comprised the rest of the kill-team. Running at the Chaplain's side was his ever-present bodyguard Koldo, boltgun held low in front of him, ready to dispense a stream of whickering fire should any oppose him or his master. Behind them came the white-armoured Brother-Apothecary Bliant and the rest of the original Squad Wolfram – Brother Lairgnen, Initiate Hebron and Brother-Initiate Gildas.

Then came Baldulf, Huarwar and Larce, with Veteran Brother Kemen and heavy weapons trooper Brother Clust effectively forming the rearguard.

Brother Jarold was the last out of the rear of the Land Raider that barely seemed capable of containing his immense bulk. The dreadnought had to duck to pass through the exit hatch of the tank and even then the spiked iron halo cresting his machine body grated against the roof of the armoured vehicle.

With Brother Jarold stomping through the swamp behind them, calling down the divine vengeance of the Emperor upon the heads of the savage greenskins, the newly-formed Squad Wolfram moved at engaging speed towards the borders of the jungle and the feral orks' refuge, splashing through the stinking stagnant surface water of the mire.

The Space Marines all heard the whining roar, the rapidly increasing volume telling them that an object was closing at high velocity.

A heavy munitions shell hit the swamp in front of the Templars with concussive force. It threw up a wall of filthy water four metres high, drenching the Space Marines, showering them with sods of black mud and peaty clumps of reeds. But the Templars, filled with righteous zeal, did not falter and pressed on towards the dark, amorphous backdrop of the treeline. It was there that the brooding darkness of the jungle met the mist-shrouded expanse of the swamplands that formed a buffer zone between the Green, as the indigenous ork hunter regiments called it, and the crawling waterway of the Minos River.

Through the mists – the indistinct outlines overlaid with orange wire-frame models by the arcane auto-senses built into the laurel-wreathed helm of the Armour of Faith – Ansgar saw huge snorting behe-moths advancing to meet the Imperial tank lines and striding war walkers. The beasts' rumbling bellows and guttural lowing were muffled by the mist, which gave it an even more unsettling, unearthly quality.

Warning runes started to flash at the periphery of his visor. One of the wire-frame models was blinking red, the suit's cogitator trying to reconfigure as some-thing large began to move at speed towards the Space Marines.

It was too close, too large and, incredibly, too fast for them to take evasive action, weighed down as they were by their armour in the boggy marsh.

And then it was on top of them, all tusks, horns and splayed crushing hooves.

Squad Wolfram split left and right, Koldo, Lairgnen, Hebron and Gildas peppering the scaly, armoured hide of the monster with bolter fire. With a screaming roar of its own, Brother Jarold gave fire with his assault cannon, the spinning weapon becoming obscured by smoke and muzzle-flash. Empty shell cases rained down around the dread-nought and splashed into the swamp as Jarold's ammunition hoppers maintained a ready supply of explosive bullet-shells to the cannon. The dread-nought's assault tore great chunks of meat and muscle from the squiggoth's flanks but did nothing to slow the beast.

And then the monster was past them, running down a trotting sentinel squadron.

'Brothers, onward!' Chaplain Wolfram commanded. It was not their place to see this battle through to its conclusion. They had even greater goals to achieve. There was more a stake here than strategic control of the Plague Marshes.

Servos protested as the Marines' armoured suits compensated for the sucking grip of the swamp as the Templars struggled to keep pace with their Chaplain.

Inside their all-enclosing suits of power armour, each Templar's body temperature was regulated so that he did not overheat in the extreme humidity of the jungles or cook in the direct heat of the sun, when it actually managed to break through the miasmic cloud hanging over the marshlands.

Then there were orks swarming towards them out of the fumy fog.

Ansgar swung his crackling sword, cutting down an ork as it ran at him out of the mist. His blow bifurcated its body from neck to hip, the two halves sploshing into the filmy brown water.

Clouds of insects buzzed angrily around the Black Templars and their adversaries. But the sting-flies did not trouble the Marines, enclosed within their power armour. Neither did they trouble the orks, the aliens' war-painted hides apparently as tough as leather armour.

And then the sodden mire began to give way to firmer patches of ground as it rose towards the gnarled shapes of mangrove trees that appeared out of the marsh-mist in front of them. The lowing of squiggoths, the harassed barks of their goaders, the revving engines of the armoured units and the clamour of the battle being fought behind them was being swallowed up by the insidious mists.

Squad Wolfram met little resistance, however, cutting through the last lines of the noticeably weaker rearguard of the feral ork force.

And then the Templars, including Brother-Dreadnought Jarold, were through and into the thickets of mangrove trees, the forest floor underfoot becoming more solid with every emboldened, striding step. Tendrils of greasy vapour slithered between the wet black trunks as if to ensnare them within their clammy coils.

They were past the last line of resistance.

The squad paused for a moment in the gloom enveloping the sheltering black trees and the lingering mist, Brother Jarold on overwatch behind them like some adamantium colossus amidst the spindly trunks and capering root-boles, as the Chaplain checked Koldo's auspex readings. Then he pointed with the bladed head of his crozius through the trees into the cloying gloom.

'Brothers,' Wolfram said, 'time is now our adversary if we are to recover the holy treasure we seek – the flesh of our flesh. The seed of our brethren of Fighting Company Gerhard waits to be found, somewhere in these jungles, at the heart of darkness.' Now their mission could really begin. 'We head for the last known position of Castellan Gerhard's company in the hope that we will find the place where they fought and where they fell, consecrating the ground there with their holy blood.'

'Forward, brothers!' Ansgar declared, raising his gleaming black blade above his head, its keen edge already glistening with the sticky ichor of butchered orks. 'For Fighting Company Gerhard. For Solemnus. Forward we go in the Emperor's name!'

'No pity,' Wolfram declared, his voice like steel.

'No remorse,' Ansgar intoned.

'No fear,' the kill-team affirmed, concluding the mantra.

And then they were gone, into the mists, into the jungle, into the gathering gloom, to face whatever fate Ansgar's visions promised them.

NINE
INTO THE GREEN

STRANGE ECHOING CRIES and mammalian hooting sounded through the ethereal otherworld of the Green. Sergeant Borysko had called a halt within an area thick with cypress and quoia. The ground beneath their booted feet was semi-liquid, pools of soupy green water standing in stagnant hollows between the massive root networks of the giant trees. What little solid ground there was, was dusted with dead leaves.

'Right, take the weight off,' Borysko told the fifteen men of his platoon. 'Ertz, Masursky and Hawkeye, you're on sentry duty.'

An hour and a half into their trek into the all-enveloping jungle, and the ork hunters didn't need to be told twice. They immediately unloaded their packs and weapons, whilst Troopers Ertz, the surly

Masursky and 'Hawkeye' Gunderson spread themselves out around the trailing root systems.

'Klim, report our position to Cerbera. The codeword is...' The sergeant paused and grimaced as if there was a foul taste in his mouth. 'The codeword is "birdman".'

'Message received and understood,' Vox-trooper Klim responded, already removing the vox-set from his back and making the necessary adjustments to signal the camp they had left ninety minutes before.

They hadn't seen any sign of ork activity in all that time. Rumour was that the feral tribes were making a big push out towards the Minos River and the Plague Marshes bordering the continent-slicing waterway.

Still, it paid to stay alert out in the Green. There were more things than just orks that could take a man down within the primordial depths of the festering forests, and some of them were a darn sight worse. There were vicious carnivorous strains of flora that were possessed of an insidious and malign intellect. And there were the predatory creatures that had been native to the region before the arrival of the greenskins with Ghazghkull Thraka's last invasion attempt, fifty years before.

The orks were a fairly recent arrival on the planet, but within the last five decades it seemed that the feral tribes had made the jungles their own. In fact there didn't seem to be a place on the planet that they weren't suited to. From the sulphurous Fire Wastes to the frozen Deadlands, and everywhere in between, the orks thrived. There was something grotesque about their alien physiologies that meant that they could quickly adapt to extremes of environment, including many that would kill a man, if he was without the appropriate protective gear and breathing apparatus, such as the toxic deserts of Armageddon Secundus.

It sometimes seemed that there were signs of the greenskins everywhere within the equatorial jungles. Scenes of savage battles where ork hunters and their offworlder Guard allies fighting alongside them had died to protect the environs of Cerbera Base and stop the orks making any further advances on the Imperial station.

As Borysko's Boys made the most of the opportunity to relax and rest their feet before continuing with their mission, Trooper Kole moved to join the platoon's commanding officer where he stood next to a projecting tree root. The root formed a natural buttress supporting the towering quoia, the root alone rising to a height of three metres where it joined with the massive trunk. Layers of woody strata were visible within the built-up root and the others like it that surrounded the skinners.

'Sarge,' Kole said. 'Why have we stopped here?'

Borysko continued to gaze out into the darkness of the jungle beyond the platoon's position. It might be only an hour from noon, but this far beneath the shrouding canopy it was as dark as at dusk or dawn. Swathes of the forests were locked in a permanent verdigris twilight; the only time there was ever any change in the light levels being when night fell. Even then the jungle was darker than anywhere else on the planet with the overlapping branches and palm leaves keeping out the light of the stars that elsewhere peeked through as pinpricks of diamond light between the effluent clouds of industrial pollution.

'You don't want to know, Kole,' the sergeant said without looking at his second-in-command.

'Sergeant?' Klim called, raising his voice to get Borysko's attention.

'What did Cerbera have to say, trooper?' the sergeant asked, cutting Kole's next question off before it could be voiced.

'Cerbera report message received and understood, sir.'

'Was there anything else?'

'Yes, sir,' Klim confirmed, a tone of uncertainty in his voice, as if he had not fully understood the message he had received himself. 'They said the birdman has landed, sir.'

Borysko scowled. 'Marvellous. So it begins.'

'Sarge?' Kole asked. 'What begins?'

'This is where we make our rendezvous.'

'Rendezvous?'

'You'll see.'

The skinners waited, the sentries tense, anticipating the appearance of a threat – orkish or otherwise – at any moment. Even those men who were apparently relaxing before their sergeant gave them the order to resume their trek through the clinging jungle had half their senses tuned to the possibility of any sudden disturbance. Not that they were consciously thinking about it. It was a subconscious skill that anyone fighting to survive out here in the claustrophobic forests learnt very quickly. That, or they died before they had a chance to.

Hearing a rustling in the canopy above, Borysko and the others looked up. Eyes adjusted to the deeper gloom above them and then a grey shadow unfolded itself from the darkness and resolved in a recognisable shape.

A cloaked figure perched on one of the lowest branches jutting out from the trunk of the quoia, still a good seven metres above the hollow where Borysko and Kole stood.

More than a dozen lasguns, shotguns and other weapons were aimed up at the figure on the branch, the ork hunters reacting on instinct. But something held them back.

Automatically, Kole's laspistol had come to train on the cloaked figure balanced on the protruding branch, but the sergeant just stood where he was, his laspistol still in its holster, his chainsword remaining inactive in his hand.

Sergeant Borysko had not reacted to the appearance of the figure at all.

It was not just Borysko's curious response to the appearance of this stranger, effectively in their midst, that unsettled the skinners and prevented them from following the usual course of action in such circumstances – that of blasting the jungle apparition out of the tree.

Despite the fact that it was crouched on the branch, one hand gripping the barrel of a curious rifle which it was using like a walking stick to help balance itself, the hunters could tell that the figure watching them from within the cowl of its cloak was not one of their usual enemies. Kole could see that, under the apparently camouflaging cloth of its cloak, the new arrival was tall and thin. It was not an ork.

Neither had the figure attacked them yet. But it was watching them intently, its head twitching from side to side under its hood, its face still unseen. And it remained silent, the only sound other than the tense shallow breathing of some of the men being a twittering, whistling bird call coming from the vine-strewn canopy above.

From where he stood, still targeting the figure with his laspistol, his aim unwavering, Kole dared risk a glance more directly at those few parts of the stranger that were not hidden beneath the shadows of its cloak. The hand holding the rifle was wound with strips of hide or cloth, but Kole had an impression of horny nails at the ends of the long fingers. The figure's feet looked even more like claws.

Kole blinked and strained his eyes to pierce the gloom further. The feet appeared to be incessorial, the talons hooked around the branch on which the figure perched.

'Sarge,' Kole said, disbelief colouring his voice, 'what is–'

'Hold your fire,' Borysko said languidly, as though disappointed that he was having to give such an order.

The sergeant put a hand on Kole's laspistol and forcibly pushed it down to point at the ground. Stunned, his second-in-command did not resist.

'Stand down, all of you,' Borysko said with more force this time. 'This is our rendezvous.'

The muzzles of lasguns, shotguns and the rest unsteadily dropped towards the forest floor. But even though his men followed his order automatically, some of the troopers' minds were taking a little longer to catch up with ingrained instinctive reactions.

'Rendezvous?' the ratty Raus said indignantly. 'You never told us about any rendezvous.'

'No, I didn't, did I.' Borysko's stern response was a statement, brooking no question. The implication was clear: Pavle Borysko was the commanding officer here and he would not have his actions brought into question.

An uneasy stupefied hush descended over the men. The chirrups of insects and the croaking of forest birds invaded the silence; the jungle sounds slowly reclaiming their territory, just as it the undergrowth tried to take back the ground around Cerbera Base.

Borysko looked up at the cloaked shadow still perched motionless on the branch above them. 'You'd better come down,' he called up to the figure.

Without making a sound, the figure dropped from the branch, landing on the raised crest of a root. From there, the creature made a last agile leap to stand in front of the skinner sergeant, at the centre of the platoon, knees bending to absorb the kinetic force of its landing.

The figure straightened, the curious rifle held in its right hand. The weapon looked relatively primitive in its design and manufacture, certainly compared to the shotguns and las-weapons of the skinners. It had a curved wooden stock and sported two hunting knife blades, one at the base of the stock and another under the muzzle of the rifle. The gun had been given additional decoration in the form of feathers and small bones that had been tied to it, for some savagely primitive reason.

Now that it was standing upright in front of Borysko, it was clear to all the hunters that the stranger was almost a head taller than the sergeant, who was himself of greater than average height. That the stranger was so lean and thin merely seemed to exaggerate its height. It was probably taller even than Coburg.

The skin of the figure's arms was brown like leather. Quill-like protrusions poked through the discoloured skin in places on the lower arms. The long fingers ended in hard, talon-like claws. But, more disturbingly, there were only a total of four digits on each hand, curiously arranged. The stranger's face remained hidden by the obscuring cowl of its cloak.

To Kole's mind this creature had to be a mutant of some kind.

'Come on then,' Borysko said wearily, addressing the gangling cloaked figure, 'show yourself.'

Still the figure said nothing. Instead it put its free four-fingered claw to the hood and with slow, deliberate actions – its other hand gripping the rifle tightly, as if ready to swing it like a scythe – pulled back the hood.

An audible gasp rippled through the platoon, accompanied by a few stunned curses, the racking of shotguns and the hum of las-cells charging.

'A KROOT? AN alien?'

'Do you have a problem with that, Borysko?'

'With all due respect, sir, damn right there's a problem. I am an ork hunter. A xenos hunter. I hate frikkin' aliens! Aliens have been a blight on our world and have brought it to its knees.'

'Ah, war makes strange bedfellows of us all, Borysko. You know that.'

'Have you ever heard the phrase "Sleeping with the enemy"? I kill aliens. It's what I do.'

'Ah, I would remind you that this particular alien is a sanctioned agent of His Imperial Majesty's Holy Inquisition,' Vine warned, his voice an angry hiss.

'And what the frikk do the Inquisition think they're doing sniffing around here sticking their noses into our business?'

'It *is* their business, Borysko. Ah, whatever they *deem* to be their business is their business.'

Borysko couldn't believe what he was hearing. This was getting more ridiculous by the minute.

'What kind of mission is this you're giving me, Vine?'

'Look, I told you. I need someone out there I can trust. While the agent's watching you, I want you to be watching the agent. Don't let anything get past you. I don't like this anymore than you do, but this comes from the top, and I don't mean Armageddon High Command. This comes right from General Kurov's war council.'

Borysko was dumbfounded. Shock was taking its toll.

'The kroot are expert trackers,' Vine said appeasingly. 'The presence of this creature will speed up your quest and hasten your platoon's return to Cerbera for a tour of duty here at the base.'

Borysko still said nothing.

'Ah, Emperor damn you!' the marshal snarled. 'If you don't do this I'll have you up before the Commissariat, and I think you'll find that they're not as understanding as I am!'

'HOLD YOUR FIRE!' Borysko commanded. Guns wavered.

'But, sarge,' Tannhauser spluttered, 'it's a freakin' alien!'

'I do have eyes,' Borysko snapped back.

The kroot shifted the rifle to hold it in both hands. The skinner sergeant raised an eyebrow.

'I wouldn't do that if I were you,' he said coldly. 'There's only so much I can do to keep this lot at bay. I could lead them into the Emperor-forsaken Fire Wastes without so much as a complaint, but if you point that gun of yours at any of them I won't be able to stop them blasting you back to whatever alien hell spawned you.'

The kroot put its head on one side and blinked twice. The orbs of its eyes were milky white and pupilless. Faced with the avian appearance of the kroot's head, there was no doubting its alien nature or its genetic heritage. It had a blunt beak and a shock of banded black, brown, yellow and white quills – the remnants of vestigial feathers – stuck out from the back of its head. When the creature had shaken its head free of the cowl the quills rattled hollowly.

Kole had heard campfire tales of the alien mercenaries known as the kroot. They were primitive creatures and practised all manner of barbaric alien rituals. Word was that Guardsmen fighting alongside the kroot on frontier worlds, or against them in the Imperium's battles with the nascent Tau Empire in the Ultima Segmentum, had witnessed acts of depraved head-hunting and even cannibalism. Even their mercenary units were referred to as carnivore squads, and rightly so. But what troubled any right-thinking Imperial Guardsman, more than the fact that the kroot were happy to consume their own dead and that of other xenos races they killed, was that they would, if given the chance, just as readily devour the remains of human beings, even if they had been fighting on the same side.

The kroot were most well known for selling their services to the growing empire of the equally alien Tau, but it was not unknown for the forces of the Imperium to make use of them as canon-fodder in their campaigns against mutual enemies.

'This is the Inquisitorial agent that I was ordered to hook up with before we progressed any further on this mission,' Borysko broke off. 'I take it you have some proof that you're allied to the Inquisition?' he said, addressing the alien again, with the sort of look on his face that suggested he was chewing dung.

The kroot reached inside its cloak. Kole caught a brief glimpse of the accoutrements of its trade. Under the cloak it was wearing a basic loincloth and a harness formed out of bamboo cane and cured animal hide. Hanging around its neck on a leather thong were all manner of feathers, and primitive alien totems carved out of wood or bone.

Amongst the clutter of objects was one that was obviously Imperial in origin. It looked like a letter 'I' crossed by three bars – representing the three main ordos of the Inquisition – and bearing the image of a jawless human skull at its centre. It was an Inquisitorial rosette, presented to those in the employ of an inquisitor – daemonhunter, witch hunter, or alien hunters – of the various ordos.

The kroot held the rosette out to Borysko. Such objects were more than just badges of office; they were also often potent devices in their own right, capable of storing as much information as a data-slate, including details of security clearance codes and encrypting comm-interfaces, and containing all manner of other useful devices such as lock overrides, digi-weapons and signum trackers-cum-homing signals.

Sergeant Borysko turned to take in the incredulous faces of his platoon again. 'I am assured that this… mercenary is an expert tracker.'

'Probably kill us all in our sleep,' Ferze muttered. Borysko didn't rise to the comment this time; it wasn't worth it. The men were edgy enough as it was.

Scout Trooper Tannhauser snorted derisively.

'You have something to say on the matter, Lucky?' Borysko challenged. This was too much. He might not like the presence of the alien on this mission, but he wasn't about to start tolerating anyone questioning his orders, whether they were initiated by him or passed on from a higher authority.

'Yes, sarge,' Tannhauser dared. Kole sighed inwardly: when would the arrogant idiot learn? 'We don't need no tracker. You've already got the best in the regiment right here. We don't need no freakin' alien.'

'I don't like this any more than you do, you must know that. But if I tell you this xenos-thing is coming with us, that's how it is, whether you like it or not. Even if it is a stinking alien.'

'Stinking alien,' the kroot trilled suddenly, as if mimicking Borysko's words.

The sergeant turned on the creature, anger flaring in an instant like the blast of a melta gun. 'Did you speak?'

'Speak?' the kroot chirruped.

Kole had heard tell from some of the grizzled off-world Guardsmen that sometimes served alongside the ork hunters at Cerbera Base, that kroot were able to learn the languages of other species at an astonishing rate. They were able to achieve this through a combination of bird-like mimicry and knowledge of language gained, it was said, from consuming the brains of other creatures. In the case of Low Gothic, human beings.

The longer a kroot lived in human society, the more competent and assured it became at using the common tongue of the Imperium and its associated dialects. Until they achieved that level of surety, they had to make do with communicating in a form of pidgin Gothic, parroting the phrases and speech of others.

'I might have been ordered to have you on this mission,' Borysko snarled, 'but it doesn't mean I have to like it.'

Kole glanced around the group. Priest was fiddling nervously with the icon hung from his dog-tag chain and muttering catechisms under his breath. Ertz stood staring with disdain at the alien, straight-backed and formal-looking, even in the fatigues of an ork hunter. The brute Coburg was crouched on the ground toying with his necklace of ork teeth as if it was a prayer-bead rosary. Yeydl's hand was hovering over the ignition stud of his melta, while Kasarta was tossing one of the many blades from his crossed knife-belts in his hand.

He could have cut the atmosphere with a blow-torch. Someone was going to have to break the ice if they were going to get anywhere with this mission.

'What do we call you?' Kole asked, with one wary eye on his sergeant.

'Yeah, what's your handle?' Geist asked, an evil smile playing on his lips.

'Handle?' the kroot croaked.

'What – is – your – name?' Joker then said with exaggerated slowness – the way of all men speaking to those whose first language was not Low Gothic, assuming that speaking more slowly, or loudly, would somehow make them more understandable.

'Name Pangor Yuma,' the kroot suddenly butted in, 'of Toru Kindred.' The Low Gothic it spoke was strangely accented and clipped as if its beak-like mouth was finding it awkward to form the correct sound-shapes. Truth be told, Kole still wasn't used to hearing the bird-like humanoid speak at all.

The other troopers continued to eye the kroot warily, the Kid looking more twitchy than the rest of them put together. There were times when it was painfully obvious why Bukaj was called 'The Kid'.

'Kroot will do,' Borysko said cruelly. He turned away. 'Come on, let's move out,' he told the platoon. The skinners made ready to set off again.

'Which way we headed, sarge?' Vanderkamp asked. Vanders was notorious for having no sense of direction whatsoever.

The sergeant looked back over his shoulder at the gangly birdman. 'You're the tracker, kroot. Which way?'

The alien tracker squatted down at the centre of the clearing, one hand holding the haft of its rifle as though it was a staff. It spread the other taloned appendage out in the dirt, closed its eyes and sniffed sharply twice.

'I hate frikkin' aliens,' Borysko's curse was little more than a weary sigh.

The avian narrowed its pupil-less white eyes at the skinner sergeant. 'Frikkin' aliens!' it squawked.

'That's enough of your filthy xenos disrespect!' Borysko turned on the kroot with the fury of a cyber-mastiff. 'We are subjects of His Most Glorious Imperial Majesty, members of the greatest species – and, I might add, the dominant species – in the galaxy, not some mercenary scum like you.'

'...like you,' the kroot parroted.

Borysko flashed the alien a look of burning fury and looked like he was about to lash out at the Inquisitorial agent, but then thought better of it. A frustrated growl escaped from between his gritted teeth instead, as if it was all he could do not to strike Pangor Yuma to the ground.

The kroot calmly pointed an extended claw in a south-westerly direction. 'Way we go,' it croaked.

THE PLATOON REACHED the crash site within three hours. Kole couldn't help wondering whether they would have got there quite so quickly without the alien's help. The kroot had led the way, spending half the journey up in the branches of the crowding trees.

Pangor Yuma directed the snaking line of skinners as they trekked through the profusion of fan-palms in single file, weapons slung from their hips, making continual sweeping arcs to the side. The alien kept its distance, remaining in the trees, making flying leaps from bough to bough.

The first warning the ork hunters received that they were about to come upon the place where the Valkyrie went down was a shrill whistling call from the kroot tracker. Pangor Yuma clung to a woody creeper halfway up a poga tree as it pointed with a talon into the oppressive jungle ahead of the ork hunters' advance.

And then the men had seen it too. A rip in the forest canopy, allowing the natural light of the sun entry to the green otherworld, through which could be seen the smudged blue firmament above. Branches and leaves had been shredded by the impact of something large and heavy, hurtling groundward at high speed.

The men blinked in the bright sunlight and felt the sun's scorching heat on their skin. The culmination of their mission was in sight.

Three kilometres further on, having followed a worsening trail of devastation, they found the grounded Valkyrie. The craft was recognisable as such, but only just. It was now nothing more than a large, bullet-shaped airframe. The wings had been torn from the hull of the craft as it hurtled towards the ground through densely growing trunks. Holes had been ripped in the Valkyrie's hull, the carapace of the flyer being shredded by the unkind attentions of tearing branches. The windshield of the cockpit and every viewing port in the craft had been shattered: not one piece of armaglas remained intact. Pieces of the downed flyer were scattered throughout the thickets of red-barked trees.

The majority of the platoon spread out around the wreckage of the Valkyrie. Borysko, Kole, Kasarta and Vanderkamp clambered inside, through the lowered rear hatch-ramp, to search the wreckage of the fuselage. The kroot remained at a distance from the others, keeping watch from a higher vantage point perched on a branch, its cloak wrapped tightly around it wiry body.

'What's this doing open?' Vanderkamp wondered aloud.

'Must have opened after the craft crashed,' suggested Kasarta.

'I don't think so,' Kole said, looking at the huge hydraulic assembly required to deploy the ramp. 'Somebody opened this on purpose when the craft was still in the air.'

'Not usual operating procedure as I understand it,' Borysko cut in, 'unless on a grav-chute drop mission, and Vine didn't say anything about that.'

Although the Valkyrie had reportedly only gone down a matter of hours before, water was already dripping down from the top of the grounded craft. Amazingly, despite the catastrophic crash, it was still upright. Pieces of ragged leaves, vines and branches also littered the interior of the Valkyrie, blown inside during the flyer's dramatic descent through the rain-forest canopy.

They found three bodies within the passenger hold, strewn between the hard-backed metal seats. The bodies were all dressed in black and grey camo fatigues. The hellguns they had been holding lay on the buckled grille floor nearby. They were instantly recognisable to the skinners as Imperial stormtroopers.

'Glory boys,' Kasarta sneered.

'Correction,' Borysko said. 'Dead glory boys.'

Each of the stormtroopers had died a violent death. One of the men was still slumped in his seat, his body held upright by his restraining harness. His head hung down on his chest. At a cursory inspection it looked like this stormtrooper had bled to death, or been the victim of shock, thanks to having his face impaled with the glass of his helmet visor. There may well have been other internal injuries that the skinners couldn't have known about as a result of the crash.

It was more obvious how the other two had died. Both the men had been shot through the head at close range.

'What the hell went on here?' Kole wondered. Kasarta swore and Vanderkamp made the sign of the aquila. The sergeant said nothing.

Borysko and the others passed through the belly of the craft and climbed the iron-runged steps that led towards the front of the Valkyrie. They entered the crumpled shell of the cockpit.

A shot to the head had also exploded the pilot's skull. Pieces of brain matter and bone shards still adhered to the twisted, structural struts of the windshield – although none of the armaglas panes remained intact – and ruddy gore painted the instrument panel.

The co-pilot had been impaled on a tree branch during the crash. The splintered spar brought down by the flyer still transfixed the corpse to its seat.

There was no one left alive amidst the wreckage of the Valkyrie, nor was there any sign of the officer they had been sent to find.

'Shit!' Borysko said, rubbing his temples with a roughly calloused hand.

'This isn't over yet, is it, sarge?' Kole said in a hushed voice.

'No, it's not. It was never going to be that simple. War never is.'

'HEY, KID. TELL me I'm not seeing things.'

Nal Bukaj took his eyes off the forest for a moment and looked at the chief scout trooper standing a couple of metres away from him to his left. 'What is it, Tann?'

'I thought I saw something moving in the trees.'

Bukaj's gaze snapped back to the dense jungle before him. Strange chirruping cries and an ominous croaking echoed through the jungled darkness. 'An ork?'

'No. Something else,' Tannhauser was peering myopically into the unrelenting gloom as well.

'Can you see it now?'

'No. It's gone.'

'You sure it wasn't the kroot?' the Kid was as unnerved as any of the skinners by the presence of the alien mercenary in their midst.

Tannhauser glanced up at where Pangor Yuma was perched in the treetops, staring intently at something away to the south-west. 'No. It wasn't him.'

'Probably a tree-shrew then.'

'Yeah, probably,' Tannhauser replied, although he didn't sound like he believed it.

He was sure he had seen something. The merest suggestion of a figure. A shadow of a shadow. But he couldn't be certain. The Green could do that to a man; make him see blurred, indistinct figures in the rippling shadows of its emerald gloom, where there were none.

At that moment Tannhauser was distracted by Sergeant Borysko emerging from the wrecked fuselage of the assault carrier again.

'They're all dead in there,' he told the platoon, 'but there's no sign of the ACG bigwig.'

Several of the skinners sighed in disappointment. They too had hoped that this mission would be over soon so that they could return to Cerbera for some well-deserved R and R – or at least as close as you got to R and R on tour in the equatorial jungles.

'Spread out,' the sergeant commanded. 'Search the area. Find me a dead lieutenant.'

Borysko cupped a hand to his mouth and looked up into the towering quoia trees.

'Hey, kroot!' he shouted. The avian's head snapped round. The kroot put its head on one side and regarded the sergeant with predatory interest. 'If you're such a good tracker, tell me if anybody walked away from this mess.'

ELSEWHERE...

THE ORK twitched in its vision-wracked sleep. Sparks of green static energy fizzed and sparked from the ork's head. It created a corona of eerie light around it, not unlike a mane of fizzing, sparking hair that shorted and fizzled out in the leaf mulch around it with a scorching smell of burning plant fibres.

An outcast, its potent power too wild and uncontrolled even for the feral tribes from which it had originated, the wyrdboy dozed beneath the roots of a poga tree, alone. It was clothed in furs and animal hides, and like others of its kind, its skin was marked with blue war paint. But unlike many of its kind it had also adorned its garb with all manner of unusual trinkets and totems: raptor skulls, beetle wing cases, yukama feathers, crudely carved teeth. Spent bullet casings rattled together on a vine cord around its thick neck as it swore and grunted in its unsettled sleep. And clutched in one meaty paw, even as it slept, was a gnarled and knotted staff of quoia wood, which had the remains of a human skull tied to it.

In its mind's eye the ork saw smoky green billows swirling between midnight blue and oblivion black massing thunderheads. Crackling purple lightning split the cloudscape, vaporising wisps of blood-red cirrus in an explosion of light and ozone, leaving a stinging pink after-image. The burnt air tasted of tin. There was the smell of a psyker-storm redolent in the atmosphere.

The clouds parted. The ork saw the hives of Armageddon as mountains of rubble, burning under a blood-red sky. It saw the bones of millions of human beings spread out across the burnt, cracked plains of the planet. It saw the smouldering, twisted wreckage of war machines brought to a standstill by war. The skies rang and echoed with the screams of the dying and the monstrous, cackling roars of their slaughterers. And amidst it all the wyrdboy saw the conquering armies marching to victory, claiming Armageddon as their own world. A world of death and pain. A world of agonising torture and endless slaughter. A world drowned in blood.

The ork's ugly, tusk-filled mouth twisted into an unpleasant smile as it dreamed. Such visions had to be a message sent by its savage primal gods, Gork and Mork. Ghazghkull's invasion had already crushed this world beneath its green fist. War had spread its bloody mantle over this world. But the wyrdboy's dreams spoke of a time of even greater war coming to Armageddon.

And this outcast – Ruzdakk Blitzgul – had been chosen as the vessel of the ork gods' will. It had been given the responsibility of spreading their message to all the tribes, and rallying them to do as Gork and Mork desired. And the orks would not want to miss out when a new deluge of destruction descended on the planet.

The final battle for the planet would be fought here, amidst the equatorial jungles. The end was nigh. The conquest of Armageddon was at hand.

TEN
ROGUE

THE CHIRRUPING OF insects and the insistent buzz of rad-midges, accompanied by distant mammalian hoots and croaking bird cries filled the green-dark depths of the jungle as thickly as the endless undergrowth. The hulking black and white armoured giants moved with practiced ease through the thick vegetation covering the forest floor beneath the overarching, light-depriving canopy of dense leaves and branches above them. Only the hum of suit servos, the whisper of fern fronds brushing against their armour as they were swept aside by their passing, and the crunch of their heavy ceramite boots betrayed their presence in this twilight world.

Since leaving the battle for the Plague Marshes and entering the rainforest, beyond the half-jungle of the misted mangrove stands, the Black Templars of Kill-team Wolfram had maintained the same order of deployment. Emperor's Champion Ansgar himself led the team, his sword raised at shoulder height, occasionally using the blade to sweep aside branches or particularly pernicious creepers that hung down over their path.

Not that they were following an established track of any kind. The Marines were having to make their own path through the jungle as they advanced. As far as they knew, they may have been the first humans ever to penetrate this part of the forest. Ork hunter patrols left secret markers on routes they had taken through the jungle – knotted vines, marks cut into the bark of trees, arrangements of stones – should they ever pass that way again and to tell their fellows that they had scouted an area before.

Orks left their own markers too, if they had claimed an area as their territory. The signifiers left by orks were much less subtle, however: staked skulls, animal or otherwise; skulls plastered with mud and feathers; skulls painted with woad. There was a common theme to the signposts left by the feral greenskins. Ansgar had seen no such objects, or any sign of ork hunter activity, for the last ten kilometres of trudging through the relentless rain-forest.

After Ansgar came Chaplain Wolfram, who was using his bladed crozius like a machete. Numerous persistent woody vines had felt the bite of the power axe's disrupter field-sheathed blades. Then there was the Chaplain's sworn protector, Body-guard Koldo, his auspex readings keeping the Templars on track for their target destination.

Next came Brother Lairgnen, his boltgun sweeping the forest to the right of the line of Marines, and behind him Brother Hebron, the scorched muzzle of his bolter sweeping in an arc to the left. Brother Baldulf, chainsword at the ready, his thumb hovering over its activation stud, followed. After him was Bliant, his white armour given an emerald cast by the unnatural jungle light. Then came Gildas, Huarwar and Clust.

After Clust, his heavy bolter cinched to his armoured suit, came the other heavy weapons specialist, the mighty Kemen and his lascannon. Eleventh in line was the flamer-toting Brother Larce.

Naturally Dreadnought Brother Jarold brought up the rear. Low hanging branches snapped as they were forced aside by his passing, lengths of creeper-vine becoming tangled around his weapon-arms and the iron halo that crested his massive body.

Brother Ansgar peered ahead through the green gloom. He could see flickering breaks of yellow light between the trees. The vegetation underfoot and around them was beginning to change too. The fat, fleshy pods of nascent cycads emerged from the fern fronds and cinder-ferns.

'How far do you estimate it is now, Brother Koldo?' he asked.

'According to my auspex readings and the last signal received by the fleet, we should be almost there.'

The kill-team advanced for another two hundred metres through the dense green growth, and then Ansgar stepped through a screen of vines and into a clearing. The green shadows gave way to dazzling sunlight. For a moment Ansgar was blinded as the auto-senses of his helm visor adjusted to the dramatic change in light levels.

The clearing was roughly circular in shape with a diameter of seventy metres at its widest point. It had been formed when a series of dead, dark quoia trees, their heartwood rotted away, had fallen, exposing the forest floor here to the sky again. As well as the dead trunks of the quoia trees several large boulders and rocky outcrops emerged from the wet soil of the glade.

It was from this location that the Solemnus fleet had received the last communication from Fighting Company Gerhard. After that time nothing more had been heard from them, the only evidence Marshal Brant having of their fate being Ansgar's painful visions. Kill-team Wolfram could see the subtle signs that meant their battle brethren had been here, although they did not know from which direction they had entered the clearing. Neither did they yet know how Castellan Gerhard's warriors had left the clearing, for there was no sign of them here now.

'So where did they go?' Brother Lairgnen asked, voicing the question that was on many of their minds.

'This is not where they died,' Ansgar said plainly. 'This is not the place I saw in my vision.'

'Then let us pray for guidance,' Chaplain Wolfram decreed, 'and search for what traces our brothers may have unwittingly left us as to what happened to them from this point in.'

The Templars had been able to do little more than quickly survey the open space when a reverberating bellow echoed through the jungle, from the direction by which they had entered the clearing.

All of the kill-team turned, weapons at the ready. Brother Jarold swivelled on the hefty joint of his waist, the chambers of his assault cannon cycling up to speed. Auto-loaders whirred into operation.

Ansgar could see something – something huge – thundering towards them through the black-wet trees. A shadow was looming between the trees, out of the suffocating gloom of the jungle depths, and it was growing as it neared the clearing. Ansgar's heads-up visor display was attempting to calculate the speed and trajectory of the approaching threat, overlaying its image with a flickering orange-barred wire-frame of lines and polygons, as his ancient artificer helm's cogitator made adjustments to keep up with the rapidly approaching leviathan. The deep-throated bellows rumbled through the gathered Marines as they readied themselves for the inevitable, and were accompanied by the splintering crash of more trees coming down. The ground beneath the Marines' feet shook as if convulsed by seismic tremors.

Two towering quoia smashed through the branches of their neighbours, the leafy morass of their canopies coming down inside the clearing, heralding the arrival of something monstrous, terrible and alien. A cluster of poga trees at the edge of the glade bent and snapped, uprooted by the battering they received, and the squiggoth burst into the clearing in an explosion of leaves and trailing vine-tendrils.

The beast was enormous, a good twelve metres tall at its heavily muscled shoulder, so big that it would have been classed as an orkeosaurus by the xenos-genetors of the Adeptus Mechanicus. Underneath the brow of its armoured helmet, the monster's face was a blunt, horned visage – not unlike that of an ork itself – set in a permanent expression of bestial anger.

Incredibly, despite its furious charge through the forest, the squiggoth's weapons platform was still attached to its back by the heavy chains, which had been hooked directly into the armour-like hide of the animal's sides and wrapped round under its belly. It soon became apparent that the howdah was actually the recycled body of a Krieg-pattern Siegfried tank, minus its locomotive traction units. The shoulders of the orkeosaurus were covered with interlocking plates of beaten plate. The rattling armour covered much of its flanks and templum-pillar legs as well. It was only really the creature's head and underbelly that had been left unprotected.

Creepers that had attempted to ensnare the beast as it charged through the jungle had been pulled clean away from the root-boles to which they had been parasitically attached.

The ground shook beneath the orkeosaurus's massive feet and the Black Templars scattered before it. All except for Brother Jarold.

The gargantuan squiggoth-beast dwarfed the awe-inspiring figure of the dreadnought.

'In the name of the holy triumvirate, of Emperor, Primarch and Founding Father, I abjure thee, monster!' Brother Jarold cried, his declaration booming from the vox-casters built into the hull of his dreadnought body.

His assault cannon roared into life. Almost instantaneously, Ansgar saw chunks of flesh vanish beneath clouds of bloody pink mist as the alien animal closed on the Templar veteran. Brother Jarold's heavy weapon had managed to evade the monster's leg-armour and tear through its thick hide. The monster bellowed again, its stinking carnivore's breath washing over the ancient crusader as a hot wind, splatters of stringy saliva splashing the scarred, black adamantium hull.

But the dreadnought's barrage did not even slow the colossal creature. Weighing in at around sixty tonnes of almost solid muscle, a few blasts from an assault cannon were not easily going to stop the enraged beast.

The remainder of the kill-team gave fire as well. Bolter rounds spanged off the riveted adamantium and wrought iron sheets of the beast's armoured plating. But if the dreadnought's deadly arsenal could do little to trouble the orkeosaurus, what hope had the other Templars with their markedly less powerful weaponry by comparison? Weapons that could vaporise a man or bifurcate a body with one explosive shell seemed little better than slings and catapults against the resilient gargantuan squiggoth.

Brother Jarold pivoted on his hip joint again, in an attempt to raise the angle of fire from his weapon. A headshot was all that was going to bring the brute down. But the orkeosaurus was charging towards him with startling speed.

The assault cannon roared again. A bullet ricocheted from the broken spur of a tusk, like a fractured stalactite, a broadside of high-velocity shells chopping through the dangling lobe of a flapping sail-sheet ear.

And then the monstrous behemoth was on top of Brother Jarold and there was nowhere for the dreadnought to go.

A galloping mastodon-like foot swept towards Jarold. For a moment it looked like it was going to miss him and sweep over the armoured hull. But a two-tonne, four-metre tall colossus of adamantium, ceramite and steel was hard to miss. A snagging nail clipped the iron halo that the dreadnought proudly bore, a symbol of the great bravery Jarold had displayed on Solemnus more than a decade before. There was a flash of shorting energy fields, a resonating metallic clang and the dreadnought was sent hurtling backwards, smashed off its metal-clawed feet.

The heavy dreadnought body crashed down amidst the cycads, pulping and popping more of the fleshy stems beneath its crushing weight.

But Jarold was spared by the same savage momentum of the beast that had tumbled him backwards through the cycad patch. Rather than pause to crush Jarold beneath a foot as big and as heavy as a Mechanicus forge pile driver, the orkeosaurus was not able to slow itself enough to stop and continued straight forwards.

A massive hind foot swept over his prone, sky-facing body, mere centimetres from the protrusion of the sarcophagus inside which Jarold's mortal remains were forever interred, hooked into the dreadnought's systems. The shadow cast by the massive beast blotted out the patch of sky visible above the clearing.

But Brother Jarold had not escaped from his encounter with the monstrous squiggoth totally unscathed. The iron halo that had adorned the crown of his machine body had been torn free of the adamantium hull.

Jarold's assault cannon attack might not have slowed – let alone stopped – the squiggoth, but it had certainly attracted the great beast's attention and given its previously undirected anger a focus.

The squiggoth's tiny yellow eyes fixed on the black and white armoured figures milling around its massive clomping feet. It felt the sting of their weapons against its tough hide and it felt the raw pain of the injuries it had sustained during the battle for the marshes. It needed an outlet for its agony. A malicious streak a kilometre wide had the squiggoth wanting to take out its furious bestial rage on something. The irritation of its harrying attackers would be the ones to suffer the full fury of its wrath.

The enormous squiggoth turned, presenting its left flank to Ansgar. The action slewed it to a halt, the platform on its back hawing violently to one side.

Ansgar could now see the older massive gouged wounds quite clearly, dark and raw, burnt to a fatty crisp at the edges, the legacy of a lascannon blast, he guessed.

In the battle for the Plague Marshes, Ansgar had seen a squiggoth gutted by a blast from a Leman Russ, thick cables of intestines pouring from its guts. It looked like the orkeosaurus had only barely escaped such a fate itself.

Nonetheless, the injuries were terrible indeed, enough to drive the orkeosaurus into an uncontrollable, pain-induced rage; but not enough to finish the monster. It must have been these injuries, sustained during the battle against the Rüstung Armoured Fourth and their Steel Legion supporters, that had caused the squiggoth to go rogue.

The rogue's ork handlers were still clinging desperately to their positions inside the adapted howdah, unable to guide the temperamental brute any longer. If they had been able to, the feral greenskins would have doubtlessly steered their mount back into the battle to commit further acts of glorious mayhem.

The orkeosaurus had a stub of tail, which helped balance the massive bulk of its body, but proved no direct threat to the Space Marines. However, the studded ball and chain – the size of that employed by a hive demolition servitor – did.

The squig lashed its tail and the heavy wrecking ball swung round, ever so slowly but inexorably. The spiked steel orb swept over the heads of Brothers Huarwar, Hebron and Kemen, as they laid down covering fire, making the Marines duck instinctively.

The ball continued on its course and collided with a tall, thin trunk. There was the wet splintering crunch of timber followed by an ominous groaning, as the tree toppled down into the clearing. Brother Kemen looked up to see the lengthening silhouette of the thirty metre-tall tree toppling towards him. He only just moved in time. The cage of the tree's topmost branches crashed down in a flurry of vegetation, sending detached leaves up into the air around it, barely two metres from the lascannon-wielding warrior.

'Sigismund be praised!' Kemen exalted, realising how close he had come to death.

Recovering himself again in the next instant, the thankful Kemen turned his lascannon on the orkeosaurus and its gun carriage. His shoulder-mounted weapon flashed as something akin to man-made lightning ripped from the muzzle, lashing the armoured plates of the monster, scorching paint and rust from the jerry-rigged carapace and lacerating the paler flesh of its lower flanks, so that the smell of cooked squig-flesh threatened to overwhelm the Marines' enhanced olfactory organs.

There was the whistle and *zing* of whickering gun-fire all around Ansgar now. Cycad pods burst around him, throwing sprays of sticky sap into the atmosphere in a fine drizzle. The Emperor's Champion looked up and through the las-wrought air, through the clouds of cooking sap-smoke, to the howdah swaying precariously atop the broad back of the belligerent orkeosaurus.

Poking over the jagged lip of the howdah were ugly ork faces and the muzzles of a plethora of weapons. There was a large gun emplacement affixed to the platform too. From Ansgar's previous experience of fighting orks he thought it looked like what had been dubbed by the Imperial Guard as a zzap kannon.

There was a mirrored flash of light above Ansgar that became a flickering, spinning shadow. He deftly dodged to his left as the ork-thrown axe thunked into the ground next to him. Ansgar instinctively raised his sword, as if ready to parry the shots fired by the greenskins, or whatever else the aliens decided to throw at him.

But against these orks and their monstrous mount, it seemed that there was little Ansgar could do with his Black Sword. He briefly contemplated attempting to climb up the plates of its armour onto the beast's back, but he almost immediately abandoned the idea. The overlapping, linked metal sheets did not reach down to the orkeosaurus's feet. And besides, the great beast was still on the move, trampling through the cycad clearing, squashing the pods to a greeny-white pulp beneath its heavy hoof-feet.

It looked to Ansgar like this was going to be a heavily unbalanced battle in which the Emperor's Champion was going to have to let his battle-brethren come to the fore instead. As a brother of the Black Templars Chapter – whose battle doctrine favoured engaging with the enemy in close combat – it was not an approach to fighting that Ansgar was used to, or comfortable with. The Black Templars were not proponents of fighting a ranged war, like certain other Astartes Chapters. They believed that honour in battle came from delivering the Emperor's divine justice hand-to-hand, and face-to-face.

There was nothing more satisfying than seeing an alien coughing up blood as it was impaled on the end of his blade. The knightly Brother Baldulf was similarly restricted, with regard to the use of his consecrated chainsword – itself an ancient treasured relic of the crusade. He was having to settle for spraying the squiggoth with fire from his bolt pistol, but it was not his preferred method of combat, and he might as well have been attacking the squiggoth with a fly-swat. The same went for Apothecary-Brother Bliant.

Brother Clust was having greater success with his chugging heavy bolter, the furious fusillade he was managing to keep up with his weapon tearing chunks from the orkeosaurus's pale underbelly. Viscous black blood ran from the holes peppering its side. But the orkeosaurus had turned itself so that its head was out of range of their guns.

If Clust and Kemen could sustain this level of damage for long enough, the giant squiggoth would eventually succumb and fall. But the monster wasn't going to simply stand there and take such a beating without trying to defend itself.

Ansgar heard the jerking, clattering snap of the crushing ball-chain. Over the roars of their weapons, Clust and Kemen did not. Even as Ansgar was screaming a warning into the comm, the spiked orb smashed into Brother Clust, carrying him into the air with it on its arcing journey.

Incredibly, none of the cruel spears of steel projecting from the rusting mace ball pierced his body. Clust found himself caught between the metre-long spikes instead. Then he and his heavy bolter were flying through the air unaided, to come crashing down on top of a sundered tree trunk.

As Clust was launched into the air, he involuntarily struck Brother Kemen with one ceramite boot. There was a distinct clang as the boot smacked into Kemen's helmet. The tall Marine was spun round into a thicket of fern-fronds, his aim ruined, his lascannon falling into a bed of gourd-pitchers.

The orkeosaurus was now swinging its head from side to side, trying to catch a glimpse of the scurrying figures at its feet. The animal snorted irritably, raising its great feet, one at a time, to stamp down again in an effort to crush the Marines beneath its pile-driver legs.

Ansgar looked on in angry frustration. But perhaps there was a way that he could still play his part in this battle and help even the horrendous odds stacked against the Space Marines. He was reminded of the words of the first Overlord of Solemnus, vaunted Marshal Emrik: 'One can always find a way if one has faith.'

The squiggoth was starting to charge.

'In the name of the Emperor of Mankind, in the name of the primarch and in the name of Lord Sigismund,' Ansgar declared as he began to run towards the terribly tusked and horned leviathan, the Black Sword raised, the skirt of his robe flapping around the greaves of his armour, 'I swear that His almighty fury and vengeful wrath shall bring you low!'

As if in response to the champion's challenge, the orkeosaurus bellowed again. Its rumbling roar shook the ground at Ansgar's feet and made the Templar feel as though he had been transported through time to an era when the rest of the planet was as primordial as its untamed jungle.

The orks responded by enthusiastically taking pot shots at the Templars.

Then Ansgar was aware of the Chaplain keeping pace with him as he charged the alien behemoth.

'No fear! No pity! No remorse!' the war-cry litany of the Black Templars spilled from the Chaplain's lips as words of inspiring fire. The cross-axe of his crozius was raised over his right shoulder guard, ready to deal the squiggoth a dolorous blow.

The two warriors ran at a tangent to the lumbering beast, their suit servos whining as they closed the gap between them and the giant animal. The orkeosaurus was getting up to speed again now. There was little distance left to accommodate the monster's charge. In a matter of moments, unless the squiggoth persisted in running down the Black Templars, it would break through the trees describing the edge of the glade and disappear back into the forest.

Ansgar knew that he could not let that happen. He had sworn to bring about the end of the orkeosaurus. If he did not make good that vow, he would no longer be fit to wear the Armour of Faith or be the bearer of the blessed Black Sword.

Ansgar threw himself forward as one of the monster's front feet crashed down only a metre from him. He landed in a roll, energised blade in hand all the time, and then rose into a crouch beneath the squiggoth's head, the Black Sword pointing directly towards the heavens.

The fractionally slower Chaplain suddenly found himself separated from the champion as the monstrous mass of the orkeosaurus swept past in front of him. With a furious cry of righteous anger, he brought his crackling crozius down. The flared blades of the cross-axe struck the chains that passed underneath the beast's belly.

Ansgar pushed himself up into a standing stance as the beast thundered over him, plunging his immediate surroundings into twilight shadow. The vast columns of the orkeosaurus's legs passed either side of the champion, the span formed by its bunker-sized ribcage. For a brief second it seemed to Ansgar as if he was inside an Ecclesiarchy shrine, only one papered with pachyderm hide.

With a cry of, 'For the Emperor!' Ansgar thrust the Black Sword upwards. He felt a brief moment of resistance. He locked his arms, holding them firm. He saw the reflected luminescence of the blade's energy field as it blazed blue on coming into contact with the underbelly of the squiggoth. He heard the electrical discharge of the sword and the wet slicing sound of internal organs being punctured and cut open.

A torrent of foul, stinking blood and other fluids poured down over Ansgar in a sudden deluge, as if a dam had been breached and a stagnant lake, full of rotting fish corpses, had flooded out of the beast's guts.

The scream that rose from the cavernous throat of the squiggoth was like no other sound the Templars had heard since they had encountered the rogue war-beast. It was an agonised bellow of anguish that ripped through the glade and curdled the blood in the Space Marines' veins.

The orkeosaurus staggered almost to a halt, lurching as it pawed the air with one colossal foot. The monster was trying to rear up, to somehow escape the pain of its lacerated belly.

The chains loosed, the howdah shifted, scraping against the rough hide of the orkeosaurus's back. With a terrible inevitability, the Siegfried tank-shell slid sideways, the orks giving yelps and barks that translated as exclamations of shocked surprise in any language.

Some of the greenskins threw themselves from the carriage, landing awkwardly amongst the broken trunks and nascent tree ferns. They realised that it was only a matter of moments before the squiggoth itself keeled over, and hoped to avoid being flattened beneath its massive bulk, or the howdah gun-platform when it came down after them. As the aliens dropped to the floor of the clearing, only metres from the Black Templars, the Marines gunned them down where they stood. Some of the orks tried to fire back.

Larce's flamer belched and two of the greenskins died screaming, caught within its cone of fire. Their stinking green hides blackened and crackled as they first cooked and then burned under the intense, inescapable heat.

Seven of the aliens had attempted to make their escape in this way so far. A massive brute of a beast, its face half painted blue, landed almost on top of Brother Lairgnen. As the initiate brought his boltgun to bear the ork brought its heavy club – fashioned from a tree branch and an old munitions casing – down on Lairgnen's arm, knocking his weapon askew. But before the ork could follow up its attack, Brother-Initiate Gildas was there. His bolter coughed in his hand and the alien's shoulder and half its head was vaporised in a cloud of green mist.

The salvaged frame of the gun-howdah crashed to the ground and broke apart. The zzap gun, the main weapon it had carried, broke the skulls of another pair of orks. Moments later, the unstable power cells of the primitive laser – fractured by the fall – went critical. The zzap kannon exploded, bathing the smashed cycads in a searing green-tinged ball of expanding energy.

Ork bodies raining down across the clearing, Ansgar suddenly found himself facing the leviathan again. Despite the fell blow he had dealt it with his sword it was simply too stubborn to die. It had wheeled round again and was now gunning for the Templar that had caused it such a grievous injury, massive coils of its intestines unravelling from the hole in its belly. The monstrous beast kept lumbering forwards, threatening to trample the Emperor's Champion directly in its path.

One more carefully placed blow should do it, Ansgar considered. All he had to do was dodge the swinging head of the squiggoth and its gaping maw, which was quite capable of swallowing a Space Marine whole, and roll under its neck. A sweep of his crackling blue-sheathed blade and, with its throat cut, the beast would have to die.

Twenty metres.

The beast was closing.

Ten metres.

All he had to do was avoid the huge tusks as the monster swung its head from side to side.

Five metres.

Ansgar raised his sword and–

...HE WAS STANDING at the edge of a crater. Behind him and on every side of the crater the unnervingly quiet forest was made of up grey, twisted trunks, the withered trees clinging to some semblance of life, but one that Ansgar would have expected to see on some daemon-ruled hell-world, touched by the warp or within the Eye of Terror. It was as if the physical corruption that had taken hold of the jungle was a manifestation of the metaphysical corruption of Chaos.

The wind howled like a ravenous predatory beast, tearing leaves and branches from the trees.

At the centre of the dark crater stood an even darker ring of stones. It seemed to Ansgar that the monoliths ran with blood, the ravening daemon-faces carved into the pitted surface of the stones, writhing and howling, licking at the crimson liquid with unnaturally formed granite tongues. The blasphemous Chaos monuments crackled with a sick, purple luminescence: warp-energy. Crimson thunderheads swelled overhead and the crater was bathed in scarlet light. The air was thick with the malign sickness of the warp.

Thunder rumbled overhead. A storm of untold, unnatural power was awakening.

Black lighting streaked down from the storm clouds, lashing the sacrificial stones with its unkind caresses. Blood fell from the riven sky like rain. And as the storm broke overhead and around Ansgar, a hole of dark oblivion began to open and expand at the heart of the monolith circle, tearing open within the very fabric of reality.

Now he could see things moving within the hole in reality. Armoured shapes. Horned things. Bloodthirsty creatures of utter evil.

And all hell was let loose…

ANSGAR OPENED HIS eyes.

He felt groggy. Something was wrong, he knew that. He could feel pain, as if he had been hit by a tank head-on. But the grogginess wasn't caused by the pain; it was a consequence of the lingering vision that had dragged him from the battlefield into a distorted future where, quite literally, all the horrors the warp had to hold had been loosed upon the world. It felt as if his soul were still somewhere else, disjointed, out of time. The gaping hole of the clearing in the jungle canopy spun into focus above him. That was something else that was wrong; he was on his back.

The copper-streaked sunlight was blotted out again by a rapidly descending circle of darkness.

Brother-Apothecary Bliant was suddenly there, dragging the disorientated Ansgar from danger as he automatically scrambled to his feet. Koldo was giving them covering fire, as were Hebron and Clust, the heavy bolter-bearing crusader also on his feet again.

The foot crashed down. The force of the impact threatened to throw Ansgar and the Apothecary to the ground once more.

The Emperor's Champion stumbled. He felt dizzy. His head was still spinning. He took another half a dozen staggering steps before he felt that he had truly regained his balance.

But Ansgar wasn't the only one who was suffering. The squiggoth was also becoming noticeably slower and more sluggish and unstable in its movements. The monster loomed large over him, swaying bodily. Any second now it would come down, almost certainly on top of him.

Willing his body to behave, Ansgar turned back to the unsteady tree trunk leg next to him. He swung and the Black Sword bit again, sinking into the calf of the forelimb and severing the tendons.

Roaring, the squiggoth went down on one knee. Sprays of crimson burst from its flanks where the bolter fire continued to harass it. Ansgar realised that the dreadnought was back on his feet as with a booming war-cry of his own, Brother Jarold let fly with his assault cannon, the spinning barrels becoming obscured by smoke and muzzle-flash, empty shell cases raining down around him. The whirling assault cannon blasted great chunks from the orkeosaurus's haunches. Another leg buckled beneath the squiggoth, the brute beast screeching in animalistic agony.

Ansgar and the other Templars ran to escape the death-throes of the fatally injured beast.

The remaining orks howled, seeing the mighty orkeosaurus bested in battle. Where the armoured fight of the Rüstung Fourth and the Armageddon Steel Legion had failed, the most devout warriors of the Adeptus Astartes had triumphed.

With a long, low guttural bellow, the squiggoth toppled forwards, toppling down onto the floor of the clearing with a ground shaking crash. Several of the surviving orks were crushed beneath the monster's bulk as it toppled onto its side, the greenskins too shocked or already too badly injured to affect an escape.

Emperor's Champion Ansgar stopped running and turned to face the dying monster.

The orkeosaurus's head flopped forwards, crushing a boulder under the weight of its mighty tusked jaw, just metres from where Brother Ansgar stood.

The monster's massive purple tongue lolled from its mouth. The mess of its innards was soaking the peaty soil of the clearing with its foul fluids. A ghastly exhalation of foetid air gusted from the collapsing lungs of the beast, flapping the skirts of the champion's robe around his armoured legs. Its furious yellow eyes closed.

Ansgar took a step forward.

The creature's eyes flicked open. The orkeosaurus opened its terrible jaws, trying to lift its head.

The hilt of his Black Sword held tightly in both hands, Ansgar flung himself bodily forwards. His servo-powered leap took him over the squiggoth's widening maw, over its snout and onto the crown of its skull.

'By the Golden Throne!' the Emperor's Champion roared as he brought the coruscating blade down. 'For Armageddon and for Solemnus!'

The tip of the Black Sword burst one of the orkeosaurus's blazing eyes and with Ansgar's full might behind it, coupled with the servo-strength of his ancestral armour, the blade sank deep into the squiggoth's brain. But it still took almost thirty seconds, with Ansgar hanging on dearly to the Black Sword as the gargantuan squiggoth lashed its head from side to side to free itself of the lancing white hot pain, for the monster to realise that it was, in fact, at last dead.

And with that, a stillness descended over the glade.

ELEVEN
AN HONOURABLE MAN

STRANGE, ALIEN CRIES and sounds unfamiliar to a hive-born ACG officer haunted the darkening forest. The jungle was as oppressive now as it had ever been. Lieutenant Nimrod Tremayne halted, holding up his right arm, laspistol in hand. 'Did you hear that?' he asked, glancing at the darkness between the trunks on either side of them.

Kurn merely grunted, as much as to say that he didn't.

Tremayne looked at him, taking in the ex-ganger's upper left arm, now bound with a bandage made from the torn sleeve of his shirt and stained a rusty red where the knife had been buried in the muscle.

They had both suffered during the scuffle on board the assault carrier. Tremayne himself had more than just a sore neck, where his collar rubbed against the abraded skin, to worry about now.

'I definitely heard something,' he hissed, almost accusingly, as if he had taken Kurn's response to mean that his bodyguard didn't believe him. 'Something other than the chirrup of insects and those damned croaking bird calls.'

The jittery lieutenant cautiously lowered his pistol and they moved off again, Tremayne still favouring his right leg. He had come off little better than Kurn during their short yet dramatic flight on board the Valkyrie. As well as the injury he had received to the small of his back, he had also jarred his right knee during the final impact, when the flyer had eventually hit the ground. The craft had thrown its passengers around – both those alive and dead – as it ploughed through the jungle undergrowth until it ground to a halt in the tangled heart of the forest.

Tremayne had been temporarily knocked unconscious. He had come to – after how long he was not certain – head down, slung over Kurn's back, the stink of the man's sweat in his nostrils, as his bodyguard carried him clear of the wreckage.

He had been minded of an old naval expression he had once heard from a flyer trainer: *Any landing you could walk away from is a good landing*. Well at least Kurn had been able to walk away from it even if he personally hadn't.

His peaked cap hid a bump on his forehead that felt as large as an egg. At least the cuts on his face, from where the exploding view-port had lacerated his flesh, had crusted over.

'Stay alert,' he commanded, wiping a grimy hand across his sweat-run brow.

He and his loyal bodyguard had survived their first day in the insane green hell of the jungle, and that was achievement enough on a world such as Armageddon. But he was not quite confident that they would survive a night so easily. They would have to find shelter, and soon. A cave would be best, or the cavernous root bole of a quoia tree; somewhere where they could make a fire with only one entrance to secure.

Neither he nor Kurn would get much sleep, but that was not what was important. What mattered was that they survived to complete the mission that had been entrusted to them. It was not going to turn out to be a simple in-and-out retrieval mission after all. It had become something much more challenging, thanks to the machinations of the traitor that had been in their very midst.

Thinking of the treacherous stormtrooper and the attempt on his life made Tremayne go over the events that had led to the crash and its aftermath for the umpteenth time that day. Truth be told, he couldn't get it out of his mind. It was a miracle that he and Kurn had survived at all.

Sometimes it was all a blur to him; at others it seemed like those violent events had all played out in slow motion.

They had been flying for just over an hour, well into the airspace over the jungle. Then the assassin had struck. Sergeant Keifer and his men had died, suddenly and violently, as .had the pilot. Kurn had struggled with the traitor, Tremayne had deployed the rear hatch, the assassin had been sucked out by the rushing wind and the flyer had gone down.

The Valkyrie had crashed through the forest canopy like an ordinatus doomsday shell, breaking branches, and Tremayne wouldn't have been surprised if it had brought down a few trees as it hurtled to ground. Shredded foliage had whipped in through the smashed windshield of the cockpit. The flyer had lost its wings, and part of its tail section, and then all that remained of it had rattled on still further through the dense jungle before grinding to a halt at last. It must have been at this point that, already winded by the crash, Tremayne had been knocked unconscious. The next thing he remembered after that was being carried to safety by the hulking Kurn.

In stupefied shock the two of them had collapsed in a bed of sponge-moss, recovering their breath and trying to make sense of the whirlwind of experiences that had assaulted them as the Valkyrie had come down. They must have remained like that for a good half hour before Tremayne had composed himself enough to evaluate the situation they now found themselves in. First they had treated their injuries as best they could. Then they had returned to the wreckage of the flyer and recovered what weapons and other useful pieces of equipment they could find.

Tremayne had recovered his laspistol, although the fine tooling of the barrel and the ivory handgrip were now terribly scuffed and chipped in places. He had also retrieved his chainsword, which had been stowed in a secure locker under his seat.

As well as his own lasgun and combat knife, Kurn had equipped himself with one of the stormtrooper's hellguns and a spare chainblade. In the rucksack he now carried on his back he had spare ammo clips and power cells, as well as a couple of det-charges. There was also what food, water rations and med-supplies they had been able to find on the Valkyrie.

Armed to the teeth, with enough rations to keep them going for several days, if necessary, and with Tremayne's wrist-chron still intact, the lieutenant and his bodyguard had all they needed to complete their mission. Once they reached the target – even if it was on foot and a few days late – they would be able to signal for a retrieval team to pick them up.

So the two of them had set off, using the position of the sun and Tremayne's chron together as a compass, to work out which direction they should be heading in. They had made their cautious way through the jungle, ever alert to orks, traps, carnivorous forest plants and scab-flies, and the like.

They were currently following a stream as it trickled through the star-bracken beds carpeting the floor of a shaded gully. The sides of the defile were steep and stony, the poga trees clinging to the edges of the pass arching over above them to form an all-enclosing roof of interlocking branches.

Tremayne looked Kurn up and down, and then took in what he could of his own appearance. How dramatically had their sudden misfortune changed them. When they had set out at dawn, Tremayne had been expecting to be back in time for luncheon and medals.

He had removed his stiff starched shirt in the sweltering heat of the jungle and torn it into strips to form bandages for his back injury, the bump on his head and Kurn's arm. He was now down to his sweat-soaked undershirt, braces and britches. His braided and buttoned jacket was tied around his waist. From his belt hung his pistol's holster and his deactivated chainsword. He would be glad of his leather boots too with the sort of terrain they were going to have to negotiate, with the sodden ground hiding stabbing thorns and poisonous biting insects.

Kurn was also down to his vest-shirt and combats. His close-cropped blond hair glistened and his face shone with sweat. But where the lieutenant was thin and wiry, Kurn's sleeveless shirt merely emphasised his massive physique even more – the bulging biceps, the clearly defined pectoral muscles, his thick neck. He was also a good head taller than the lieutenant, standing in his high-laced combat boots. He had smeared his face and arms with green mud, Tremayne assumed for camouflage purposes, but it made him look even less human and more like an ogryn.

They were both soaked to the skin with sweat in the humid atmosphere, and were making fast work of their water rations simply to keep themselves suitably hydrated.

They moved off again but hadn't even reached the foot of the gully when Tremayne froze.

'There,' he hissed back at his bodyguard. 'I definitely heard something then.'

The lieutenant suddenly realised how exposed the two of them were in the bottom of the gully. Jungle fighting wasn't what he was used to. He had honed his combat skills in the derelict domes of Volcanus Hive, as had Kurn. They were street fighters, not Catachan deathworld veterans.

Tremayne's sharp mind processed quickly. The close-packed trees above and ahead of them, and the winding paths between, were not so different from the crumbling streets of a battle-wrought hive. So surely the rules of engagement out here weren't so different either.

'On my mark, we sprint for the end of the gully. You give covering fire behind. If we get pinned down,' he scanned the boulder-strewn defile, 'take cover behind that outcrop.' He pointed quickly with the barrel of his laspistol, clicking the safety off as he did so.

Then they both heard it: the crack of a dry twig snapping underfoot.

'Run!' Tremayne hissed.

The two men, ACG officer and indentured trooper, sprinted for the end of the gully, Tremayne ignoring the sharp pain in his knee. There was a commotion in the trees at the top of the bank to their left and solid slug fire whickered along the trench of the gully after them. The greenskins had found their target.

The first of the feral orks burst from between the trees in front of Tremayne, howling in insane glee, a monstrous machete held in the meaty paw of its right hand. While the greenskin was still in the air Tremayne fired his laspistol, the zinging high-powered shot hitting the creature in the arm. The ork hit the ground, howling in pain, and dropped the machete. The lieutenant took aim again. There was the roar of an autogun opening up behind him and the ork fell, arms flailing, as solid shot rounds opened up its chest in a spray of alien blood.

But it was only the first. The forest seemed to explode around them as green-skinned bodies, covered in garish blue war paint and clad in a curious assortment of furs, ammo-belts and armour-plate, launched themselves from the top of the defile at the two lone wanderers.

Only two metres from the rocky outcrop that formed a buttress-like shield across the bottom of the gully, Tremayne leapt for cover. He flung himself sideways, around the edge of the rock, grazing his knees as he landed. A second later, with gunfire spitting stone chips from the ridge of the outcrop, the hulking Kurn landed next to him.

The Emperor must have been smiling upon them that day, for not a single one of the rattling shots found its mark in their flesh.

Tremayne looked at his bodyguard. Kurn grunted. The lieutenant did not need to give the order. Crouched behind the rocky barrier, guns in hand, the two men peered over the stone parapet and began shooting; he with his laspistol and Kurn with both his autogun and the scavenged hellgun. Only half the orks running towards them down the gully actually appeared to be armed with anything other than hand-axes and spiked clubs – not the most effective long-range weaponry. Their heads were bare, or adorned with feathered head-dresses, or battered helmets, or even hollow animal skulls. Bones and bamboo canes tied to their jerkins and harnesses rattled as the tribal orks loped towards the Imperials' position, barking and hooting like jungle primates.

The laspistol whined, winging a bounding greenskin that tumbled head-over-heels into a clinging bed of mosses. The autogun coughed twice and an ork fell, the top of its skull exploded by the solid shot cartridges. The hellgun spat and another brute dropped, a smoking, cauterised hole blasted through its open mouth.

Gunfire rattled and zinged back at them. Tremayne and Kurn ducked down behind the outcrop. The lieutenant had counted twelve ferals still closing on their position: going by his and Kurn's current hit rate that shouldn't cause them too many problems. They would be able to deal with all of the tribal orks before time ran out for them.

Then the blood in Tremayne's veins froze, despite the desperate heat, and his pounding heart skipped a beat as he heard the sound of feet running up the defile from behind them.

He snapped his head round and a split second later his laspistol followed. All those hours of target practice in the shooting range were paying off now. Tremayne had won numerous competitions for marksmanship run between the regiments of the ACG. But for every trophy or medal he had won back in the barracks of Volcanus Hive, each kill shot he made now was worth a dozen of the worthless, gilded trinkets.

A mob of war-painted feral orks – made up of another six hostiles – was pelting towards the outcrop from the bottom of the gully. Their position had been compromised. Suddenly the odds didn't seem so favourable.

Kurn was aware of this new threat too. Dropping his autogun, he unslung the pack from his back, still firing back up the pass with the stormtrooper hellgun held in his right hand. His intention was plain: he was going to try something more drastic to even the odds again, by eliminating one of the ravening mobs altogether.

Tremayne focused his fire on the new arrivals, but things weren't going so well for the Imperial agents now. With only one gun trained on the first mob, those orks were almost on top of them and were in danger of taking the outcrop. Then first one las-shot and then another rebounded from the shoulder armour of another feral – ceramite shoulder pads that looked like they had been scavenged from more than just dead Imperial Guardsmen, the black and white curved plates soaking up the damage.

They were surrounded and outnumbered, and at any second it would all be over.

The sound of discharging weapons echoed from the walls of the defile; only Tremayne was still alive, and so was Kurn. The weapons fired again and now Tremayne realised that the staccato rattle of the throaty ork weapons was being echoed by the *crack* and *zip* of lasguns and the higher pitched chugging fire of shotguns. There was the *whoomph* of a melta-gun firing. There was even the animal roar of what sounded like an autocannon opening up at the head of the gully.

Tremayne heard a distinct *choom!* A second later an ork bearing down on him with a nocked cleaver raised above its head disappeared in an explosion of dirty smoke and stony soil, as if it had trodden on a land mine.

As another ork fell, one arm torn from its body by a hail of autocannon fire, the lieutenant dared a glance over the top of the outcrop.

Striding down the gully behind the orks were human soldiers – obviously Guardsmen, obviously jungle fighters – keeping a clear order of deployment. Tremayne could see more of them positioned in the trees at the edge of the defile. The men had turned the tables on the orks, trapping them in the gully.

Hearing the rapid *zip-crack* of las-weapons again, this time from the bottom of the pass, Tremayne saw yet more of the troopers advancing towards them. Tremayne made a swift head count. There were thirteen or fourteen at least, perhaps more.

Now it was the feral ork mob that was outnumbered, outgunned and outmanoeuvred. Their hoots of excitement and battle revelry turned to barks of panic and despair. The greenskins were falling to the implacable assault of the Guardsmen – ork hunters, Tremayne realised. Encouraged by their abrupt appearance and example, he returned to blasting the orks.

Another grenade hurled an ork, wearing a horned skull, back down the gully. A chainsword, wielded with no little skill by a grizzled, scarred, unhandsome man, with close-cropped greying hair, eviscerated an ork. Kurn's hellgun blasted a hole in the side of a greenskin and took its gun-arm off at the elbow.

One of the ferals hurled its axe at a brute of man, who looked not unlike an ork himself, thanks in part to the necklace of teeth around his thick neck. The brute actually caught the axe-cleaver, snatching it out of the air with a meaty paw. Then in four strides he was on top of his attacker, the autocannon slung from his shoulders quiet for a moment, and returned the axe, taking the greenskin's head off with it.

There was a sharp cry as a stray ork bullet hit one of the hunters in the leg. The dark-haired man went down, clutching the bloody mess of his calf, screaming through clenched teeth at the pain. Tremayne saw a cloaked figure, half hidden by the trees at the top of the gully, return fire with what looked like a primitive, black powder rifle. But the rifle's appearance belied its deadliness and he was startled when a pulse of charged energy tore from the muzzle of the gun, streaking down the side of the defile in a blaze of brilliant blue-white light and caving in the ork sniper's thick skull with its powerful punch.

As abruptly as it had started, the clamour of battle ceased. The orks were all dead.

The grizzled veteran made his way down to where Tremayne was still hunkered behind the rocky protrusion along with the sweating Kurn. The lieutenant rose to his feet, dusting himself down as best he could, despite his dishevelled appearance, and then straightened, as if about to throw a parade ground salute.

'You're ACG, aren't you?' the man asked roughly.

'Lieutenant Nimrod Tremayne of the Armageddon Command Guard, actually,' he replied sharply. 'And you are?'

'We're the ones who have just saved your arses.'

'WHAT DID YOU say?' Sergeant Borysko stared at the lieutenant in disbelief.

The man had a hawkish, raptor-like quality. Here was a man, thought Borysko, who wouldn't let anything stop him catching his prey, and who would never give up before he had done so. The presence of his ogryn-like bodyguard would help see to that.

The sergeant was minded of the infamous quote attributed to General Krylus at the liberation of Quixote IX, and borrowed by a hundred commanders since: *I don't know what the enemy will make of him, but he scares the hell out of me.* If Lieutenant Tremayne was on your side, you had a loyal officer for life. But if he was against you?

The stink and smoke of cooking ork corpses wafted up the defile to where Borysko and the lieutenant were arguing. The hunters had collected the bodies of the greenskins at the bottom of the gully and Yeydl had ignited the bonfire with a heat pulse from his meltagun.

'I said it is imperative that I complete my mission. It is a matter of global security. And I would appreciate it if you would address me as "Sir", sergeant.'

'My orders – sir – are to take you back to Cerbera for pick up by your colleagues, lieutenant.'

'Then I am countermanding that order, sergeant,' said the lieutenant, 'and I think you'll find I out-rank you.'

'Not out here, you don't,' sneered Raus.

'Shut it, Weasel!' Borysko snapped.

If there was one thing that Borysko most definitely was – even if his superiors back at Cerbera Base had trouble believing it – it was fiercely loyal, to Armageddon and to the structure of command, even if he might speak disrespectfully about it. If a superior officer gave him an order, even if he needed a little persuading, in the end he would ultimately do what he was told.

He was a xenos hunter and yet tolerated having an alien kroot along as part of his team, because he had been ordered to do so. Compared to that, relinquishing one set of orders in favour of those given him by Lieutenant Tremayne was nothing.

And besides, he had to admit a grudging respect for the ACG bigwig. The lieutenant was a ruthless man, but then he had needed to be to survive even one hour out in the Green, let alone a day as he had.

'So what is this mission of yours that's going to make such a difference to the whole stinking war for the planet?'

'You are to accompany me to the location of a lost research base of the Adeptus Mechanicus Xenos-Genetor sub-cult.'

'A research base? Out here?'

'That is what I said.'

'I thought I'd heard of all the bases our side had out in the Green.'

The lieutenant sighed with impatience. 'Obviously not this one.'

'And why do you need to go there?'

'That is on a need to know basis, sergeant.'

'And, let me guess, I don't need to know.'

'No. You don't.'

But Borysko still wasn't comfortable being challenged by some hive-born politico. 'And if I refuse, sir?'

'You won't refuse. You are an officer of the ork hunters' regiment, one of the most loyal of all the forces defending our home world from the greenskin menace, and, as a result, I believe you are an honourable man. You won't go against the orders of a superior officer.'

Damn him to the Fire Wastes and back, thought Borysko. How dare this man use that one against him? Yes, he was an honourable man, but how dare the lieutenant play that card on him!

Borysko scanned the faces of his boys gathered round him. He saw the weariness in their eyes, the disappointment, the fatigue, the desire – indeed, the desperation – to be on their way back to the familiar surroundings of Cerbera.

The moment he made his decision he knew what he was letting them all in for. 'So which way are we headed?'

Lieutenant Tremayne, half his face a mess of fresh scars, fixed Borysko with his bird of prey gaze. 'South-west.'

Borysko cast his eyes to the ground, rubbing his temples with calloused fingers. The smell of the ork bonfire caught in the back of his throat like bile.

'I'm going to have to call this in. Marshal Vine will need to–'

'No. You're not going to call this in.'

'But it's protocol.'

'Protocol be damned. I'm the one giving the orders now. This is a shadow operation. There will be no comm-traffic to Cerbera Base.'

Borysko raised his eyes to the canopy, exhaling loudly in irritation.

'Klim, patch me through to Cerbera,' he said wearily.

'Message received and understood.' The platoon's vox-trooper eased the precious vox-caster and its harness off his back, pulling his arms out of its harness straps, and set it down on the ground. Crouching next to it, he began flicking switches and fiddling with knurled dials.

There was the sudden fizz and subsequent bang of a las-bolt exploding the caster.

Borysko turned to Lieutenant Tremayne with genuine shock written all over his face, his mouth agape. He saw the aimed laspistol gripped tightly in the officer's right hand. The sergeant's brow furrowed and hatred burned in his eyes.

'You idiot! What in the name of this green hell did you do that for?' It was the usually taciturn Klim who had exploded in anger at the lieutenant.

Borysko held out a cautioning hand to the fuming vox-trooper. 'Message received and understood, trooper,' he cautioned. 'Message received and understood.'

'My mission, the mission I have just seconded you for, is top secret. I would like it to remain that way.'

Borysko stared at the smoking vox-caster. 'My men and I just saved you from certain death,' Borysko snarled, 'and all we get is a "Here are your new orders" spiel and the "You're coming with me" routine.'

'I'm sorry, sergeant. Thank you for saving my life and that of my bodyguard,' the lieutenant said, tilting his head in deference to the ork hunter. 'Now, as you would say, can we get a frikkin' move on?'

THE HUNTERS MOVED off, the mark and his bodyguard going with them.

He watched them go, hidden by the quoias, as they set off down the defile, the alien – the birdman – bringing up the rear of the column now, until the jungle swallowed them again.

He waited, controlling his breathing, listening to the buzz and chirrup of the local wildlife.

Night was coming, and with it a whole new facet of the forest came to life.

Then, having checked the charge on his weapon, he too left the shelter of the treeline, no more than a swiftly darting shadow in the dusky gloom of the forest.

Ignoring the stabbing pains in his back, the lacerations on his legs and the aching bruises of his shoulders, he followed after them, scampering down the defile, past the smouldering ork pyre, and back into the clinging, foetid jungle. After his mark.

After his prey.

TWELVE
DOOMSAYER

KILL-TEAM WOLFRAM paused at the lip of the rocky escarpment, auto-senses compensating for the sudden increase in light levels. Having been able to see no further than a few hundred metres at most through the green gloom of the jungle, suddenly the Templars were looking out over a vista that stretched for a hundred kilometres to the horizon in the harsh glare of the planet's sun.

The stink of the jungle was on them now. Wolfram felt that after a day hacking their way through the sticky forests they were truly of the jungle now. As a consequence of their battle with the orkeosaurus, and a day and night of trudging first through the swamplands of the Plague Marshes and then chopping their way through the dense swathes of creeper-clung rainforest, the Templars' black and white power armour was sticky with sap, wet with condensation and caked with still-wet mud.

It saddened the Chaplain to see the ancient ancestral suits, handed down over the centuries from one generation of warrior to the next, looking like this. He would not be happy until they could return to the fleet in orbit and see to the upkeep of their armour, washing them clean and seeing to any other repairs as necessary. The intricately tooled Armour of Faith worn by the Emperor's Champion, with the sculpted iron laurel wreath of its helmet and the aquila wings on the chestplate pinioned around a memento mori skull bearing the cross of the Chapter, was as soiled as any other, but in the case of Brother Ansgar the sight was even more painful to the old priest. Such feelings served to fuel his continually smouldering hatred of their alien enemy: that the foul xenos savages had caused them to sink so low and do this to themselves.

The morning light was steadily crawling across this hemisphere of the planet as it spun in its lazy orbit of the system's star. At its golden touch the endless swathes of rainforest were transformed from a misty blue, through a brazen tinged turquoise, to a lush iridescent palette of emerald, jade and verdigris.

The Templars had walked on through the night, always on the lookout for ork traps, the greenskins that had set them, and the notoriously deadly flora and fauna native to the planet. The combination of the Space Marines' biologically enhanced eyesight and the auto-senses of their power armour meant that they were hardly disadvantaged by any lack of light. If need be, their eyes alone could see well enough to know where they were in almost total darkness.

They also didn't need sleep, at least not as a trooper of the Imperial Guard would understand it. It was another trait inherited from their primarch Rogal Dorn, bequeathed them by their genetically manipulated heritage. The Marines could consciously switch off one half of their brains at a time, passing all autonomic functions and reactions to one hemisphere.

Such incredible genetic manipulation was beyond the genetor-magi of the Adeptus Mechanicus, the medicae of the Imperium or even the Apothecaries of the Astartes Chapters. Such superhuman medical accomplishments now seemed so incredible and unfeasible as to be like magic.

Chaplain Wolfram had called a halt during the watches of the night for a brief moment's prayer in recognition of vespers and compline. The Black Templar crusaders were in the middle of a holy mission and it was worth asking the Emperor for His continued vigilance and guidance at such a time. The Chaplain's chanted litanies were accompanied by the choirs that sang their own haunting plainsong in the jungle night: curious trills and shrill whistles underscored with the ever-present clicks and hums of insect life.

On those two occasions, the battle brothers had formed into a circle and knelt on one knee – apart from Brother Jarold – resting their hands on their weapons. They bowed their heads as Wolfram led them in their prayers, the dreadnought keeping his monitoring auspex arrays alert for unwelcome guests or any other signs of danger. They had put their faith in the visions that the Emperor had sent to his champion Ansgar and it paid to keep their minds focused and open to His word, should He deign to speak to them through waking vision-dreams again.

But, that said, there was one thing troubling the wise old Chaplain.

There was no doubt that Ansgar had been marked out by the Emperor. Wolfram had seen Ansgar, clad in the Armour of Faith and wielding the Black Sword, in his own dreams, even before the battle-brother had come before Wolfram and Udo on the eve of Fighting Company Adlar's first planetfall mission to Armageddon. Neither was there any doubt that the visions Ansgar had been given that night had been true, for they had led the Black Templars to victory against Morkrull Grimskar and the orks of the Blood Scar tribe. And hitherto, as far as Wolfram could tell, Ansgar's more recent visions were showing them the true path that their new divinely inspired mission should take.

But there was one aspect of the visions that concerned him and, if he admitted it, that one aspect troubled Wolfram deeply. It was the way in which the visions devolved into the madness and anarchy of Chaos.

As the Chaplain understood it, from Ansgar's recounting of what he had seen when keeping prayerful vigil in his cell aboard the *Divine Fury*, everything was clear up until the gathering of the fell storm above the very jungles they were now penetrating.

It was not like Wolfram to question his faith, but one small part of him couldn't help but wonder if these visions Ansgar was now receiving were really coming from the Master of Mankind. Was it possible they had their origin from somewhere darker, perhaps even within the warp?

First there was the way in which the visions relapsed into insanity – the meaning of the revelations becoming more indistinct and unfathomable – and Ansgar's apparent experiencing of his own death. The start of their mission was clear in His champion's vision, but there was no clear conclusion to their quest, at least not as far as Ansgar had seen.

And then, of more immediate import, there was the seizure Ansgar had suffered during the kill-team's battle with the rogue orkeosaurus, just when the battle had been swinging the orks' way and when Ansgar had been in the ideal position to shift the balance back in the Templars' favour.

At that moment, for no discernable reason and without any warning precursors, Ansgar had been struck down. One moment the Emperor's Champion had been standing tall and proud, facing off against the gargantuan squiggoth like some epic hero from the mythical days of the founding of the Imperium. The next moment he had thrown his arms out to the sides and toppled backwards. In no time at all he had gone from being on the verge of felling the terrible beast, to being seconds away from death, crushed beneath one of the monster's massive hoofs. Apothecary Bliant had put his own life in jeopardy to haul Ansgar out of the path of danger. At that moment Ansgar had not seemed so much the champion.

Then the Emperor's Champion had recovered himself and *did* fulfil the vocation to which he had been called, bringing down a monster that had even threatened the mighty Brother Jarold, with a final, fatal blow from his crackling Black Sword.

With the orkeosaurus and its crew dead, and with the Marines' own injuries having been tended to, the kill-team had scoured the clearing for signs of Fighting Company Gerhard's passing. It was clear to all that this was not the place where the vaunted castellan's company had made their last stand, even though it was the place from which they had successfully communicated their position to the fleet for the last time.

As a consequence, Koldo's auspex was of little use to them directly now, in terms of helping find the lost company. Koldo had been using the augury device to lead them to the coordinates of that last crucial transmission. The way ahead was a mystery to them now. They could pray for guidance and trust in the visions of the Emperor's Champion. But for the time being they were also going to have to rely on the skills of the scout, as taught to the warriors of the Chapter during the endless hours of training and indoctrination they endured on board the ships of the fleet, and honed during the long days, weeks and months spent traversing the Empyrean.

It had been Brother Huarwar who had chanced upon the days-old footprints in the mulch and mud at the westerly edge of the clearing, where a stream coursed its way down a boulder-strewn slope into the gloom of the trees beyond. The marks had been almost lost to them thanks to their encounter with the squiggoth. During the battle the Marines and orks, but more particularly the gargantuan orkeosaurus itself, had trampled the glade clear of the evidence that the kill-team required to show them the way forward.

Ansgar had seen the battle for the Plague Marshes and the rising of some dread storm at the heart of darkness, but how one was connected to the other had not been revealed to him. And Wolfram knew that another part of the visions would be preoccupying Ansgar's thoughts more than any other: the rise of Chaos and his own demise. But how could the warping hand of Chaos have a part to play in the greenskins' invasion of Armageddon?

And it was herein that the Chaplain faced a new and unsettling dilemma. Trust in the visions as the word of the Emperor or be beguiled by the insidious confoundings of Chaos.

The Emperor's Champion had confided in his confessor, revealing what he had seen at that terrible, crippling moment in the battle, as the Marines continued their slow but steady advance through the jungle, Brother Jarold taking the lead. He had told Wolfram of the crater, the blasphemous henge of stones, the appearance of the warp gate – everything.

And now, here they were, a day and a night into the equatorial rainforests, with Brother Ansgar standing apart from the rest of the group, as though distracted, absorbed in a world of his own troubled thoughts.

'Brothers,' Wolfram said, addressing the Templar party, 'we will rest here a while. Let us spend a moment in prayer, that the Emperor or the primarch might look upon our venture and confirm the rightness of our onward path.'

It was an excuse: there were still discernable signs that Company Gerhard had passed this way, and there could be no mistaking the intrusions of the Astartes with the unruly passage of greenskins. Not that Chaplain Wolfram did not believe the Emperor and Rogal Dorn would grant them the guidance they needed, when they needed it. It was just that before he committed his kill-team to travelling any further on this path, to who knew what, he wished to speak to the Emperor's chosen one again.

As the other Templars enjoyed a few minutes' rest from their relentless march – slowed by the difficult, overgrown terrain and made even more protracted by the slow-striding Brother Jarold – the kill-team's leader and spiritual inspiration crossed the bare rock of the outcrop to stand at Ansgar's side, looking out over the interminable jungle.

'Brother, you appear troubled,' Wolfram said. 'What vexes you?'

Ansgar sighed heavily. It was a sigh full of the guilt and anxiety and doubt that Wolfram had feared.

'It is the visions you have witnessed, is it not?'

Ansgar turned to look at his confessor. His face was lined with worry.

Wolfram had become so used to seeing Ansgar as the Emperor's Champion, his face hidden by the helm of the Armour of Faith, that he was still not used to his new appearance. Since being singled out as the channel of the Emperor's divine will, Ansgar had taken on an even more penitent attitude. Part of this attitude of contrition manifested in the way in which he had shaved his head after the destruction of the gargant factory.

And it had only been after that same battle, when what remained of Fighting Company Adlar had returned to the *Divine Fury* in orbit over the war-torn planet, with Apothecary Bliant examining the battle-brothers to assess the level of their injuries and the subsequent medicae care they would need to make a complete recovery, that Ansgar had made another shocking revelation. During his titanic clash with Morkrull Grimskar, Ansgar had suffered a grievous blow from the warboss's power claw that fractured the visor plate of his helm and cost him his right eye. The scar tissue around the newly implanted augmetic was still pink and tender-looking.

The Chaplain's devotional death mask – the ominous memento mori skull – looked back at Ansgar dispassionately.

'Pray for me, father,' he said, using the Chaplain's formal honorific. In spite of the deep, basso timbre of his voice, Ansgar still sounded like an anxious child.

'Pray for you, my son? But I always pray for those whose spiritual well-being is entrusted to my care,' Wolfram replied. 'What would we be without the power of prayer and the divine guidance of the Emperor?'

Suddenly Ansgar was down on his knees before the Chaplain. 'Pray that these doubts might be taken from my mind. Pray that I might be focused fully once again on the mission He has in mind for us.' Ansgar paused, bowing his head. 'Father, pray for the absolution of my soul.'

'It is not for a Templar to have doubts,' Wolfram said, his tone reproachful. 'Our faith is our shield. Without it, we are nothing.'

'I know that, father. I know that better than most. And my faith is sure.' Ansgar looked up again into the faceted crystal eyes of the Chaplain's skull-helm. 'So why am I beset by visions of this world all gone to some daemon-spawned hell?'

'There is no question that in the past these visions of yours have led our noble crusade to victory over our detestable foe. And these most recent visions came to you first when you were aboard the *Divine Fury*, in watchful prayer. There is no reason to believe that these are any different to those granted you before our last glorious campaign.'

'But since setting foot on this world again I have seen nothing but an ignominious end to our venture, amidst the triumph of the fell forces of Chaos. And never before have I suffered such crippling visions when the Emperor, and my battle brothers, have need of me most. That fact troubles me more than any other, father.'

Silence hung in the air between Chaplain and champion, priest and penitent. It was this same fact that had troubled Wolfram as much as the details of Ansgar's ill timed, crippling vision.

'What does it mean?' Ansgar looked up imploringly into the death's head face of the Chaplain. His eyes – both organic and augmetic – traced the fine detailing of Wolfram's ornate, devotional armour, the repeated pattern of carved skulls on the trim of his shoulder pads, the embossed wax stamps of his purity seals and the careful embroidery of his monkish habit.

He looked like such a tragic figure, kneeling on the bare rock of the escarpment before the Chaplain, the harsh morning light reflecting dazzlingly from the white painted portions of his armour's shoulder pads, and illumining the passages of devotional scripture in letters of golden fire.

'We must trust that its meaning will become clear when we have brought the Emperor's divine retribution down upon His enemies with cleansing fire and righteous zeal,' Wolfram said, taking hold of the rosarius, hanging on its chain about his neck, in one gauntleted hand.

'Then what must I do to atone for my lack of faith?'

'You must trust in the Emperor. It is all any of us can do. For without faith we are nothing, even we battle-brothers of the mighty Adeptus Astartes. But with faith we shall conquer the galaxy in His most glorious name.'

With his other hand, Wolfram held out the tip of his crozius arcanum towards Ansgar. The Emperor's Champion closed his eyes and put his lips to the Chaplain's holy staff of office. Making the sign of the Templar cross over his breastplate, he whispered a prayer of heartfelt contrition to the Emperor.

'We shall show our enemies no pity,' Wolfram intoned.

'We shall show no fear in the face of whatever perils may be set before us,' Ansgar vowed.

'And we shall show no remorse when we have persecuted our crusade to its bitter end, no matter what it might cost us, or what sacrifices we have to make, in His glorious name.'

'In His glorious name.'

'For the Emperor, for the primarch and for Sigismund,' they both chanted together.

'Brothers, gather round,' Chaplain Wolfram commanded as Brother Ansgar rose to his feet once more and replaced his helmet. 'Before we continue on our divinely-inspired quest, let us renew the oaths we made when we first set ourselves upon this holy quest.'

THE BLACK TEMPLARS made slow progress through the jungle. Firstly they had to keep checking that the path they were following was still correct. In the last few days, since the confirmed disappearance of Fighting Company Gerhard, torrential downpours had continued to wrack the rainforest. Heavy rains could change the very shape of the landscape, reshaping the terrain with devastating mudslides and causing rivers to break their banks and describe new courses through the sodden jungles. It could only have been thanks to the guiding hand of the Emperor that there were still tracks left by the passing of their battle-brethren for them to follow.

And then there was Brother Jarold.

None of the Marines would wish the veteran gone from among their number, not for one moment, but, as had already been noted aboard the battle-barge *Divine Fury*, it was not usual for a dreadnought to join a kill-team mission; such missions usually being marked out by their stealth and swift execution.

The Templars could not have done without him in their encounter with the orkeosaurus, or earlier in the battle for the Plague Marshes. But there was no denying that the dreadnought was slowing them down. And there was an element to this mission where speed could be a crucial factor. The longer they were in hunting down their missing brethren and their precious gene-seed, the more likely it was that their mission would prove to have been futile. If they took too long, even if they did recover the gene-seed, the narthecium could keep the progenoid glands stored within it healthy and in a usable condition for only so long. And if the stasis vessel had been damaged, for proportionally less time.

And then a new threat arose to test the already slow progress of Kill-team Wolfram.

As the Templars' second day in the interminable jungles wore on, rain-heavy grey clouds rolled across the firmament over the dripping jungles and the skies darkened. By noon, it was as dark as at dusk and the first, heavy drops of rain had begun to fall. But this was as nothing to what awaited them, deeper into the jungle realm.

After a further two hours, the downpour had passed, leaving the jungle that enclosed the Marines once again within its deadly verdant clutches, smelling strongly of damp rot, leaf mould and wet soil. Long, red-bodied centipedes, as big as Catachan vipers, scuttled through the bark and leaf mulch that their feet sank into with every step, while clouds of dazzlingly patterned butterflies came to rest at the lip of strikingly coloured jungle orchids, lapping at the runny nectar held within, with unrolling, whip-like tubular tongues.

With the passing of the sudden deluge there came a change in the atmosphere of the jungle. Red lightning crackled across the underside of the darkly massing, monsoon clouds away to the west. West – that was the direction in which their objective lay.

'It looks like a rad-storm is blowing up ahead of us, at the heart of the jungle,' Ansgar said. 'Like that meteorological beast we narrowly avoided in the toxic wastes out beyond the defensive guns of

Clain's Stronghold. But how could there be such a thing, out here, over the equatorial rainforests?' he wondered.

The radiation storms of Armageddon were the result of millennia of unchecked industrial pollution on a planet-wide scale and several ecology-devastating wars. Ansgar had understood that for the most part, rad-storms were restricted to the polluted wastes of Armageddon Prime and Secundus.

'That is no radiation storm,' Chaplain Wolfram said darkly. 'Can you not feel it? That sensation of sickness in the air?'

Ansgar *could* feel it. He had endured such feelings before, but it had not been in the presence of the crusade's ork enemies.

He had felt it at the Gate of Duranon on the relic-world of Kazalus. He had felt it at the defence of the Shrine of the Immortal Emperor on Macaris Tertius. And he had felt it on board the *Red Slaughter*, as Marshal Brant's Black Templars had pursued their own boarding action against the Carnage-class cruiser.

It was the revulsion felt when confronted by the repulsive, insidious presence of Chaos.

And then all the doubts and fears came flooding back, and his mind was dragged back to the traumatic visions he had suffered at the height of the kill-team's battle with the rogue ork battle-beast.

…Standing at the lip of the crater, on every side the unnervingly quiet jungle become twisted, withered trunks… The wind howling like a ravenous beast, tearing the forest apart… The ring of stones, jagged-tipped menhirs raking the sky with their gore-clogged talons…

Leering daemon faces hungry for blood... The profane monuments crackling with the sick, purple luminescence of the warp-magick... Thunderheads, stained the rusted colour of blood, swelling and boiling overhead... The air thick with the malign sickness of the warp... The death-drum roll of thunder, like the hammering of desecrated weapons against fused and corrupted armour... the birthing of the hell-storm... Black lighting lashing the stones, abattoir-blood falling from the sundered sky like scarlet rain... The rent in reality and all the horrors of the warp unleashed upon the world...

'It is just as I experienced it in my vision: the words you spoke, everything,' Ansgar gasped, as though taken aback by the veracity of his own visions. There was still that element of doubt, which had to be overcome, one way or another, or it might spell the end of them all.

His battle brothers turned to regard the stupefied champion, their obvious unease apparent. Several made their own supplications to Sigismund, their primarch and the Master of Mankind, touching the holy icons of their battle-suits as they did so.

'Then we must be watchful,' Chaplain Wolfram warned them all, 'for the Emperor knows what is afoot here. He prepared us to be the instruments of his divine judgement and bring his wrathful retribution down upon those that would profane this sacred world, no matter what their origin or intent.'

And then the doubts were gone, the fears, even the guilt Ansgar had felt at confessing his chaotic visions to the Chaplain. Now he knew that what he had seen – no matter how terrible – was the truth. The Emperor had sent them a warning of the dangers to come. There would be greater dangers to face yet. This was the mission for which they had really been chosen. And now they would be prepared for it. The fell hand of Chaos was at work on Armageddon, under cover of the Great Beast's invasion. And when the time came, the Emperor's Champion and his devout brethren would not be found wanting.

URGLUK GURLAG LOOKED up from his work, finding the bonesaw missing from the metal gurney next to the operating slab. The painboss snorted angrily, then barked something into the gloom at the corner of the underground room. The walls were crumbling rockrete, the plaster hanging from them in broken sheets like the flayed albino hide of some leviathan creature.

A much smaller greenskin scampered out of the shadows. It was wearing a filthy surgical gown, which touched the floor at its feet, and a facemask, which did nothing to hide its large, hooked nose and pointed bat-like ears. In its hands it was holding an appliance that looked not unlike a large pair of pliers. The painboss snatched the instrument from his reluctant assistant and then hurled it at the creature, which shrieked in fear. The pliers flew over the gretchin's head. The creature remained transfixed, quaking on the spot, rubbing its hands nervously on the filthy skirt of its apron.

The painboss said something to the runt in obvious annoyance. The ork said something else in the base alien tongue of its kind and, as the grot orderly turned to depart, gave it a vicious kick with one ironshod foot. The gretchin fled into the fitful darkness yelping in pain.

In the flickering light of the temperamental glow-globes, Urgluk looked down at the massive, prone form in front of him. The wan sodium light revealed the green and red stains discolouring the surgical table and the wet detritus and oil leaks covering the floor around it, evidence of the great work that was taking place here.

The painboss's own body was mostly a self-customised mechanical rebuild, but it was as nothing compared to the hulk harnessed to the steel table in front of him now. It was at least twice a good head taller than Urgluk and as broad across its heavily augmented shoulders as a dray-squig.

The warboss had been a mess when Urgluk had brought him to his hidden den within the foetid jungles of the planet. It had not been built by the orks, merely taken over. The former masters of this place had been the first to experience the unique benefits of the painboss's initial 'eksperiments', although none of them had survived the process. The humans were pathetically weak and had a tendency to break far too easily, not like the rough and resilient boyz of his own kind.

But now it was the warboss who was enjoying the attentions of the most notorious and celebrated painboss active amongst the massed tribes of Ghazghkull Thraka's invasion of the human world. It was not his fault that his biological and technological advances were not understood or appreciated by the majority of tribes operating on Armageddon at that time.

Not that it mattered. He was a dok of such renown that he had gathered his own retinue around him. His gretchin slaves were a continual aggravation to him, but a necessary evil to the successful execution of his work. It was his bodyguard, which he had quite literally built up around him, of which he was most proud. The cyborks in particular, with their unique upgrades, were his greatest achievement so far.

And Urgluk had done an incredible job with the warboss, even if he did say so himself. His patient had been virtually dead when the painboss had recovered his body, and would have died at the hands of any other mad dok. But Urgluk had repaired the ork's savagely broken and burnt body with the pieces of armour his cyborks had recovered from the jungles beyond his hideaway.

Even after his ministrations, the stark black and white patterns could still be seen upon the scuffed ceramite. They were war-badges that Urgluk had seen on this world before, and it amused him that they were now being used to help raise the warboss from the dead. The irony had not escaped the brutal ork dok. The augmetics that had been salvaged from the same source certainly seemed more reliable than those he had previously been able to utilise in his renovations, even if it did take some clobbering to get them to work with the more conventional pieces of ork technology that still made up the majority of his patient's reconstructed body.

For the time being the warboss was still unconscious, Urgluk having not yet re-activated the part organic and part newly improved 'mekanical' brain. The painboss would not make that final connection until he was ready. And when that time came, with a pet warboss under his control, Urgluk would gain all the power and influence his greedy alien mind could hope for. When Armageddon felt at last to the green-skins, as it so surely would, he would be recognised at last as the greatest of his kind and even the dread war-lord Ghazghkull Mag Urk Thraka would seek him out to work his wonders on the overlord's already mighty frame. Then he would have all the subjects he could hope for to 'eksperiment' on to his heart's content.

THIRTEEN
TARGET TREMAYNE

'HERE, RUB THIS on your skin,' Kole said, passing Lieutenant Tremayne a round, purple fruit he had just picked from a drooping branch. The exposed flesh of its interior was a pinky-yellow and oozing with small, hard seeds. Kole couldn't help smiling to see how the ACG officer wrinkled his nose and gagged at the foul stench of the sackran.

'It smells disgusting,' Tremayne managed whilst trying not to retch.

'Yeah, but it will keep the stab-flies and mosquitoes away,' Hawkeye Gunderson threw in.

'Keeps everything away,' Vanderkamp added.

'"cept orks,' Ferze said.

'Yeah, only thing that smells worse than a sackran – apart from Coburg – is a greenskin,' Geist laughed mirthlessly.

245

Tremayne began apprehensively rubbing the cut half of the fruit over his bare arms. Some of the juice dripped onto his sleeveless undershirt, but it made little difference; what had once been white was now at best stained a filthy brown.

'Better that you stink like an ork than you attract the attentions of some of the Green's less friendly denizens,' Kasarta said.

'Yeah,' Raus butted in. 'There's all sorts of things out here that'll kill you and eat you soon as look at you,' he said in delight. 'And I don't just mean critters like the cisorfish or tree-scorpions.'

'Not all of them wait until you're dead to do it either,' Vanderkamp added as they negotiated the barely buried root system of a quoia tree. 'The brain fluke – that's a nasty one.'

'Did I ever tell you I knew a fella who got a brain fluke?' Ferze said, the morose trooper uncharacteristically cheerful all of a sudden. 'The medicae thought he got it from falling in a mosquito breeding pool. Got in through his nose probably and then ate its way into his frontal lobe. Poor bastard went mad and ate his own feet before it finally killed him.'

'Really?' the Kid asked, horror and morbid fascination written large on his innocent face.

'Death was a mercy, when it came,' Ferze added with a wistful look in his eyes.

'The liverworm's one nasty little frikker too,' Tannhauser said through a mouthful of ration bar.

'And the tsetsu-fly. They're practically all carriers of Doseyne's disease. If one of those bastards infects you with that – and it only takes one bite – your blood will thicken to pus in three days. But don't worry, you won't live long enough to suffer that. You'll drown in the mucus that'll fill your lungs before that happens.'

The sullen Priest, a haunted look in his eyes, made the sign of the aquila and kissed the relic hung around his neck.

'Then there are the plants,' Kasarta said, tossing a knife end over end in his hand as he puffed on a lho-stick. 'There's the strangler vine, Vego's death-trap, not to mention the deceptively named Emperor's Blessing.'

'Yeah, you've got to respect the Green,' Yeydl said conspiratorially, taking a swig from a battered hip flask. There was a faraway look in his drink-glazed eyes.

The party had stopped for Sergeant Borysko to study the platoon's maps Ertz carried with him, comparing their position to readings he was taking with a hand-held auspex. They were all glad of the chance to rest and get some rations inside them, none more so than the half-crippled Masursky and his human crutch Coburg.

There was no sign of the kroot. Pangor Yuma hadn't bothered to stop and rest when Sergeant Borysko had called a halt for five minutes. Kole imagined the avian had gone on to scout the surrounding area, keeping an ever-watchful eye out for orks.

'Tremayne!' Borysko called. 'Show me again where you think this genetor base is.'

'That's Lieutenant Tremayne, or a simple "sir", to you, sergeant,' Tremayne said, getting to his feet and approaching the tree stump that Borysko was using as a makeshift map table.

Kole yawned. He hadn't slept well. He'd been glad when Ertz had shaken him in the dry hollow where he lay under the webbed canopy created by the snare-spiders, watching the crimson, ochre-striped arachnids scuttling about above him in the near dark. He had been less pleased to discover he was on duty with the obsessive Priest.

The kroot had spent the night in the branches of the mottle-barked quoia tree above them. At times during the noisy night Kole had heard a strange hooting cry followed by a trilling warble, strange clicks, and whistles and hoots. He had wondered whether it was the kroot and, if so, what the alien tracker had been doing. Was it calling to others of its kind out in the jungle? Was it singing of past exploits, or re-telling the fable-tales of its ancestors?

He had seen how the ACG officer looked at the alien, and it was with even more reproach and disgust than how he looked at the skinners.

'Okay, let's move out.' Borysko's command stirred Kole from his reverie.

'Yeah, on your feet. You too, Masursky,' Kole chided.

They had been making slow progress thanks to the limping Masursky's messed up leg. The only way he had been able to get so far was because Coburg was effectively carrying him. The brute of a man was supporting Masursky with his right arm, his left hand holding Masursky's around behind his huge neck. The lieutenant and his equally strong bodyguard had not offered to help in any way.

Kole couldn't help wondering what awaited them at this lost genetor enclosure, cut off, out in the

Green. But he dared not ask; the lieutenant had already made it plain that the matter was not for discussion. Borysko himself hadn't pushed the matter. Either he didn't care or he was bothered and was simply keeping his opinions to himself. So Kole followed the example of his superior and said nothing. They would find out one way or another in the end.

'Doesn't say much, does he?' Geist said, gesturing to the hulking Kurn.

Kurn turned his head and fixed Geist with a penetrating stare, a low growl escaping from the gargoyle-twist of his mouth.

'He can't,' the lieutenant said, replying for his bodyguard. 'Not since he had his tongue cut out in a hive gang-fight as a juve.'

'Come on, Geist. Move it,' Kole said.

'There's a long way to go before we spend another night out here in the Green.'

'Yeah, you've got to respect the Green,' Yeydl said, stowing his flask again and shouldering his meltagun. 'As soon as you stop respecting it, that's when it gets you.'

TREMAYNE WAS SICK of the jungle. He was sick of forever having to brush palm fronds out of his face. He was sick of the constant irritation of buzzing insects that all seemed to want to use him as a reluctant blood donor. He was sick of the constant chittering noises of the forest. He was sick of the heat and the oppressive humidity, feeling as wet as if he'd jumped in a lake. And he was sick of the ork hunters.

The morbid religious obsessive, the practical joker, the sneering, ratty scout, the sulking vox-operator, their wisecracks, their sarcastic comments, their bickering and their disparaging looks. He could quite happily shoot the lot of them. But he had a feeling he would be glad of their assistance in the end. Nonetheless, the sooner this mission was over, the better.

And then there was the presence of the alien mercenary. That unsettled him more than anything else, more than the knowledge that there were potentially orks on all sides of them, lurking in the jungle hollows, more even than the knowledge of what he was trying to accomplish out here in the emerald-darkness of the forest. What in the name of the Hero of Hades Hive was a platoon of ork hunters doing with a xenos breed anyway? And what had Tremayne inadvertently got himself mixed up in?

The sooner this mission was over, the better.

THE ASSASSIN LAY motionless inside the hollow tube of the rotted log. From here he could look down on the hunter platoon's position, from between the unfurling fronds of the star-bracken ferns. Most of them were grouped around the buttressed-base of a quoia, where the exposed, soil-washed roots of the surrounding timber giants made a labyrinth of sandy pathways between the trees.

He played the cross-hairs of his gun scope over the figures, one by one. There was his target, standing next to the skinner sergeant, and his adjutant, the three of them poring over the charts spread out in front of them. If he moved forward a fraction he would have a clear shot.

But this was not the time. There was too much movement amongst the party. If one of them blocked his line of sight for one second, his shot could be ruined and he would lose the advantage of anonymity. The longer the mark thought he was still dead, the better.

He had hoped to make his move during the night, but with so many skinners on sentry duty at any one time around the root-bole of the quoia tree they had the place sewn up tight. If he had still had the det-charges with him he might have been able to take the whole lot out, but the explosives had been left on the flyer when he had been forced to make his untimely departure. Instead, he had spent the night dozing fitfully in the crook of a tree, keeping half an eye out for tree snakes.

He couldn't see the mercenary either, the freakin' alien. He wasn't going to do anything unless he was certain where that freak was and what it was up to. For the time being he would stay where he was.

Tentatively, he stretched and tensed his leg muscles, his back and his arms, in an effort to avoid the onset of cramp. His body still ached from his rather unceremonious landing, but then he was lucky to have been able to walk away from it at all.

When he had been sucked out of the back of the Valkyrie, the assault craft had been flying low, just above the jungle canopy. The spreading palm leaves of the cycads had broken his fall, as had the network of whiplash branches beneath. He had plummeted through the canopy, sending ibises flapping away, squawking in panic. His ribs and limbs had taken a battering, in spite of the body

armour he was wearing, but his helmet had pro-
tected his head.

His crazy descent had come to an abrupt stop several metres from the ground, with him trussed up in
a tangle of creepers and liana tendrils.

He had hung there for several minutes whilst he
recovered his breath, stunned by the battering he had
received, cursing himself for not taking the shot on
board the assault carrier sooner. Incredibly he still
had his weapons intact, the hellgun still cinched to
his harness. When he was ready, he had eventually
carefully cut himself down, using his knife, swinging
down into a natural avenue between the trees on the
end of a knotted woody vine.

From that moment on he had been able to re-
evaluate and continue his mission. First he located
the crash site but discovered that his mark had
somehow made it away from there alive. Not only
that, but the assassin soon discovered that there were
others on his target's trail.

The assassin froze, feeling something long, seg-
mented, and possessing more legs than he could
believe scuttle over the back of his legs. He held his
breath. In a moment it was gone.

The skinner sergeant signalled for his men to move
out again. The moment had passed. But there would
be other, more auspicious occasions. Besides, the platoon was making slow progress, thanks to their
insistence on dragging their wounded with them.

The assassin would wait a few moments to be sure
that all of the party were on their way again. Then he
would follow, scout out the trail ahead, get in front of
them, find a suitable sniper position from which to

target them and then – and only then – would he strike and take out his mark.

BORYSKO'S BOYS, AND their three new comrades, continued on their way through the jungle. The sky was becoming more visible above them now with every hundred metres they progressed along the worn, animal track they seemed to be following. It appeared as sparkling facets of azure, streaked with stratospheric pollution trails, like shards of imperfect sapphires between the crazing patterns of the twisting branches.

The scouts were at the head of the snaking line – Raus, Tannhauser and the Kid – although, of course, the true pathfinder was out of sight, further ahead along the trail through the forest.

After them came Borysko and Kole, with Adjutant Ertz, followed by Ferze and Gunderson. Then there was the mission's new commander and his bodyguard, with Vanderkamp keeping a close eye on them from behind. After the scowling, silent Klim, still carrying the mangled, scorched wreck of the vox-set on his back, came Coburg and Masursky, with the witchy-looking Priest and uncharacteristically sullen Geist. Kasarta and Yeydl brought up the rear.

Unseen birds sang in the canopy and from away ahead of them came a burst of clicks and whistles that were becoming more familiar to the group as their time in the jungle on this mission wore on. It was at moments like this, Kole thought, that it was almost possible to believe that they were caught up in a world-consuming war.

Klim suddenly came to an abrupt halt, so much so that Coburg, still supporting Masursky behind him, cursed as he almost walked into him. Klim turned to face the blaspheming brute, a finger pressed to his lips.

The others looked at him.

'Water,' he said.

The platoon continued for another hundred metres, senses straining, by which point they could all hear it.

Another fifty metres brought them to the edge of the ravine, the jungle falling back behind them, the sun beating down on this rocky scar in the jungled landscape.

A river swollen from the previous day's downpour, white water crashing through a precipitous gorge, the roar of it as loud as a Basilisk barrage, amplified by the confining walls of the echoing, misted chasm.

The platoon gathered at the cracked edge of the cliff. Kole edged forwards cautiously and peered over into the shadow-dark depths of the gorge. A hundred metres below the water boiled and heaved, churning and racing through its twisting channel, like an angry beast that would not be contained. A thousand years of its fury had cut this precipitous gash through the bedrock of the jungle. There was no more terrifying or powerful force on the planet – not amongst the armies of the Imperium or the forces of Ghazghkull's invaders – than that of the seas, rivers and rains of Armageddon.

The river wound torturous bends and wild meanders that almost completely doubled back on themselves, giving it the appearance from above of an anaconda slithering through the tropical rainforests, as if the water course had tried to take the most indirect route on its journey through the equatorial heartlands.

The kroot squatted on a rocky promontory jutting over the edge of the cliff, staring out over the gorge, its milky white eyes fixed on something the rest of them couldn't see in the treeline on the other side.

But there was a way across the precipitous, thirty-metre gap. At some point in the past a massive tree had fallen across the ravine – whether thanks to a monsoon storm lightning strike, the erosion of the river, its own weight unbalancing it, or the efforts of orks. The crown of its topmost branches had fallen on the near side of the gorge, its half-unearthed root system anchoring it securely on the far bank, in the face of the cliff. Its bark was grey and weathered, and the stubs of branches jutted out at points along its length. Although its surface was knotted and uneven, the tree-bridge was a good two metres in diameter.

'That wasn't on the map,' Tremayne complained.

Ertz scowled. 'I'm sorry, lieutenant, but they're not the most accurate charts on the planet. Reconnaissance out here is not an exact science.'

Tremayne was used to the hive-cities and their networks of servitor-surveyed streets, hab-blocks and trunk highways. It showed.

THE ASSASSIN CROUCHED in the crook of the massive branches of the tree, a screen of vines and leaves hiding him from his target but, at the same time, allowing him a clear line of sight.

He shifted himself slightly, making sure that he was totally comfortable before taking the shot. Although time was of the essence – he could see that this was the best chance he was going to get – the ork hunters and their wards were taking care not to rush their crossing of the fallen tree, but then of course his target did not know that the assassin was still on his trail.

Only three of the skinners had so far successfully negotiated the obstacle, the kroot watching from its boulder-perch at the lip of the precipice. And besides, his mark was only halfway across the tree-trunk.

Closing his left eye, the assassin put the scope to his right and lined up the crosshairs on top of the lieutenant's peaked cap. The range was good.

Regulating his breathing – long, deep and slow – his body locked in position, only the muscles of his right index finger moving, he gradually increased the pressure on the trigger.

TREMAYNE TOOK ANOTHER step forward and, catching the heel of his boot on a knotted protrusion on the log, he stumbled, his legs slipping out from under him. He was only dimly aware of a passing zing of heat.

His heart racing, Tremayne fell forward, hugging himself to the trunk with both hands. He heard shouts of surprise around him.

It was only then that he became aware of the hot pain in the meat of his right arm and realised that he had been shot.

THE ASSASSIN FORMED an oath in his head. He had missed. The barrel of his gun must have been knocked out of alignment during his own crash landing. It was hardly surprising if that was the case. He had checked it but, without wanting to test it and give himself away, obviously not carefully enough.

No matter; he was an expert marksman. He would compensate. With a hastily formed prayer to the Emperor, he squeezed the trigger again.

Giving a growl of anger, the lieutenant's hulking bodyguard threw himself down on top of his master, shielding him from the sniper. The two of them lay pressed flat on the tree trunk, a hundred metres above the thundering water pounding through the gorge beneath them, as another sizzling shot impacted against the tree-bridge, exploding the bleached bark where it struck.

Almost as one man, the ork hunters reacted on instinct, just as they had on meeting the kroot mercenary, training their guns on the trees that clung to the edge of the ravine. Whatever the hidden sniper had originally intended, the gunman now had all of them to contend with.

The assassin snapped off a third searing round from his position within the verdant foliage. With a soundless cry, Ferze pitched backwards off the log, shot through his throat. His grenade launcher popped, launching a krak grenade, which described a sharp parabola through the air.

The kroot was already moving as the assassin took out Ferze. In a matter of seconds the alien tracker had bounded back into the jungle. 'Freakin' coward,' Kole heard Tannhauser shout after it.

Only a handful of the hunters exposed out on the bridge realised what was happening and tried to scatter. The grenade came down in front of the turning Klim. It struck the trunk a glancing blow and exploded.

The whole bridge shook, sending the other skinners on the bridge stumbling as they tried to maintain their balance, or falling flat onto the rough bark of the trunk, hugging it as though their lives depended upon them keeping a tight hold, which they did. For the unfortunate Klim, however, it was another matter. His legs peppered with shrapnel, he fell forwards, out over the raging torrent in the shadows below. Screaming, he plummeted the hundred metres into the raging river. His cries were cut off as the waters claimed him, and then he was gone.

An autogun opened up with a clattering roar. Masursky, usually so cool-headed, was straddling the log, firing into the undergrowth on the near side of the ravine, yelling like a maniac. His injured leg making him feel even more vulnerable, panic had seized him and he had lost it completely. Some of the other skinners joined him in futilely blasting the treeline.

Over the cacophony produced by the autogun there was the *zing* and *zip* of a high intensity las-shot and Masursky, suddenly silent, slipped off the bridge. His autogun fired for a full five seconds before it emptied its ammo clip. Masursky's body hung beneath the bridge, snagged on a protruding branch by the webbing of his fatigues, swinging lifelessly over the yawning gulf.

There was a sudden flurry of activity within the thicket of cycor trees, branches and leaves shaking violently. The hunters heard a thrashing crashing followed by a distinct thud.

Something hurtled from the undergrowth before the fallen trunk and hurled itself at the bridge. The fact that it was a man dressed in torn black and grey camo fatigues and body armour – the exposed skin of his arms and legs covered in grazes and contusions – and not an ork, surprised the hunters enough to make them hesitate, and let him get closer than they otherwise might. The man had a scuffed black hellgun held in both hands in front of him. As he sprinted for the tree spanning the ravine, he raised the gun to his shoulder, sighting through the target-scope wildly as he ran.

The kroot burst from the trees after the man, landing in a crouch, his bladed rifle slung on his back. There was blood on its talons. The Inquisitorial agent had flushed out the assassin.

Ignoring the ork hunters, barging Geist and Priest aside, the sniper – dressed in the garb of an Imperial stormtrooper – sprinted onto the still swaying bridge, obviously gunning for Tremayne.

Pangor Yuma sprang like a savage feline predator, the muscle of his wiry body uncoiling like a taut spring. He gave his own screeching war-cry as his impressive leap carried him over the heads of Coburg, Gunderson and Vanderkamp.

Then the hulking Kurn was on his feet again, blood welling from the semi-cauterised hole of a las-wound. His bellow an unintelligible roar of fury, the massive bodyguard thundered forwards to meet the assassin. The trunk flexed and shook beneath Kurn's pounding steps as he closed the distance between the two of them.

Yuma landed behind the sprinting sniper, his grasping claws missing the man by mere centimetres. As the man twisted to evade the kroot, Kurn spread wide his arms to catch the sniper and wrestle him down onto the trunk.

The hellgun spat. The back of Kurn's skull blew out in a spray of blood, bone and brain matter, but the assassin had left his shot too late again. Momentum carried the bodyguard's body forward three more stumbling steps and Kurn's shambling corpse collided with the assassin.

The kroot lunged again but the dead weight of Kurn's corpse pushed the flailing assassin backwards off the tree, the sniper losing his footing on the log, its mossy surface slippery from the rain. The entwined sniper and ACG trooper, both now dead or as good as, dropped like stones into the gaping chasm. The two of them fell for three seconds through the void before the river claimed them.

The kroot was left holding a torn strip of the stormtrooper's black fatigues, its body stretched out over the side of the makeshift bridge.

A stunned calm descended over the ork hunter platoon again. Three of their number were dead, along with Tremayne's bodyguard, the sniper gone into the angry river with him. Death had come suddenly and violently amongst them and reaped a savage harvest, as was the way out here in the Green, which was, after all, just another theatre of war in the battle for Armageddon. But the lieutenant himself was alive, sitting up in shock in the middle of the log-bridge, as were the rest of them. The assassination attempt had failed and to Sergeant Borysko's mind, pragmatic as ever, there was still a mission to complete.

'Cut him down,' the sergeant said, indicating Masursky's corpse hanging limply from the buckling branch, his face a scowling grimace. 'We've got a job to do.'

FOURTEEN
EMPEROR'S WILL

THE SHADOWS OF the twilight cloud-forest gave way to dazzling sunlight. Away to the west the sky remained stained an ominous red and heavily overcast, but directly over the Black Templars the sun beat down, relentless as ever. The auto-senses of Angsar's helm visor adjusted to the dramatic change in light levels, and the images before his eyes resolved into a scene that was all too familiar to him.

The moss-limned tree trunk lay at the centre of the cycad-carpeted glade, its rotten bark scarred by weapons fire. The columns of the wet black scale-barked trunks demarcating the edge of the glade also showed signs of battle damage.

Saplings had been splintered by the charge of something, and cycads exploded by sustained solid shot cannon-fire. There was barely a single one of the primeval plants left intact. The loamy soil of the clearing had been churned up by booted feet and deep claw marks had been gouged in the disturbed ground. It was unnaturally quiet: the stillness was eerie and unsettling.

The entire clearing was a testament to the fact that a devastating battle had taken place here, amidst the cycads beneath the mantle of the forest. And, as if to confirm the fact, amidst the gently swaying fern-fronds and fallen quoia trees lay the bodies of the dead. Black and white armoured bodies, everywhere the image of the Templar-cross and the Imperial eagle defaced by deep, ceramite-splintering claw-marks, the scorch marks of missile detonation, cracked open by rocket fire and splattered with the Marines' congealed blood. The fallen crusaders all wore their death-scars as they would campaign-won medals.

In the copper-stained sunlight permeating the glade between the tree trunks, Emperor's Champion Ansgar and the other members of Kill-team Wolfram stared in stunned silence at the scene of devastation.

As if mentally wresting himself free of the stupefying anguish he felt on seeing the bodies before him, Apothecary Bliant went about his business.

'By Sigismund's Black Sword,' Initiate Hebron breathed in disbelief.

'What madness occurred here?' Chaplain Wolfram snarled as he surveyed the clearing.

'This is the work of the accursed xenos,' Brother Jarold declared, panning his weapon-mounts across the treeline in front of him. 'And, I swear by Sigismund's Sword, when I find them I shall repay them for their sacrilege a hundredfold!'

For a fleeting second, the vision-memories returned to Ansgar, assailing his waking mind like a desert rad-storm assaulting the hives of Armageddon Secundus…

…*Castellan Gerhard standing atop the fallen tree, Standard-Bearer Pelka at his side… Alien weapons discharging in the sticky air… The few valiant survivors of the lost fighting company returning fire… The black cross of the Black Templars, flapping from a banner-pole above the beleaguered Marines… Crazed, tattooed orks charging their position, and dying as incandescent bursts of plasma fire enveloped them…The noble cry of the Templars' battle-cant sounding over the roar of rockets and exploding shells… Smashing their way through the treeline, emerging from the smothering green twilight beyond, were a mob of hulking cyber-orks, their bodies modified with rusting alien augmetics and scavenged Imperial components… Cycad stems exploded under a withering hail of weapons fire… The stink of boiling sap and burning plant fibre filled the air… Then there was blood misting the air too… Whirling chain-blades clashed with Templar blades and bolters… Missile launchers screamed as they fired… Crackling green lasfire, like earth-bound lightning, streaked across the glade… The ancient wax of purity seals melted under the wash of flamer fire, parchment ribbons becoming red-glowing cinders… Warning runes flashed across his visor display, amber burning to red… A mechanical claw bit deep as another scythed towards his neck…*

The physical trauma of the psychic echoes of the Marines' deaths was too much for the Emperor's Champion. Overwhelmed by a flood of raw emotion and psychic agony, Ansgar fell to his knees, his grip on his sword relaxing.

'Brother Ansgar, what is it?' Veteran Brother Kemen asked, hastening to Ansgar's aid.

'This is where they died. All of them,' he said, emotion making his voice sound small and desperate. He felt drained by the force of the recollections.

'Emperor's oath!' Chaplain Wolfram gasped. They were standing at the spot where the men of Fighting Company Gerhard had made their brave last stand against the unforgiving greenskin menace.

This marked a dark moment in the history of the Solemnus Crusade. It reminded all the Templars present that this would be their last crusade. The inevitably of the situation weighed heavily upon the Chaplain in particular. They were of a dying breed.

'If this is where Castellan Gerhard's fighting company made its last stand,' Brother Baldulf said, 'in the name of Sigismund, this clearing should be littered with the carcasses of the orks.' He took in the clearing with an expansive gesture of his chainsword. 'I will not believe that our brethren died in battle without taking even one of the foul greenskins with them.'

'That was not the case. They took their fair share of ork lives,' Ansgar said. 'I saw that it was so.'

'Very well then,' said Brother-Initiate Gildas, 'so, in the name of the Golden Throne, where are the bodies of the greenskins?'

'Isn't it obvious?' Clust said. 'The vile xenos must have taken their fallen with them.'

'Koldo,' Wolfram said dourly, his tone dark and threatening as a building thunderstorm, 'signal the fleet. Let Marshal Brant know what we have found.'

The Chaplain dropped to one knee beside the body of a Templar whose chestplate had been fractured and scorched by what looked like a direct rocket impact. The name picked out in red on the scroll-worked ceramite of a shoulder pad read 'Heorot'.

'May the Emperor go with you, Brother Heorot,' Wolfram whispered, as he made the sign of the Templar-cross over the dead Marine.

'Father, tell me,' said Brother Kemen. 'How many were there in Castellan Gerhard's company when they entered these jungles?'

'I believe it was reported that the fighting company numbered twenty-three devout brothers when Castellan Gerhard led his men into the jungles to confront the enemy.'

'So where are the rest of them?'

A careful search of the cycad clearing by the kill-team confirmed what an initial scan had suggested. There were no more than fourteen bodies lying strewn about the clearing. The members of Kill-team Wolfram gathered again before the moss-limned trunk. Bliant continued with his gene-harvest.

'What is the word from the fleet?' Wolfram asked his bodyguard.

'I do not understand it, father, but I have been unable to contact the *Divine Fury* or any of the other vessels of our crusade,' Koldo replied, a quiver of anxiety underlining his words.

'What do you mean, brother? Is the fleet still there? Has some tragedy befallen our space-borne brothers whilst we have been fighting here on the planet's surface?'

'No, I do not have any evidence that it is that, blessed be the primarch,' Koldo said, allaying the Chaplain's immediate fears. 'It is just that I am receiving nothing but static, and appear to be unable to transmit our position either.'

'Have you checked your long-range comm transmitter?'

'Yes, Chaplain. Three times. It should be working within operational parameters.'

'Then what do you suggest is the matter?'

Koldo paused. 'I know this is going to sound like foolish ravings of a madman, particularly when you consider that we are out here, at the wild, untamed, primordial heart of the planet, but I believe the signal is being jammed.'

'What could possibly do such a thing out here in the jungle?' It was Initiate Hebron who spoke this time.

'I know, brother. But that is all I can suggest could be doing this.'

'Check the comm again,' Wolfram stated solemnly, the final comment on the matter. 'So, what happened to our missing brethren? Suggestions?' Wolfram asked, opening up a new discussion to the group gathered round him.

'Perhaps, by the grace of the Emperor, some of Castellan Gerhard's warriors survived,' Larce said, a tone of optimism in his voice.

'No.' The Emperor's Champion uttered the word with such finality that none of the others dared challenge him. 'They all fell here. I have felt it.'

'Then only one explanation remains,' Brother Jarold said, his clear, augmented voxponder tones cutting through the oppressive stillness of the glade. 'The greenskins took the bodies of our brothers with them, for some unfathomable evil purpose of their own.'

'So where did the greenskins go?' Wolfram asked.

'They left one of two ways,' Huarwar spoke up. 'There are signs that orks travelled from this point further west, heading deeper into the jungle. But there are also signs that a much smaller force went this way, heading north-east.'

'Then by which way shall we continue our own journey?' Lairgnen asked.

No one answered.

'Orks went both ways,' Huarwar repeated inconclusively.

'Well, Emperor's Champion?' Chaplain Wolfram was looking directly at Ansgar, the glittering ruby-eyed stare of his ceremonial death mask seeming like it could see through into a warrior's very soul. Ansgar then realised that the rest of the kill-team was looking at him too. 'What do the visions reveal? Which way should we go?'

'I...' Ansgar hesitated. 'I do not–'

...A HOWL REVERBERATED across the clearing over the heads of the warriors of the ravening, blood-hungry warband. Fury and an unadulterated bloodlust rose from them like an animal pheromone excretion. Just one fragment of a legion of murderers, but terrible to behold – a formidable force in their own right – the jungles of Armageddon burned behind them, painting the sky black with smoke. Flames leapt high into the tortured sky.

Ansgar could feel the insidious presence in the place crawling under his skin, like burrowing maggotworms. There was the bitter taste of bile in his mouth.

The host filled the wide crater and at its middle, atop the altar stone at the centre of the ring of monoliths, stood one warrior, more terrible than all the others among a legion of barbaric killers. The champion's head was thrown back as he bellowed his fury to the blistering sky.

Ansgar beheld the champion standing before his assembled warband in all his tarnished, daemonic glory, and he was awesome to behold. His ancient power armour of ruddy brass and bolter-cratered crimson ceramite was crusted with black gore, caked with dried gobbets of meat and wet with recently spilled blood. The suit was finished with blasphemous runes and icons, from the kneepads and the armoured greaves to the gorget and the embossed roundels of the knuckles of its gauntlets. A skull image had even been fashioned into the faceplate of his helmet, formed from chiselled bone, tarnished brazen metal and chipped ceramite.

In one gauntleted hand the warrior held a massive chain-axe, the serrated metal teeth protruding from the belt-feed looking like hooked crocodilian teeth. In the other hand, the warrior carried an archaic bolter, bristling with spikes, its barrel an open dragon's mouth. Sheathed at the warrior's waist, in a scabbard of rusted iron and brass, was a gutting knife that looked more like a sword in size and purpose.

And finishing this terrible image, the savage champion's armour was bedecked with skulls, taken by the warrior in battle.

Blood misted the air before him and over the heads of the berserk warband that was now also bellowing battle-cries and curse-oaths in frenzied delight, the warriors revelling in the savage sound of their own dog-bark voices…

ANSGAR OPENED HIS eyes. Chaplain Wolfram's death-mask face swam into focus in front of him, the facetted ruby eyes reflecting back the faceplate of the Emperor's Champion to his own sight a hundred times.

'Father,' he said, his voice manic and exhilarated. 'The Emperor has a different destiny mapped out for us now.'

'What did you see, Ansgar?' There was concern in the Chaplain's voice. 'What did you see? What did the Emperor show you?'

'Terrible things. The fate of this world in the balance. The horror that mankind is capable of, as if a dark mirror had been held up to our own devout brotherhood.'

'And we have a part to play in this?'

'Oh yes. We have the greatest part of all to play.' A dreadful conviction had taken hold of Brother Ansgar's voice.

'Then which path did He show you to take?'

'We should continue to head west, father.'

Wolfram looked up at the sky to the west. The evil storm had swollen since the day before so that the sky there looked almost as dark as night.

'Into the heart of darkness?'

'That is the way we should go. That is where we are needed.'

There was an unsettled muttering coming from some of the other brothers. Chaplain Wolfram turned his terrible glittering gaze on those dissenting members of the kill-team.

'What is it, Brother Clust?' the Chaplain challenged.

'I merely voiced the question we are all thinking, father. How can we be certain that these visions of Brother Ansgar's are coming the Emperor? He usually speaks to His servants through prayer, during the hours of the vigil. To my knowledge His visions have not struck down a recipient in such a way before.'

Wolfram responded with words of holy scripture: 'If any man doubts the Emperor, He will withdraw His favour from him.' And that was an end to the matter.

Bliant, his white armour crossed by bars of shadow from the waving fronds of an intact cycad arching over him, returned to his brothers.

'Brother-Apothecary,' Wolfram said, 'are you done with your holy work?'

'Indeed I am,' Bliant replied, his voice heavy, suggesting that the worries of the world weighed heavy on his shoulders, 'although approximately half of the bodies have already had the progenoid glands harvested from their bodies.'

'By Apothecary Colber,' Ansgar said, his voice distant.

'Where is the Brother-Apothecary?' Wolfram asked.

'Colber is not here, father.' It was Brother-Initiate Gildas who answered the question.

'And his narthecium? What of that?'

Ansgar took in the clearing yet again, through the armaglas of his helmet's visor. For a moment he felt like he wasn't really there in person. And then he wasn't, and the memories came flooding back to him.

... A battlefield of churned mud and mulched rotting vegetable matter amidst the all-enclosing forest, devoid of the hoots and trills of jungle animals and birds, strewn with the bodies of black Templars, a sealed box bearing the helix seal of the Apothecarion half buried in the mud...

'It is not here,' the Emperor's Champion replied, before Bliant could speak.

'That is correct, father,' the Apothecary confirmed. 'Brother Colber's narthecium is missing.'

'Is there any way of tracking it?'

'There might be if we still had Colber with us, a tracker unit in his suit linking to a matching one in the stasis box. But as it stands? No.'

'Then, it would seem, if we are to save the genetic heritage of our Chapter, we must find Brother-Apothecary Colber and his precious narthecium. We go west. And when we find our xenos enemy we shall show them no pity,' the Chaplain growled. 'We shall not feel any remorse as we repay them for their blasphemous crimes against our Chapter by taking our recompense in ork heads. But before we do, we will cleanse this place of the taint of the greenskin with holy fire.'

'What of our fallen brothers, Chaplain?' Initiate Hebron asked.

'We shall gather their bodies together here and it shall be their funeral pyre that shall light the fires that will scour this place of all evidence of the xenos.'

The bodies were gathered and the pyre formed. The kill-team knelt in a circle around the mound of crusader corpses as the Chaplain intoned prayers of thanksgiving and blessings for the fallen fighting company.

When he was done, Wolfram turned to Larce and Jarold.

'Burn it!' he instructed them.

SO THE SPACE Marines continued westwards, following the trail left by the departing orks. There were tracks and footprints here that concerned Chaplain Wolfram and Emperor's Champion Ansgar, signs that not just one tribe of feral orks but several whole tribes were gathering somewhere nearby, within the oppressively humid jungles.

The further Kill-team Wolfram advanced, the more regular were the signs they saw of the presence of orks.

And that inevitably led Wolfram to wonder what manner of orks they might find when at last they caught up with the massing greenskins. Were they even now steadily catching up with one of the surviving cells of the Solemnus Crusade's sworn enemy, the Blood Scar tribe?

Brother Jarold also wondered what fate awaited them, and prayed fervently to the Emperor, the primarch and blessed Sigismund that he might be granted his only real desire: to be revenged upon the hated orks that followed the grim alien icon of the scarred ork.

The dreadnought struggled on in the wake of the advancing crusaders, his massive body not designed for a prolonged march in such an environment. Branches snapped against his adamantium hull and rocks were crushed beneath his stomping steps. But his assault cannon would be ready, as would his power fist, when the time came.

It was not just Brother Jarold who was finding that the unforgiving environment of the equatorial jungles was starting to take its toll. As the Black Templars progressed through the jungle, their ancient suits of power armour maintained a stable, comfortable body temperature for the Marines locked inside them. But since the battle with the orkeosaurus and the fell blow Brother Clust had suffered from the massive spiked wrecking-ball, the veteran's suit's systems were struggling to regulate temperature and humidity for the warrior.

And there was something else about the environment of the rainforests that troubled Chaplain Wolfram and Brother Ansgar in particular. It was a subtle yet ominous change which was only increasing in its effects the more kilometres the Space Marines continued on westwards.

At first the alteration in the trees and shrubs around them was barely noticeable, it seeming simply that different species of flora were dominant in this part of the jungle. But the warping of the rainforest continued and worsened, becoming more and more obvious as the kill-team advanced within range of the threatening, tainted storm.

It was also something that troubled the rest of Kill-team Wolfram. Once their objective had seemed so clear, but now, the further they progressed into these dark, forbidding jungles, the less clear it became to the likes of Brother Clust and the veteran Kemen. When they had left the *Divine Fury*, bound for their rendezvous point with the Land Raider Crusader *Avenger*, it had been clear that they were engaged on a search and rescue mission, to find the lost Company Gerhard.

And yet now, although that was what Brother Ansgar still claimed they were doing, there seemed to be another, conflicting objective coming ever more to the fore, and it seemed that the inimical hand of Chaos was drawing them ever further from their pre-destined path, weaving their destinies with another, altogether more sinister fate entirely.

LIGHTNING CRACKLED and burst across a threatening sky as black as the hearts of the aliens that would see Armageddon brought to its knees. Peals of thunder rolled over the wind-lashed forest canopy, sounding like the bellowing of angry, primal gods. Rain fell with all the ferocity of a tropical monsoon.

Ansgar looked around him and as he saw the corruption afflicting the forest, at the same time, through his mind's eye, he saw another vision of the corrupted jungles.

…Trunks grey and withered and yet still clinging to unnatural life, twisted into even more bizarre shapes than they ever had before, an alien outlandishness that was a total anathema to strong, vigorous life itself, as though actual physical corruption had taken hold of the jungle…

'What has happened to the forest?' Brother-Initiate Gildas was asking.

'The time is drawing near,' Brother Ansgar stated, sounding as if his words came from another time and place.

'Drawing near to what?' Clust challenged.

'The end,' Ansgar said, turning his helm's expressionless faceplate on his battle-brother, an ominous aura radiating from his body and the Armour of Faith.

At that moment it seemed more ominous and threatening than Chaplain Wolfram's skull-masked image.

ANSGAR HALTED, THE rest of the line of Templars coming to an abrupt stop behind him. The Emperor's Champion stared at the path ahead of them.

...A precipitous path hugging an almost sheer-sided cliff face, a raging torrent of filthy ochre water cutting its way through the jungle a hundred metres below...

The onward path was barely wide enough for Brother Jarold to negotiate with his dreadnought body. To the left the hillside rose up above them, a rocky cliff decorated with precarious plant growth, bristling ferns clinging to the rock face by means of anchoring taproots. To their right the path ended at the lip of a cavernous river gorge, that same river boiling and foaming as it bounded over the boulder-formed rapids just beneath the surface of the water.

There was a moment's hesitation as Chaplain Wolfram considered the best way to continue. There was always the option of retracing their steps and finding another path onward, but that would mean losing precious hours.

It had already taken them several days to push this far into the jungled depths of the equatorial rainforests, and there was no guarantee that any other route would be any easier or save them any time. They would continue on their current path, the one that had been shown to Brother Ansgar in his vision-dream.

But Ansgar had not witnessed the ork ambush.

The orks attacked with insane abandon, despite the torrential downpour that beset them all, revelling in the wild savagery of battle. Clad in furs and scraps of pilfered armour, adorned with bones and teeth, hollow cane sections and toof jewellery. Armed with everything from clubs, spears and bows to guns, stickbombs and axes, the crazed orks thought nothing of taking on the superior might of the Black Templars.

They came at the kill-team from both directions along the precarious cliff-path, the earth rippling under their charge, the ground made unstable by the deadly cloudburst. The greenskins even came at the Marines from the cliff above, bounding from rock to rock or swinging their way on ropey lianas, like ape-men of the sodden forests.

Restricted by their position, Chaplain Wolfram's men could not make the best use of their battle skills as they would have wished against their poorly-armed and even more poorly-armoured attackers. They were surrounded on all sides.

Orks were thrown from the path, batted aside by Wolfram's whirling mace-like crozius, or sent plummeting to their deaths in the river below by Ansgar's crackling Black Sword. Baldulf's whirling chainsword removed the limbs of anything that strayed close enough, whilst the bolters of Lairgenen, Koldo, Hebron, Gildas and Huarwar scythed through the orks bounding down the cliff-face towards the Space Marines, barbspine-tipped arrows slicing through the air towards them, and gun barrels spitting high velocity shells at the Marines.

Larce brought his flamer to bear as best he could, sending one blazing, fur-clad alien hurtling into the hungry river a hundred metres below. Kemen tried to get a bead on any viable target with his soaking lascannon.

Dreadnought Brother Jarold's assault cannon drowned out the roar of the untamed river crashing through the gorge below, as the ancient brought down screaming greenskins, blasting great, gaping holes in their stinking alien carcasses. The ground visibly vibrated beneath the dreadnought's adamantium feet.

Jarold was unaware of something that Brother Ansgar could see clearly from where he fought at the head of the Templar line.

A mob of orks was closing on the dreadnought from above, reckless in their descent of the rock face. A pair of the creatures had stopped half way down, still six metres above Jarold, and was worrying at a jagged rock protruding from the cliff with their axes, trying to break it loose. And they were succeeding; Ansgar could see the cracks appearing in the base of the outcrop.

Ansgar leapt past his fellow Templars, Jarold's name booming from the vox-speaker of his laurel-wreathed helmet. Jarold heard him and following the line of the champion's sword as it pointed towards the hazard above him, fired the rocket launchers that topped his armoured hull.

The shelf of rock exploded, blasted into a million tiny fragments, as did one of the orks kicking away at it. A shower of stone shards and other debris rained down amidst the pouring rain, clattering from the dreadnought's scripture-inscribed hull.

And then Brother Ansgar's part in the battle was over, as was Brother Jarold's.

Ansgar felt the ground shift beneath him, and then he was seeing the exposed face of the cliff hurtling past his eyes as the path fragmented and gave way, weakened by the rain, the weight of the dreadnought and the vibrations of the battle provoked by the ork ambush.

Greenskins, Dreadnought Jarold and the Emperor's Champion fell into the void of the gorge as the side of the cliff slipped away in a catastrophic landslide. Chaplain Wolfram could do nothing but watch in appalled horror as the crusade's Champion and the dreadnought dropped hundred metres into the churning, turgid water below.

THE ORK DOK'S patient stirred and the warboss opened one piercing red eye, the auto-responsive lenses of the other – a newly grafted augmetic – whirring into focus. The first thing the warboss saw was the ugly, smiling face of Painboss Urgluk Gurlag staring back, one eye enlarged by a surgeon's head-strap mounted magnifying lens.

Images and recollections of experiences came back into the re-booted memory of its improved bionic brain like old pict-reels.

…The belly-hold of the mega-gargant – Gork, or Mork, made flesh – on the verge of being launched against the mountain-cities of the humans… The black and white armoured challenger, daring to face it on its own ground, dwarfed by the might of its mega-armoured body… The shimmering, black blade of the

*champion's sword...Their titanic struggle within the
kannon-chamber, the clash of metal ringing on metal
echoing within the cavernous space... Blue sparks flying
from the armour plating sheathing the warboss's torso
as the sword impossibly sliced through the metal and
into its chest... Acrid black smoke rising from the fissures in the exoskeleton as its circuits shorted out,
sheathing the warboss in its own field of unleashed
lightning... The electrical feedback and physical pain of
his right arm being removed at the shoulder... The
winding impact of the shockwave of the explosion, as
the munitions stored within the belly of the gargant-
beast were touched off by the chain reaction consuming
the idol-titan... The swollen chamber filling with roiling flames as the warboss's vision faded to black...*

Morkrull Grimskar sat up and immediately looked
at his right arm. Servos ground and screeched as it
flexed the new bionic replacement – synapse signals
relayed via a thought-impulse transmodulator –
opening the shearing claw and then snapping it shut
again in one brutal action.

It was only then that Morkrull Grimskar, Warboss
of the Blood Scar Tribe, Conqueror of Conloach
and the Scourge of Solemnus, turned to take in the
cowering painboss.

Whatever the self-serving ork dok had intended
by recovering Grimskar's ruined body from the
firestorm-ravaged ruins of the caldera, he would
soon learn that this warboss would not be a pawn
in another's plans. He had his own plans to bring
to fruition. The half-death he had suffered at the
hands of the Templar champion had only delayed
things temporarily.

Soon all of Armageddon would know and fear the name of Morkrull Grimskar. Beginning with Painboss Urgluk Gurlag.

FIFTEEN
GREEN DEATH

SERGEANT BORYSKO HELD up his right hand and the ork hunters behind him immediately fell silent. Lieutenant Tremayne followed suit.

Since their encounter with the Imperial assassin they had made better progress, no longer slowed by the injured Masursky, even though the fatigue they were feeling was becoming more acute. It had also taken a good half hour to dress wounds and recover from the shock of the sniper's sudden attack. And then there had been the questions.

The hunter sergeant had been full of them. It had been obvious that Tremayne had been the target, but his presence amongst the platoon had cost the lives of three of Borysko's Boys, not to mention the loss of his own bodyguard. No one had else had mentioned the dead men since they had cut the wounded

Masursky's body from the tree to let it drop into the hungry river. Tremayne was not sure if their silence was a sign of their grief or embarrassment.

He had considered it best to tolerate the sergeant's questions and let him get it all off his chest, although even if he had known the answers, he would not have shared them with him.

And Tremayne had his own questions. He could guess why he had become a target. He had known the risks of what would happen if a rival faction found out about the covert operation when he had accepted the mission.

But there were other questions which remained without an adequate answer, and that made Tremayne nervous, because it made him wonder who else knew about his mission. It made him wonder who else he could trust.

Why had Borysko accepted his change of orders so readily? Was it because he was a loyal servant of the Golden Throne, a steadfast soldier who followed orders to the letter? Or was it because he had his own orders of what to do once Tremayne achieved his objective? What part did the alien mercenary have to play in all this? It was a shame that the assassin hadn't disposed of that unknown quantity for him at the ravine crossing.

And who *had* the assassin been working for? Who else knew about his killing brief? And who would be monitoring his progress? Who would know that the assassin's mission had failed? If Tremayne did get through to his objective alive and manage to complete his own mission, what would be waiting for him when he reported back to his employers? And what would Zephyrus have to say about how it had gone?

The mercenary had tried to take the assassin alive. And if he had succeeded, Tremayne would certainly have had some questions to ask him, after he had personally given him a good beating. But why had the kroot been so desperate to find out more? The lieutenant again found himself wondering what part the alien had to play in this great game that they were now all caught up in, uncomfortable allies in a far-reaching conspiracy.

But what were they supposed to be listening out for now? Tremayne suspected orks. In fact he was surprised that in the space of two days and one night out in the jungle, the only time he had encountered the greenskins was when Sergeant Borysko and his men had come to his aid at the stony defile. It seemed even more surprising when he considered that Imperial intelligence claimed that there was a proliferation of the creatures in the jungle heartlands.

He looked at the sergeant again now. His grizzled, scar-mauled face was set in a grim frown. Borysko was turning his head slowly from side to side, trying to take in the whole of the canopy above him. The skinners were nervously glancing all round too, not daring to move and draw any attention to themselves, but at the same time trying to cover every part of the suffocating forest with arcs of fire.

Mantis-bugs made their chainsword noises while bowl-like leaves heavy with rain water dripped the contents of their reservoirs onto the flat, bladed leaves of urchod palms below in an irregular drumming tattoo, every drip making a rubbery thwacking sound.

Borysko slowly lowered his fist again. Lieutenant Tremayne felt the skinners gathered around him relax, letting out their pent-up breath in a susurrating sigh.

ARMAGEDDON'S SUN WAS a dusty orange disc, staining the hydrocarbon-polluted sky the most incredible shades of red and gold, making it look like an oil slick had been spread across the sky.

Not that the skinners could see much of the sky any more. The area of jungle they were hacking their way through now, using their combat knives and las-gun bayonets like scything machetes, was particularly dense.

Borysko swore inwardly again as his chainsword snagged in the pith of a woody creeper. The parasitic vines hung in thick screening swathes here. Cutting a path through the sticky vegetation was exhausting work.

All of the skinners were feeling draining fatigue upon them now, sapping the strength from weary muscles as effectively as it sucked the morale from them.

And here they were, almost at the end of another day in the Green. The stab-flies and rad-midges were troubling the troopers more than usual as the insects came groundward as dusk crept like a stealthy preda-tor through the darkening forest. The irritation they felt at the insistent attentions of the gnats was merely adding to the general edginess of the strung-out hunters. Priest's doom-laden appeals to the God-Emperor and all His saints were doing little to help the mood of his fellows.

The sergeant knew that if they didn't make some headway soon, they would be no use to anyone when they inevitably encountered the territorial greenskins again.

But where were the orks, Borysko wondered uneasily? The platoon hadn't come across any of the feral aliens since rescuing the ACG officer and his late henchman. Something was not right, Borysko was sure of it.

Heretically, he almost wished that they would encounter some more greenskins soon. Their presence would reassure him that equilibrium was being maintained in the jungle. The fact that they weren't here could only mean that something infinitely worse was waiting for the Imperials at the heart of darkness.

Pavle Borysko rued the day the Imperium ever totally reclaimed the world of Armageddon from the greenskins, and the orks were driven out of the equatorial reaches of the planet. For the ork gave him, and men like him, purpose. For as long as there were orks infesting the jungles the skinners would still be required and their lives would have purpose. If the orks were to be purged from the planet, the ork hunter regiments would become superfluous.

And then, at last, Borysko did encounter the orks, although not how he had imagined he would.

Giving his chainsword a violent tug, Borysko pulled the blade free of the creepers, and a whole swathe of the hanging vines came down after it. The marker was behind, atop a jutting spear of rock.

At some point in the past, the stone had been roughly carved to give it a grim, leering-mouthed expression. But over the years – or more likely centuries – acidic lichen and the jungle had weathered the stone to an amorphous, pitted grey surface. Any detail there might once have been in the carving was now worn away.

Lashed to the rock with a length of creeper was a piece of tree bark. The bark had been daubed with a substance that looked like it had been concocted from guano or white mud. An experienced ork hunter, Borysko would have immediately recognised the symbol painted there even without the addition of an ork skull surmounting the rocky protrusion, the scattered bones at the base of the monolith or the splatters of dried blood and encrusted gore.

Crossed bones meant the same thing to races the galaxy over: Only death awaits you here. But what manner of death was unclear. Was it a warning that the skinners were about to enter ork territory at last? Or was it a warning put there by the orks themselves, declaring that this was not somewhere they wanted to go.

'Sarge,' came a croaking bird-cry of a voice, and then the mercenary was in front of Borysko.

Borysko flinched, hearing the alien speak, and tried to avoid looking directly at the kroot. But the skinner sergeant realised that for Pangor Yuma to join the platoon on the ground he suspected that the kroot must have something portentous to tell them.

'What is it, kroot?' he asked.

The alien tracker put its head on one side and blinked its eyes twice in quick succession. It was clutching its rifle in its right claw, using it like a staff again.

'Danger ahead there is,' the creature said in its pidgin-Gothic way. 'Greenskin signs there are many.'

'I know,' Borysko said uncomfortably, tasting bile in his mouth as he found himself agreeing with the alien. Yuma blinked again. 'Is it clear what the danger is?'

'Not clear,' the kroot replied. 'Trees are quiet. Like dead place. No birds sing.'

'Is there a problem, sergeant?' It was the lieutenant, his tone condescending, as if to suggest that if Tremayne were the one leading this expedition there would not have been a problem.

'There's this,' Borysko said, pointing to the crossed bones marker. 'And the kroot confirms more like it ahead.'

'And what is this danger?'

'He doesn't know. Says he can't tell,' Borysko sneered, answering unsympathetically for the alien.

'Can't tell yet. No birds sing there. Jungle warns us,' Pangor Yuma piped up. Borysko's frown deepened. Once again, he found himself thinking, I'm only following orders by having this alien alongside my men. It doesn't mean I have to like it.

'Then we go on,' Tremayne stated flatly, as if there was no point discussing the matter further.

To go on was certainly the more direct route, and hence technically the quicker route to their target. But even orks would not have put up warning signs without good reason. If the skinners were to fall foul of some as yet unknown threat, it might not prove to be the quicker option at all.

'You're sure you don't want us to skirt round this area?'

'No. We go on.'

'We don't know what the danger might be,' Borysko persisted. 'It could slow us up for hours… or worse.'

'We go on,' Tremayne stated again. 'This mission has taken me longer and cost me more than I had imagined it would. Time is a factor here, sergeant.' The lieutenant's manner was so calm – despite all he had been through – Borysko could have throttled him. 'We will continue to take the most direct route possible.'

Borysko loathed the haughty lieutenant more than ever now, but, stuck out here, three men down, with no vox-caster and an alien Inquisitorial agent tagging along with them, there really didn't seem to be much else that Borysko could do but keep on doggedly to the resolution of this Emperor-forsaken expedition.

He turned away from the lieutenant and, with one last disdainful glance at the ork marker, strode on into the forbidding jungle beyond. As he did so he pushed past the kroot.

'That way danger,' the alien squawked again.

'Don't I just know it,' the skinner sergeant snapped back. 'Do you think I'm an idiot?'

'WHAT DID THIS?' the Kid asked, his voice a harsh whisper.

'I don't know, but do you get the feeling we're about to find out?' Geist asked humourlessly.

The jungle had continued to darken, thanks in part to the red sun sinking into the molten sky at the horizon and in part due to the increasing density of the foliage all around them.

And suspended from the greenery was skeleton after skeleton. Some of the largest and most obviously recognisable to the platoon were the intact skeletons of skins, immediately identifiable because of their oversized skulls. There were almost complete skeletons knotted within the creeping vines, bound together by the constricting tendrils.

There were not only ork remains hanging from the impenetrable branches. There were the strung up remains of what looked like forest primates, bird carcasses and even a panther-like felid.

And not all of the remains amongst the blood-red orchid blossoms had been entirely picked clean of flesh.

Was this the work of some terrible forest predator or some homicidal ork shaman creature?

The unsettled ork hunters towards the rear of the advancing line shared their concerns regarding the location they found themselves in, their insistent voices barely more than urgent whispers.

'Surely the sergeant's going to call a stop for the night soon,' the Kid said.

'Not here, I hope,' Kasarta replied, glancing up at the macabre abattoir branches. 'Not with whatever did that around here.'

'What do you think it was?' Bukaj asked, persisting with his line of questioning.

'Could have been a clawmoset, an adult male,' Yeydl mused.

'It would take a pack of them to do this,' Kasarta said.

'Could be something the orks brought here that we haven't seen yet.'

'Maybe it's a mutant of some kind, a consequence of all the industrial fouling this planet's suffered over thousands of years,' Gunderson suggested. 'I've heard that there are manta sharks in the Tempest Ocean that have been changed by the chemical effluents that have been pumped into the seas. They've grown abnormally large over the centuries so that they're now so big they can swallow a submersible. Couldn't there be things that are just as bad lurking in the depths of these jungles now?'

'An Ecclesiarchy-sponsored missionary once told me,' Vanderkamp said conspiratorially, 'that there are parts of this jungle – only at its deepest parts – where it has been corrupted by the power of the warp.'

Priest hastily made the sign of the aquila across his chest. 'Speak not of such things lest you bring its stain upon your soul,' the sniper said, sounding like he was quoting Imperial literature.

'Perhaps it's the work of *his* kind,' Tannhauser said, nodding towards the kroot now striding forward through the forest at the head of the skinner platoon.

There were mutters of agreement from some of the other men.

'A kroot carnivore squad? I don't think so,' Yeydl said, eying the kroot as suspiciously as anyone else.

'Why not?' hissed Tannhauser. 'How do we know he's not leading us into a trap?'

'He's a sanctioned agent of the Inquisition, Tann. Besides, can't you see how jumpy he is? He's as freaked by this as the rest of us, in his own alien way.'

'I'm not convinced.' Tannhauser regarded the mercenary with hooded eyes.

And at that moment Pangor Yuma turned and looked back down the line, directly at him.

THE GROVE BORYSKO'S Boys found themselves in would have been considered a clearing if the foliage had not formed an effective barrier over the sacristy-like vault that had formed beneath the spreading boughs.

The knotted tree roots created a natural bowl in the hollow at the centre of the green-dark space, some twenty metres across at its widest point. The only colour other than green here was the occasional white nub of bone protruding from the rich, dark soil, and a proliferation of the blood-red flowers.

The hollow was filled with soupy, green water. Emerging from the centre of the pool, to a height of three metres, was a fleshy trunk two metres across, ripe with tuberous pods. The top of the trunk formed a lip and was thick with the red flowers, although the petals had begun to draw themselves shut as dusk spread its dark mantle over the twilight gloom of the forest. The boughs above the skinners' heads were draped with trailing creeper-vine, more of the flowers budding amidst the lianas.

Spilling over the top of the trunk, amongst the bloody blossoms, were a number of pallid fleshy tendrils. Sergeant Borysko followed the path of the thick cables as they emerged from the fat, fleshy stem and coursed through the water, to emerge again amongst the roots of the surrounding mahogany and adagas trees. But the tendrils did not stop there. They divided, latching onto the trunks of the surrounding trees, snaking around the branches above them until they hung down from the canopy.

The boggy glade was eerily quiet, as the ork hunters were used to a constant background hubbub of animal and insect sounds day and night in the jungle. The only sounds disturbing the eerie peace of the glade now were the chainsword-buzzing of leech-ticks, the steady drip of rainwater that was ever-present in the damp rainforests and the slither of the creeper-vines as they were moved by the gentle evening breeze.

But there was no breeze: the air in the hollow-glade was still.

'What in the name of the Golden Throne is this place?' the lieutenant wondered aloud, displaying true unrestrained astonishment as he brushed aside a dangling, bristle-haired vine.

The attack came so suddenly that the first Borysko knew about it was when first the lieutenant, and then a split second later both Raus and Vanderkamp, disappeared up into the canopy.

Then the silence of the shaded glade exploded with a cacophonous roar. Coburg's autocannon opened up, the hulking trooper drenching the canopy and its hanging foliage with shredding fire. The rest of the skinners followed suit, doing what little damage they could with their las-weapons and racking shotguns. Yeydl was taking considered shots with his meltagun at the trailing tendrils, closer to the base of the fleshy stem, the pallid tendrils blackening and shrivelling.

A barbed creeper shot out from the gloom of the boughs above towards Yeydl. Hearing the rasp of the vine's hairs pushing through the leaves he spun round, his meltagun already firing. The malign creeper withered and burst into flame. But the fire soon died, doused by the damp conditions of the grove.

The kroot went for the writhing creepers like a whirling dervish, spinning athletically out of the way of the plant's lashing tendrils. The alien was using its twin-bladed rifle as if it were a quarterstaff.

Other than Coburg's wild assault and Yeydl's more composed attack, the skinners' weapons didn't appear to be particularly effective against a plant this size.

Borysko peered up into the darkness of the adagas boughs above him, trying to find a viable target in the gloom. Tremayne, Raus and Vanderkamp hung there, struggling in the constricting coils of half a dozen of the bristling vines. Their movements were already becoming less vigorous. The longer they remained trapped there, more vines continued to wind themselves around their bound bodies.

'By the Emperor!' Borysko swore. He should have known it: the blood-red orchid-like blossoms, living semi-parasitically among the other trees, the constricting autonomously moving lianas, the thin hair-spines. He had heard other men talk of this plant but had never encountered it himself. Carnivorous and possessed of a rudimentary, yet unerringly malign, intelligence, *haemovora labrusca* was its Administratum archivum catalogue name. But amongst the ork hunter regiments it was simply called the vampire vine.

Having snared its prey, the plant would pierce the flesh of its victims with the hollow, hair-like, hypodermic needle spines that covered its tentacle tendrils and then absorb the nutrients from the bodies. To drain a corpse would take it days, but in a matter of minutes its victims would already be dead, their windpipes crushed by the rapidly constricting creepers.

The two ensnared troopers and the ACG lieutenant cried out – perhaps as much in fear of their lives because of the apparently indiscriminate firing of the autocannon as because of the plant's unexpected assault. But their cries were already becoming muffled and Raus's face had been smothered by the writhing creepers entirely.

The other skinners would have to act fast to save their companions and the lieutenant. Much as Borysko would have liked to let the man die, the sergeant was, as Tremayne had so unfairly pointed out, an honourable man at heart, and he couldn't bring himself to do it. After all, the completion of Tremayne's mission could have far-reaching consequences for the War for Armageddon. Despite his own fears regarding to his personal fate, should Ghazghkull Thraka's invasion actually be repelled, he could not jeopardise the lives of who knew how many millions, all because of a personal grudge. And now he knew how to resolve this situation.

'Concentrate your fire at the stem,' Borysko shouted over the roar of the autocannon and the *whoomph* of the meltagun, turning his own laspistol on the tuberous trunk at the centre of the stagnant glade.

The trunk of the plant was shredded, roasted and blown apart under a hail of autocannon shells, sizzling las-rounds and the inferno-heat of a melta firing at maximum intensity. Blood-red petals filled the hollow with a blizzard of wine-dark flakes, looking like frozen drops of plasma suspended amidst the whirlwind of the plant's destruction, as if spilled by the vampiric plant itself.

The blood-sucking vines whipped around above the ork hunters in a frenzy, as the trunk of the plant, which contained what passed for a nervous system, was killed off. The rudimentary ganglia running the full length of every one of the deadly creepers were denied the signal they needed to be anything more than jungle creepers and were stilled at last.

The constricting knots of the vampire vine holding its three unfortunate victims sagged. Tremayne dropped out of the adagas boughs, his motionless body splashing down into the stinking water. Kole darted over to the lieutenant.

'Is he alive?' Borysko asked tersely.

'He's alive, sarge,' came Kole's matter-of-fact reply.

Moments later, a cursing Vanderkamp pulled himself free of the ensnaring coils and descended too. Borysko could see tiny pinpricks oozing blood on the exposed skin of their arms and faces.

But there was no such descent for Raus. The scout trooper's body hung where it was, his fat tongue protruding from the whiskery man's purple, puffed face. Raus had already been throttled to death by the plant. The vampire vine had claimed another of Borysko's Boys.

'Cut him down,' Borysko commanded. 'Let's not leave him hanging up there like one of those feral ork's corpses. And then, let's get out of here. Coburg, bring the bigwig.'

Trooper Yeydl looked up at the hanging corpse swinging between the boughs of the tree and took a long pull on his battered hip flask. 'Yeah,' he muttered to no one in particular, 'you've got to respect the Green. Soon as you don't, that's when it gets up and bites you on the arse.'

SIXTEEN
NEXUS

NIGHT FELL, LIKE a purple-dark shroud being drawn over the world. Chaplain Wolfram gazed up at the midnight-blue firmament. Smudges of ochre pollution smeared the dome of the sky, appearing as black streaks. The patterns of star clusters covered the higher heavens, far beyond the stratosphere of the planet, stained red by the ruby-visor of his helmet, looking like the blood-splatters of gunshot wounds.

He found himself wondering which of those spots of light were the ships of the Solemnus Crusade. He wondered what role the Emperor had chosen for them, what awaited them in these twisted forests. He wondered how the orks of the Blood Scar tribe fitted in to all this. And he wondered what had happened to Ansgar and Jarold, and whether they were still alive.

The place where the Templars had regrouped after the ork ambush was a clearing within the warped wilderness where the trees and plants appeared even more sickly and corrupted than any they had seen so far. The forest in general had also become sparser, there being larger and more regular gaps between the trees, the remaining jungle less dense than the kilometres of wilderness the Space Marines had pierced to reach this far.

The silhouettes the trees threw against the purple-blue sky made it look like the quoia were frozen in agonised death-throes. It was as if the forest was decaying without ever actually being granted the release of death.

The devastating rains, which had taken the most terrible toll on the kill-team, had stopped. The discoloured thunderheads continued to mass to the west, their mass and nature unchanged by the cloudburst, and an oppressive pressure remained in the atmosphere.

There was not one among the crusaders who had not been shocked by the loss of Brother Ansgar and Dreadnought Jarold. As well as losing two of their number, and two of the most celebrated battle-brothers of the Solemnus Crusade at that, with their loss, the Chapter had also lost a number of irreplaceable treasures, including Brother Jarold's dreadnought war walker body as well as the crusade champion's Black Sword and Armour of Faith.

But what had at first stunned the Space Marines had the next moment driven them on to best the voracious feral orks.

Wolfram had shouted, 'Make sure our brothers have not died in vain! No fear! No pity! No remorse!'

Roused by the Chaplain's impassioned words, those battle-brothers remaining charged the greenskins on the path ahead of them, the threat behind them gone, those orks having fallen to their deaths along with Ansgar and Jarold, to have their skulls smashed open on the rocks at the bottom of the gorge or drown in the roiling waters of the ferocious river. The Black Templars had fought their way clear of the feral creatures, taking down every last one that remained in their righteous wrath.

Now numbering eleven warriors, there was nothing Kill-team Wolfram could do other than pray for Ansgar and Jarold, that the Emperor might take them into his care, before going on to fulfil the oath they had sworn at the beginning of their enterprise – to recover the gene-seed of their brethren – with renewed vigour and steely determination.

And it was at this point in the sickening jungle that the Black Templars had re-grouped and reassessed their losses.

There was something else about the oppressive atmosphere around them now. As the Marines neared the centre of the meteorological disturbance, so it worsened. The sickness in the air. The taint of Chaos. It was almost as if something was watching them. That was how it felt.

It was then, and only then, that Chaplain Wolfram caught sight of the figures waiting beyond the treeline. Figures over two metres tall, clad in power armour, like the Black Templars – Space Marines.

The Marines emerged from the jungle all around Kill-team Wolfram as one man. There was the rack of bolters on both sides, the hum of weapons charging and the furious whine of chain-blades running up to speed.

And then a voice cried out through the darkness: 'Hold your fire!'

THROUGH THE NIGHT-SIGHT setting of the magnoculars the nighttime world was revealed in shades of green and black. Where illuminators glowed like cadmium and tungsten stains in the darkness, through the night-sight they blazed flaring white.

The platoon lay flat on their bellies on the protruding edge of the cliff, or hunkered down at the foot of the bank, sheltered beneath the clumps of sunburst palms. Only Pangor Yuma was missing, the sergeant having sent the kroot to scout the perimeter of the complex.

'There it is,' Lieutenant Tremayne hissed at Borysko, who was lying next to the ACG officer amidst the fern-fronds.

The skinner sergeant put the magnoculars to his eyes and peered over the crest of the rise, moving a drooping frond gently to one side with an outstretched hand.

The genetor base lay spread out below them at a wide, meandering bend in the river. From the foreshore of a sandy beach, and the remains of a dilapidated jetty, a well-worn trackway led up to the watchtower-protected gates of a large fenced compound. Gun posts stood at the junctions and razor wire topped the doubled fences, the forest encroaching as far as the first chain-linked barrier. The sandy space between that and the second was being reclaimed by the probing tendrils of the jungle.

However, in places the vegetation had been uprooted or burnt down to black patches of scorched earth. Elsewhere it was clear the fence had been rent apart and then repaired in a haphazard fashion.

But there was something else, something more sinister and alien that had already claimed the compound as its own. Suspended from the lookout towers on either side of the gate were ugly, metal icons. And there were other signs that the base was now under the command of another race. The most obvious of these were the sentries on duty at the watchtower gun-posts. The barrels of heavy stubbers and cannons could be seen poking out from under camo-net awnings of the roofed wooden platforms.

The compound beyond the mined fences was overgrown with fast-seeding ferns and pernicious constrictor-vines. Lianas and flowering screens of vegetation were scaling the featureless walls of the low buildings that spread out across the centre of the compound, their ground plan looking like a letter 'H'. The structure broke into two distinct wings off a central, heavily fortified rockrete rectangle. Here and there armacrys domes emerged from the smothering greenery covering the roofs of the base, most of the rhomboid panes cracked or missing entirely.

Bullet holes pockmarked the pitted walls of the base, like the scars of some disfiguring jungle disease, and in places the rockrete had been burned by the unkind attentions of a flamer assault. Most of the east wing was a blackened shell, having been gutted by fire.

On the other side of the compound, crouched on an asphalt square, was a Valkyrie-class airborne assault carrier – like the one that had brought Tremayne to these mosquito-haunted jungles in the first place – although it was obvious that the craft had been captured and put to their own use by the green-skins. Its once-sleek gunmetal grey bodywork was now defaced with ork glyphs, black and white check bars, and had more generally been given a fresh coat of red paint. Additional pintle-mounted cannons had been mounted at the open side hatches of the craft, making its insect-like form seem even more unbal-anced and ungainly.

'What happened here?' Tremayne gasped. What he saw before him now was not what he had been expecting to see.

'It was overrun.' Borysko didn't need to know the exact details of what had happened here; it had been the same all over the planet and throughout the equa-torial rainforests. In the first days of the invasion, following the first rok landings, the feral orks had risen up and marched from Plateau Greenskin to claim the last few Imperial bastions that stood out here in the green wilderness. 'First to fall was Wolf Outpost and the orks made a play for Cerbera Base too. This Mechanicus research facility must have fallen at around the same time. The skitarii tech-guards posted here clearly weren't prepared for such a colossal and coordinated attack from the greenskins. If it was the ferals, of course?'

'What do you mean?' Tremayne asked, his interest piqued.

'I'm not sure, but it's not like ferals to take over a place like this. They'd be more likely to just loot the place and then be gone. But the orks that seized this place have stayed. Besides, I wouldn't have expected feral orks to have the resources to besiege and conquer an Adeptus Mechanicus base.'

'So what manner of ork could have achieved this?'

'We'll just have to wait and see.'

Borysko looked out across the base. Now it was his turn to ask a question. 'What were they doing out here? Why build a facility here?'

'Diseases,' Tremayne said, a twinkle of excitement in his eye. 'These jungles are teeming with life and, surprisingly, most of it exists on a microscopic level.'

'Bacteria?'

'They are the most adaptive, durable and successful life form in the galaxy. There was a great deal that the genetor-magi could learn from such effective killers. And then of course there was the ready supply of spores within the vicinity.'

The sergeant looked at the lieutenant again. There was something more that Tremayne still wasn't telling him, and it was the point of their costly mission into the Green.

'We're talking about biological warfare here, aren't we?'

Tremayne looked at him from beneath the jutting peak of his battered cap but did not answer Borysko's question.

'And you have dragged us here because?'

'The object of my quest, the culmination of my mission, lies inside. We are going to have to infiltrate that base.'

'So how are we supposed to get in there?'

Tremayne looked at the skinner sergeant. By the green reflected light of the magnoculars, Borysko could see the unnerving expression distorted by the red weals of the scars that raked the left side of the lieutenant's face. It was a smile, and the sight of it unnerved Borysko more than any man-eating plant or ravening skin.

'I was rather hoping you would be able to provide the solution to that problem.'

THE BLASTED CRATER stretched for half a kilometre across the face of the tormented jungle. Vegetation only encroached as far as the lip of the crater. On every side the trees were grey, twisted and withered. They looked like no kind of flora that should ever exist anywhere other than the daemon-worlds of the Eye of Terror.

Nothing grew within the crater itself. The ground there was infected, sickly in colour, parched and purged of all nutrients that might have allowed plants to grow.

At its centre, at its very base where the ground was flat and cracked like an arid plain of the chem-polluted ash wastes of Armageddon Secundus, stood a circle of eight stones, each at least four metres tall. The monoliths appeared black, as if they had been carved out of obsidian. Each one bore worn features and, despite the unkind atten-tions of acid rain and more esoteric weathering effects over the centuries, what they had once been carved to resemble was still clear. The faces of the menhirs bore the forms of cruel, daemonic visages – all fang-filled maws and darkly twisted features.

Other things had been carved on the surface of the sacrificial stones too: writhing sigils and unnatural runes that stung the eyes and made stomachs knot to look upon them. But the vile images seemed not to affect the orks and the leering daemon faces merely excited them all the more at the prospect of battle.

The ork host filled the space within the circle of standing stones and spilled out across the crater floor beyond. There were the greenskins of several feral tribes gathered here, including amongst their number boar-riders and even a runt squiggoth.

Standing at the very centre of the circle, astride the altar stone, was the ork wyrdboy, the one-time outcast returned to be amongst his kind again. Clutched in one meaty paw was its gnarled quoia-wood staff. The alien shaman gazed up at the tortured sky above, green fire crackling in its eyes.

Strangely, the gathered greenskins were unusually quiet, where normally one would have expected a bellowed 'Waaagh!' to fill the crater with cacophonous noise. All were staring up at the heavens, like the wyrdboy that had brought them to this place and this propitious point in time. And there they watched and waited.

Above them the warp storm writhed and spiralled, mountainous blood-red thunderheads boiled and seethed with unbridled energies, bathing the greenskins in the strobing light of crackling amethyst lightning flashes.

Wind howled around the crater with the fury of a ravenous predator. Thunder rumbled as if the sky was splitting apart, the residual crackling aftershock of the rumbles echoing away over the canopy of the rainforest.

And Ruzdakk Blitzgul and the feral ork tribes of Armageddon, waited for the end of the world.

PART III
NO FEAR

SEVENTEEN
LEGACY OF THE DAMNED

AN UNEASY SILENCE hung over the twisted, tainted clearing as the two Space Marine forces regarded each other. Having commanded his men not to fire on the other Space Marines, his crozius held firmly in his hand, Chaplain Wolfram watched to see what their counterparts would do next.

One of the grey-armoured warriors stepped forward. Wolfram caught a glimpse of the white skull emblazoned on one of his shoulder pads.

'Captain Oberon Eurys of the Relictors,' the warrior said, his own power sword still held tightly in one gauntleted fist, ready to defend himself if the situation demanded it.

'Chaplain Wolfram of the Black Templars Solemnus Crusade, gene-son of Sigismund and Rogal Dorn.'

The two sides continued to regard each other as suspiciously as if they had each been orks to the others' eyes. Something had to be done to break this impasse in which they now found themselves.

'Blessed be, brother,' Wolfram said, making the sign of the aquila as he held the cross-head of his crozius up in front of him.

'Strength of will, courage of will,' the Relictor said, holding his power sword in both gauntleted hands by its blade, so that its skull-embossed hilt and pommel formed their own cruciform shape before his bowed head.

'By the Throne, it would appear that we are of the same intent,' Wolfram declared.

'Indeed. Well met, brother Templar.'

INTRODUCTIONS DONE WITH, at the mutual command of their leaders, the combined Black Templar and Relictor force had decided to make camp within the clearing, to make preparations and discuss their mission goals. The Space Marines numbered twenty-three warriors in total, made up of the eleven survivors of Kill-team Wolfram and the twelve of Captain Eurys's warband.

Although the Black Templars did not need to sleep, they needed to take time to assess the damage they had suffered and Apothecary Bliant needed time to treat the wounds they had received in their battles with the tribal orks. The other brothers needed time to make what repairs they could to their battle-damaged power armour. They needed to make sure that their bolters were blessed, and with a full clip in place, ready for the ultimate battle that they were sure to face as they advanced inexorably towards the centre of the massing storm to the west.

And although the two forces were now united, they still distanced themselves from one another in the camp, forming two distinct groups within the glade. Separated from both groups, the commanders of the two Space Marine warbands met in heated conference.

'These are propitious times,' Oberon Eurys said, gazing distantly into the sickly trees of the withered jungle.

'These are dark times,' Wolfram said, an edge of anger in his voice. His counterpart had sounded far too pleased about the prospect that these days were anything other than a dire black mark on Armageddon's long and war-scathed history.

'Granted, Chaplain Wolfram,' the Relictor agreed, 'but they are propitious nonetheless. This is an age of signs and portents. The omens are there. As the forty-first millennium draws to a close, the Imperium is facing the dawn of a new age.'

'These are the last days of an old millennium, I grant you that,' Wolfram affirmed, 'but these are also the last of our crusade. The last twelve years have cost us so much, we will be lucky to see the dawn of the forty-second millennium.'

'Such fatalism in one of the Emperor's Chaplains.' The Relictor's tone was almost chiding in its boldness.

'Fatalism, perhaps. We have had to face so much, and have so far prevailed, but it has come at a terrible price,' Wolfram said, his mind replaying the events of the last twelve years, the last few weeks on Armageddon, the matter of days their mission to recover the seed of their brethren had so far lasted. But more particularly he went over what had happened in the last few hours of that very mission. 'Blessed be the Emperor, I prostrate myself before His wondrous majesty, but I prefer to call my attitude pragmatism. This war for Armageddon will see an end to us all, but before that time when we shall come before the Golden Throne to be judged by the Master of Mankind, we will do all we can to fulfil the vows we made to Him on the eve of our part in this conflict.'

'We will all have to atone for our sins before the Golden Throne, when the Emperor demands it, father. But no life given in the service of the Emperor was ever... given in vain.'

'I know the creed, Brother Eurys, and better than most,' Wolfram growled, the ire clear in his voice.

'But all I am saying, Chaplain Wolfram, is have faith. We are warriors of the immortal Emperor of Mankind.' A sinister smile played across Eurys's thin lips. 'We have eternity on our side.'

The Chaplain turned aside from the leader of the Relictor party and turned his gaze on the remainder of his own warband gathered within the clearing.

The grey-armoured warrior made him feel uncomfortable. He had heard rumours about the Relictors. Talk of Inquisitorial interest and a curse upon the Chapter, brought upon the Relictors thanks to the precarious position of their home world in the galaxy. Torva Minoris was said to be situated within an area of the Segmentum Obscurus notorious for the intensity of its warp storms.

Wolfram looked to where his Black Templars were gathered, kneeling in a circle. Their other preparations complete, the crusading brothers were now preparing their hearts, minds and souls for the inevitable conflict that awaited them, chanting together litanies of vigilance and sure-firing.

'The roles we have to fulfil in the events that are playing out on this one world could determine how we embrace this new age,' Eurys said. 'Whether we enter it as champions, inheritors of the legacy of our forebears, and fulfil the plan laid out for us by our Emperor-father. Or whether we enter it as slaves of the myriad forces that are set against mankind.'

'And what is this role that you believe we have to play on the verge of this new dawn, captain?'

Eurys regarded the gathered battle-brothers around them with conspiratorial glances, as if ensuring that none were close enough to hear the sensitive information that he was about to share with the Black Templar.

'Chaplain, you cannot have failed to notice the dread storm that is brewing over the heart of these foetid jungles.'

'Indeed, we have been aware of its presence ever since we entered these forsaken forests.' *And before*, he added to himself.

'But do you have any inkling of why such a manifestation should occur here, and at this time?'

Wolfram thought back to what Brother Ansgar had told him of the chaotic visions that had beset him on this most recent campaign of their last crusade. 'I suspect you are going to tell me what this portends, captain.'

'The masters of our Chapter have indeed acquired certain information. There lies within these dark jungles the legacy of another time – another attempt to conquer this world. An attempt made in the name of the profane gods of the outer darkness.'

Wolfram suppressed a gasp of horror. He was already aware of that particular dark episode in the history of Armageddon. In his position as a spiritual guide and guardian of his Chapter, he was party to certain otherwise prohibited information. But he did not want to reveal this to Eurys – not yet. So he said nothing.

'What kind of legacy?'

Eurys met the blood-red gaze of the Chaplain and his own eyes seemed to darken. 'Monuments,' the Relictor said.

In his mind's eye, Wolfram saw a circle of savage, black stones. *Like claws raking the bleeding sky,* Ansgar had said.

'Raised by the servants of a daemon prince who sold their souls to the warrior god of Chaos ten thousand years ago, to honour the Blood God's twisted divinity and bring his favour upon them.'

It was as the Black Templar had begun to suspect on hearing the revelations of the Emperor's Champion.

'They lie further to the west,' Eurys went on, 'at the eye of the awakening storm. And it is the growing warp-power that is awakening their blasphemous potential. They in turn are drawing more warp-power to them.'

'You say these monuments are the legacy of another aborted attempt at conquest. What do they have to do with the greenskins' invasion at the close of the forty-first millennium?'

'What do you know of the First War for Armageddon?' Wolfram saw that the Relictor's hand was fidgeting with the power sword that was scabbarded at his side.

'You are referring to Ghazghkull Thraka's first invasion fifty standard years ago?' Wolfram said, intentionally evasive. This was to test the captain, to judge what manner of man he might be by seeing how much Oberon Eurys would openly reveal to a battle-brother he had met only a matter of an hour before.

'No, Chaplain,' the other said, eyeing Wolfram darkly. 'And I suspect you knew that already. Your kind are so suspicious.'

'Our *kind*?'

'I refer to the cultist uprising and the whole-scale planetary invasion initiated by the Traitor Primarch of the World Eaters Legion, the Fallen One.'

Eurys paused to let the shocking nature of his words sink in, and to give Wolfram time to make sense of the implications of his words.

'Tell me everything,' Wolfram said, the fire of righteousness burning in his eyes behind his crystalline eye-sockets.

REBELLION GRIPPED THE hives. Myriad cultist cells of the Dark Gods emerged from their hiding places to make open war with the leaders of the planet. The fighting was bloody and intense. Armageddon's Planetary Defence Force was forced to suppress the populace with increasing regularity. Across Armageddon Secundus the rebellions were swiftly put down but on Armageddon Primus it was another matter altogether.

The waste zones surrounding the hives of Tempestora, Volcanus and Death Mire stretched further, isolating the great mountain-cities from one another. Geography itself therefore helped to hamper the loyalist forces attempting to restore Imperial rule of law to the continent. And then, into this lawless state of emergency came the cursed legion of the Blood God.

As their world was locked in the throes of insurrection and disorder, the forces of Imperial order were caught completely unawares by the arrival of the hulk the *Devourer of Stars*, at the heart of the Armageddon subsector, their attention consumed by the anarchic uprisings wracking their cities.

Aboard the vast derelict-cum-spaceship, the massed forces of the Blood God's primarch hungered for the lives and souls of a population billions strong. Angron the Accursed, daemon primarch of the World Eaters Space Marines, stood at the head of this awe and terror-inspiring Chaos army; the stuff of nightmares made unholy flesh, driven by a terrible appetite for blood.

As the unholy primarch's savage hordes of darkness swept across the face of the war-torn planet – twisted daemonic creatures joining with mutants, cannibalistic cultists and ancient traitor sons of the Emperor in their savage slaughter of the Armageddon – the Imperial forces once again faced rebellion as fully half of their number defected to join the ranks of the enemy.

The few loyalist defenders that remained were efficiently routed from Armageddon Prime. The all but defeated remnants of the Imperial defence forces fell back through the thick equatorial jungle, eventually joining forces with scattered pockets of survivors from Armageddon Secundus. It was this collection of troops that then regrouped and prepared to make a last stand along the banks of the sluggish rivers Styx and Chaeron.

With Chaos in the ascendant, the one thing the Imperial forces had on their side at this time was that, despite the heavy defeats they had so recently suffered, they were well organised. This defence was further bolstered when the Wolves of Fenris arrived on the sulphurous shores of Armageddon to aid the harassed defenders in direct response to widespread distress signals, sent as Angron's armies made planetfall.

The presence of the battle-brethren of the Space Wolves Chapter, assigned to this sector only recently, was unknown to the forces of Chaos. The defenders gained valuable time when Angron – complacent following one successful conquest after another – spent weeks erecting blasphemous monuments in homage to the Fell Powers rather than pressing home the advantage his hordes had won him.

The daemon primarch's failure to run down the shattered fragments of the Imperial armies and destroy them utterly would prove to cost him the ultimate prize when the final reckoning came. Emerging from the sweltering jungles at last, his army found a well prepared, dug in force of defences reinforced by the Space Wolves, commanded by the Chapter Master Logan Grimnar himself.

Battles raged on a titanic scale right along the front line as tides of Chaos soldiery smashed into the unyielding banks of Imperial troops. On the banks of the River Chaeron the Imperial line stood firm, and at last the broken forces of Chaos were thrown back in disarray.

Further to the west, the outcome of the battle did not bode so well for the loyalists. It was here that Angron the Accursed, the Blood-soaked, the Fallen One, personally led the Chaos attack. Supported by a bodyguard of no less than twelve greater daemons of Khorne, the daemonic primarch carved a bloody path through the Imperial lines, urging his forces towards the hives of Helsreach and Infernus.

But it was at this crucial point that the Great Wolf Logan Grimnar committed the one force he had left in reserve to the battle. An entire company of Grey Knight terminators – superhuman warriors of the Ordo Malleus's Chamber Militant, rigorously trained to deal with otherworldly, soul-taking threats such as those of Chaos manifest – teleported directly into the midst of the traitor primarch's host.

Only the unique abilities of the Grey Knights would be able to truly defeat a monstrosity such as Angron. Rematerialising at the very feet of the Chaos demigod, at the pulsing heart of the roiling mass of corruption that was the daemon prince's unholy army, the knights joined in battle with Angron's brass-skinned bloodthirsters.

Of all the company of crusading Ordo Malleus warriors that Grimnar committed to the conflict that day, only ten Grey Knights survived, their commander having paid the ultimate price in his personal battle with the daemon prince. But regardless of the price that had been paid, Angron of the World Eaters had at last been defeated, his tainted spirit banished back to the hellish miasmic unreality of the warp.

Their figurehead destroyed, the massed forces of Chaos fell back in confusion, consumed by infighting or driven mad by the seemingly unconscionable fate that had befallen their master. The Space Wolves launched a massive counter-attack. As a result Angron's hordes were routed utterly. Only the frenzied Berserkers of the World Eaters Legion managed to fight their way back to the *Devourer of Stars* and thus, in time, the safety of the warp.

THROUGH THE CROAKING jungle night the weird warping effects continued to the west.

His story done, his revelations made, Oberon Eurys said nothing more. The Chaplain, incredulous at the horrific details of what Armageddon had suffered five hundred years ago, the scars of which it still bore, was unable to say anything.

They were close to the epicentre of the disturbance now; Wolfram could sense it in the air about him, in his very soul. He knew it to be true just as certainly as he knew that he lived and breathed and walked on the surface of this contested world. They were so close, in fact, that their camp was almost in the shadow of the wild esoteric effects they were witnessing.

It seemed to Chaplain Wolfram that amidst the swirls of red and massing purple thunderheads he could glimpse half-formed faces, snarling in animal hunger or perhaps perpetual torment.

As well as the malevolent cloud formations overhead, darkly underlit by the crackling warp-light of unearthly black lightning, bars of twisting, ethereal luminescence – in a spectrum of colours that surely could not exist beyond the Empyrean – lit the night like some dislocated aurora.

Strange crackling sounds like static energy discharging in the ionised air *crick-cracked* across the dome of heaven. It did not take a warp-seer to be able to tell that something terrible was coming, that something of world-shaking significance was waiting to come to fruition.

When the storm broke, as inevitably it must, a magnitude of force would be unleashed upon Armageddon akin to that of an orbital strike, devastating enough to surely tear open a hole in reality, a rift between times, between universes.

'So what happens now?' Wolfram asked, slowly turning to face the Relictors captain again.

'Of the fact that the stones are awakening there can be no doubt. As a consequence, it is clear to me that we are on the verge of something potentially planet-shattering – something apocalyptic. The forces of Chaos are not yet done with this world. The resources for the defence of Armageddon are already stretched beyond measure.

'We can either let this new and possibly greater threat arise and take holy Armageddon from us once and for all, or we can face this challenge head-on and take the fight to our enemies before they can gain a foothold on this world again.

'I beseech you and your men to join us, Brother-Chaplain, for I fear what fate might befall this world if this emerging threat goes unchallenged.'

'We have our own mission to complete. We swore sacred oaths that we would not rest until we had hunted down the last of the greenskins of the Blood Scar tribe and freed Armageddon from the oppression of ork-kind,' Chaplain Wolfram pressed.

'Have I not convinced you of the seriousness of this situation?' Eurys asked incredulously. 'If we do not act now there may be no world left for us to save. And that means you will be rejecting your holy vows if you do not act now to help us.'

The hackles on the back of Wolfram's neck rose. How dare this Relictor speak to him of his holy vows, in such a way, and challenge the strength of his faith? And the Chaplain a champion of His creed amongst the most devout brotherhood of all His holy armies!

'The vows I have sworn mean more to me than life itself,' the Chaplain growled.

'Then join us now,' Eurys reiterated. 'I fear what will happen if we do not present a united front to defeat whatever awaits us at the heart of darkness.'

Wolfram turned away from the captain again.

All the signs that the Black Templars had seen with their own eyes were that a massive ork force had passed this way. Perhaps the greenskins had been somehow drawn to the awakening of the Chaos monoliths that Eurys spoke of, drawn by the concentration of warp-power.

Casting up a heartfelt prayer to the Emperor for guidance, Wolfram let out a world-weary sigh and turned back to his own spiritual challenger.

'Then it would appear we have no choice, do we, brother-captain?' Wolfram said, feeling uncomfortable as he made such a confession before the Relictor. 'My brothers and I will join with your warband to eradicate whatever threat it is that faces us here on this darkly inauspicious day.'

And in the process, Emperor willing, we will discover what has befallen our brothers among

Castellan Gerhard's company and recover that most precious treasure – the gene-seed of their Emperor-wrought bodies, Wolfram added to himself.

Or die trying, he thought, gazing at the shadow of the massing warp storm reaching out over them all.

EIGHTEEN
H-363

THE EXPLOSION TORE the pre-dawn night apart, bathing the compound in the hungry orange glow of an expanding ball of roiling promethium. Roosting golvers rose squawking from the dark forest in panicked flight, their white bodies luminescent against the colouring sky. At the gated entrance to the ork-controlled base, the wooden structure of a watchtower began to burn.

A second echoing detonation ripped through the jungle night and this time the hunters could hear the desperate barks and angry snarls of the greenskins, as a portion of the doubled chain-link fence was blown apart in an explosion of stony earth.

A scuttling figure, keeping low even in the darkness, rejoined the skinners where they were hunkered down in the thick undergrowth.

'One distraction, as requested,' Vanderkamp said, the white slash of a slick grin on his face.

'That should get their attention,' Borysko said, his face set in a stony mask. 'Half the greenskins in there will now be rushing to join in the fun at the front gate.'

'While we sneak in the back,' Tannhauser chuckled quietly to himself.

'As it were,' Ertz added.

'Beneficent majesty, look upon us sinners with compassion,' Priest half-whispered, putting the icon to his lips.

Borysko held up a fist and his men were immediately quiet again. To the south-west, threatening storm clouds were gathering. Their legacy was a thunderous pressure in the atmosphere over the compound.

The noises of the forest had returned to fill the vacuum of sound left by the rippling explosions; insect chirrups, primate shrieks and bird cries.

One warbling cry came more clearly and from closer than any other. The sound came again. The kroot had given the signal.

Two sharp jerks of Borysko's hand moved them forwards, in a low scuttling line over the blackened turf up to the fence where Geist – no more than a camo-fatigued shadow – crouched waiting beneath one of the watch-tower gun-posts. The trooper had re-opened a section of damaged fence that the orks had repaired badly following their seizing of the genetor-base. There was a hole there now big enough for a man to pass through easily – even one as large as Coburg.

The twelve men covered the ground beneath the gun-tower almost soundlessly.

Kole was the first through the fence. There was no danger of mines; the blasted area around this section of the barricade showed that the orks' initial assault had detonated the devices buried here, and Geist's trained eye had confirmed that the skins hadn't replaced them with mines of their own making. Then came Ertz, the Kid, Tannhauser, Kasarta, Borysko and Tremayne, followed by Yeydl, Coburg, Gunderson, Priest and finally Vanderkamp. Geist joined the rear of the line, giving the treeline one last sweep with his shotgun before he followed the rest of the platoon through.

They didn't have long before the orks realised the explosions that had drawn them to the main gates were merely a decoy action. Once they realised that, even primitive-minded greenskins would start looking for where the real threat lay. Before that happened, Borysko's Boys needed to be inside the base, ideally with the prize already in their hands. At least they had a sure-fire escape plan.

The fire-gutted rockcrete buildings of the east wing of the base rose up before the hunters. In the lee of the windowless structure, Kole brought the platoon to a halt. There they waited until all the skinners had joined them in their position. His back to the side of the building, Kole glanced right towards the gates. From this position they couldn't be seen, but he could hear the orks barking at one another in annoyance and confusion.

Borysko peered up at the gun-post they had all just run past, eyes narrowed. There was a suggestion of movement beneath the camo-awning there, and then the kroot emerged. Pangor Yuma perched on the edge

of the lookout post and then dropped the four metres
to the ground, landing tensed like a feline, without
making a sound. Rifle in hand, the mercenary covered
the ground to the hunters' position with long-legged
strides.

The hunters joined the kroot as it scaled the side of
the building in front of them. The task was made easier for the weary troopers by the straggling lianas and
woody vegetation that had proliferated with the
demise of the base's original occupants. It was as if a
naturally growing scaffold covered the rockcrete.

In no time at all they were on the roof. Scuttling
between ventilation outlets, comms aerials and the
ruined crystal domes, which glittered with what little
starlight broke through the hydrocarbon clouds circling the world above the equator, the troopers made
their way across the eastern wing towards the central
block of buildings. Without the aid of spot-beams
any orks watching from the other sentry posts
wouldn't have been able to see the hunters as they
made their mad dash across roof of the base. In the
gloom of night, they would appear as shadows
against the pitch-black structure beneath them.

The roar of high-calibre gunfire abruptly tore
through the night. Kole threw himself down flat on
the roof. The rest of the party copied him without
hesitation. Had the orks found a target on which to
vent their frustration?

Looking up, only another ten metres away, silhou-
etted against the rich ultramarine of the sky, Kole
could see the bulge of an armacrys projection. They
did not have far to go before they could actually get
inside the base.

There was a dull boom and then the swelling sphere of an explosion rose into the sky above the parapet of the building.

'What the hell was that?' he heard Vanderkamp gasp behind him. 'That wasn't one of mine.'

Kole tried to crane his head to see what was happening at the front of the base. Shuffling towards the edge of the roof on his stomach, he was able to look over the edge and down onto the gated entrance to the compound.

Another of the watchtower gun-posts was aflame and as he peered over the parapet, he saw a greenskin wreathed in flames tumble off the platform and plummet to the ground below. Other skins were closing on the gates, which were coming under heavy fire from the direction of the river.

Sergeant Borysko had been right. These were not your ordinary feral greenskins. From the looks of their armour and the weaponry they were carrying, these were orks of an altogether more sophisticated kind – probably off-worlders, rather than spore-grown skins from the jungles. All of them wore some manner of plate ceramite armour and all of them carried primitive firearms and fire-throwers.

But then the opponent they were facing was of an altogether greater ilk as well. Shells spanged off sheet-iron ork glyphs affixed to the gates, in what could only have been an assault cannon barrage. A huge shape was moving up the worn track with heavy, clanking steps. A weed-dripping hull gleamed blackly in the reflected light of muzzle-flare and the resulting explosions.

Then Ertz, Borysko and Vanderkamp were next to Kole.

'What's that?' Ertz hissed.

'I'd call that a distraction,' Vanderkamp suggested.

'Agreed,' Borysko said. 'Now let's move and get inside before we're spotted.'

The wattle-combed head of Pangor Yuma could be seen in silhouette against the awakening early morning sky, at the lip of the shattered dome. Then they were all at the jagged edge of the broken armacrys protrusion and Coburg was lowering a coil of rope into the darkness below. And then they were in.

By means of stealth, subterfuge and rank cunning worthy of a feral skin, Borysko's Boys had penetrated the compound. Now the prize they sought lay within their reach.

'IN THE NAME of the primarch, death to the blasphemies!' Brother Jarold's augmented voice rang from the vox-speakers of his dreadnought body. His booming cry carried over the scream of his assault cannon and the rattling fire of his storm bolter.

The orks manning the gates of the compound returned fire; some of the aliens even managed to hit the dreadnought. Their bullets rattled harmlessly off the adamantium shell of Jarold's body like hailstones.

'Vile xenos scum!' the veteran roared, river water running off him. 'Thou shalt not oppose the holy Templars of his Imperial Majesty. May you rot in whatever alien hell spawned you!'

Brother Jarold's symbiotic machine-spirit chimed a warning, alerting him that weapons-lock had been gained on him as, through artificial eyes, he saw the exhaust flare of the rocket launcher fired from the remains of a watch-tower.

Jarold had no time to do anything other than brace for impact. The rocket struck him a split second later, its warhead exploding in a flash of oily flame. The dreadnought was enveloped in a thick cloud of greasy smoke that completely obscured him in the pre-dawn gloom.

The sound of orks hooting in grisly satisfaction made strange echoes within the derelict compound.

A gentle yet insistent breeze blew from the river through the jungle. The smoke cleared. Brother Jarold still stood, a last persistent wisp of fumy vapour clinging to his tank body. The left hand flank of his armoured hull was dented and cracked, the devotional passages of scripture that had been inscribed there burnt away and unreadable now.

'Thou shalt not oppose a brother of the Black Templars! For by our faith are we made strong; strong enough to resist anything that the enemy might throw against us,' Jarold roared in anger.

The dreadnought had received a direct hit from a crashing ork plane and survived to recount the incident. Did these stupid greenskins really think that a simple rocket attack would halt his indomitable advance?

With mighty crushing steps, the dreadnought resumed its tank-like charge towards the gates. Ork bullets rattled from his hull again. They troubled the veteran brother no more than if they had been mosquito stings against his impenetrable steel hide.

'No pity!' Jarold's voice rang across the shrinking space between him and the genetor-base.

Sensory impulse grafts rotated the dreadnought's own hull-mounted rocket launcher to lock onto the gate gun-tower.

'No remorse!' he roared.

His machine-spirit notified him of target-lock just as the chime-alert warned him that the orks had acquired weapons-lock on him again as well.

'No fear!'

With the shriek of rocket engines firing, three Retribution-class rockets were launched. For a moment their spiralling flight seemed haphazard and chaotic, then tiny cogitator relays kicked in and the three missiles turned groundward again.

They hit the gun-post in quick succession. The watch-tower exploded outwards, utterly destroyed as the triple detonation in turn set off the orks' own gun-post ammunition dump.

Jarold's rocket launcher fired again and the ork-defaced gates of the compound buckled and burst inwards.

Striding through the roiling smoke and flames, Brother Jarold entered the ork-held base like some dreadful avenging angel of the Emperor's holy wrath.

HE WAS DROWNING; his body sinking like a stone, weighed down by the dead weight of ceramite and plasteel that encased him. Fractured, rippling light penetrated the darkening azure depths. There was a rushing throbbing in his ears. He felt a swirl of movement around him and his body spun as it sank deeper into the smothering inky darkness.

There was another buffeting change in the current and something surged under him, shapeless in the impenetrable gloom. The light above him was fading. He opened his mouth to cry out in defiance at the hungry water that was dragging him down into this watery abyss. Brackish water poured into his throat and lungs.

He riled against the water's invasion, expelling the foul-tasting stuff with a violent diaphragmatic spasm. The roar that followed the water made bubbles of rippling silver in the muffling darkness that ascended to the distant surface again.

In a sudden flurry of movement he kicked out. Powerful leg muscles propelled him upwards. Hands and arms pushed against the resisting water and he rose further. Encouraged now by his upwards progress, he kicked out again with sharp rhythmic thrusts.

The sparkling, light-shot swell swam into focus above him, like the guiding beacon of the Emperor's glorious golden light of true faith, until he could see distinct shapes beyond the surface. Upwards he swam, coming closer and closer to the broken wave-chopped surface, until–

ANSGAR OPENED HIS eyes and blinked. Above him, a cracked rockcrete roof faded into focus out of the shadows. He realised that he was not seeing the ceiling through his helm's visor. Either he had lost his helmet or someone had removed it.

Ansgar tried to move but felt resistance where his wrists and ankles were restrained. Incredibly his arms felt weak; his legs too. The Emperor's Champion riled and snarled in angry frustration. He tensed his body again, twisting and pulling against the resisting clamps. Still his efforts were to no avail.

Trapped on his back, gazing up at the cracks covering the ceiling of the chamber, memories began to return to the restrained champion.

...The path crumbling and dropping away beneath him... The cliff face a blur tearing past his eyes... Hitting the churning white water, the hungry river closing over his head... The sharp pain of concussion flashing through his skull as he was battered against the rocks of rapids as the surging force of the water dragged his body under and along... Flashes of recollection as he was swept through the churning, disorientating darkness, alternating with blinding bubbling froth... Another moment of lucidity, lying amongst the mud and reeds at the shore... Brutal hands taking hold of his limbs and dragging him ashore... Then nothing but the black oblivion of unconsciousness again and dreams of drowning...

More calmly this time, the restrained Space Marine tried to move again. Pushing his chin down towards his chest, he could see something of the dilapidated room in front of him. He could see still more by turning his head to left and right.

The spacious chamber was littered with pieces of rusting, ill-kept equipment. There was something of the Apothecarion about many of the pieces, but just as many looked as if they would not be out of place in the tech-workshops of Forgeship *Goliath*. But everything about the place was united in its drab and ill-cared-for appearance. The tools, the equipment benches, even the walls and pillars of the room itself all were dilapidated and deteriorating. Water dripped with all the acoustics of a cavern.

Ansgar was secured to an operating slab, with what looked like thick clamps of adamantium holding his wrists and ankles secure. He was aware now that, as well as his helmet, his right gauntlet had been removed, the flesh of his wrist stuck with stabbing,

tingling electrodes. There was also a thin plastek tube,
dark with his blood, emerging from his forearm. He
became aware of other probes connecting to his neck.
He could not see what the tubes and wires connected
to in turn.

'B-Brother?'

Ansgar was suddenly alert and focused, hearing the
thin voice.

'Brother Ansgar?'

The voice was coming from somewhere over his
right shoulder and sounded like its owner was trying
to talk through a mouthful of spittle or blood. Neck
muscles straining, Ansgar craned his head round. And
there, highlighted by flickering illuminator strips, he
saw a second operating slab, and the poor wretch
secured to it.

This second slab had been elevated so that it was
almost on the vertical plane. The figure strapped there
had been a Space Marine once. The Marine's dermis-
bonded black carapace was still partially intact,
disconnected neural sensor and transfusion points
cut into the hardened shell beneath his flayed skin.
Of his armour there was no sign.

The man was only still upright thanks to the
restraints holding him in place. He was a physical
wreck. His body was a mess of open wounds and,
from the nature of some of the voided clefts, it looked
like the Marine had had some of his internal organs
removed. His right leg was missing altogether. It
seemed incredible that he was conscious at all.

He was hooked up to a crude monitoring device,
via a tangle of plastek tubes and electrode wire-
bundles. The auspex-monitor, all discoloured metal

and tarnished brass, looked like it had been cannibalised from a piece of equipment of Mechanicus origin.

It seemed to be all the other Marine could do to lift his head to look at Ansgar, and his appearance was a terrible sight.

'Solemnus weeps,' Ansgar gasped. Even after all that he had seen in his years of service to the Golden Throne of Terra, the terrible condition of the surgically savaged Space Marine still shocked and appalled him.

'I had almost given up hope of ever being found alive,' the dissected man slurred. As he spoke, Ansgar saw that seemingly half his teeth had been removed. 'Now seeing you here, bound to that pain-table, our crusade's champion brought low by the enemy, I know that all hope *is* gone. This must truly be a sign that our holy venture is over at last.'

'Do I know you, brother?' Ansgar asked, unable to identify the Marine from his disfigured face or by his cracked voice.

'By the primarch, I doubt it,' the other coughed. 'Not now.' The Marine paused as he hawked a gobbet of bloody matter from his lungs. 'I am – or rather, I was – Apothecary Colber of Castellan Gerhard's company.'

'Sigismund's sword!' he gasped. His quest was over; he had inadvertently been brought to the place where he might discover the fate of the lost fighting company. 'Are there any other survivors?'

'There were,' Colber said weakly, hanging his head again, 'and I would weep for them, had I still the means to do so. But they are all dead now, their corpses defiled by the filthy fiend that claims lordship of this domain. I am the only one left.'

Ansgar's mind was left reeling. That some craven, filthy-clawed alien could do such a thing to a brother of the Solemnus Crusade.

But then again, that the alien greenskins could carry out such an act of desecration should not have surprised him, especially not when he remembered what they had done to his home world. It was just one more reason why every last one of the xenos breed had to be eradicated. Ansgar swore again that he would not rest until the whole of ork-kind had been driven from the surface of Armageddon, even in his current situation.

'Where are we?' Ansgar asked, trying another tack.

'It seems to have been an Adeptus Mechanicus base operated by the Divisio Biologis. I have seen the caducal helix within these walls, along with the motto: *disposito divinus ex corporeus.*' The broken Apothecary laughed darkly. 'The greenskins have made a mockery out of that noble sentiment here. Divine order out of flesh? It should be *turba ex corporeus* now.'

Ansgar realised that he was staring at the broken suspended figure of Brother Colber.

'What did this to you?' Ansgar asked.

'The defiler of sacred flesh, the desecrator of our holy gene-seed,' Colber said, his voice wavering.

'But your wounds–'

'It called them… the word sounded like *eksperiments.*

'–look like the work of some malevolent surgeon. They do not look like the handiwork of the ork savages. So what manner of creature did this to you?'

Both the bound Templars heard the shuffling steps over the drips leaking from the damp-rotted ceiling. Both looked to their right.

'That,' Colber stated flatly.

Ansgar's breath caught in his throat. Approaching the makeshift alien operating theatre was a creature that was undoubtedly an ork, although the Emperor's Champion had never seen a greenskin like it in the twelve long years of the Solemnus fleet's Crusade, or before Marshal Brant's Black Templars embarked on their holy mission.

There was something about the ork's attire that reminded Ansgar of the medicae of the Divisio Biologis, but the ill-fitting, gore-stained gown was clung to the body of an alien that was as tall as a Space Marine. Much of the ork's body had been rebuilt with customised bionik replacements. Such body parts included the ork's left shoulder – giving it an almost hunchbacked stance – the lower part of its right arm – the hand an unexpectedly fine piece of craftsmanship with several extra multi-jointed needle-digits – and one leg. The creature was also wearing a head strap-supported magnifying lens.

Its green flesh was criss-crossed with knotted scars and stapled flesh wounds; signs of other procedures carried out to replace the internal portions of its body. Unusually for an ork of this size and obvious standing within the hierarchy of ork society, the creature's build was more lithe than Ansgar would have expected of a brute of such a height, even in spite of its mechanical customisation job.

As if the appearance of the ork medic, and the realisation that it was this freakish, sideshow surgeon that had taken Apothecary Colber and his battle-brothers apart piece by piece was not enough, there was something even more unsettling about its abrupt appearance.

Ansgar could practically smell the fear coming off the alien like a foetid musk. And it couldn't be afraid of its two helpless experimental subjects, of that Ansgar was sure.

The ork medic barked something in its unintelligible language and strode up to the crucified Colber. Raising its left paw it dealt the Apothecary a vicious backhanded swipe across his abused face. Colber's head lolled unconsciously on his chest.

Drawing a gobbet of saliva into his mouth, Ansgar forced his head down and, having taken careful aim, spat on each of the metal cuffs holding his arms tight to the table.

The ork uttered something else and moved towards the operating slab on which Ansgar lay trapped.

Acrid wisps of smoke stung the champion's olfactory senses and Ansgar was able to discern a hissing, fizzing sound. Tired muscles tensed, flexing on instinct rather than because Ansgar had any particular plan in mind to act upon.

A low growl, deep as the Tempest Ocean, as grating as the glacial ice sheets of the Deadlands, and as threatening as a rad-storm, drifted from the clinging shadows beyond the ork. It was a sound that chilled even the Emperor's Champion to the marrow.

There was something else again here with them in the laboratory.

With clanking, piston-hissing steps, a hulking mass of solid shadow stepped out of the gloom into the flickering strobe-light of the inconstant illuminators.

There was nothing the bound Emperor's Champion could do but watch as the monster revealed itself. The warboss seemed even larger than Ansgar remembered from their duel aboard the gargant-titan.

…Something huge stepped out of the gloom, clad from head to toe in cumbersome power armour, a low rumbling growl emanating from deep within its barrel chest, iron-shod feet clanking on the grilled metal floor… Three metres tall and almost as wide, the bulk of its already massive green body was enhanced by the metal exoskeleton armour it wore… Piercing red eyes fixed Ansgar from beneath the brow of a long-horned helm, the banner pole rising from its back topped with a metal ork-face, the blood-red scar bisecting it clear in the dim light… With heavy clumping steps the warboss pounded towards him… Metal rang on metal as the Templar's sword struck the oversized, crackling power claw… The savage brute dropped its head and charged… Ansgar howled in pain as the warboss lifted him off the ground, skewered on the end of a horn, feeling bones shatter beneath his armour… Hefting the Black Sword in his right hand, placing its tip against the torso plating, he pushed down hard, the blade slicing through the thick armour and into the monster's chest… With a yell of righteous fury and pain, the champion brought the Black Sword down on the warboss. The energy-sheathed blade cut cleanly through armour plate, alien flesh and thick bone… The ork's arm fell to the floor with a resounding clang…

The warboss was even more mechanised than it had been before. Where before the mekanisation had been in the form of the heavy ork armour it wore, the monstrous alien war-leader was now a true cybork. Its augmentations included an entirely bionik right arm that ended in another shearing claw, both piston-driven legs and a cracked-lens ocular implant.

But most horrible of all, Ansgar could see that some of the ork's modifications had been accomplished using distinctive black and white ceramite and plas-teel plates, cannibalised from the power armour that would have been worn by Ansgar's battle-brothers among Fighting Company Gerhard. A shoulder plate even bore the red helix of Colber's stolen armour.

The evidence of such sacrilege right there before his eyes filled the Emperor's Champion with an insane rage, but it was one which his weakened body was unable to turn into righteous retributive vengeance.

The warboss – that should, by rights, have been dead – had been rebuilt using parts scavenged from the honoured dead of the Black Templars.

The warboss of the Blood Scar Tribe. The nemesis of their last crusade. The Scourge of Solemnus.

Morkrull Grimskar.

NIMROD TREMAYNE STOOD, staring in mute wonder at the vault door before him. Behind him the ork hunters were whispering to one another, keeping a tight grip on their guns and other weapons, as they watched the far end of the blackened corridor for any sign of the enemy. But the ACG lieutenant couldn't care what the skinners were doing, or what they thought of him. The prize that he had braved the green hell of the jungle for was finally within his grasp.

From somewhere far away came the unreal echoes of gunfire and the guttural cries of greenskins. At irregular intervals dust and ash would shower down from the ceiling as the building was shaken by what sounded and felt like a full-blown orbital barrage. The hunters glanced from the shaking ceiling to the other end of the corridor and back to Tremayne and their sergeant in equal measure. Only Borysko's adjutant, Ertz, did not take his eyes from the auspex he held tightly in his hand. The alien kroot crouched at the rear of the party, unmoving, with the carved stock of its rifle held tightly to its shoulder.

They were within the abandoned east wing of the base where fire had taken its evident and costly toll. The platoon had gathered within a bare square room at the end of an arterial corridor, from which other archways, all bearing the caducal helix of the genetor-magi, led to other burnt out medicae bays, experimental laboratories and once secure, sealed test environments.

But Tremayne had ignored all of these as he had led the party through the base, apparently following a map that he had somehow called up on his wrist chron, as if it were a conventional data-slate. It was what lay beyond this massive, circular vault door that he desired.

The adamantium-shielded door had been partially melted by the fire that had ravaged this block, but the opening mechanisms appeared to still be intact. There were signs that the new occupiers of this facility had tried their best to open it; the uneven scars of lasfire and great scorch marks attested to the various methods the greenskins had used to try to force their way into the vault. All had failed. After all, the vault had been built to withstand everything other than a direct orbital blast from a battleship in low orbit over the planet.

There was only one way of opening the sealed vault door. To the right of the huge portal was the genetors' caducal helix icon – combining the image of a serpent-entwined staff and the double helix – mounted on a sunken circular plaque.

'So, this is it?' Borysko asked. 'This is what we came here for?'

'What lies beyond this door, yes,' Tremayne confirmed.

'Just one more question,' the skinner sergeant sneered. 'How are you going to get in when the green-skins couldn't?'

'It helps if you have a key.'

Tremayne's peaked cap was still firmly on the lieutenant's bandaged head. He removed it now and wiped the ACG badge upon its brow clean of grime and jungle filth. Removing the pin badge, he held it up in front of the caducal helix, passing it over the gleaming crystal eyes of the twin serpents wrapped around the staff.

There was a distinct click, followed by a gentle hiss of compressed air, and the genetor symbol slid out of the wall, on the end of a cylindrical metal plate. Tremayne allowed himself a cautious sigh of relief. As he understood it Zephyrus had gone to a lot of trouble to acquire that little piece of tech.

Set into the plate was a terminal console board, the individual keys bearing the numbers and gothic alphabet utilised by the Imperium of Mankind.

'That's some key,' Borysko admitted.

'Oh, that's not the key,' Tremayne corrected the sergeant. 'The real key is the access code that will unlock the secrets of this hermetically-sealed vault.'

With Tremayne on the verge of opening the vault, Borysko suddenly seemed to feel that their position was even more exposed than before. 'I want this place secure,' he barked. 'Vanderkamp. Take Coburg and make sure we have this area sealed up tight.'

'Send the kroot,' Tremayne cut in darkly.

'What?' Borysko didn't like having his orders countermanded.

'You heard me, sergeant.'

Borysko's scarred face turned even uglier thanks to the expression he pulled.

'Kroot.' The alien mercenary snapped its head round, fixing the sergeant with the orbs of its milky white eyes. 'Go with Vanderkamp.'

After a moment's uncomfortable hesitation, the trooper and the alien set off down the passageway out of the antechamber.

Tremayne turned back to the console. Fingers darting over the sprung keys, the lieutenant entered the code that thirty agents had died to procure. He just hoped that it worked.

For several painful seconds nothing happened. Tremayne held his breath, his heart pounding a tattoo of agitation against his ribs.

There was a click, a thrumming whirr of hinge-servos activating and, with a hiss of escaping frozen air, the massive door swung open. A wash of cryogenic mist cascaded over the stepped lip of the portal and across the fire-marked floor of the antechamber.

Tremayne paused at the entrance to the vault, as if coming before the Golden Throne of Terra itself. Then, taking a deep breath, he stepped inside.

Before him, amidst the swirling ice-blue mists of the hermetically sealed vault, stood row upon row of individual cold-stasis containers: gleaming stainless steel cylinders bearing the caducal helix, the intersecting crescents that warned of biohazardous material, and stencilled reference codes. This was the legacy the genetor-magi had left behind.

Tremayne shivered, but it wasn't against the sub-zero chill of the vault. He shivered in excited anticipation.

His eyes scanned the rows of numbered cylinders before him. And then, there it was, right there before him, the long-sought-for prize. The prize he had risked his life, and the lives of a platoon of ork hunters for. The prize that had cost the lives of his bodyguard Kurn, a squad of stormtroopers, the crew of a Valkyrie assault carrier and several of those self-same ork hunters already.

It was a row of canisters marked with the same code reference, and the universal biohazard warning symbol. The code read: *H-363*.

Hybrid pathological agent 363.

NINETEEN
HEART OF DARKNESS

THE COMBINED BLACK Templar and Relictors force
advanced through the stifling, sickness-gripped jungle
in mutual silence. To keep his mind focused, Chaplain Wolfram recited prayers of contrition to the
Emperor, asking for his guidance and protection in
the conflict that undoubtedly awaited them. The
Emperor alone knew what was occupying the mind of
Captain Oberon Eurys as he and his Relictors made
their way through the putrefying cloud-forests.

Around them the jungle continued to deteriorate,
the trees and other vegetation becoming more and
more misshapen and unhealthy-looking. Pallid epi-
phytes drooped from branches like dead men's
fingers. Unnatural fleshy black tubers grew in the
foetid mulch that covered the forest floor. Trees rose
from the sodden, contaminated ground, bark cracked

and peeling, as if they were sloughing diseased skin. Cankerous growths hung from their frail bending boughs looking like shrivelled fungi.

Wolfram couldn't help but give voice to his opinions of the place. 'This warp-damned place is corrupted beyond all reason, an affront to the Emperor's holy purpose for Armageddon and His Imperium.'

'This area is *purgatus*. It has been so declared by order of the Inquisition,' Eurys told him. 'The equatorial jungles saw an unprecedented level of fighting during the first invasion of this world committed in the Blood God's name. This place became tainted and has remained so ever since despite the best work of exorcists of the Ministorum.'

'Then, by the Golden Throne, they did not pray hard enough,' Wolfram opined coldly.

'We were fortunate not to run into an Inquisitorial cordon, although how the Inquisition can seriously expect to cordon off the rainforests of Armageddon is anyone's guess,' Eurys went on, ignoring Wolfram's outburst. 'And besides, they are focusing all their attention on the blasphemy that is Angron's monolith, further to the south. They probably don't even know about the focus of this apocalyptic storm. There are not enough of them to cover all of the monuments left by the daemon primarch's armies all those centuries ago. I'd wager they have not even all been charted.'

Above them the malevolent mass of the menacing warp storm seethed and boiled, filling the sky. Crackling fingers of lightning skittered across the battered ceramite of their armour in skittering cascades of obsidian, amethyst and crimson.

The unholy cloud cover pushed down on top of Wolfram, as though the weight of them was resting directly across his shoulders.

The malignant clouds were as ominous as the events they portentously foretold. Wolfram prayed that this was what the Emperor truly willed. With Ansgar no longer with them, they could not be so sure of the path the Master of Mankind wanted them to take.

And so the Marines continued, heavy ceramite boots clumping over the diseased terrain until they reached the crater.

THE CRATER MUST have been at least half a kilometre in diameter, a hollow bowl carved out of the once verdant cloud-forest long ago. Whether it had been created naturally as part of the topography of this area, blasted out of the ground by a meteorite impact or intentionally dug out of the bedrock by ancient hands, there was no way of telling. All that they knew about the crater was what they could see of it.

The sickly trees grew thickly up to the edge of the blasted bowl, but within the crater nothing grew. The precipitous sides dropped down sharply before the base of the hollow levelled out.

Even though Chaplain Wolfram had been alerted to the existence of the crater by Brother Ansgar's tormenting visions, the appearance of the feature still came as quite a shock, so stark was it. But what drew Wolfram's glittering ruby gaze to the centre of bowl were the circle of jagged stones and the occupants of the crater.

They rose from the ground like twisted black stalagmites, ten metres tall. Their acid-eaten faces bore weathered carvings that looked like they might once have been faces and mouths, before Armageddon's ravaged climate took its toll.

Wolfram now saw that there were other markings upon the stones, lines of writhing runes and sigils. The longer he looked upon them the more they seemed to shift and crawl across the obelisks like scuttling centipedes.

He looked away and when he returned his gaze to the stones, the sigils were still, having returned to their original positions. There could be no question that the eight monoliths had been raised as part of some greater plan.

Neither was there any doubt in the Chaplain's mind that these stones had once been adorned with the viscera of sacrificial victims and washed in their blood; the bound souls of the desperate victims cried out to him from the menhirs.

The stones crackled with esoteric energies. Wolfram could feel it setting the hairs on the nape of his neck on end, tingling his flesh unpleasantly, smell it burning off the monoliths, the stink of ozone like hot tin in the air. It was the same soul-sickness that had beset them for days now, intensified almost beyond tolerable levels.

As the storm crackled and seethed overhead, the towering monoliths seethed and crackled with tainted heliotropic corposant. Simply looking upon the blasphemous monuments filled Wolfram with a stomach-tightening nausea. He cast another prayer to the Emperor, and another to his primarch, that he might be granted the strength to overcome and conquer in the inevitable battle to come.

For the Black Templars' enemies were already here in this place. Wolfram's heart pounded with anger to look upon the ork tribes gathered within the stone circle, and he knew that his brothers must share his feelings.

Wolfram felt genuine surprise at seeing the gathered ork horde and yet, at the same time, he was not surprised. It was just like the greenskins to be drawn to something as insidious and corrupting as a monument dedicated to Chaos. It certainly went a long way to explaining why they had encountered so few orks as they marched right through their domain, and explained the signs of mass migration the Space Marines had seen during their days traipsing through the jungle.

It also gave credence to Ansgar's confusing visionprophecies. It would appear that the Emperor had indeed called them to this place, to dispel the malignant Chaos power growing here and to be revenged upon those greenskins that must have slaughtered their brethren amongst Fighting Company Gerhard.

There were all manner of ork troops here too, all of them sporting the banners and adornments that denoted their wild nature. Scanning the flapping hide standards mounted atop poles, Wolfram judged there to be elements of at least four different tribes here. The vast majority were axe and machetewielding warriors, but there was a substantial component of ork cavalry – brute savages straddling ill-tempered wild boar.

Some of the greenskins were armed with something more deadly than axes and cleavers. Some had guns and cannon-weapons, scavenged from the Imperial defenders of Armageddon or left behind by Ghazghkull's trial attack fifty years before. There was even a runt squiggoth battle-beast among the gathered horde.

This massed ork army might be primitive in its armaments, armour and even its approach to war, but to underestimate such a force would be the worst thing the Space Marines could do. The greenskins might be among the most backward and uncivilised of the Imperium's enemies but there was no disputing that ork race had subjugated entire systems beneath their tyranny.

Some might like to believe that the Imperium was one solid mass of star systems, covering the five segmentae of the galaxy, but in reality it was no more than a series of loosely-connected sectors and planets, separated by the unimaginably vast gulfs of wilderness space and the domains and dominions of a myriad other races.

On all sides disparate worlds were beset from within and without the boundaries of Imperial space by countless alien races, all of which sought to extinguish the divine light of the Emperor's knowledge and civilisation. The voracious entity that was the utterly alien, extra-galactic tyranid race. The ancient, unfathomable eldar. The young, yet aggressively expansionist tau and their kroot carnivore kindred allies. The skulking hrud. The spear-ship fleets of the sheed. The demiurg. And more recently, in terms of the ten thousand-year history of the Imperium, the insidious evil of the awakening aeons-dead necrontyr and their vampiric star gods.

And yet currently there was no greater sustained threat to the dominance of the Imperium of Mankind than the pugnacious resilience of ork-kind. On a thousand worlds the greenskins had waged war with asteroid-fortresses, death-ships, gargants, squig war-beasts, improvised firearms ands axes. There were just as many worlds that were already under ork rule, clusters of these worlds forming the petty tyrannies of the mightiest warlords of their savage, warring kind.

Of course, the orks had practically brought the bastion world of Armageddon to its knees twice in the last half century as well. Their grip was tenacious and their willingness to let go non-existent.

But the orks gathered here were not behaving as Wolfram would have expected. On every other occasion when he had confronted the greenskins, they had given up their 'Waaagh!' battle-cry and the more there were congregated in one place, the louder the bellows and the more frenzied the mob. The tribes gathered here were unnaturally quiet and calm. Every ugly tusked face looked heavenwards at the portentous meteorological effects raging above them.

The assembled orks were might be unsettlingly still, but the wind was not. A gale howled around the bowl of the crater, whipping the leaves from the warp-altered trees that crept up to the lip of the Chaos-consecrated hollow. It tugged at the Space Marines, as if looking for any vulnerable spot by which to seize hold and penetrate the shield of their armour. And it danced around the desolate hollow, lifting clouds of dusty soil and ash from the ground.

Thanks to his enhanced eyesight and the auto-senses of his death's-head helmet, Wolfram could see the lone ork around which all the others were gathered, as if this woad-daubed, feather-headdressed, skull-staff wielding creature was the shamanistic inspiration behind this massing of the jungle tribes. Wolfram could sense the emanations of power coming off the creature, like steam rising from the slime of a foetid swamp. It made his skin crawl. That and the warp-magick saturating this place. In fact it was just as if the psychically charged ork wyrd was the focus of the untamed essence of the warp massing at this spot within the potential of the storm.

The cracks of thunderclaps shook the jungle, sending rippling shockwaves across the discoloured vegetation that formed the jungle here. Wolfram felt each crack reverberate within his helm. The migraine-inducing pressure ground down at his contained anger, threatening to unleash it before he had even engaged with the enemy.

None of the greenskins were aware of the presence of the combined Templar-Relictor force. The Space Marines – all twenty-three of them – lined the crumbling lip of the crater, emerging from the shroud of the forest like vengeful ghosts.

There was Bodyguard Koldo, auspex in hand, despite the obvious presence of the maelstrom consuming the crater before them. Veteran Brother Kemen had his lascannon ready, aiming it at the heart of the distant stone circle. Brother Baldulf stood, chainsword in one hand bolt pistol in the other, the safeties of both weapons disengaged. Huarwar, Hebron, Lairgnen and Gildas held their boltguns close across them. Brother Clust stood with legs braced to help him balance the cumbersome bulk of his heavy bolter and absorb the recoil of the weapon. Brother Larce gripped his flamer firmly with gauntleted hands, primed with a fresh canister of fuel, the pilot flame an intense blue cone of heat.

Apothecary Bliant stood out most distinctly from the line of grey and black armoured figures, his slime-stained white armour bearing the striking black cross of the Templars on one shoulder pad and the scarlet helix pattern of the Apothecarion on the other.

And then there were the gunmetal grey-armoured forms of Captain Eurys's warband: the brothers Cynewulf, Deogol, Pleoh, Nerian and Kirkor; the veteran Relictors Durinc and Edred. The ruddy-armoured Techmarine Govannon. Eurys, his power sword unscabbarded now, its blade humming with resonating power. Assault Marines Rodor and Slecg, equipped with jet-powered assault packs

And lastly there was the one called Abrecan, the Relictors' Librarian. Wolfram had not realised that there was a practitioner of warp-craft amongst Eurys's party until they had reached this place. His presence among their number made the warp sickness pressing upon him from the atmosphere seem even worse.

To have a user of the warp-magick in their midst would have made Wolfram turn his men around and march them away from this place, were it not for the fact that those the Black Templars had sworn to conquer awaited them within the circle of daemonic monoliths, and that the Emperor Himself had called them to this place to act as instruments of His immortal vengeance.

'What would you have us do now?' Wolfram challenged the Relictors captain.

'We wait.'

'But our enemies are ranged before us. It is our duty to bring the Emperor's justice down upon them and smite them with our consecrated wargear.'

'To attack now would be suicide, brother. We must bide our time and strike when our enemies are at their lowest ebb.'

'We have bested such odds before.'

'Are you sure? In these primal conditions? I do not think so. Besides, I feel that there are others who have yet to arrive at this apocalyptic hour to join the battle to end all battles.'

'What do you mean, Relictor?'

'I mean, Brother-Chaplain, that the final actions of the first planet-wide war for Armageddon are yet to be played out.'

It now felt as if the entire rainforest was being smothered under a seething blanket of viscous black cloud. That which, by rights, should only have been agglomerations of water vapour in the atmosphere appeared to have impossibly taken on more solid form. At its horizon-distant periphery, other rags of cumulous scudded across the sky to join the apocalyptic storm, as the cloud mass began to spiral over the desolate crater and the warp-channelling stones.

At its heart faces seemed to appear briefly amidst the cloud-shapes before evaporating again as the thunderheads roiled and raged.

Staring up at the unnatural phenomena manifested above where they stood at the very eye of the storm, Chaplain Wolfram fancied he saw an eye, a kilometre

across, open amidst the cyclonic vortex. The iridescent forks of lightning crackling across its cornea were
like broken blood vessels, its pupil the black of the
void.

Wolfram tried to shake the image from his mind,
for surely it was just an illusion, the malign influence
of the maelstrom working on an overactive, yet tired,
mind. But when he looked again, the seething orb
still stared down from the tempest-wracked sky, gazing down on the tiny, insignificant warriors and their
even more insignificant enemy with its corrupted
gaze.

And then the monstrous eye blinked.

With a crack like a hundred orbital barrage reports,
the warp storm broke. Lightning struck in as many
places across the face of the rainforests, setting trees
aflame or felling their sundered twisted trunks with
their lashing ionic discharges. Hurricane gusts and a
deluge of diluvian proportions lashed the jungles
from the splintered sky.

Chaplain Wolfram scanned the unreadable helm-
faces of his kill-team. He was convinced now more
than ever that this would indeed be their last crusade.
The Emperor had a purpose for all His loyal servants
and this was theirs. They had been called to this place,
at this time, to put a stop to the Adeptus Astartes'
most ancient and enduring of enemies – their own
fallen kin – no matter what the cost.

Ansgar had seen himself here, at this time and this
place. But he was not here, so did that mean that his
visions were now meaningless? Was the future that he
had witnessed an unknown country, unwritten in the
annals of time once again? Was the only future they

had to look forward to the one that, through their own actions, they would make for themselves? How much of what Ansgar had seen had been the truth, as mapped out by fickle fate? How much of it had been mere illusory fantasy?

And then the warp portal opened, a door between realities, between times, between planets; one the Armageddon of today, at the brink of destruction at the hands of the foul greenskins, the other the Armageddon of five hundred years before, when the planet lay ravaged by the murdering hordes of the Blood God's armies.

At first it was almost indiscernible amidst the fury of the writhing tempest, a black hole in the sky. But as the storm raged on, so the doorway expanded, stretching out towards the clawing tips of the eight standing stones. It shimmered as though seen through a volcanic heat haze. At its spiralling vortex edges, the view of the standing stones beyond appeared broken and fractured, distorting the image as a whirlpool would distort the smooth surface of a lake with its ripples.

The gate opened onto a scene very different to the dark-shrouded stormscape of the crater, but it was recognisable as an equatorial rainforest nonetheless. Where the stifling jungle here was warped and mal-formed, the trees that could be seen through the hole in the sky were vibrant green specimens, like those the Space Marines had become used to beyond the limit of the warp's corruption here at the heart of darkness. Where the sky beneath which they waited was as dark as night, thick with suffocating black clouds, torn at by the primal fury of the tempest, through the gate the jungles were lit by flames rising above the tops of the trees as the forest was consumed by a fiery holocaust.

Two different worlds, two different – and yet not so dissimilar in their ultimate outcome – apocalypses.

And where the Black Templars and their untested Relictor allies waited on this side of the warp beach, as the forty-first millennium drew to a close, across the gulfs of time other superhuman armoured colossi also waited with bloodthirsty impatience for the portal to fully form.

What blasphemy was this, Chaplain Wolfram wondered? What foul warp-magick was at work here? The Marine's veins and arteries pulsed with the righteous wrath of the wronged.

There was no question as to whom these bloodied warriors served. Theirs was the ultimate warrior god, a deity whose eternal thirst for slaughter could never be assuaged, not even with the blood of the countless billions who had already perished in his unholy name.

That the World Eaters all followed the same depraved cult was clear, for the blasphemous iconography of their accursed legion was prevalent upon their armour, their wargear and the battle-standards they carried with them.

But just as they were similar in appearance to one another, so were they dissimilar. After almost ten millennia fighting the Long War, these Berzerkers of Khorne had altered their armour through choice and necessity, personal heraldry vying with the skull rune of the daemon-god to whom they had sold their immortal souls and the planet-devouring maw icon of their dark legion.

Most were helmeted, the head-armour sprouting flared, recurve horns. The design of their faceplates ranged from brazen skulls, through overlaid Khornate runes, to the beaten visors of ancient knightly orders. The palette of their attire was similar too, restricted to various shades of red, black, burnished brass, beaten gold and the off-white of actual bone-carved adornments.

Their power armour, although archaic in design, had been customised by the warriors in veneration of the Blood God. Here a ceramite kneepad had been fashioned to resemble a leering gargoyle face: there a shoulder plate had been emblazoned with the profane eight-pointed star of Chaos. Others had skulls hanging from their armour, or skewered on the tips of their helm-horns, or loops of hooked chains dangling from their armour.

All sported recently-won battle-scars, paradoxically acquired five centuries before, as the Fallen One's attack on Armageddon collapsed in the wake of the daemon primarch's death at the hands of Captain Aurelian's Grey Knights' last rites suicide squad. On a daemon-held world, any one of these Berzerkers would have the status of a Chaos lord, with countless cultist-slaves to send to their gruesome deaths in battle. A warband of such warriors was a formidable threat indeed.

The orks were giving cry to their own pent-up battle-hunger now, the roar of the 'Waaaaagh!' resounding across the crater.

Raising scything chain-axes above their heads, howling with insane fury, the Chaos warriors set about the orks blocking their exit from the reality-rupturing gate.

Their bellowed battle-cants carried over the typhoon wailing of the storm to chill the blood pumping in the loyalists' veins, like hounds baying for blood. It was one simple word – one syllable – repeated over and over with growing passion and fury, the name of the blood-soaked abomination they worshipped. 'Khorne! *Khorne!* KHORNE!'

'No pity! No remorse! No fear!' the Templars shouted as they charged down the steep slope of the crater, into the screaming daemon winds, no longer able to contain the righteous fury boiling within them. Truly was it said that no man had the capacity for hate like a Space Marine. And of all the Emperor's loyal Astartes, the Black Templars were the most vengeful.

The Relictors followed the Templars' lead, throwing themselves down the crumbling scree slopes of the crater towards their enemies, giving joyful voice to their own battle-cry: 'Strength of will, courage of will!'

SUCH PORTENTOUS TIMES, Oberon Eurys thought. To be standing here, at the threshold of a new age, an age of understanding and knowledge. An age of conquest. An age to rival the Great Crusade that had seen the founding of the Imperium.

The Relictor luxuriated in the surging power of the warp storm. It held within it such possibilities, such potentialities, for he who had the courage to turn it to his advance, to the Imperium's advantage.

A scant hundred metres ahead of them the brutal orks had engaged with the horn-helmed warriors. Oberon Eurys threw himself into the fray, and suddenly he and his Relictors were in the thick of battle where the otherworldly portal blistered the ground at its threshold, having torn a hole between realities that should never have coincided.

The World Eaters warband still emerging from the hole far outnumbered the combined Relictors and Black Templars force of twenty-three loyalist Marines. But the Berzerkers themselves were outnumbered three-to-one by the massed tribes of the feral orks.

But where the greenskins enthusiastically threw themselves into battle, so were the World Eaters revelling in the brutal yet systematic slaughter of the greenskins. It was a chilling reminder that these ancient warriors had once fought for the Emperor at the founding of the Imperium. The realisation made Oberon pause and think: there but for the grace of the Emperor go any who would be made as gods compared to other men and then live their whole lives in servitude to such lesser, worthless wretches.

As the Relictors found themselves swallowed up by the battle, so too were the Black Templars. Eurys saw the one called Baldulf chopping down a pug-faced greenskin with his chainsword and the towering Kemen – tall even for a Space Marine – hammering the runt squiggoth with searing blasts from a lascannon as the imbecilic beast rampaged through the chaos and confusion reigning at the core of the ork army. The Chaplain flew at the orks, his bladed crozius whirling around his skull-helm and into torsos, limbs and heads. He was supported by his bold bodyguard whose chugging boltgun was taking its own toll of shredded ork bodies. And the Apothecary, the one called Bliant, dealt out death to their enemies, rather than administering the Emperor's Mercy to all and sundry.

A snarling warrior leapt in front of Eurys, its bared canine teeth visible beneath the cut helm that masked the rest of its head. With his own shout of, 'Strength and courage!' Eurys brought his power sword up in his right hand, the blade's energy field singing. There was a crackling burst of sparks as the power blade was halted by a shimmering glaive. Eurys's eye caught the polished surface of the glaive blade and, as it twisted in the World Eater's grip, thought he saw a snarling leer writhe across it.

His bolt pistol was in his left hand. Eurys raised the gun and fired as the Berzerker pressed home his newly won advantage. At point blank range the high velocity mass reactive shells, blessed by the Relictors' own warp-aware reclusiarchs, exploded against the Chaos warrior's shoulder guard, detonating on impact. The sudden, unexpected force of the bolter blasts sent the World Eater staggering back. Power sword and Berzerker glaive parted.

With a savage snarl of, 'Maim and kill!' the traitor Marine charged back in, the blood-frenzy consuming the warrior robbing him of all reason. Eurys's sword cut in under the World Eater's guard, screeching as it sliced in under the Berzerker's arm and into his chest. Even as the energised blade exploded the lunatic's frenziedly pounding hearts, his bolt pistol unloaded the rest of its clip into his snarling mouth.

Only a matter of a few strides from Eurys, Govannon smote ork skulls with his thunder hammer, whilst the writhing arms of the Techmarine's servo-harness deflected strokes of axe and sword. As Eurys's dead foe fell to the darkening, blood-soaked ground, the Relictors captain saw the Techmarine's plasma-cutter, flaring magnesium white, burn a dripping, liquid metal slice across the face of another of the emerging Chaos warband. As the World Eater's face-plate exploded in a welter of burning blood, the warp-tainted canine-beast it held straining on a leash of rusted chain leapt at Govannon. Looking like some avatar of the god of the forge, Govannon swung his lightning-headed hammer and shattered the monster hound's ribcage, batting the monster aside to die with its blasphemous master.

Librarian Abrecan delivered vengeful psychic death upon the Dark Gods' chosen. The features of his face a knot of concentration, the hood of his armour flared with psyker witch-light as the augmetic crystals of its construction and the conductive wires penetrating his brain channelled and focused the esoteric energies of the warp, that they might become a tool of destructive power in Abrecan's hands. Lightning flared from his fingertips in a welter of volcanic light.

One Chaos warrior, the mark of his blasphemous deity picked out in gold on the forehead of his reptiliad-horned helm, threw himself to the ground, tearing off his helmet and crushing his skull between his own gauntleted hands to stop the screaming torture consuming his frenzied brain. Another World Eater turned on his Berzerker brethren, barking rabidly, his cracked lips slick with blood and drool.

Veteran Brother Durinc wrestled with a heathen as each tried to use the Relictor's multi-melta on the other. Brother Cynewulf's arcane lightning-sheathed claw ripped apart the carcass of something red-skinned, scaled and unearthly, while Deogol staggered back under the relentless axe work of a World Eater, the chain-weapon describing a lethal figure-of-eight pattern in the air in front of him quicker than even the eye of a Space Marine could follow.

THE TUMULT OF battle was all around them. Chaplain Wolfram looked to his devoted Black Templars. They surrounded him, in the thick of battle, delivering the Emperor's divine judgement upon His enemies with holy vengeance. To his left, Brother Larce ignited the flea-ridden hide one of the primitive aliens was wearing. To his right, Brother Baldulf sent a bellowing ork head spinning from the creature's hunched shoulders. Behind him his finely augmented hearing detected the whine of the machine-spirit of Brother Kemen's lascannon achieving target lock, soon followed by the white noise of the heavy weapon firing.

In front of Wolfram the Black Templars line broke against the tumult that was the massed feral tribes of the southern jungles – or so it seemed. The greenskins formed an effective barrier between the Space Marines and the predations of the Chaos worshippers. But the maniacal warriors of the unpredictable Captain Eurys had broken through the already preoccupied orks with their initial charge. They were now locked between the ferals and a squad of savage axe-wielding World Eaters. But they appeared to be making a good account of themselves, laying about them with bolter, sword and hammer as if they were divinely inspired themselves.

Their mutual enemies were effectively reducing each other's numbers in a brutal war of attrition, aided by the Relictors' efforts and the Templars' vengeful wrath. Ork corpses littered the spaces between the crackling stones and there were even several rust-armoured figures lying among the dead. In places there were so many dead that the Space Marines could not help crushing them underfoot in order to reach those of the enemy still standing.

And all the time the rain lashed down around them. Bolts of black lightning, birthed by the monstrous storm above them, ravaged the crater. Where they struck, the ground was ripped open by zigzagging fissures. Where they struck living tissue – whether ork, Marine or Chaos warrior – victims were vaporised where they fought, or, if they were lucky, hurled through the tumult, minds reeling, armour scorched and flesh smoking.

Wolfram turned to face the barrelling charge of a hulking greenskin, as tall and as heavy as he was in his power armour. The Chaplain stumbled backwards, reeling from the collision. But in the next moment, he was bringing his right arm up, crozius in hand. The flaring blades of the power-axe flashed as they connected with the tough knots of muscle over the creature's midriff and sliced through them, gutting the beast.

Kicking the dying ork from him, the ropes of its intestines unravelling, Wolfram gave voice to the unforgiving battle-cant of the last crusade. 'No pity! No remorse! No fear!'

And the survivors of Kill-team Wolfram took up the cry.

THE GREENSKIN CHIEFTAIN fell apart before him, divided into eight pieces by Deathbringer in honour of Khorne, and suddenly Hrothqar Furor found himself at the becalmed eye of the maelstrom of battle raging around him.

He snarled in bloodlust, anger and delight, the bestial sound escaping from between the grinding fangs of his lipless mouth. On all sides his warriors were engaged in violent battle to the glory the Lord of Skulls.

And what was this place that their carnage-slaved patron had brought them to? It was like the jungle they had left when they entered the sacrifice-summoned gateway, only changed now to better suit the Dark Gods' purpose. Not that it mattered. Khorne had brought them here, praise his name. And wherever 'here' was, it was a place of battle and apocalyptic war. Where better for the Foresworn to gather skulls in the name of their martial god?

Deathbringer hissed and writhed in the restraining grip of his hand. Furor raised the chain-axe before him, letting it sniff the battle-wrought air, letting it seek out its own target. Then, the warp-cursed weapon straining to be free, Furor let the bound daemon lead him through the press of orks and the servants of the false emperor.

Furor once more threw back his head and howled in macabre joy at the carnage he was committing in his warrior god's name. As if in response to his animal battle cry, rain lashed down from the heavens, rain that was viscous drops of blood. It was as if the very sky itself was torn and bleeding, ravaged by the Chaos-wrought tempest.

An agonised bellowing cut through the clamour of battle. The war-beast's death screams coursed through him like molten fire, sparking off satisfyingly grisly synaptic sensations deep within his brain as they triggered impulses in the buried bio-neural implants.

Furor saw the squiggoth straining its neck upwards, trying to be free of the Berzerkers that set about it on all sides. He watched as the monster was brought down by the chain-axes of half a dozen of his blood-frenzied warriors.

Isakar Savagehand, the celebrated Slaughterer of Kairn, sliced through the mobbing feral orks with the obsidian blades of his lightning claws. Volkarr, the Herald of the Skull Lord, blew another resounding funereal note on the brass carynx horn that was forever welded to the faceplate of his armoured helm. The mournful sound cut through the gale, grasping the lap-dogs of the false emperor in the stifling grip of fear but, at the same time, filling the devoted of Khorne with renewed vigour, sending their overwrought minds into a frenzy of blood-letting and limb-lopping.

Baruch charged into the throng – a full head taller than any of the others present, his warp-charged body barely contained by his ancient power armour, his bulging-muscled arms bare of armour – and began to tear the greenskins limb from limb with his bare hands. The insane creature that the Foresworn knew simply as the Reaper, its allegiance to Khorne marked by a skull-rune brand repeated all over its filthy, bristle-haired flesh, dragged its gore-clogged talons through ork bodies and ripped the throats from their boar mounts with slavering, shark-like teeth.

A squad of World Eaters marched towards a pack of cleaver-wielding ork savages, in marital order, led by

Zalel Eazar. The Chaos warrior's sutured skin rippled with the daemonic essence of the entity he had invited to share his physical form, and in the shadow of the damned icon carried by Brother Orrax, the Bearer of the Eye of Kharnath, the Berzerkers set about them with chainsword and axe, taking yet more brain-pans for the brass throne of the Lord of Skulls.

Khorgha the Chosen engaged one of the grey-armoured Marines – who appeared to venerate skulls as much as their own legion did – in single combat. Sparks flew where the aspiring champion's dread-axe clashed with the insubstantial chainsword of the Marine. But in his eagerness to prove himself to Khorne, Khorgha was proving to be the stronger, pressing home his advantage until the grey skull-marked Marine stole an assured victory from him by retreating from the fight, launching himself skywards on jets of smoking flame, like the coward all servants of the corpse-husk were.

But this day would be theirs yet: Furor was certain of it. With a portal open to the realm of daemons, it could only be a matter of time.

A DYING ORK falling apart before him, Chaplain Wolfram looked to the portal again. It filled the field of view ahead of him now. Its outline had expanded, writhing and flexing, distorting the vista beyond it. The portal's writhing was accompanied by a snarling of tortured air, as if the warp gate were the maw of some warp-born entity, growling hungrily for flesh and souls. But rather than consuming, the warp-mouth was vomiting out the daemon hordes of the most blood-thirsty and savage of all the Traitor Legions.

But the view of Armageddon's burning jungles of five hundred years ago was becoming more and more indistinct as it was replaced by a red haze, like blood misting out of the air. And now other things were forming within the roaring maw of the warp gate, congealing out of the blood-mist. Horned things, fanged things, cruelly clawed things, wielding unnatural blades of pure darkness that screamed for blood just as their bearers gave cry with shrieking, high-pitched animal voices that should never have been heard beyond the place of Chaos from which they had been birthed.

Prowling from the warp-hole now came canine forms, coalesced from the bloody matter of the Immaterium. Larger than wolves, the flesh hounds of Khorne padded towards the Templars on cruelly-clawed feet, teeth like bayonets bursting from their snarling jaws. Their rough hides were covered by a combination of reptilian scales, rank black fur and steaming skinless flesh, the musculature of their unnatural, and yet disturbingly familiar, forms clearly visible, full of the promise of savage energy, lightning speed and murderous strength.

If Chaplain Wolfram had not been so sure in his faith, he might have begun to believe that they could not prevail this day against such odds.

Oberon Eurys's men had set themselves up as an effective challenge to the World Eaters' invasion of this Armageddon, but the tide of Chaos warriors, and even darker things born of the same emotions that had manifested their dread war god from the warp, seemed never-ending. For every one of the servants of

Khorne, felled by the Relictors and even the rogue greenskins, yet another would march or crawl or prowl from the otherworldly aperture of the warp gate.

As long as the gate remained open, the Relictors and their allies would ultimately find themselves fighting a losing battle. Whatever else they hoped to achieve here, their priority now had to be to close the portal, to heal this rent in the fabric of reality that was allowing the malignant essence of the warp to leak into the world.

But what could be used to battle a Chaos-conjured warp gate? There was no physical weapon in their arsenal that could accomplish such a task. There was no demagogue of the Blood God who had performed some savage rite to open the hole in time, a focus of the evil power at work here, who the Relictors could focus their own attacks against. The focus of the warp-spell was the monstrous maelstrom raging above and around them. Whatever warp-magick had been worked to affect the opening of the portal had been achieved five hundred years ago, on the other side of the gate.

To attempt to fight their way through the massed Khornate hordes to the gate would be an honourable death indeed, but also suicidal and ultimately futile. It was not the way of the Relictors – with their proud history as the Fire Claws Chapter behind them – to throw their lives away in such a wasteful way. Their wargear, their armour and indeed their very gene-seed were too precious. They were instruments of the Emperor's will and as such it was as much their responsibility to enter battle with an eye to their own survival as it was to learn all they could of the ways of the Great Enemy and mete out His wrath against the minions of the Dark Gods. Certainly there were times when a situation demanded the greatest sacrifice a warrior of the Emperor could make, but this was not one of those times, not yet. There were still other things the Relictors could try before taking that course of action.

From Oberon Eurys's decades of hallowed study, on the battlefield as well as in the Librarium of Torva Minoris, the only way to fight warp-magick was to bring to bear a little psyker-sorcery of one's own.

EVEN OVER THE wind, rain and warp-turmoil of the cataclysm consuming the monument crater, Chaplain Wolfram could sense the unnatural sorceries of the Relictors' Librarian. It was like bone ash in his mouth. It was the acrid aroma of ozone catching in his nostrils. It was the bitter taste of copper on his tongue. It was the crawling of gooseflesh across his skin. He did not know whether it felt worse because he was already reviled by the sickening emanations coming from the stones or because he knew it was one of the Emperor's own sons that was bringing such profane power to bear.

Wolfram watched as, the Librarian's head sheathed in a crackling warp storm of its own, tendrils of coruscating warp-energy spun from the Relictor's outstretched hands. Disgust and revulsion surged through him in nauseous waves. The discomfort he felt was much worse than any physical fatigue he had suffered as a consequence of the trials the Templars had been forced to overcome to reach this Emperor-forsaken place.

The Librarian's warp-spell seemed to pull and worry at the inconstant shimmering heat-haze outline of the portal. Ribbons of roiling rainbow-hued light spasmed and coiled where the streamers of energy met.

And Wolfram had the sensation of another psyker-presence nearby, amidst the mayhem. Where the Librarian's powers felt like a caged carnodon to the soul-shriven Chaplain, and the madness of the storm was like some insane, ravening daemon itself, this third presence was like a mindless alien thing, possessing none of the strict chastising discipline of the Relictor or the sick intelligence of the soul-slaughtering essence of the Blood God. In fact, it was just as primitive as the combined race-warp imprint of the primitives that had created it and of the tribal shaman that channelled it.

The waaagh – the distilled warring nature of the orks – boiled over the crater like an invisible spreading fungal growth, tingeing the whirling warp storm with a pustulent luminescence.

And then there was a void where before Wolfram's mind had been trying to fathom what he had been sensing. The power unleashed by the Relictor's Librarian was gone. In its place a blackness festered, like that left by a soul swallowed by the capricious currents of the Sea of Souls.

The Chaplain scanned the battlefield described by the Chaos monoliths. His own deathly red gaze locked onto the hulking totem-bedecked gunmetal grey armour of the Librarian again. He saw the boar-tusked greenskin, naked except for a hide loincloth, looming over the collapsing mass of the Relictor. He saw the blood-dulled curve of its oversized cleaver. He saw that the miniature psychic storm surrounding the Librarian has dissipated. He saw that the Librarian's head was no longer attached to the rest of his body.

In the confusion of the battle, the Relictors' own warp-manipulator had been killed by the most primitive of xenos creatures. So is the fate of all who would expose themselves to the evil of the warp and attempt to use its malign power to their own ends, the Chaplain considered, with no little grim satisfaction.

OBERON EURYS WAS a blur moving through the press of green, red and black bodies. As Librarian Abrecan's head rolled to a standstill at his feet, Eurys had already drawn and quartered the creature that had so heretically dared slay a psyker hero of the Relictors Chapter.

Assessing his situation more carefully, Eurys looked around him, shaking the vile blood-rain from his armour. He was only a matter of metres from the shimmering warp portal through which the Blood God's followers still flowed – lithe-limbed bloodletters, snapping daemon hounds and the last of the Khornate warband.

Through the blood-mists he could see the still burning jungles of five hundred years ago, and a part of him yearned to have been at the climax of that first battle for Armageddon all those centuries ago, to confront the daemon primarch face-to-face, to really know what such unbridled warp-power felt like; to know what it could do.

But pressing in around him was also the confused and excited throng of the feral orks. And next to him, atop a Chaos-consecrated altar stone, was the focus of the orks' power in this place, the outcast that had managed to unite the tribes of the jungle here, in the name of their own war-loving tribal deities. It had decorated its exposed skin with ork glyphs, realised in woad, and wore a patchwork of animal hides. Clutched in one meaty paw was its gnarled and knotted staff. The alien shaman was gazing up at the storm-wracked sky, transfixed. Green fire sparked in its eyes and ethereal emerald smoke billowed from its gaping mouth.

Eurys could feel the waves of power rolling off the wyrdboy like ocean waves beating against a lone rocky promontory. But of course he was a warrior of the Adeptus Astartes, the Emperor's finest, and he had the strength, both physically and the strength of will, to overcome.

With a cry born of anger, desperation and a holy zeal, leaping from the press of greenskin bodies onto the altar stone, Captain Eurys swung his humming power sword over his head, double-handed – the blade screaming as it cut through the psychically-charged air, the splatters of blood-rain cooking off its white-hot cutting edge – and brought it down on top of the wyrdboy's simmering skull.

It seemed to Eurys that there was a moment of uncanny silence, before he was hurled from the altar, across the circle of standing stones, by a blast like an orbital strike.

The battling Marines, traitors and greenskins, the lightning-scarred standing stones, the crater, the portal and even the warp storm boiling above were consumed in an explosion of cold, green fire, as the energy of the ork waaagh was released in one cataclysmic explosion.

Warriors on every side were knocked flat like grass-stems in a storm. Fully half the remaining orks died as their skulls exploded under the force of the psychic shockwave.

Eurys lay where he had fallen against the side of a black granite monolith and looked back across the scorched ring of stones. Apart from the momentarily halted battle, something else had changed. It took him a moment to realise what it was as he gazed across the altar stone to the clawing menhirs beyond and the withered, hurricane-devastated treeline on the opposite side of the crater.

He could no longer see the burning jungles of Armageddon from half a millennium ago. The warp portal was gone.

TWENTY
EVOLUTION

ALL AROUND THE dreadnought the ork-infested compound burned. The vile xenos had attempted to resist him but all had fallen before his wrath, orks wired into their own crude imitations of power armour and their less technologically-enhanced, but nonetheless violent and battle-hungry, green-skinned kin.

But by far the majority of his holy work had involved orks cybernetically adapted in some way by the inclusion of crude bionics and augmetics that were too delicate to be of alien design – in fact those pieces looked like they had been manufactured by the tech-adepts of the Cult Mechanicus or that they were even the handiwork of the forge-ships of the Adeptus Astartes. Jarold's fears were horribly confirmed when he saw the unmistakable arm of a flaring cruciform emblem picked out in black and white on a piece of a shoulder guard that made up another of the blasphemous aliens' suits of mega-armour. The cyborks snapped at him with steel-trap mouths and raked at him with adamantium claws crackling with barely-controlled electrical discharge.

Jarold passed another arched doorway in the crater-riddled corridor, and spun on his grinding waist-joint to counter any ambush awaiting him there. Three cyborks were guarding drums of flammable chemicals carelessly stored in the anteroom behind them.

The rounds that rattled from the barrels of the cyborks' guns spanged off the dreadnought's resilient hull like iron rain. The cyborks could hardly miss. Three times the height of a man, the doorway could barely contain the dreadnought. As Jarold turned in the sundered passageway, his massive weapon-arms scraped chips from the facing stones of the walls.

Jarold trained his assault cannon not on the charging cyborks but at the drums behind them, the whirring barrels spinning up to speed. The drums disappeared under a blaze of cannon fire as the arm-weapon itself was obscured by smoke and muzzle flare. Their contents touched off, enveloping the chamber in a furious inferno. The last of the river-weed cooked off his scarred hull under the gouting flames of the conflagration that roasted the orks like suckling pigs.

The dreadnought crashed on through the wreckage of hastily erected barricades and abandoned defences. Orks fell before the withering fire of cannon and storm bolter, the more lightly armoured aliens giving up one defensive position after another, before the inexorable advance of death-dealing adamantium and steel. And all throughout, wrathful statements of holy Astartes scripture spilled from Jarold's speakers; a tirade of retributive pronouncements.

So the dreadnought descended deeper and deeper into the base, following the interference-like vision that bypassed the mechanical senses through which Brother Jarold experienced the world and scratched unrelentingly against the surface of his organic mind. It was like a small insistent voice that had been grating against the edges of his consciousness ever since he had emerged from the silt-choked waters of the river, washed clean again to carry out the Emperor's work in His most glorious name.

Jarold could not explain it. It was like a calling, simply an instinct that he had to act upon, as though the Emperor Himself had called him to perform a specific task, as though he had a part to play in fulfilling His holy plan for the Black Templars and their crusade for Armageddon.

The might of the river had carried even his tank-like form with it, until, beyond the fury of the tumbling rapids, the watercourse had become a much gentler creature altogether. Passing beyond the chasm of the gorge it had widened and, although it still moved at a flood-engorged pace through the jungles, the journey was much smoother and something as large and heavy as a boulder – or a dreadnought – could break free of its inexorable pull. So Brother Jarold had done.

During his journey through the churning white water, the linked machine-spirit of the war machine had struggled to process the flood of information that the mechanical senses relayed to Jarold's brain. For much of his journey through the gorge – bouncing from the submerged rocky walls and the boulder-strewn bed of the river – he had not known which way was up, let alone project trajectories, speed, and direction or accurately assess damage sustained by his ancient dreadnought body.

But once the river had relinquished its hold on him he was able to stagger free of its clasp, leg-servos and hip-joints grating, gears and ball-races penetrated by the sand and silt that he had churned from the river-bed at his passing.

He looked a wreck of his former magnificence. The passages of scripture adorning his hull had been scraped down to the bare metal in several places. Even the cross insignia of his proudly devout Chapter was scuffed and scarred by the unkind attentions of scorcha blasts and the crater impacts of heavy weapons fire.

And then the last of the orks opposing him fell, crushed to a greasy green pulp beneath an iron-shod foot, and Brother Jarold entered the vault of the underground laboratory.

The echoing chamber was in a derelict state, all manner of detritus littering the floor and great slabs of plaster peeling from the walls and ceiling. The flickering of illuminator bulbs bathed the laboratory in strobing flashes and flickering shadows.

Scanners took in his surroundings in minute detail – everything from the dimensions of the room and the number of accessways into, or out of, the chamber – ventilation ducts and arched openings – to the configuration of the symbols carved into the walls. But what Jarold's mind focused on was the rough-and-ready operating theatre at the far end of the room and the figures standing there.

There were two operating slabs and both were occupied. What little blood that was left in his mortal remains interred inside the coffin of the dreadnought body boiled as his mechanical eyes took in the insignia of his own Chapter displayed on the still-armoured portions of one of the wretches secured to the surgical slabs.

Jarold took another clunking step into the room and the hunch-backed creature wearing a blood-and oil-stained surgeon's apron that stood over the wreck of one of the bodies turned to regard him, one bloodshot eye distorted behind the disc of the magnifying lens strapped to its head.

The foul greenskin howled, strings of saliva flapping from the yellow ivory of its tusks, raising the primitive device it held in one meaty fist with all the care of a spaceport docker, as if it were a makeshift club and not a surgical instrument.

Even as he advanced into the grisly vault, Jarold's artificial senses told him that the ork's victim was dead.

Jarold's storm bolter fired and the Painboss Urgluk Gurlag was hurled backwards, smashing into a steel gurney cluttered with bloodied tools and bizarre surgical instruments. The tools clattered noisily to the floor.

But incredibly, the ork surgeon was not dead. The creature staggered drunkenly to its feet again, despite the holes torn in its barrel chest and the fact that its left arm was missing below the elbow.

Jarold fired again. And again. And again. This time the ork could not return. Torn apart under the hail of bolter fire, the creature was now no more than a bionic mechanical frame and shredded gobbets of bloody green flesh.

Jarold turned his attention to the Templar fastened to the second slab, and he knew him at once to be his brother in battle, Emperor's Champion Ansgar. There was no mistaking the artificed Armour of Faith, even after the damage it had obviously suffered in its churning passage through the crashing river and after the sacrilege the painboss had committed against it since. But Jarold's auto-senses told him that Ansgar still lived.

The impact came as unexpectedly and as violently as a lighting strike. His dreadnought body shook as, at almost point blank range, it was struck by a barrage of heavy munitions fire.

His body shaking under the continuing onslaught, Jarold turned to face his attacker. And there before him stood the nemesis of the Solemnus Crusade resurrected as a metal-formed avatar of mechanical mayhem.

For a moment even Brother Jarold was stunned into inaction. So the tyrant warboss of the Blood Scar tribe had not died within the nuclear inferno that had consumed the Mechanicus caldera. Instead he had been reborn, evolved into something greater, something worse.

Then, all the rage Jarold had felt over the last twelve years – all the anger and hatred and remorse and guilt at the deaths of so many of his brethren and the fall of the proud chapter keep of Solemnus – erupted with all the wrath of a furious volcano.

His own assault cannon screamed again, auto-loaders protesting as they hurled rounds into the

emptying barrel breeches. This burst of shells batted
the ork's gun arm aside. And then Morkrull Grimskar,
the Scourge of Solemnus, was upon him, scissoring
shears trying to sever the shielding of the power-feed
cables and nerve impulse bundles connecting Jarold's
sarcophagus to the rest of the dreadnought war
machine.

The crude artistry of the painboss had re-made the
Templars' nemesis as a bio-mechanically bonded
cybork. The dreadnought's machine-soul read the presence of bionic components bonded to the warboss
implanted throughout its abnormally adapted body,
including its right arm, one eye and even one hemisphere of its tiny, primitive brain.

At last Brother Jarold was confronting the creature that
had ultimately been responsible for his incarceration.
But what made Jarold revile the warboss more than anything else – even more than the knowledge of what
Grimskar had done to his home world and his battle-
brethren – was that here the beast stood, re-made,
sporting components of his brother-Templars' power
armour, wearing the Apothecary's auto-responsive
shoulder plate and the heraldic devices of the Black
Templars as though they were trophies of war. And
above them all, atop a rusted banner pole, the scarred
ork stared down at Jarold with blasphemous pride.

The colossi grappled with one another in a reeling
dance around the vault, crashing into columns and
carved stone walls, bulwarks becoming heaps of rubble
at their bulldozing collisions as if they were made of
nothing more than rotten fibreboard.

Dust filled the stale air of the laboratory in great billows as the dreadnought and the warboss laid blow

after blow against each other. After his battering by the river, Jarold's robotic power fist was no longer functioning, but it still made an effective club with which to bludgeon the ork.

Since entering the equatorial jungles Brother Jarold had endured encounters with gargantuan squiggoth war-beasts, survived a fall from a precipice into the raging torrent of a river, and broken into a cybork-defended stronghold single-handedly. And slowly but surely, Jarold was prevailing against the warboss. Would this battle see the end of Morkrull Grimskar, the Slayer of Solemnus, at last? Was it the Emperor's divine purpose that Brother Jarold exact revenge for all the wrongs done to the Black Templars of the Solemnus Crusade from the alien-inspiration of that invasion, here in the bowels of the overrun genetor base?

Dull booms came as muffled rumbles from above, particles of crushed rockcrete cascading from the chamber roof as explosions ripped through the complex. Were those detonations the legacy of Jarold's rampage through the base, or were they down to some other agency?

Mechanical senses detected the hull breach the warboss had somehow achieved against the veteran's sarcophagus, registering in Jarold's machine-linked mind as a flare of knifing white-hot pain. But in the same moment Jarold brought his cannon to bear and the shock of cerebral pain caused the dreadnought's impulse-link to fire the weapon. The warboss was thrown backwards, across the lab, towards the pain-boss's surgery, propelled by the force of the assault cannon fusillade.

With a yawning heave, the rockcrete of the ceiling – the structure of the vault weakened by their titanic and unrelenting onslaught and the explosions ripping through the base above them – bulged inwards, and then fully half the ceiling came crashing down. The rockcrete broke into a thousand pieces on top of the beleaguered Brother Jarold, burying the dreadnought under several tonnes of rubble.

For a moment Jarold suffered total sensory blackout. Servos ground and muscle-bundles strained against the crushing weight. It would take more than a building collapsing on top of him to stop the Hero of Solemnus. He had survived a drop pod crash and a head-on collision with an ork warplane. A cave-in was nothing.

The fused fist of Jarold's left arm punched through the rubble surrounding him and burst through into clear space. Flailing with the attachment of his assault cannon as he swept chunks of masonry aside with his monstrous mechanical hand, even the action of him swivelling on the ball-joint of his waist helped shift the larger slabs of rockcrete on top of him. Brother Jarold pulled himself clear of the rock fall.

There was the warboss, but he was not where the veteran brother had expected to find him. Grimskar stood at the end of the laboratory next to Ansgar's restraining slab, only now the limp form of the Emperor's Champion hung like a lifeless marionette from the metal claw of the scarred ork. In his other hand Grimskar held the champion's holy wargear, the Black Sword and his bolt pistol. And something else: a blunt metal tube, its tip a flashing beacon light.

Not wanting to risk the life of his battle-brother with weapons-fire, Jarold bore down on the warboss again with clumping steps. Grimskar said something unintelligible in the guttural language of his kind, his alien voice a basso growl. A malevolent animal cunning burned in the ork's remaining organic eye. This was not the final climactic battle Jarold had expected to fight against the creature that had brought Solemnus to its knees, and whose Blood Scar tribe still harried sulphurous Armageddon. His mind boiled. This was not how it was supposed to be. He would not let it be.

As Jarold closed on the alien tyrant, a sphere of crackling emerald light surrounded the ork and his unconscious prisoner. The dreadnought did not slow his pace but watched helplessly as the green glare of the crackling shield intensified.

And then, as the dreadnought's crashing steps brought him within reach of the warboss, with a subsonic boom the sphere of light disappeared, plunging the ruins of the laboratory into sudden comparative darkness, leaving nothing but a retina-searing afterimage on the sensor-linked optic nerves of Jarold's physical body.

Of the Emperor's Champion and the alien warboss Morkrull Grimskar there was no sign.

Brother Jarold's augmetic voice gave vent to a swelling roar of tortured mental anguish and enraged frustration. The despicable ork had activated some kind of alien teleportation homing beacon and had himself dragged away from a battle he knew he could not win. So, once again, the Scarred Ork had made his escape, only this time taking Brother Ansgar with him as a trophy of his continued defiance of the Black Templars. The Emperor alone knew where they were now and what would happen to the crusade's fallen champion.

Brother Jarold opened up with every weapon in his arsenal, assault cannon, storm bolter and rocket launcher lending their voices to his hymn of rage.

BEYOND THE DISMAL dungeon of the painboss's laboratory dawn was breaking over the jungle, the cloying moisture of the night's precipitation steaming from its green depths as the sun struggled through the storm-bruised heavens.

Another explosion shook the cold grey walls of the magi-genetor complex and a second sun rose over the compound, a ball of hungry flame rolling up into the sky.

Sergeant Borysko could see the landing pad painted in shades of purple in the violet light of dawn: a rectangle of daylight beyond the smoke-shot gloom of the interior of the compound. Behind him his boys followed, each bearing one of the precious canisters, the Kid carrying his as though it was a krak grenade on a motion sensor hair trigger. And for all he knew that was exactly what they were.

The ACG lieutenant hadn't deemed it necessary to tell them exactly what it was they had liberated from the orks' occupation of the devastated complex. What Pavle Borysko did know, however, was that he and his men had practically completed their mission and in a matter of minutes they would be on their way back to the sweaty, stinking – yet most welcome – embrace of Cerbera Base.

But it didn't stop him being curious as to what H-363 was, that it should have been developed here, in the depths of the unforgiving jungles by the flesh-manipulating genetor-adepts who, by their actions, had dared mimic the legendary creative powers of the Emperor Himself.

Tannhauser ducked into cover at the archway that was all that stood between the skinners and the exterior of the compound. Borysko immediately did the same, waving his men back against the wall with a silent hand gesture. At his shoulder Tremayne put up his laspistol and did the same.

Their flight through the base had been surprisingly unhindered by the orks. The arrival of the avenging Astartes angel of death had drawn their attention away from anything that Tremayne, Borysko and the ork hunters might have been up to. Further explosions tearing through the base and any element of surprise gone, Coburg's autocannon did for any orks still intent on challenging the skinners' escape.

However Kasarta was no longer with them. In the adrenaline-rush of their flight, carrying Tremayne's precious prize, and not receiving the sort of attention they had been expecting, they had become careless. That carelessness was cruelly highlighted when an ork booby-trap had done for Kasarta, stickbombs hidden in the general detritus littering another arched doorway, blowing the trooper messily in two. Once again Borysko cursed himself for their complacency.

But now they were only a matter of thirty metres from where the hunched insectoid-form of the ork-desecrated Valkyrie crouched on the warming landing pad, its hard black surface crazed by the green tendrils of jungle pushing up through the rockcrete. Geist eyed the assault carrier hungrily.

Something moved, almost imperceptibly, in the shade of a fuel-dump lean-to. The kroot was virtually camouflaged by the twilight still clinging to the awakening forest. At the mercenary's signal, Tannhauser turned and motioned the rest of them forward again.

Hawkeye Gunderson and Priest moved up to flank the exit and cover the ork hunters' escape. Then, with a quick glance at the plaza before him, Sergeant Borysko led his men out to the crudely re-painted and re-fitted flyer at a run.

He heard the report of Gunderson's lasrifle before he heard Priest's warning oath to the Emperor.

Pounding around the western wing of the complex were a pair of the largest orks Borysko had seen in a long time. For a split second the question crossed his mind as to why these two were not involved in the battle for the compound elsewhere. Perhaps the Astartes' avenging angel had eventually succumbed to the greenskins' determined resistance.

As well as being half a tonne of alien muscle each, already their bodies had been surgically augmented with crude mechanical components. With servo-powered legs and arms, weapons built into their metal exoskeletons, and snapping iron mouths, they looked like they would present a warrior of the Emperor's finest Adeptus Astartes with a challenge. To any ordinary soldier of His Imperial Majesty's armies they were terrifying examples of how serious the xenos threat was to mankind.

But ork hunters, and Borysko's Boys at that, were not just any other unit of Imperial Guardsmen.

Gunderson snapped off two more zinging las-rounds, both finding their mark in the middle of the unprotected forehead of the first of the augmented greenskins before the creature could bring its own weapons to bear. Ork skulls were notoriously tough, reputed to be as hard as ceramite, but the sniper's longlas could penetrate the hull plating of a Leman Russ. With dark blood running from the clean puncture wounds in its head, the cybork's mechanised body powered forwards for another ten metres before it crashed to the ground, its pistoning legs kicking futilely against the weed-cracked rockcrete.

By then the second cybork had engaged its cannon, the whirling primitive weapon still managing to hurl explosive shells at the escaping ork hunters at a frightening rate. But the unencumbered ork hunters were quicker than the slower cyborks, and as the solid shot rounds of their gun attachments chewed up the rockcrete between them, the ork hunters' feet barely touched the ground, always keeping ahead of the shell impacts.

Too quick for all of them except Ertz. Borysko's adjutant suddenly performed his own flailing dance of death as bullets punched through kidneys, lungs and the coils of his intestines. His body crumpled to lie on the heating rockcrete with limbs out at unnatural angles.

But Borysko, Tremayne and several of the other skinners had also been able to bring their shotguns and las-weapons to bear. Gunfire whickered across the plaza, spanging off the armour of the charging cybork. The furious bellowing of the beast was cut off as just as many las-rounds and shotgun shells bypassed its protective exoskeleton and cut through its body. Trooper 'Ox' Coburg, bellowing in an almost perfect imitation of an ork, was the one who finally did for the brute, the belt feed of the autocannon clattering through the breech, spent shell cases pinging off the cracked landing pad.

And then Borysko passed into the umbra of the dawn-long shadow of the assault carrier.

The alien mercenary was already perched inside the open side of the craft, regarding Borysko with its blind-seeming eyes, its head on one side. It made the grizzled sergeant's skin crawl. 'Metal bird empty,' it chirruped.

Borysko barged past the kroot and into the shadowed chill of the flyer's belly. The others piled into the Valkyrie after him.

Borysko turned to the trooper who had boarded the assault carrier after him. 'Geist, can you fly this heap of junk?'

'I think so,' the skinner grinned.

'Don't *think* so. Now's not the time for thinking, Joker. It's not your job to think.'

'Yeah, leave the tricky stuff to the sarge,' Kole quipped.

'Don't think so. Know so.'

'Let's just hope the frikkers haven't done anything to stop it flying,' Geist muttered to himself in annoyance.

There was a promethium cough and then the thrumming of powering engine turbines. Either the orks had left the original human controls of the flyer intact, or Geist had managed to make sense of the meks' clumsy customisations.

The orks had opened up the sides of the Valkyrie, exposing the interior of the craft to the elements, so that they could fit their bulky cannon attachments inside, giving the overburdened craft increased fire-power capabilities.

Borysko was glad the jet-wash of the engines swept through the belly of the bird: it blew out the musky, vegetable stench of ork and blew in the far more preferable stink of promethium fuel.

The skinners settled themselves inside, hanging onto webbing straps and crudely welded roll bars. There was plenty of room for them all.

'Everyone on board?' the sergeant barked, taking a quick head-count as he tried to remember how many of his men remained. There was Vanderkamp and Kole. The Kid was huddled in a corner behind an ork cannon at the gaping side of the flyer, Coburg next to him, hanging ape-like from a roll bar by one hand, the other supporting the weight of his autocannon. Geist was up in the cockpit where Yeydl had joined him. Tannhauser was just scrambling on board, leaving only the two snipers who had covered their escape.

There should be twelve of them left, he decided, including Tremayne and the alien. Tremayne had strapped himself into a steel seat, clasping a stencilled canister tightly in his lap. Borysko cast the kroot a withering look through hate-narrowed eyes. Pangor Yuma stood there in the open hold, rifle in hand, able to keep his balance thanks to the way his taloned feet gripped the grilled floor.

No matter what the alien mercenary had done for them during their latest mission into the jungle, or how many orks it he had killed, Borysko still couldn't get away from the fact that Inquisitorial agent or no, the kroot was still an alien, an abomination in the Emperor's sight. Given another time and place, under different circumstances, it was just as likely that Borysko would have found himself fighting against the avian freak.

The sergeant was brought back to the here and now again by a shout from the cockpit.

'What is it, Yeydl?'

'Geist says we're ready for dust-off.'

'Understood. When Hawkeye and Priest are on board we go.'

Borysko swung himself half out of the hatchway. With a simple hand gesture he signalled the two snipers to join the rest of the platoon aboard the flyer.

Borysko allowed himself a moment of unalloyed self-satisfaction. They had almost made it.

The last two of his men onboard, along with the lieutenant's precious cargo, turbine engines screaming, fighting the pull of gravity, the heavily-laden Valkyrie rose ponderously off the rockcrete.

As Borysko scanned the compound, slowly dropping away below them as Geist turned the flyer towards the north-east, the sergeant caught sight of a disturbance in the leafy undergrowth, where his own party had entered the compound only a matter of hours before.

A figure, clad in black and grey stormtrooper fatigues burst into the open at the back of the enclosure, moving with a curious limping gait, dragging one leg behind him. As he ran, the stormtrooper put his hell-gun to his shoulder and pointed it at the ascending Valkyrie.

The sergeant was so surprised that it took him a second to realise that he recognised the man, that he had encountered this individual before. It was the assassin who had tried to kill Tremayne and who had been responsible for the deaths of three of his men as they crossed the tree-bridge over the river-chasm.

Borysko thought he felt the searing pulse of a las-round pass by his head. The kroot suddenly squawked loudly, and the report of its alien firearm discharging filled the hollow cabin.

Below them, the stormtrooper fell forwards onto his face on the rockcrete, his hellgun under him, and didn't get up again.

The Valkyrie's nose tipped forwards, Geist urged the flyer towards the perimeter of the compound, the lumbering craft only just clearing the razor wire topping the chain-link fence.

Borysko turned to Tremayne. He barely registered Tannhauser speak as the trooper swore.

The lieutenant still sat strapped in his seat, the gleaming silver container held in his lap. Only now his chin rested on his chest, his cap lying between his feet.

'Throne,' the skinner sergeant himself gasped. Several of the other hunters uttered their own expletive curses.

They could all see the semi-cauterised exit wound oozing dark blood, and smell the acrid reek of ozone and cooked brain matter. There was no doubting that Tremayne was dead.

Before any of the ork hunters could stop it, or even really knew what was going on, the kroot was on top of the lieutenant, a scalping blade gripped between the four claw-fingers of its hand pulled from the harness across its chest. There was a sharp crack followed by a horrid sucking pop.

'What in the name of Terra do you think you're doing, you freak?' Borysko screamed, all his xenophobic hatred and fury suddenly unleashed. There had been no love lost between the skinner sergeant and the pompous ACG officer, but Borysko wasn't going to stand for this act of violation from the alien. The rest of the troopers were silent as they observed the commander's challenge.

Pangor Yuma turned to regard him with the dead white orbs of its eyes. The Ministorum padres sent to work within the camps of the ork hunter regiments said that the eyes were windows to the soul. Borysko saw nothing within those pupil-less alien eyes now. It was as he had always suspected: the xenos spawn were soulless creatures.

In one hand the kroot held the bloodied knife, in the other the top of Tremayne's skull.

'I asked you a question, freak!' Borysko was on his feet now, trying to keep his balance as the Valkyrie sped over the canopy of the rainforests, through swirls of evaporating morning mist, bumping over the thermals rising from the warming forest. 'What in all this green hell gives you the right to defile this man's body? I've heard of what your kind get up to. Give me one good reason – any reason – why I shouldn't kill you now?'

Borysko wanted to finish the kroot more than anything else at that moment, but something stayed his hand. That something was his own trenchant curiosity. Yes, he had heard how the kroot devoured the flesh of their enemies, but in all the time he had been forced to spend in the alien mercenary's company of late, he had never witnessed it eat from the corpses of any of the orks they had killed, and it had also left the bodies of those troopers who had died during the course of the mission. So why do so now, in front of all of them, and by doing so put its own survival in jeopardy? Surely it could only be because doing so had somehow become part of its own vile undisclosed agenda.

The kroot paused, glancing back and forth from the exposed grey flesh of what was left of the lieutenant's brain to the red-faced Borysko with obvious unease. Pangor Yuma indicated the Inquisitorial rosette hung amongst the other totems around its neck.

'Is enough you know this is work of Inquisition,' the birdman said in its grating pidgin-Gothic. 'Stop me now and mission a failure.'

'What do you mean?' the sergeant growled, swaying as the Valkyrie hit another thermal updraft.

'Officer wanted shiny silver things. Only he know why. Only he know what they for. If I not do this they will be useless. Sarge want to tell Master Klojage why they now useless and why mission fail?'

Although it jarred against his moral sense of what was right and just in the Emperor's sight, like any right-minded Imperial citizen Borysko had a healthy dread of His Majesty's Holy Inquisition.

'Do what you must then,' he said, the words like bile in his mouth.

The foetid green expanse of the steaming jungles slipping past beneath them, like some emerald sea beneath the prow of an ocean-going vessel, Borysko turned away, unable to watch. The slurping gulping sounds were almost too much to bear as it was, even for this hard-bitten ork hunter. He could not stomach such barbaric behaviour. It was enough that he had effectively condoned such a disgusting heretical act of hubris. He was appalled at himself for allowing such an appalling desecration of a human body to take place. He could hear Priest whimpering to himself in the corner of the belly-hold. The rest of the party remained in horrified silence, and it took a lot to horrify an ork hunter.

'So?' Borysko asked when the kroot was done. 'What did you learn?'

Pangor Yuma swallowed noisily. 'Learn much,' the creature said, almost proudly.

'I bet you did, you frikkin' alien bastard,' Borysko growled. 'But what did you learn about the canisters? What is it we're carrying back to Cerbera?'

And the kroot told him.

Borysko's expression hardened to an impassive mask of steely resolve. 'And you learnt all that by eating a man's brain?'

'Yes. By eating flesh of dead kroot can know what they know.'

'So we can now tell your masters in the Inquisition what the genetor-magi managed to forcibly evolve, and let them do the rest.'

'Pangor Yuma tell his master,' the kroot trilled.

'I don't think so,' Borysko growled, 'not when Pangor Yuma died during the mission.'

For a fleeting second an expression of avian curiosity creased the alien's hawkish features.

Before it could react, Borysko put his laspistol to the side of the creature's head and fired in one slick action.

The kroot's body folded in half and tumbled almost lazily out of the gaping hold of the Valkyrie to be claimed by the predatory jungle below.

Borysko calmly holstered his pistol and turned to see the shock-slack faces of his men. 'I hate frikkin' aliens,' he said with a shark's smile turning the corners of his tight-lipped mouth.

And the Valkyrie sped on over the sea of the jungle canopy towards the still climbing sun and Cerbera Base.

TWENTY-ONE
EMPEROR'S WRATH

HROTHQAR FUROR, RAVAGER of Worlds, Champion of Khorne, threw back his head and bellowed his blood-lust to the tempestuous sky. The howl reverberated across the crater, rebounding as an echoed growl from the altered stones. The last of the greenskins fell, bifurcated from crown to groin by the ravening Deathbringer, as Furor brought his axe down in one final scything motion.

Wrath boiled inside him, blazing through his veins like molten magma, the volcano of his killing rage ready to erupt. His Lord Khorne had brought them to this place that they might continue to take skulls and souls in his name and had found themselves confronted by the degenerate alien horde. But it had been the Blood God's will that the World Eaters reap a harvest of these unworthy vermin and had proved this was his intention as his daemon-spawn servants had manifested within the physical realm to join their murderous assault.

Ungodly pleasure had sparked his cerebral implants when he set eyes on the whelps of the false emperor running to join the abattoir carnage. Dim and distant memories, rising from his mind like tiny bubbles rising to the surface of a seething bloody ocean, told him that the heraldry of these pitiful fools were of the Black Templars and Relictors Chapters – neither of which had even existed when the World Eaters had made their final, glorious assault on the false emperor's palace on Terra ten thousand years ago.

The souls of these upstarts would be more to the Blood God's taste. The Ravager of worlds would ensure that their skulls joined the mountains of bones that were as foothills to the macabre monstrosity of Khorne's great throne of brass.

But the gate to that other Armageddon had been closed, and in that one apocalyptic slamming of the portal between worlds the daemons' link to the warp had been severed. The storm still raged above, although its terrible fury was beginning to blow itself out, and the physical forms of the bloodletters, flesh hounds and other ravening daemon-things that had joined the Berzerkers in their battle for this new Armageddon, were rapidly de-stabilising. But they fought on ruthlessly to the end nonetheless, until sword and bolter of the World Eaters' enemies cut them down and their flesh dissolving in bubbling puddles of slime on the spoiled ground of the crater, evaporating back into the ether.

His rage unleashed in a frenzied orgy of bloodletting, Hrothqar Furor and his Berzerker brothers like him, had fought on against the greenskin horde with renewed savagery in their desire to bring the battle to the misguided loyalist Marines.

Attacked from both sides, those among the ork tribes that remained, following the devastating death of the wyrdboy, had found themselves outnumbered by the World Eaters, Relictors and Black Templars, and were soon wiped out to an ork.

Having cut a bloody swathe through the forces of the feral orks, Furor and the survivors of his warband came face-to-face with their true enemy at last: the whelp-pups of the weakling primarchs that had cowered behind their false emperor when the true masters of mankind had revealed themselves to them.

The Dark Gods had offered them power beyond measure, if only they would kneel before them: and Khorne was the mightiest of all the fell powers and most worthy of a warrior's fealty. It was the Astartes legions that had forged the Imperium in the false emperor's name and then they had been expected to debase themselves to serve those who were not fit to lick the excrement from their boots. Why should such as they serve when they could be masters of the galaxy?

Hefting Deathbringer in both hands once again, the possessed axe screaming with blood-greed, Furor charged across the corpses of the fallen greenskins towards the leader of the Relictors. And he wanted his enemy to see the face of the one who would take his soul in the name of the Lord of Skulls. He wanted him to look into the face of Khorne when he died, wide-eyed and befouling himself.

Ripping his helmet from his head, his lipless mouth formed in a permanent predator's snarl and eyes so bloodshot that none of the white remained, Furor bore down on his hated foe the bloody badge of his loyalty, plain for the whelp to see.

ON EVERY SIDE Relictors battled the devotees of the insane, carrion-hungry warrior god of Chaos, but at a terrible cost.

Brother Edred fell, his head cleaved in two by the snarling maw of a heavy rusted blade, the plasma cannon he carried going critical seconds later – its power cell ruptured by another axe blow – killing the creature that had put an end to the veteran Relictor.

Brother Pleoh laid the killing blow to a Berzerker with a daemonic leer formed into the grille of its helmet faceplate, his bolter rounds puncturing the glassy eyeholes of its visor and exploding inside the Chaos warrior's brain, as the hellish minion took off the Relictor's right leg at the hip.

Another of the daemonic-offspring of the fallen primarch beheaded Brother Kirkor with its executioner's blade whilst Brothers Slecg and Rodor, both now airborne, harried their battle-brother's killer from the air with bolter fire and frag grenades.

Brother Nerian squeezed the unholy life from a World Eater as he crushed the warrior's helmeted head between the oversized fingers of his punishing power fist.

With a screaming of grating metal, Captain Oberon Eurys's power sword broke through the armoured carapace of the gore-streaked warrior before him, the crackling disruptor field generated by the blade exploding the monster's black hearts inside its chest. The Chaos worshipper was immediately gripped by violent, twisting death-throes, its body making impossible shapes as it reeled away from its slayer.

So violent were the sudden paroxysms Eurys's sword was tugged free of his grasp even as the Chaos creature's own grotesque blade was hurled free of nerveless fingers to stick, point first, in the spoiled ground at the Relictor's feet.

Before Eurys could recover his own weapon from the twitching corpse of the World Eater, a daemon more savage than any he had so far encountered came charging down on him, its howling chain-axe raised above its head.

The crimson ceramite and ruddy brass of the warrior's ancient power armour was crusted with black gore, the remnants of the many kills made by the savage. Everywhere the profane skull rune of his hellish legion could be seen side-by-side with the maw-enclosed planet symbol of the World Eaters. Human skulls rattled from a crude leather belt, on a rusted chain about the warrior's bulging-veined neck and the exhaust ports of his armour's generarium.

But it was the savage's face that attested to where this monster's fealty lay, more than any war-trophy adorning his foul armour.

His head was devoid of all hair and he had the scar-twisted face of a killer. His nose had been debrided down to the cartilage and most repulsive of all, Eurys saw that the champion's lips had been removed. His teeth were sharpened yellow fangs and his gums bled as he ground exaggerated incisors together. His eyes were darkly smouldering pits of hatred and bestial bloodgreed. And writ large across his hideous features was the blasphemous mark of his inhuman god. His face looked most like a death's-head skull.

The barbarous aura of a killer poured off him in a torrent of brutality made tangible. There was no doubting, in Eurys's mind, that this murderous beast was the master of this insane blood-hunt.

In only a few precious heartbeats the World Eater would be upon him. There was not time to think: there was only time to act.

Reaching out a gauntleted hand he grasped the hilt of the infernal weapon still quivering in the ground at his feet. And his mind was assaulted by indescribable, blasphemous images. He saw...

...*Monstrous hell-titans, daemon-possessed gods of death, stalking the ash wastes, their hellish cannon lacerating the ancient armour of Titanicus Legionnes land battleships... Living creatures of brass and iron, with molten fire coursing through their steel veins, crashing through the lines of beleaguered hive-militia.... Daemons born of bloodshed and bilious rage cutting through the flesh of Guardsmen and Marines with smoking black swords, the monstrous hounds that came in their wake lapping up the gallons of spilled blood... Butchered corpses strung from Chaos-consecrated monuments raised to the glory of the god of genocide and his fallen son... Unbridled slaughter on a planetary scale... A voice like murder itself screaming in the oblivion of despair... A landscape blackened and dead, running with rivers of blood... Wreathing clouds of crimson smoke parting before his eyes and amidst the acres of bones, dwarfing the mountainous slopes of the skull-mounds, he was barely able to comprehend the legs of the colossal brass and iron construction,*

enthroned upon in, luxuriating in its primal savagery, a
soul-searing vision that no eye should ever fall upon... And
everywhere the echoing cry of tortured souls, and their dae-
monic canine tormenters, the same... 'Khorne! Khorne!
KHORNE!'

It was a hymn of blood and sacrifice sung to him by
the daemon-possessed sword, and the Relictor's
bared soul rejoiced in its song of slaughter.

As if awakening from a nightmarish dream, Eurys
was only dimly aware of the battle still raging around
him and of the Chaos champion before him bellowing the name of his hell-god over and over, again and
again.

Hell-sword and daemon-axe screamed as they
clashed and tore at the armour of the two suddenly
warring colossi. But against a daemon-weapon consecrated to his own dark patron, Hrothqar Furor found
himself to be more vulnerable than he ever could
have imagined. Khorne did not care from whence the
blood flowed in his name, only that it was shed, and
in oceanic quantities.

It took all Eurys's strength to finally stay his hand
once the screaming hell-sword had delivered its fatal
executioner's stroke, and the Chaos champion lay in
a dozen bloody pieces on the ground around him.

WOLFRAM FELL TO his knees, his grip still tight on the
haft of his blood-splattered holy axe, and stared
dumbfounded around him at the corpses of his
brethren, those who had paid with their lives among
the Relictors warband, and the mounds of alien bodies. Looking around him he could not see a single
one of the Khornate warband still standing. In fact,

not many amongst his battle brethren still stood, nor amongst the Relictors.

Oberon Eurys's Relictors.

He was the reason for the shock now seizing Wolfram's body, not the euphoric aftermath of having conquered not only the desecrating orks but also the murderous legacy of the Fallen One's first invasion five centuries before.

Wolfram had witnessed Eurys pull the hell-forged daemon-sword from the despoiled ground and watched in disbelieving horror as the captain had cut down the Blood God's champion with the selfsame weapon.

Of the thirteen Templars who had set out on an oath-sworn mission to discover the fate of Fighting Company Gerhard and recover the precious geneseed of their battle-claimed brothers, only five remained.

Of the twelve Relictors they had encountered during their fateful mission, six now remained.

The orks might be dead, as were the Blood God's savage servants, but the Black Templars' work was not yet done here.

His grip sure on his thrice-blessed crozius arcanum, Chaplain Wolfram rose to his feet. Righteous fury blazing like a halo around him, like some avenging angel of the Golden Throne, he strode across the slaughter-field of the crater to confront the Relictor.

Eurys stood there, in defiant arrogance before Wolfram, the smoking hell-sword still tight in his hand.

'Brother-Captain,' Wolfram fumed, 'what have you done here this day? How could a loyal servant of the Emperor consider taking up a weapon consecrated to the foul Gods of Chaos? In the Emperor's name, explain your actions if you can!'

'Chaplain Wolfram,' Eurys said, his voice as cold as the icy interstellar gulfs, 'it would appear that you are labouring under the delusion shared by so many of our brother Astartes Chapters.'

'By the Holy Throne of Terra, what can you mean? What delusion do you speak of?' Wolfram growled, raising the cross-head of his crozius before him as if to ward against evil.

'I speak of the fact that you do not understand the true nature of the power that we call Chaos.'

Dying peals of thunder rolled across the landscape as the Relictor spoke. 'You, a man of faith and intelligence, still hold to the tenet that it is Chaos itself that is inherently evil, rather than that it is a power put to use by *those* who are evil. In that way it is no different to the psyker power manipulated with such success by our Librarian brothers.'

'Sigismund preserve me! You would speak to me of psyker-magick,' Wolfram spat, 'when our Chapter has sworn to have no truck with the agencies of the warp? If power corrupts and absolute power corrupts absolutely, imagine what the power of Chaos can do to a man's soul, what it can do to the soul of a Space Marine.'

'But you do not understand. It is a power that can be turned against those who would seek to bring down the Imperium of Mankind as much as it is a tool used by those who would enact their malicious galaxy-shattering schemes against us.'

'When your yearling of a Chapter has forged itself a history as long and as glorious as that of the Black

Templars, then perhaps I will listen when you speak of the allure of Chaos. Now, put down the weapon and stand-down your command,' Wolfram demanded, taking another step towards the Relictor captain. 'Your soul needs to be purged with contrite prayer, in which you must beseech the Emperor for his forgiveness.'

In response Eurys raised the smoking hell-sword in front of his chestplate, showing no intention of obeying Wolfram's command and relinquishing the cursed blade.

'I pity the Imperium when esteemed Chapters such as your own are trapped in the past and cannot see the benefits to be reaped from the study and application of artefacts such as this,' Eurys said, regarding the sword in his hand.

It seemed to Wolfram that images moved and slithered across its obsidian surface, images of screaming faces that made the priest feel cold to the marrow.

'These are not your words, your opinions, brother-captain,' the Templar said. 'Can you not see that? These are the first signs of the corruption that this accursed daemon-weapon is working on your soul.'

'You are a man of faith, are you not, Chaplain Wolfram?' Eurys challenged, taking a step towards the Templar himself now.

'By the primarch, I thank the Emperor I am,' Wolfram declared.

'Then why can you not see that, if a warrior has the strength of will and surety of faith with which to shield his soul, he can resist the deceiving promises of Chaos and turn its power to His holy purpose, just like any other weapon? We stand at the dawning of a new age for the Imperium, one that would see us as the masters of Chaos or crushed beneath the heel of those who would use it where you, and your kind, would not.'

'Such heresy!' the Chaplain barked. 'Your faith is weak, Relictor. You have already been swayed by its lies and half-truths.'

'No, priest, it is you who is weak,' Eurys said darkly. 'It is you who lacks the courage to turn such weapons against those who would otherwise use them to bring about the end of all that we would gladly lay down our lives for.'

By now the followers of the two opposing leaders had regrouped and gathered behind the Chaplain and the captain.

'The myriad evils that harry the walls of the Imperium – the alien, the heretic, the traitor – threaten to engulf the galaxy and snuff out the guiding light of the beneficent Emperor. Their very existence merits the use of such weapons. These are desperate times,' the Relictor went on, his voice sounding hollow. 'How little is your love of the Imperium that in your cowardice you would not use every weapon at your disposal to hold back the tide of evil that would drown His realm in its malignant depths? How weak *your* faith?'

'By Sigismund's sword, you would dare to call me a *coward*?' Wolfram roared.

Behind him, the survivors of his holy band brought their own weapons to bear. From the line of Relictors could be heard the hum of weapon-cells charging and the *click-clack* of bolters being readied. The captain's men showed no sign of disputing the verity of their commander's claims.

'I command you, in the Emperor's name, drop the sword,' Wolfram declared, his voice carrying across the stone circle and rebounding from the stilled monoliths.

'I cannot do that, Templar,' Eurys growled. 'It is my sworn duty to recover just such treasures that they might be studied, so that we might understand the machinations of the Great Enemy all the better.'

'Just as it is my sworn duty, in the name of the Emperor, the primarch and Lord Sigismund, as a Chaplain and a Black Templar, to bring about the end of all those who would deal with daemons and thereby threaten the stability of His galaxy-spanning realm. I forbid you to take that weapon from this place of *purgatus*.'

'Then I have nothing more to say to you, Templar,' Eurys declared, unrepentant.

'But I have something to say to you,' the embittered Chaplain stated solemnly, 'and it is not something I do lightly and without great sadness eating at my soul. But it is the only resolution to this matter that can be of the best for the Imperium.'

The Black Templars Chaplain swung his crozius arcanum up to his shoulder in one hand, ready to bring the power axe to bear in battle once more. In his other hand he grasped his rosarius. The ruby-quartz eyes of his death's head mask bore into the Relictor captain, laying Eurys's warp-stained soul bare.

'The Emperor has looked upon you and found you wanting in His sight,' Wolfram declaimed, 'and his wrath is terrible. By the grace of the Holy Emperor and in His name, I cast you out. I declare you *diabolus*.

It is written that by his actions may you know the heretic, so I know you, Oberon Eurys. I declare you *hereticus*. May the Master of Mankind have mercy on your eternal soul.'

The last fitful lightning bursts of the dying storm shook the oppressive air festering above the Chaos circle, its last gasping breaths tugging at the Templars' ruined robes, as Chaplain Wolfram of the Solemnus Crusade led the Black Templars against Captain Oberon Eurys of the Relictors Chapter and his brethren.

'Brother Templars!' Wolfram declared, his voice having the quality of a tolling death-knell, 'in the name of the Emperor, in the name of Dorn, in the name of Sigismund, in memory of our fallen brothers, suffer not the unclean to live. No pity!'

'No remorse!' his loyal crusaders responded, taking up the chant.

'*No fear!*'

Priority level: Amethyst Alpha
Transmitted: Cerbera Base, Equatorial Jungles, Armageddon
To: Battle-cruiser Valiant, Task Force Sparta, geo-stationary orbit above Hive Tartarus
Date: 3904999.M41
Transmitter: Astropath Prime Kaballas
Receiver: Astropath-terminus Reis
Author: Interrogator Maximo Rivera
Thought for the Day: Intolerance is a blessing

My Lord Inquisitor Klojage,
*   I write with news regarding the artefact code-named H-363 and the attempt to steal the same said artefact by agencies outside of the Officio Inquisitoria.*
*   It transpires that H-363, or hybrid pathological agent 363, is a biological weapon developed by the genetor-magi of Biologis Facility VI since the last ork invasion. The pathogen combines anti-fungal agents with other aggressive self-replicating bacteria. However, it remains an*

untested anti-ork weapon. There has not been the opportunity to carry out a test confirming its authenticity.
Neither do we know why the genetor-magi did not use H-
363 themselves when their base was attacked, and
consequently overrun, by the orks during the opening
stages of the invasion prosecuted by the Great Beast's
forces. What we do know, however, is that agencies other
than our own were prepared to go to great lengths to
acquire the pathogen.

This brings me to the matter of the notorious criminal
Hastur Zephyrus and the rogue trader's attempt to capture
H-363 for himself, through the use of agents acting on his
behalf. I am sure you will agree, my lord, that it is con-
cerning to note that Zephyrus's operative in this endeavour
was an officer of the Armageddon Command Guard, one
Lieutenant Nimrod Tremayne. Seeing that Zephyrus's
influence has reached so high within the echelons of the
very authorities that have been charged with the protection
of this vital, strategic world, I would be so bold as to suggest that you authorise a more in-depth investigation of the
ACG without further delay.

I have been able to ascertain that Zephyrus was seeking
to recover Hybrid Pathological Agent 363 with the intention of selling it on to the highest bidder elsewhere, and
possibly also intending to use it as a safeguard for himself
and his agents whilst operating under cover within the
Armageddon subsector. It sickens me, my lord, that during
times of war there are those supposedly faithful servants of
the Immortal Emperor who would gladly see themselves
profit from the suffering and desperation of others.

There was also an unfortunate incident that I feel duty-
bound to report, regarding two of our own field agents, in
that they did not realise that they were operatives working

for the same faction. But secrecy is the way of the Inquisition and I myself take sole responsibility for this error. However, there was too much at stake to risk informing them of their mutual missions and exposing their cover. I shall try to explain.

Our operative planted amongst Keifer's stormtroopers had been thought lost and so the alien mercenary was then deployed. However, between losing contact with the first agent and assigning the second, I came into possession of further information that changed the parameters of the mission. It was no longer simply a case of trying to take out Zephyrus's agent but necessitated that we discover what H-363 was and why the renegade wanted it.

It now transpires that our two agents encountered one another in the field, without realising that they were in the employ of the same master. Both operatives have now been registered as fatalities and it is ultimately thanks to the efforts of a platoon of Armageddon ork hunters that we now know the nature of H-363 at all. This situation does, of course, necessitate the removal of the said ork hunters and I shall be seeing to this matter myself directly.

I trust that this communiqué finds you in good health and your own ongoing investigation into the practices of the Black Templars of the Solemnus Crusade progressing as you would hope.

I remain ever your obedient servant

Rivera

[Message ends]

ABOUT THE AUTHOR

Jonathan Green has been a freelance writer for the last thirteen years. In that time he has written Fighting Fantasy and Sonic the Hedgehog gamebooks for Puffin, and atmospheric colour text for a variety of Games Workshop products. His work for the Black Library, to date, includes a string of short stories for *Inferno!* magazine and six novels. Jonathan works as a full-time teacher in West London.